MW00463378

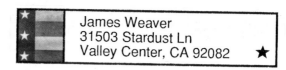
HMS *Comet*

DEFEAT AND VICTORY

This book is dedicated to Lieutenant Colonel Forte, United States Marine Corps (Ret.): warrior, confidant, and instructor. His uncompromising professionalism and operational excellence provided the strength to tell this story.

Prologue

Southampton, England, August 1717.

"Christ," slipped from Earl Von Hunter's lips before he realized he had said anything. His eyes continued to scan down the letter he held. The tremor in his hand, while slight, was distinctive enough for his servant to notice.

"Is something the matter, sir?" The servant's question was sincere, if not somewhat detached.

"It seems the Spanish Fleet is on the move from Cadiz toward the Mediterranean Sea. No one on the Imperial Council knows why."

"Is that our concern, sir?"

"Yes, if only because Captain Darroch has asked for me to meet him at the Red Fox Inn in Portsmouth to discuss pending developments. I owe the young Captain much."

"Is that the Royal Marine Captain, sir?"

"Yes, the very same," replied Hunter lowering the letter.

"Will the Earl be packing for this trip?"

"Yes, plan for a just a couple of days stay. If it extends any longer, I'll return and pickup additional items."

"Very good, sir. Will the Earl be traveling on horseback or in your coach?"

"I'll ride my horse on this one. Given the tight alleyways around the Red Fox Inn, it's better to keep the larger coach at home."

"I'll take care of all preparations, sir."

Hunter nodded. His servant exited the study. Picking up the letter, he read the text again. His lips moved as his eyes followed the lines down the page. He walked over to his desk. Sitting in his red leather chair, he pulled paper and quill from the center drawer. He spelled out a set of instructions for his estate

1

manager and signed the bottom. Pushing the paper aside, he settled back into the comfort of the overstuffed chair. His eyes wandered around the room.

On two walls, bookcases ran from the floor to the ceiling with selected works and reference material. The various colors of the spine on each book, combined into a random mosaic of patterns and shapes around him. On the third wall, a fireplace dominated the carved wood panels that surrounded the blackened bricks. The rich patina of oil polished oak needed no decorations to enhance its appearance. Finally, behind his desk chair were three large windows that opened to a manicured garden. Filled with finely trimmed hedges, flower beds, and shade trees, the garden was a quiet place often used to spawn meaningful meditation. Drake turned his chair around and stared into the lush green of this sanctuary.

With a few quick breaths and a match, he lit his whale bone pipe. Taking a long drag from the small tobacco bowl, he blew a smoke ring skyward. He studied its round shape expand, fade, and disappear above him. His thoughts settled in once again on the content of William's letter.

If the Spanish are heading east, into the Mediterranean, then the British fleet will have to follow. Gibraltar is too rich and recent a prize to let go. I'm sure the loss of their Italian holdings in the last war, still rubs them raw. But what, in the name of God, does Captain Darroch need my assistance for now? My militia would never stand before Spanish regulars. He must have something else in mind. But what?

*****

"Captain Darroch, this contingency planning is almost done. I fear my stay here in Portsmouth is about to come to an end. Can you make any recommendations as to what the army should ask our navy friends to do in preparation?" asked General Temple.

"General, you need to convince them to get the fleet at anchor and away from the docks."

"Why is that?"

"Once word of a pending deployment reaches the waterfront, many of the sailors not signed to a crew will vacate to avoid the press."

"The press?"

"Yes, unlike the army, England's wooden walls are crewed with many sailors not there of their own free will. They have been forced into service given the King's command and needs of the nation. Placing the fleet at anchor will secure the crews aboard and make them ready for service should the need arise."

"Does that mean I would lose access to your planning skills?"

"No. Officers and selected crewmembers will still be allowed ashore. I don't think it will be an issue General."

"Very good. I'm going to get my staff back to headquarters this afternoon and see what some of my folks think about our approach here. Who knows, we may be executing this west coast option sooner than you think."

The two exchanged salutes. The look from the General confirmed the level of respect Captain Darroch had earned during the hectic planning days that now stood behind them. The General gathered the rest of his soldiers and departed the inn. A wave or two from those departing closed this chapter in the history of the Red Fox Inn.

Captain Darroch walked up the stairs to the second floor. The handrail moved as his weight pushed against it. The center of each step was bowed with a slight depression worn down from the amount of patron traffic that had found their way to the delights above the ground level. He held his course to the last room on the left side of the hallway. He softly knocked on the chamber door.

The Royal Marine placed both hands behind his back in a failed attempt to make his stance appear less formal. He held his gaze on the wooden frame of the door and listened. The sound of

3

footsteps on the other side of the threshold announced his patience was about to be rewarded.

Annette pulled open her bedroom door. She held the door with one hand while resting her weight on the doorframe with the other. Tilting her head forward, long locks of auburn hair framed her face. A loose-fitting white cotton dressing gown covered her frame from shoulders to knees. She eyed the Marine from his boots to his collar while avoiding eye contact.

"And what would you be wanting on this early afternoon?" asked Annette. The corners of her mouth edged up revealing a smile brighter than the dawn. She now surrendered eye contact to the gentleman before her.

"Don't you ever get dressed? It must be one O'clock by now," said William.

"When I'm in my own room I'll dress, or undress, as I please. If it pleases you, enter. I don't want to be standing in the draft all day."

Captain Darroch walked into her room and positioned himself over by the window. He looked out at the ships with tall masts that dotted the quay wall and that swung at anchor in the harbor. Annette closed, and locked, the door. William could hear the metallic click of the locking mechanism engage. They were once again alone, safe, and secure in her chamber.

Annette slid up behind him and slipped her arms around the full extent of his chest. She pulled her body against his and held tight with one hand. Her other hand began to unbutton his coat from top to bottom until it opened wide. She now ran her fingers across the light cotton shirt on his chest, pressing firm against the expanse of his muscular upper body. William turned around and secured his arms around her waist. Annette now worked to unbuckle his belt. Before she could complete the task, William pulled her into a deep passionate kiss. While it was the kind of embrace this couple would often share, he never grew tired of the energy she cast upon his body.

He loosened his grip and pulled away while remaining whisper close. The two locked eyes. Hers green, his blue, each on fire. He placed a single finger on her lips.

"Annette, who is taking care of Captain Calder in your absence from *Comet*?" While the question was professional, his tone remained soft and didn't break the mood. He lifted his finger from her lips.

"He is dining with Captain Hemroni on *Royal Anne* tonight. It's not my concern and sure as hell should not be yours at this moment."

The Marine reached behind himself and pulled the curtains closed. The room was now darkened. Annette finished working his belt free. William pulled the last tie on her dressing gown allowing it to loosen and fall to the floor.

"You're right," he said.

These were the last words the couple would exchange through the afternoon. When the chill of the evening air rolled in from the English Channel, the passions between them cooled. Annette, after all, had an inn to run. This night, as every night, the deepening darkness announced the arrival of patrons eager for ale, a smoke, and perhaps a night of entertainment if the price was right.

Chapter 1 At Anchor

"Would you like another glass of wine Delmar?" asked Captain Hemroni.

"Yes, please John. Most appreciated," replied Captain Calder.

Hemroni waved to his Orderly. In a flash the cook emerged from the captain's galley and poured another glass of wine. Its red color reflected the light that danced from the rippling waters astern HMS *Royal Anne*. With the exception of a new painting, the great cabin of this First-Rate ship looked the same as Captain Calder remembered in the West Indies.

"Is the painting new?" asked Calder.

"Yes. I had it commissioned to celebrate our victory over the Brotherhood of the Coast at Nassau Bay. What do you think?"

"It's just a little dark for my liking."

"Well, it was a night action after all."

"Yes, I do have some familiarity with the engagement," said Calder. The edges of their mouths crept upward, followed by a spontaneous laugh that reflected the bonds of friendship these two professional navy men shared.

Calder took a long sip of his wine. His eyes walked around the cabin. It looked much like his home aboard *Comet*, all be it a little larger and more spacious.

"Here we are, dinner," announced Hemroni. He leaned back in his chair to allow the cook to place the plate in front of him.

"Top of the line, John. Top of the line. Hopefully, not on my account?"

"Well, yes and no. The Duke insisted I take some top end beef. Who am I to refuse? Anyway, I thought this a good occasion to break it out being the Victors of Nassau and all."

"It is much appreciated. My cook is on shore leave, so I've noticed a decline in the quality of my mess."

"Annette?"

"Yes, she is taking care of her place in Portsmouth. Hope to see her back aboard for the next cruise."

"So, do I, would never miss a meal on *Comet* when she is in charge of your galley. That's a fact."

What do you hear from the Admiralty these days?" Calder asked. He stopped cutting his meat and looked over at his host.

"Just got a letter this morning. Seems the entire fleet will have to be anchored out by Friday."

"Friday?" said Calder. The corners of his mouth pointed down.

"That's the word. I don't look forward to having all the bumboat folks descend on my ship. I can never keep track of all their wares and whores. Between the liquor and the women, it will take a full week at sea to clear the stench out of the bilge."

"Moving the fleet to anchor, normally that means only one thing."

"Yes, I fear something is afoot with Spain. They sortied their fleet toward the Mediterranean from Cadiz," said Hemroni. He set his wine on the table and looked over to lock eyes with Captain Calder. "Is your ship ready to make sail?"

"Yes. We can always use more time to fix things pier side. But that's just for convenience. We can sail the world if need be."

"Gunpowder, shot and ball, ground tackle, and rigging, all good to go?"

"Of course. The first thing I did was replenish my stocks of powder when we got home. *Comet* will be ready. Wish I could say the same for the crew."

"The crew, what do you mean by that?"

"We paid out our prize money from the last voyage. It was a good haul, if I do say myself. Anyway, many of the men will be off pursuing . . . other interests. I will be a little shorthanded if we set sail tomorrow. I can get to anchor of course. Action stations on the other hand would be a little more problematic," said Calder. He gazed at his wine glass and moved it in a tight circle on the table. The red liquid climbed the side of the glass before surrendering to gravity. He lifted the glass to his nose and inhaled a deep breath. The aroma made him smile. "Any idea what the Spanish are up to John?"

"My guess is they are going to use the fleet to take back the Islands of Sicily and Sardinia. That would be a good use of sea-power and consistent with fleet movements."

"What about the Austrians? Wouldn't they want to intervene and hold those gems?" Calder said. His fingers tapped lightly on the table. "You're the strategist here. What do you think?"

"I think they are taking on way more than they can handle," said Hemroni. He leaned forward and crossed his arms in front of him on the table. "Sure, they have at least a month head start. So, what! They can land troops, take an Island, but then what? Unless they can control the waves, we'll cut their armies ashore off from resupply. End of game."

"Do you think we can take them afloat? I've seen their efforts to build and add ships of the line."

"This is not a numbers games Delmar. Our gunnery is better. Our crews are better. We can take them in a close-in fight or at range. I don't fear the seamanship of the Don's," said Hemroni. His words relaxed them both. They each leaned back in their chairs.

"To the Empire," said Calder. He raised his glass shoulder high toward Hemroni.

"Indeed, to the Empire, my good friend," replied Hemroni. "I fear this is not the last fight you and I will sail into together."

"Nor would I want it to be," said Calder

They both took a long swig from their wine glass. Setting his empty glass on the table Hemroni nodded.

*****

Pang and Annette stood side-by-side at the bar. Annette used a white towel to dry pewter tankards. Pang flirted with a sailor at the end of the bar until he bought a round of whisky for his mates. She stuffed the shillings in the box under the bar.

Leaning over toward Annette, she whispered, "I think I just got you a new patron. He seems most interested in all the services here."

"Your services?"

"Not what I said. You know I've sort of been off the market of late."

"Well look who just walked in Mistress Off-The-Market, Midshipman Rutwell."

"Annette can you look after things, while I play with my Midshipman a bit?"

"Sure, but play nice Mistress Pang," said Annette. Her tone was just a touch exasperated.

"Nice, but naughty, that's me," shot back Pang. She pulled her open hand through long rows of brown hair and let them fall loose about her shoulders. Locking her brown eyes on Midshipman Rutwell, she walked toward him. Pang rolled her hips from side to side casting the sway of her dress in a rhythmic manner. Her movements were picked-up by Rutwell, who was dazed on her approach.

"Pang, I've missed you," said Rutwell. His bright eyes reflected the sincerity of his words.

Pang reached up around his neck and locked her hands together. With a slight leap, she jumped up on his waist and wrapped her legs around him. Michael instinctively caught her and supported her weight with both hands below her bottom. The kiss that followed drew the attention of most of those within the Red Fox Inn, but only for a few passing seconds. He lowered her to the floor, but their embrace remained close.

"Miss that did you?" said Pang, her flirtatious smile instinctively widened.

"Well of course."

"Captain Darroch is over at his table, do you want to join him?"

"I can see the good Captain anytime, I came here for you," said Michael. The muscles in his face relaxed, but he held his eyes transfixed on the depths of Pang's deep brown eyes.

"Perhaps you would like to join me upstairs? I have my own room now."

"Let's go."

Annette watched as this young couple went to the second floor. When they disappeared, she looked over at Captain Darroch. He had watched the scene unfold and when he made eye contact with Annette, he shrugged his shoulders. Annette turned back to drying the tankards.

Pang pulled Michael by the hand down the second-floor hallway to her room on the right. It was across from Annette's chamber and held a position of respect within the entertainment staff of the inn. She picked up a few stray articles of clothing that were thrown randomly across a chair and stuffed them away within a cabinet. She turned back around to find Midshipman Rutwell hovering behind her.

"Damn Pang, you're a sight for well-travelled eyes."

"I'll bet you used that line on those young courtesans in the colonies, didn't you?"

"Only the ones as pretty as you," replied Michael. The edges of his mouth rose in something short of a smile, but playful none the less.

Pang giggled. The light pitch of her voice stood in sharp contrast to the male dominated commands issued forth in an endless stream aboard *Comet*. Michael looked around the room. His eyes focused briefly on each area before locking once again on Pang.

"God it's good to be back in Portsmouth," said the Midshipman. His unblemished hand reached out and touched Pang's cheek.

10

Pang laughed and slid her hand up to cover his fingers resting against the side of her face.

"Good to be back in Portsmouth, or good to be back in my bed chamber?"

Michael blushed but he nodded while holding his smile. Pang guided his hand down from her face until it rested on her front. He pulled her close. The kiss that followed was as passionate as any Pang had ever known. She could feel him stroke his hand across her. She found his focus on pleasing her a refreshing contrast to those that had entered her chamber in an earlier time. Pang lowered her head, took a deep breath, and then returned the kiss matching his passion. Their tongues united in a delicate dance they each found exciting. Her hand lowered below his belt, seeking to raise his expectations for the evening ahead. For the first time, in a long time, Pang wanted this young man to feel her warmth. She did not seek the exchange of silver, but for something more permanent than a monetary transaction. She could feel him stiffen to her touch. It was a predictable reaction and Pang used her few years of seniority and experience to control the flow of this intimate engagement.

Belts, lacing, and petticoats fell to the floor. The pace of their breathing accelerated just slightly. Each pulled, tugged, and slid away the clothing that encumbered their conduct in proper society. As these garments were cast aside, so too were social norms that inhibited their desire to enjoy the full sensuous palette each had to offer. They fell into the soft embrace of Pang's bed. The warmth of the bed covering embraced them in the dark. In the low light of her bed chamber, the sense of touch now dominated their engagement. They each explored the full range of pleasure a touch or lick could release to the mind.

Pang had let loose the activities of the Red Fox Inn, just one floor below her. Right now, it was only Michael that defined her universe. With eye lids unbroken, she could see the flash of stars form into unnamed constellations. He rocked against her in a

11

motion as rhythmic as the waves of the Atlantic Ocean. When the muscles of Michael's legs tightened, Pang slapped his bottom breaking his concentration and extending the duration of their coupling. She wanted to expand the depth of her universe and explore new heights of pleasure with this young man that had come to be with her, and only her. She was not disappointed. The moans that followed where loud enough to be heard at the bar below.

Annette looked over at William as the sinful symphony of pleasure above them echoed in their ears. The two exchanged smirks fully aware of what was happening only a few feet above them.

"Well, it would seem our young Mister Rutwell has hit his stride," said William.

"He has hit a lot more than his stride, I would say," replied Annette. She giggled for the first time that evening. "I've not heard Pang let loose like that in a long time."

"This is not business as usual then?"

"Not business at all. I hope our young friend up there realizes that."

"On that account, I think you have nothing to fear. She is his first after all."

"How do you be knowing that?" asked Annette. Her expression dimmed as her lips flattened into a straight line.

"Michael, I mean Midshipman Rutwell, and I have spoken of it on occasion. He does after all value the advice of a Royal Marine."

The smile returned to Annette's face. She took her towel and wiped the ever-present dampness from the top of the bar. The moaning above them fell silent. Annette and William looked at each other and laughed.

The figure that stood at the entrance to the inn was out of place. His stance was formal, regal, in its posture. A red cape covered a finely tailored riding suit. Brown leather pants

12

protected the wearer's legs from the high thorns that struck a rider as they crossed the many untilled fields of southern England. His long coat was cut in the latest style with deep pockets on each side. William stood and waved for this patron to approach.

"Right honorable Earl von Hunter, you have once again returned to the Red Fox Inn," said Darroch.

"I got your letter. What's up my friend?"

"It seems—"

"Drake, you're back," said Cynthia. Her voice drowned out Darroch. She fell upon the Earl with purpose. Her hand immediately secured his hip.

"Cynthia my child, how good to see you. All of you. This is a pleasant surprise and perhaps my reward for answering the good Captain's call for assistance," said Hunter. His eyes traveled direct to the low cut of Cynthia's dress and the dual rounded forms that commanded his attention.

"Perhaps the Earl would honor me with a dance?"

Hunter looked over at Darroch.

"Do you plan to stay the night, sir?" asked Darroch.

"Yes, I'll be in Portsmouth a few days if needed."

"Sir, it is late. Enjoy some time with Cynthia. We can discuss our business in the morning. It's nothing that can't wait until then."

"Well, very good then. You'll excuse us while we take a turn on the dance floor?"

"Of course, sir. Enjoy."

Darroch watched as the two of them made their way out onto the empty dance floor. Hunter took Cynthia's hand and placed the other low on her hip. She in turn, let her hand settle to the Earl's shoulder. The two them began to swirl in a manner rarely seen at the Red Fox Inn. Formal steps were not normally used by the Inn's patrons. Their movements commanded more than a passing glance.

13

Annette briefly left her posting at the bar and walked over to Captain Darroch's table. They both watched as Hunter spun Cynthia in wide arcs in time with the music. She leaned down behind him and whispered in his ear, "Haven't we seen this play once before?"

William laughed, caught his breath and replied, "Yes, I think we both know how this little dance will end."

Hunter lifted Cynthia's chin to hold eye contact. Her black hair was held atop her head in a bun that made her appear taller. A single curl from this dark mass fell down along her neck and drew the Earl's eye downward. He found the soft white rounded flesh instinctively appealing.

"How have you been my dear?" he asked.

"Well, and you?" Cynthia said. She noted his eyes had wondered downward. The resulting smirk on her face was visible to Annette and William across the floor.

"I've been managing the family estate and running the local militia. These keep me engaged, but I've not enjoyed anything akin to the pleasure of your company the last time we danced," said Hunter. His stare returned to fix on Cynthia's eyes. He was once again drawn into the pitch black of those orbs that returned his gaze. She stroked the back of his neck.

"Enjoyment is yours for the asking, sir," said Cynthia.

"For a price."

"Of course. As are all things."

"Does it have to be like that?'

"No, you would perhaps like something more exclusive."

"Yes."

"Only you."

"Yes."

"My right honorable Earl Drake von Hunter are you asking me to marry?" asked Cynthia. Her smile foretold she knew the answer but wanted to make the Earl squirm just a little.

"I'm unable to make such a commitment at this time. My duties to King and country preclude it. I will cover your living expense and care. That would preclude your need to stay within these walls. Be my—"

"Mistress?" said Cynthia. She stroked the side of his face as she spoke.

"Yes. Mistress . . . my God I don't know your last name."

"I would be Mistress Maitland. Courtesan to the right honorable Earl von Hunter. I can live with that for a start." The imagined sound of shillings echoed in Cynthia's ears.

The Earl twirled her around and dipped her backward. The depth of this move strained Cynthia's back. Pain took her breath for a moment as she struggled to balance against this awkward position and the forces of gravity.

"Then it's agreed. You'll be mine and only mine. Mistress Maitland," said Hunter. His tone was low but forceful.

Cynthia was unable to speak. She nodded, hoping he would lift her upright once again. The couple returned to the vertical and swirled around the full circumference of the dance floor. The flow of blood to Cynthia's brain returned to normal. She thought, *what in the hell did I just agree to this time. Mistress to the Earl. Not quite a title but it will do. Hell, that's a long way from walking the Point in Portsmouth for a living."*

Alicia ran down the stairs to the main floor. She navigated her way over to where Annette and William were standing. She wore a simple dress with a peasant top. The small canvas bag over her shoulder told the two of them Alicia was off to somewhere. Half a dozen entertainers were soon clustered behind her. Annette frowned at the scene before her.

"Annette, the fleet has been called out to anchor. It won't take long until the demand for us here dries up. I guess you sort of know we have to follow the fleet," said Alicia. Her eyes were wide. Her voice trembled as she spoke.

"Damn it. Why do you girls know about this before I've been officially informed by the Imperial Naval Staff?" Darroch commented to no one in particular. "When did they order the fleet to anchor?"

"I was entertaining a sailor that said he had to hurry. Might be the last time ashore for a long time. He wasn't sure. Anyway, they always allow women aboard once at anchor. I think more than a shilling or two can be made there. It's been over a year since I went out to anchor, but at least there you get a steady customer for the duration," said Alicia. Her long blonde hair bounced on either side of her face as she spoke.

"You can't leave me shorthanded here," said Annette.

"Annette, you'll be fine. Most of your customers are sailors or Marines. They will be locked aboard them boats. A few merchant crew and officers are all that will be calling. Our services will not be needed anyway. I think you know that."

"Damn. I hate to break up such a good crew," said Annette. Her eyes fell to the floor.

"Crew, you'll be called to anchor as captain's cook and Pang will get caught holding the bag around here. We need to be looking after our own interest my love. Not because we are not loyal to the Red Fox Inn, but because we all know the flow of coin will preclude you being able to pay our way," said Alicia. Her tone was less emotional but forceful just the same with its compelling logic.

"Go then. Good luck to you all. Just know when this at anchor business ends, I expect you'll all return here. The Red Fox Inn is your home as much as it is mine. You helped build this place. All of you will be missed. Alicia, you most of all. My little lost blonde-haired sister."

Alicia leaned over to Annette and kissed her on the cheek. Then she slid close, chest to chest, compressed together with the force of her embrace. Their auburn and blonde hair mixed as

Alicia locked lips with Annette. The kiss was deep, romantic, and more than a touch inappropriate.

"I love you, Annette. I'll find my way home. I promise," said Alicia.

Willian stared at the scene. His mouth fell wide open. He had to blink hard to ensure his eyes were recording what his mind thought it had witnessed. All he could do was force some inaudible noise from his throat.

Alicia turned away and lifted her arm pointing to the main entrance. She flipped her hair back over a shoulder and announced, "Ladies, the bumboat is waiting on the wharf. If you want the pick of the litter, you'd better get your asses aboard the nearest warship." This small herd of women started out of the inn. Alicia grabbed up an unattended tankard of ale and threw it back with a long gulp. Silence replaced the clatter of the stampede as fast as it had appeared.

Pang and Michael descended the stairs as Alicia led her pack out the main doorway. The two of them joined Annette and William.

"Did you two hear us down here?" asked William.

"No," said Michael.

"We sure as hell heard you two carrying on upstairs," said William laughing.

Michael's cheeks turned bright red. He pointed to the wake left by Alicia and her crew.

"What was all that about?"

"It seems the fleet has been called out to anchor. Alicia wanted to get out ahead of the other entertainers and stake out her turf. Service to the fleet and all," said William. He looked over at Annette.

"What does it mean for *Comet* and crew?" asked Annette.

"Nothing until we get the official recall notice. I suggest we all get a good night sleep ashore. For many of us it could well be our last for a long while."

The crowd on the first floor of the Red Fox Inn soon thinned out. Only a drunk sailor stayed. He was resting face down on his table. The fingers of his hand still wrapped through the handle of his tankard. William went over to lock the front door.

Looking out into the alleyway he noticed a steady stream of ladies walking down to the waterfront. These human shapes were bent over under the dull glow of the whale oil lamps that illuminated their path. Most carried a bag or satchel. Many of the taverns were emptying out their entertainment staff. The downward cast of the eyes told most of the tale. Uncertain futures gripped a dark industry that fed on the coinage of those able to scrape a living from the sea. Sailor's wives, with no means of support when their husbands went afloat, fell into this moving mass to trade the value of their flesh to glean out a meager existence. William slowly closed the door. He turned the key to ensure the lock went home and those outside would remain so.

Alicia reached the quay wall to find two older women loading up a bumboat. The elder one was grey haired and stood at the back of the boat. She studied each passenger with a critical eye before allowing them to board. She eyed Alicia from head to toe.

"You, blonde hair. You're in my boat."

"How much?"

"Oh, you'll not be paying a pence. They will pay gladly for you sweetie. Please take a seat back here with me. You'll be last off. A little eye candy to sweeten a sailor's appetite."

Alicia squeezed her ass between the cases of rum and whisky to settle in near the boat captain. The old lady looked down and smiled at her. Not in a motherly fashion, but rather with the affection of a cattleman leading the heard to slaughter. The bottle soon found its way to Alicia's hand. She took a long swig of the clear liquid. The burn went well down her throat.

"What in the hell was that?" coughed Alicia.

"Rum," squawked the old lady.

"That's terrible."

"Some of the worst my dear. But the price is right. The sailors like it. My guess is you will too by the time you work your pretty little ass off that ship."

Alicia passed the bottle down the line. The young ladies, girls for the most part, were eager to drink as much as they could as fast as they could. The burn in the throat was replaced by a dulling of the senses. The cold of the night air seemed less intrusive. The selling of fallen virtue, perhaps less of a sin. A warm, uncaring glow was the best defense against the stark chill of their individual reality.

Two more from the Red Fox Inn boarded the old woman's boat. As the third lifted her foot to board, a cane slapped her knee.

"Not you sweetie. Not on this boat," said the old lady. Her voice was level, business like, but firm. Alicia looked on at the exchange. She took another swig from the bottle as it continued to make its rounds.

"Why not?"

"Can't make any money with you my dear. Too fat. Too ugly. Too old. Can't sell fat, ugly, or old. I don't want to waste a boat space to take you out to the fleet, only to have to bring you back with no profit. In your case it's more like two boat spaces."

The lady burst into tears.

"Maybe another boat. Move along now. I've got to get this boat loaded and out to the fleet before someone beats me to it," said the old lady. She held a hard stare on this soul until she drifted down the waterfront.

"Let's go now. Get aboard, I've not got all night," said the old lady. Her tone was as gruff as any sea captain.

The boat pushed away from the quay wall and started to stroke out toward the fleet. Alicia took another nip of rum. She looked over at the girl next to her and offered the bottle. The lass tipped it back and took a long gulp. She leveled the bottle, wiped her mouth with the back of her hand, and coughed a few times. She passed the bottle on, shook her head, and tried to straighten up in the boat. Her dark brown hair looked black in the night. Her eyes were as blue as Alicia's. She thought, *unusual mix of eye and hair color.*

"What's your name dear?" asked Alicia. She spoke softly so the old woman couldn't hear.

"Sadie."

"First time, Sadie?"

"Yes."

"No family, dear?"

"No. My father was killed in a mining accident in Cornwall. Mother ran off with a man from up north. He didn't want a child in the bargain."

"How old are you, Sadie?"

"Twelve."

"Twelve?" asked Alicia unbelieving.

Sadie nodded.

"Have you ever been with a man before?" whispered Alicia. She was surprised to see her hands shake waiting to hear the answer.

"No," replied Sadie. She shook her downward cast head as she answered.

"My name is Alicia. If you need any help aboard, you find me."

"Yes, madam," said Sadie. She pulled Alicia's ear closer. "How does all this work?"

Alicia rolled her eyes. The warm numbness of the rum faded. This little girl was forcing her to face the reality of her situation.

Alicia said, "When we get to the ship, each of us will be sold to a sailor. Some will take two, others only one. Since you are a virgin, you'll command a large price. I'm sure that will please our boat captain. Then you'll have to keep your sailor happy. As long as he wants you, he will feed you and give you a place to sleep. If he tires of you, you'll have to find another interested in your talents. Then they will take care of you."

"Talents, what do you mean by talents?"

"Oh, sweetie. You'll be asked to do their laundry, sew and mend their clothes, and swab and clean their living spaces. When he is drunk and passed-out in his own vomit, you'll clean him up and roll him into his hammock."

"Is that all?"

"No."

"What else, Alicia?"

"You will have to satisfy his every whim. In his hammock, on the deck, or in the dark of the cargo hold. You're his, period. He will teach you what he likes. That's why he bought you to begin with. Have you ever seen two dogs' couple?"

"No, but we did have sheep back in Cornwall."

"Yes, like that."

"Do you mean from behind?"

Alicia took another long swig of rum. She handed the bottle to Sadie, who did the same.

"Behind, on top, on bottom, or with your mouth. Whatever he wants. Just keep him happy and there be no trouble."

"What sort of trouble?"

"A drunk sailor can be a mean sailor. I've seen our kind beat because they didn't do what was expected. Learn your sailor. Make him want you more than anything else. That's the path to stay the hell out of trouble, beatings, and pain."

"What's it like below decks? All I've ever seen is the ship under sail passing along the coast."

"Below decks is an odd place. After the meal, you'll get part of his ration, some of the sailors will dance with their women folk. At night the place finds everyone coupled together making all manner of strange sounds. Moans and groans dominate the deck. Then, as the hour grows long, the snoring starts.

Sometimes it's so loud you have to stuff cotton balls in your ears to block the clatter."

"That sounds bad."

"Even worst are the smells. Stale vomit penetrates the air. I've slept with a perfume scented handkerchief over my face just to reduce the obnoxious odor. The acidic smell of urine combines with gunpowder residue, to burn your eyes and nose. Not even a scented handkerchief can help with those."

"How do you endure all this?"

"Strong drink is your best defense. Why do you think that rum bottle is making the rounds so freely?"

Alicia took Sadie's hand and squeezed it. Their blue eyes locked in the night. She lowered her lips next to Sadie's ear and whispered, "I'll take care of you sweetie. You have to promise to take care of me as well." They exchanged nods. The compact was sealed on a small boat that bounced on the ice-cold waters of the bay.

The stern lamp of the warship grew in size with each stroke of the oar. The old lady yelled up toward the main deck, "Ahoy, on *Royal Oak*, bumboat coming along side."

"Approach port quarter. Use the ladder," replied the Officer of the Deck.

Sailors wearing a mix of colors gathered on deck. Looking over the rail, they sized up the talent below. The old woman started the bidding at the front of the boat and worked her way back. Many of those gathered above had drawn their focus on Alicia. Her blonde hair reflected the moonlight and foretold of someone special.

"How much for the blonde?" An unseen voice called out.

"We'll not be bidding on the blonde till the rest of this cargo is bought and paid for, is that clear," said the old woman. She knew how to control the lust of the mob above.

The front end of the bumboat sent up rum and whisky in small creates. One by one liquor was lifted aboard under the nose of the Officer of the Deck. This exchange was being run at the same time as the bidding for the services of the wenches. The bidding was fast.

Alicia shuttered as one by one the girls in front of her were purchased, climbed the ladder and disappeared onto the main deck. The old woman made sure the full payment of her share was lowered to her before letting the young lasses scale the side of the ship.

The sailors above had thinned, but the mob's intensity had held constant. Only Sadie and Alicia remained. Sadie stood in the boat and look down at Alicia.

"I guess I'm next," she said tearfully.

The bumboat woman held her hand out and motioned for Sadie to sit. Those sailors gathered along the rail, were pushing and shoving to get a better look at the prime cargo remaining. The old woman was letting the anticipation build.

She cupped her hand around her mouth and announced, "Alight you scurvy ridden sons of bitches, these last two are a pair. A fine looking blonde to warm the coldest of your nights. Skilled in the art of love making to satisfy your deepest and darkest desires. And this young thing, never been with a man before. Train her as you will, but be sure to train her well." The old woman looked down at Alicia and added, "I heard every word you two said. I will not be the one breaking you apart tonight."

The bidding went from shillings to pounds in a flash. The price climbed. Alicia, who had been through this once before, was taken by the amount as it went up. Slowly, those that could not make the mark moved away from the railing.

When only two were left, the larger man turned toward his crewmate, and said, "Let me be taking these two. If you're nice I'll lend you one on a cold night." The two men exchanged smiles.

23

Looking up Alicia was stricken to see the back shadow of only one sailor holding the rail. The bucket was lowered to the bumboat. The old woman dutifully counted the coins. She smiled.

"Up you go you two. Go meet your new boss man."

Alicia pulled Sadie up and steadied her on the ladder. She slowly worked her way up the side of the ship. When she was half way up, Alicia started her ascent. The bumboat woman didn't wait, as soon as Alicia locked onto the ladder, she pushed away heading back to the quay wall. Alicia was exhausted by the time she stood on deck. Looking at the sailor that had paid for their services she had to blink. The corners of her mouth edged up.

"Giles is that really you?" asked Alicia.

"In the flesh my dear."

"How is that possible?"

"You didn't think I would let one of those seadogs out bid me, did you?"

"How much did that cost you?"

"A hell of a lot more than I ever paid at the Red Fox Inn. That's for sure."

"Sadie, this is Giles," said Alicia. She moved her hand along Giles waist. "He is a big man, with an equally big heart. And now he has two women to attend him."

"Ladies, shall we strike below. Perhaps a dance before we retire," said Giles. He extended an arm to each of his new women. They each locked on to his powerful frame.

They strolled along the main deck drawing the lustful stare of many a sailor. Alicia looked up into the clouds, and mouthed the words, "Thank you."

As the three of them approached the ladder the smell from below permeated their senses. Sadie looked over at Alicia. Her lips were flat.

"What?" said Alicia.

"It's worse than you described."

"Nothing a shot of rum can't solve. Relax, you don't know how lucky you are my dear."

The wind pushed against the beam of HMS *Royal Oak.* Alicia's blonde hair carried to the lee, obstructing her view. The force this gust exerted on the anchor rode pushed it out to full length. The ship pointed up into the wind. The entire fleet now aligned to one compass point . . . due South.

Chapter 2 Call to Arms

The newly appointed Militia Commander of Cagliari sat in his courtyard sipping tea and enjoying a bowl of fresh cut fruit. Looking around the white stucco walls of the courtyard he felt secure within their confines. Heat waves curled up from the red roof tiles on all sides. The sun was near its full height. The Commander's wide brim straw hat provided some measure of relief from the full force of the radiant heat cast down upon him.

His servant approached holding a tea pot. The white towel folded across his forearm provided an air of sophistication not normally associated with this distant outpost newly acquired for the House of the Habsburgs. Austria's hold on this region was a direct result of their alliance in the War of Spanish Succession, and they were happy to take control in this part of the Mediterranean Sea.

"Some more tea, sir?" asked the servant. His formal posture was the result of indentured service to masters from more than one country.

"No. Too warm at this time of day," replied the Commander.

A hot wind gust across the courtyard separating the towel from the well-intentioned servant. He spilled the Commander's tea in a vain attempt to secure the towel as it flew across the table.

"Those damn Sirocco winds. They blow in hot from Tunis and the Sahara Desert raising the already overheated temperatures another ten degrees," said the Commander. His tone reflected the irritation resulting from the disruption of his afternoon routine.

"Yes, sir. I fear they will carry all sort of trouble from well beyond the horizon."

"Yes, yes. It's not your fault. You're dismissed."

"Sir, I have a gentleman from the harbor here to see you. He said it was urgent."

26

"Send him in, we mustn't keep the locals waiting you know," said the Commander. His tone was distant. He pulled the front of his grey uniform down, smoothing its appearance. He stood as the man entered the courtyard.

Waving his hand toward the table, the Commander asked, "May I interest you in a cup of tea?"

"No, sir. I must report the Spanish are approaching," said the Harbor Master. His stance oscillated between formal and relaxed.

"Spanish? How do you know? When did they appear?"

"Sir, they rounded Cape Spartivento at mid-morning. A fleet of six Ships of the Line and eight Galleys approaches. Many other smaller craft are operating in close support. There is no mistaking they are Spanish, sir. The yellow and red banners float from the tops of the ships."

"Troops?" The Commander patted his forehead to remove newly formed beads of sweat.

"Yes, sir. They started lowering away small boats this afternoon. Green uniforms have been coming over the sides for about an hour now. They are holding just beyond musket range off the beach."

"Orderly," yelled the Commander.

A man dressed in a grey uniform with brass buttons entered the courtyard. He stopped three paces from the Commander and saluted. "Sir, reporting as ordered."

"Go down to the harbor and have the Captain of the Guard call out his formation. Assemble them along the beach. Standard line formation. I'll be down to assume command in a moment."

"Yes, sir," said the Orderly. He saluted to acknowledge the order, spun around on his heels, and vanished from the courtyard.

The servant approached carrying the Commander's sword. The Commander nodded in his direction and lifted his arms shoulder high. The servant wrapped the sword belt and accoutrements around his boss's waist.

27

The Commander patted the hilt of the sword, turned to his servant, and said, "I'm going to take a look at this report. I will be back for dinner. I'll see you then."

The servant could only nod in reply. His boss was out of the courtyard and heading toward the harbor before he could say anything. The Sirocco wind tip the Commander's hat to one side before he reached up and secured it.

The Commander's mind raced, *how is it the Spanish have chosen to violate the treaty? These reports are always overstated. Let see what the harbor holds.*

Each stride of the Commander lengthened as he increased his pace toward the waterfront. The clanking of his sword against his hip kept time with his march. His posture was erect, communicating an air of superiority as he walked. A small group of chickens scattered on his approach. Some took to flight, while others scurried on stubby legs, waddling in all directions before him. Rounding the church, he froze.

The scene in the harbor drew his immediate military assessment. The grey of his militia lined the beach. Movement in the ranks indicated the tension generated by the appearance of a potentially hostile fleet in this normally quiet backwater. Boats circled beyond the breakwater, holding just beyond the musket range of the Austrians. Four Ships of the Line swung on two anchors each. Rode ran down from the bow and stern of these ships disappearing into the clear water of the bay. The rest of the fleet hovered a mile or more in the distance toward Cape Carbonra.

Being a Landsman, the Commander pondered the scene, *Boats loaded with green coats, that's the landing force. Four ships in close on two anchors. Why two? The rest of the fleet ready to support and holding distant. Sixteen boats, with about thirty plus men each, that's a battalion against my company.* He straightened his sword belt and continued toward the battle line.

"Sir, the company is formed and ready," said the Sergeant. His tone was even. His voice unbroken.

"Very good. Muskets loaded?"

"No, sir."

"It's time Sergeant, load. Let's be ready for whatever these people have in mind."

"Yes, sir." The Sergeant turned and commanded, "Company, load."

Cartridge box flaps flew back as gunpowder and ball wrapped in paper were pulled from their resting place. This deadly combination was deposited down the smooth bore of multiple musket barrels and rammed home into a compact lethal mass. One by one, these soldiers returned their ramrods to the musket and assumed the position of attention. The three ranks of the formation were razor straight along the flat sands of the beach. The men in the ranks waivered as they moved to counter the shifting forces of the Sirocco winds.

The Commander took out his spyglass and extended it to full length. First, he studied the troops in the boats. Nothing special here. Just regular soldiers, muskets held vertical, waiting. The rhythm of combat, always waiting before the full fury of the exchange of shot and shell. Next, he watched the ships somewhat more distant. Crews worked the capstans on the fore deck. Turning, twisting, and moving in circles to shorten the bow line. On the stern, sailors let loose cable to allow the boat to swing and align with the beach. He slammed the spyglass into its compact shape.

"Damn it, that's why they let out two anchors. Those are their bombardment ships, they are –"

The white smoke of the first broadside was visible before the thunder like report of the cannon reached the shore. The round shot cut through the three ranks of men sending arms and legs in several directions. The troops instinctively closed the gaps torn in the lines keeping their firing potential massed and compact.

"Sergeant fall the company back into the town. No sense standing in front of this cannonade," yelled the Commander above the din of the offshore bombardment.

The grey uniforms streamed into the recesses of the town. As if this was the cue, those circling in boats now started to stroke for the beach. The green uniforms leaped over the white gunwales of the long boats as they rubbed up on the wet sand. Sergeants with long pikes pushed, yelled, and encouraged the green uniforms to get on line. The geometry was precise. The line swept forward through the city. The rhythmic pounding of boots stomping flat on cobblestones carried on the wind down the tight alleyways. Shutters slammed shut on their approach. Women and children cleared the street ahead of the march.

Passing the last buildings, the countryside opened up before them. The grey of the Militia could be seen moving across the river and off to the north. A small detachment held the bridge. Its few ranks held muskets at the ready.

"Shall we push them back El Capitan?" dutifully asked the Lieutenant.

"No, let's not push forward piecemeal. We have Cagliari, and that sir, is a very good start. We have seven thousand more troops to get ashore. It would be selfish for us to enjoy all the fun," said the Captain. His dull smile was unmasked when his lips curled back. "Setup a perimeter and we'll hold here for the rest of the Division to land."

"Yes, sir," replied the Lieutenant. He saluted and went about the business of establishing a beachhead.

The Captain looked down the extent of the valley before him. Steep mountains on his right. Lower hills on his left. The river rushing to the sea before him. The bread basket of Sardinia waved with light caramel hues as far as the eye could see. He whispered to himself, "Home."

*****

Captain Darroch sat at his table on the first floor of the Red Fox Inn. The bell in the clock tower rang twice. He had been patiently waiting for Earl von Hunter to make his appearance but given his late-night activities he had yet to surface from room number three. If Cynthia was true to form, he could be tied up for quite some time. Looking over at the bar, he made eye contact with one of the few servers that had decided not to follow the fleet to anchor. A short nod was all it took for her to bring him a pint of ale. He stared at the dark liquid for a few minutes before lifting the tankard to his lips.

A single canon shot reverberated up the tight alleyways of Portsmouth. Every sailor and Marine knew the meaning of this odd, but solitary, burst of thunder. William eased back in his chair and took a long swig of ale. In a muffled voice, he said, "Recall. General fleet recall. Damn."

Annette scurried down the staircase wearing nothing but her dressing gown. "William, William, was that the recall signal?" She stubbed her toe on a chair as she neared the table where William was ensconced. "Damn it!" She leaned across the table to secure the Marine's attention.

Looking up William was momentarily at a loss for words. Leaning forward, the cut of her gown failed to cover her upper body. Her auburn hair fell to either side of her face framing her features in a reddish hue. His initial thoughts were far from duty, recall, or the crown. He cleared his throat.

"Yes Annette, that's the recall signal," said William.

"I'll be getting my things together," said Annette. She felt a hand pat her ass, causing her to standup and pull her dressing gown more tightly around her body. She took a step closer to William.

"The right honorable Earl von Hunter, I was hoping you would come down from your lofty chamber with Cynthia," said the Marine.

31

Annette tightened her stare on the Earl. She thought, *of all the people in this inn, he should be knowing my ass is off limits.*

"Annette, Earl, please take a seat the both of you. I have to discuss business for a moment."

The three of them sat around the small table. It only took a couple of minutes for two additional tankards of ale to appear before the joiners.

"The last time England went head-to-head with Spain, they sent an armada into the English Channel. Over a hundred ships, seeking to invade our island," said William.

"That was over a hundred years ago Captain Darroch. They don't have the ships to launch that sort of invasion again. It can't possibly happen this time around," said Hunter. He had gotten serious as the topic of conversation drifted far afield from the usual flirtatious banter that filled the smoke-filled corners of the Red Fox Inn.

"Invasion, true enough, but you should expect them to raid our coast. Portsmouth is a prime target. I would personally appreciate it if you could harbor Annette at one of your estates until this conflict is resolved," said William. Annette snapped her stare from the Earl over to William.

"What do you be meaning here? My place is aboard *Comet*. I'm the captain's cook and should be his personal body guard. Hell, I can out fence most of the crew thanks to Mister Rutwell's instruction," said Annette. Her green eyes fired a strong stare at William.

"Annette, it is one thing to chase pirates or an occasional warship. That is not what is about to happen here. We are talking about staring down multiple Ships of the Line. A solid wall of massed canons firing at point blank range in line ahead formation. Shredding wooden planking and masts like tooth picks. I do not want to expose you to such a firestorm."

"No! It's not your decision. It be mine, and mine alone," replied Annette. Her voice elevated, and auburn hair bounced around her head as she spoke.

"Earl von Hunter, can you provide Annette refuge at one of your estates?"

"William, you're not listening," said Annette.

"Yes. I have a castle in the north. Out of the way. Certainly, distant from any threats the channel will endure. It's called Eilean Donan, on the west coast of Scotland," said Hunter. He turned aside Annette's attempt to make eye contact.

"Is it safe?" asked Darroch. He was holding Annette's hand to stop her from poking him in the ribs.

"It's a bloody bastion. The fortress has thirty-foot tall stone walls and sits out on an island in Loch Duich. The damn thing doesn't need a mote, it's surrounded by water. It has a solid well and can withstand any siege. It will hold, I mean, protect Annette."

"Hell no," interrupted Annette. "I just got this posting on *Comet* and I will not be having Captain Calder think I'm some sort of coward by not reporting at the first sign of danger."

"Annette, I will tell Captain Calder I forced you to stay ashore. You have been paid-out by the purser. You owe nothing to the Royal Navy," said William.

"True, but I be owing much to Captain Calder. He took a chance on me, stood-by me when you were fighting at Nassau, and allowed me the freedom and responsibility to run his mess as I saw fit. To not report now –"

"Annette, you'll have to do it for me. I don't want to see you a bloody mess, bent and broken on the command deck after *Comet* has to take a position in the battle line. No, you will stay and travel north away from the likely targets of Spanish aggression," said William. He softly stroked Annette's hand as he spoke.

Hunter leaned closer to Annette. Under the table his hand slid beneath her light cotton dressing gown and traveled along the supple flesh of her upper thigh. He continued to study her response as he pressed farther up her leg. Annette ran her free hand down Captain Darroch's leg crawling toward this legging. She rubbed the back of his calf until she felt the hardness for which she was searching. Annette secured her grip on the rigid shaft, wrapping her fingers around the rounded top of the unseen object. In one quick move, Annette pulled William's dirk from its resting place in his legging and slammed it into the table top.

Looking over at the Earl, she found his eyes had doubled in size. The blade stood motionless given the depth to which it had penetrated the table.

"If you be wanting to keep your hand, you'd best be keeping it off me leg," said Annette. Her tone was low and controlled.

"Earl, that's the best advice given this afternoon. I think you know, if I place Annette in your care and any harm should befall her on your account. I shall cut you below the waist in a manner you'll find most unpleasant," said William.

"Well, yes. Just being a little friendly here. Remember when I told you after the fight with Jacobite, I'd do anything to help. Well, this is it. I consider our debt paid after this conflict is over."

"Done."

"Not quite done," said Annette.

"What do you mean?" said Hunter. His hand retreated to his lap.

"I will be taking my hand maiden with me. She will act as chaperon and confident. It is the only condition that will make this sojourn acceptable."

"And who would that be?" asked Hunter. He rubbed the bottom of his chin and looked up toward the roof.

"Cynthia will travel with me. She will be with me always. We each will need a couple travel trunks to pack our belongings."

"Aye, all that makes sense," said Hunter. He crossed his arms in front of him. "I'll ride back to my estate today. It will take me two days to coordinate the arrangements. Then I'll return here with an armed escort and a carriage for the ladies. While I recommend you both travel light, the only luxuries in Scotland, are those you bring."

Annette stood, and looked at the dirk in the table.

"If you gentlemen would excuse me, I best be getting dressed," she said. Annette pulled the dirk from the table with both hands. She grabbed the dirk by the blade so as to pass it handle first to Captain Darroch. She stopped when the blade went half way to the Marine. "Perhaps, I should be keeping this for our little trip. Many predators along the highways and paths to Scotland." She looked Hunter in the eye as she spoke.

Annette bumped into Cynthia at the top of the stairs. The two of them looked down at the Earl and Marine below.

"Cynthia, it seems you and I will be going for a trip north in a few days. You get two trunks, so pack accordingly," said Annette.

"Where are we going?"

"Scotland."

"Why? Nothing there but Scots."

"We are going there to stay out of trouble along the coast."

"But why do I have to go?"

Annette stood close to her and whispered in her ear, "Your job is to wear down Drake von Hunter, so he keeps his damn hands off me."

"Really, again?"

"Yes, really. I can't take it. I'm not his whore."

"Annette, what does that make me?"

"His Mistress. You get due compensation for your efforts. All I get is a scaly hand in my crotch. Wear him out or teach him to like sheep. Lots of sheep in Scotland."

"I only know one lady for that task, and she be staying here in Portsmouth," said Cynthia. The corners of her mouth edged up.

They both looked down and giggled.

35

"Yes, well Pang has to run this place. The traffic might be light, but the doors will stay open. The sailors will return. You can't stay at war forever, can you?"

Cynthia just shrugged. Michael and Pang joined these two at the top of the stairs. Looking down from their perch, they saw Captain Darroch and Earl von Hunter in conversation. The talk between them was accented with much hand waving and gesturing.

"What's all that about?" asked Rutwell pointing below.

"It seems the general recall signal is in effect. Sailors from *Comet* are starting to gather. Not all of them are sure they want to return," said Annette.

"The payout. That's right, most of those folks signed on only for the voyage. Good luck getting them back for another go."

"Annette, would you be expecting me to run the inn again on your return to *Comet*?" asked Pang. She crossed her arms over her chest.

"Well, yes and no. You'll need to keep the place open in my absence. However, Cynthia and I are heading north with the Earl. I'm not going back to the ship."

"Why?"

"William thinks with the war, it will be too dangerous for me to remain afloat. He may be right. I've seen the smoke and fury of just a few ships in action. Pure hell on the water. I can't even imagine what a whole fleet lined up and exchanging blows would be like."

"I'd better see if I can help our Marine with the recall," said Rutwell. He started down the stairs.

"Why do things look so quiet?" asked Pang.

"Most of our crew got out of here last night. They were heading to the wharf to get a ride out to the fleet at anchor on a bumboat," said Annette.

"How do you expect me to keep this place open with no entertainment staff?"

Annette smiled at Pang. She tilted her head forward.

"Oh no. I've been down that path before. Don't expect me to carry the weight of those poor souls left in Portsmouth."

"Not you. You'll have to recruit new staff. You've done all that before."

Cynthia and Annette returned to their rooms. Pang went down stairs and took up a position behind the bar. She kept one ear bent in the direction of the three men gathered around the near table.

"Midshipman Rutwell, gather up all those from *Comet* you can find. I'll see if we can get them to return for duty. That should prove interesting," said Darroch.

"Aye, aye, sir."

"Earl, I take it you'll be on your way to prepare a coach for the trip north?"

"Yes, indeed. Don't worry Captain Darroch, I am a man of my word. I'll see to Annette's safety and ensure nothing happens to her in your absence." Drake stood, threw his red cape over his shoulder and headed out the door.

On the second floor, Darroch could hear Rutwell pounding on doors and pulling crewmen from the comfort of their night's activities into the harsh daylight. The verbiage and tone of their response was about what the Marine expected to hear. He studied these sailors as they descended the stairs and milled about the dance floor. Hands in pockets, heads cast downward to the deck, and wide yawns provided insight into their mood. William tapped his fingers on the table struggling to think of the right words to address these men. *They have all done their duty, and now we are about to ask for more. More from those that have so little to give. More from the cogs that drive the markets of this kingdom. More from frail human frames, under nourished and fatigued. How is it possible they can muster more?* Darroch struggled to control his doubts.

Midshipman Rutwell joined this mass of humanity on the first floor. Looking over at the Marine, he said, "Sir, this is all the crew I could find. I'm sure others are scattered in taverns down the alley."

Darroch nodded, stood, and approached the stairs. He positioned himself on the first step. Making eye contact with each man, he lifted his hand to get their attention. He cleared his throat. It felt drier than normal.

"Men of *Comet*, I know some of you heard, or are aware that, the recall signal has been fired. Most of you here have been paid out by the Purser. Your commitment to the Royal Navy fulfilled. For your service, I'm personally grateful. We achieved much in our last voyage across the Atlantic. Most of you have lined your pockets with silver taken from distant places. That is, as it should be," said Darroch. He paused to catch his breath. He could feel his heart pounding in his chest coupled with a tightness in his stomach. Looking around he found all eyes still locked on him.

"Sir, you can't be pressing us back into service. We just got home," called out an unseen voice.

"No, I'm not here to impose the press, but consider this if you will. You all know the quality of our Captain. England is heading to war. Once that declaration is made, the press will in fact follow. You all know that to be true. Most of you have felt the pinch before. Now I ask you, would you rather sign-on with a captain you respect and trust, or roll the dice for one of those upper crust ruling elite folks. Some of you know what that service entails." Darroch looked across the crowd and found most of the heads nodding. He took one step back to gain another foot of elevation.

"Men, please know this, as a Marine I've served both afloat and ashore. I've seen all types of leaders and suffered under some more than others. *Comet* has a good crew. Well-seasoned from the last voyage. Few could stand before us. My Marines will do their part, on that you can be sure. I would not begrudge any sailor that walked away today. You've served well, and for that you have a pocket of coin, the King's thanks, and my respect. But now, I must ask you to return with me to the ship. Your country demands you, Captain Calder needs you, and I'm personally asking each of you. Answer the call."

For a moment the only sound in the Red Fox Inn was the crackling of the fire adjacent to the dance floor. Pang threw her hair over one shoulder and studied the sailors. They were looking side-to-side, hoping for someone else to speak first. A lone hand was lifted slowly skyward.

"I'm in, sir. Hell, most of the girls have gone out to anchor anyway."

"Damn, he's right. I'll go, sir."

"Count on me."

"Me too, sir."

"Midshipman Rutwell, would you be so good as to form this mass into something that resembles a formation and march them back to *Comet*. I'm sure Captain Calder could use some assistance in getting out to anchor," said Darroch.

"Aye, aye, sir. All hands let's form up in the alleyway."

The crew shuffled out of the inn under the watchful eye of Rutwell. Darroch moved over to the bar. Pang smiled at him.

"Nice speech. Powerful words to get these seadogs back to the boat," said Pang.

The Marine leaned on the bar as if a load had just been lifted from him. Pang took his hand and squeezed lightly. She locked eyes with him, ensuring his attention.

"You take care of Michael. I want him back. In one piece, if that's not too much trouble. I have plans for the young lad and I will not let a little thing like a war with Spain deter me."

"For you Pang, anything. But I think you know not all the factors of war are influenced by a mere Royal Marine captain on a fourth-rate ship of the fleet."

"I don't care. You, and only you, can bring him back. Do so."

"You'll wait for him then?"

"Of course. Him, and no other."

"I don't think I ever thought I'd hear you say that my dear. It sounds rather nice."

"Look, I know my history is a little jaded. However, I've been with enough men to know what I want. What I really need. So, while I haven't kept tally, Michael is the one. Please, bring him home to me."

"I can't promise—"

"I'm not asking you to promise. But I know if a Marine says he'll do a thing, a thing will get done."

"I take it you'll make him happy then?"

"Do you enjoy your passion with Annette?"

"Of course," said Darroch. His smile reflected a light blush.

"I taught Annette everything she knows in bed. That doesn't mean I taught her everything I know," said Pang. She lifted her finger to her lower lip and pressed down exposing the moist flesh within.

Captain Darroch took a deep breath. Straightening his stance, he said, "Pang if you are loyal to Michael, I'll return the loyalty to you. I'll get him home. Hell, I hope I can get us all home."

*****

The Earl approached his estate at a gallop. He had paced his steed along the trail and now finished the journey at a fast clip. The clip-clop sound of horse hooves announced his return to his staff. Pulling back on the reins he brought the animal to a graceful stop in front of his servant.

"Welcome back, sir. I'll take your horse over to the stable boy."

"Excellent. When you have handed him over, please pack two trunks for an extended trip. I will be away from the estate for a long while I fear."

"Yes, sir."

"Oh, one more thing. Have the stable boy prepare both my horse and carriage for a long trip north. It seems I'm going to be in Scotland for the duration."

"Yes, sir."

"What's all this talk of Scotland?" The query came from a female voice behind him. He turned to find a woman his age walking toward him. Her fully rounded face, foretold the nature of her physique hidden beneath a well-tailored dress of the finest material. The multiple layers of petticoats made the skirt extend well away from her sides. The dress bounced in time with each step and made it appear that she glided across the gravel path.

"Rachel, my dear. I've missed you," said Hunter.

"And why is my husband heading to Scotland?"

"I've been called up to send a militia troop to our northern frontier. Deterrence really. If the Jacobite see a large English force on their soil, they will be less inclined to start something."

"The militia you say. Where in Scotland will you be staying?"

"Eilean Donan castle, on the Loch."

"Eilean Donan castle, dreadful place. Cold, damp, and the wind always blows in from the north. I shiver just thinking about it. How long will you be away my dear?"

"For the duration."

"The duration of what?"

"War is coming between England and Spain. Not sure how long it will take to defeat them, but I'll be up there until they fold."

"And what of the estate?"

"Our grounds manager has things well in hand. You'll oversee the books as always. Let's not make a big stink over this, shall we."

"Are you traveling with anyone else?"

"Just the militia. Why do you ask?"

"I thought it a little odd for you to request the carriage. That's the normal conveyance of us ladies."

41

"I think you know how often it rains in the highlands. I do want to be able to get out of the weather from time to time."

"I see," said Rachel. Her slanted smile injected an element of doubt to her response.

The Earl walked over to her and stretched to get his arm around her waist. They turned and walked side-by-side up the path toward the main house. Its grey stones rose above them. The fine wood trim around the windows and details on the solid oak door, spoke to the affluence of this couple. The sheer mass of the structure provided stability, comfort, and continuity. While only a short distance in miles, it was a world apart from the Red Fox Inn.

*****

Captain Calder paced on the seaward side of the main deck. With *Comet* tied along the quay wall, he watched as the rest of the fleet moved into the Portsmouth Sound to anchor out. The sea breeze rippled white caps in the bay sending small spurts of white foam skyward. He pulled his collar up against the ever-present chill of the wind.

"Captain, you need to come see this," called Midshipman Dugins from the quarterdeck on the other side of the ship.

Calder turned his back to the bay and walked athwart ships to where Dugins was standing. Looking down to the dock, his eyes widened. A group of sailors were marching, in step, and approaching *Comet.* In the lead, Midshipman Rutwell.

"Well, I'll be damned," said Calder.

"Looks as if most of the crew is answering the recall signal, sir," said Dugins.

"So, it does. Have Mister Rutwell report to me when he gets aboard. I'll be in my cabin."

"Aye, aye, sir."

The crew filed up onto the main deck. Mister Dugins, as Officer of the Deck, ensured proper boarding protocol. Each sailor saluted the flag, then the Officer of the Deck, and requested to come aboard. It was a routine so ingrained most had done it with a belly full of ale, following a long night ashore.

"Request permission to come aboard," said Rutwell. He held a firm salute in the direction of Midshipman Dugins.

"Granted," came Dugins' quick retort. "The Captain wants to see you in his cabin."

"What's that on your face, Brice?" asked Rutwell. He tilted his head to the side.

"Lieutenant Martino suggested I wear some makeup to protect my skin from the sun and wind."

"Brice, you look like a ghost."

"I'm told it's the fashion of the ruling elite. If you want to move up the chain, it's important to look the part. Don't you think?"

"I think you look royal. Very, very royal," replied Rutwell. He had to bite his tongue to prevent from smiling.

Dugins stomach muscles tightened, straightening his posture. He advanced his left foot toward Rutwell and secured the left lapel of his blue coat with a strong grip. The flesh over his knuckles turned pale. He cleared his throat.

"Well, patronage is one path to promotion—"

"So is performance," said Rutwell cutting his contemporary off before he could finish his thought.

"You'll have to excuse me Mister Rutwell, I'm standing duty here and should not engage in such idle talk."

"Certainly, but I think you know the winds from the south are blowing battle in our direction. What do you think will stand the ship and crew in good stead during the heat of battle, patronage or performance?"

Dugins shifted his arms akimbo. His eyes tightened on his messmate. He took a deep breath, held it, and then exhaled.

"Michael, you are free to choose whatever path you want. Not all of us share your talent with a blade. I have to use every means

43

at my disposal to secure a proper posting. All I ask is you support me in my quest. Is that too much to ask?"

Rutwell extended a limp wristed salute. His lips flattened into a straight line. Locking eyes with Dugins, he said, "Brice, I wish you all the luck you deserve. I hope this works out for you."

Chapter 3 The Road North

The sun continued to climb shortening the shadows in the alleyway adjacent to the Red Fox Inn. The chill of the morning faded slowly as Portsmouth dusted off the effects of a dull dark night. Light rain drops hurried on the wind leaving the city smelling fresh in their wake. Residents moved along their way to reach appointments and comply with routines that demanded mindless obedience. Unseeing and unthinking, no one took notice of the man covered in the rich brown cape.

This figure was unassuming beneath the hooded cloak that protected him from the elements and masked his identity to those passing by. He leaned against the rough stucco wall of the inn. Its course texture held his hand firmly in its grip. He remained motionless, with head downcast toward the filth of the gutter. When the sunlight finally illuminated his stance, only the lower half of his face was visible within the recesses of his hood. Chapped lips and a thin black mustache provided little in the way of clues to his personage or purpose. He stood aside as a coach squeezed through the narrows of the alleyway and came to a stop in front of the Red Fox Inn.

Drake von Hunter rode up on his horse alongside the coach. He had to spur his ride lightly to persuade the mount to negotiate the narrows between the wall and coach. The Earl stopped alongside the coach driver. He tapped him on the boot to get his attention.

"Wait here. I'll get the ladies and be right back. Have the footman help our guests with their trunks," said Hunter.

"Are we still going up to Eilean Donan castle, sir?"

"Yes."

"That be a long way off, sir."

"Indeed. I figure it will take the better part of three weeks to make the journey. Should be worth it though. We'll be staying there until this mess with Spain sorts itself out."

"Aye, sir."

The figure in the cloak retreated to the shadows. He kept his vigil as the Earl dismounted. Hunter waved his arm to move his red cape over the shoulder and proceeded to enter the inn. His footman followed dutifully one step behind.

"Cynthia, are you ready?" said Hunter.

Cynthia ran to Drake and threw both arms around him. She pulled herself into a deep kiss. He struggled to retain his balance, given the force of her sudden impact. They separated and she settled her feet to the floor.

"I'll take that as a yes," said Hunter.

"Drake, this is so exciting. I couldn't sleep last night. I don't think I'll be letting you sleep tonight. It's only fair," said Cynthia. She giggled as she spoke.

Looking around Hunter saw four trunks neatly aligned on the dance floor near the fireplace. He pointed at them, and asked, "Are those your luggage?"

Cynthia nodded. "Well, mine and Annette's," she added.

"Footman, please load those in the back of the coach."

The footman tipped his hat in Hunter's direction. He walked over and bent down to lift the first trunk. As he attempted to straighten up, he let out a large breath. He struggled to get the chest to pass through the narrows of the doorway.

"What's in those things?" asked Hunter.

"Just a few basics for a lady on the road," replied Cynthia.

"Annette, how about you, are you ready for the road?"

"Why, my right honorable Earl von Hunter, yes. Thank you for asking," said Annette. She moved closer to the couple but hovered just beyond the implied closeness of their courtship that the loose embrace between them foretold.

"Ladies, we will be traveling in close quarters for several weeks. I see no reason why you should not address me in the familiar. Please, call me Drake."

"Drake, how long do you think it will take to reach the castle?" asked Annette.

"I was just discussing that with the coachman. I'm guessing something on the order of three weeks."

"What do you think we'll see along the way?" asked Cynthia. "I've never been more than a stone's throw outside Portsmouth."

"Well, the turnpike system is new and nowhere is it complete. I know one of the trustees managing part of the effort. We'll have a good road out of Portsmouth. So, don't think the whole trip will be like the first thirty miles. I plan to pass through Reading, up to Northampton, and then follow the mix of roads to Newcastle. Once we get north of there, the roads are little more than dirt tracks. The coach has the latest in springs, but I fear they will do little to ease the bumping. You ladies will have to be patient."

The footman returned. He lifted the second trunk. His grunts bore witness to the weight of the satchel. The two ladies giggled as he strained toward the door.

"Drake, what is beyond Newcastle? I've heard stories of robbers and highwaymen that dot the paths up into the highlands," said Cynthia. She gripped Drake's coat just a little tighter.

"My dear, do you really think I would let anything happen to you? You are my world. I will make damn sure you reach Eilean Donan castle intact, if not refreshed," said Drake. He slid his hand up from her waist to the bottom of her breast. The corners of Drake's mouth rose when he made contact with the soft flesh. This drew Cynthia's gaze from Annette, back to Drake.

Annette let out a long sigh. "I think what she is trying to say is, you're one against possibly many."

47

"Oh, I see your point here ladies. I failed to mention that a mounted escort ten strong will be traveling with us. These men are from my personal unit. Hand selected for their skill with weapons and fighting spirit. It will be fine."

The footman returned for his third trip. His breathing was measured. He looked over at Cynthia and gave a slanted smile. She nodded in his direction. The laborious process of lifting, carrying, and loading the trunk was repeated.

"Is the escort here?" asked Annette.

"No, I intend to meet them in Reading. The pike is safe all the way up to Northampton. Again, I don't think the stories that get pandered about over a pint of ale hold much truth."

The footman returned for the final trunk. His breathing was heavy now. He didn't make eye contact with the ladies as he set about his task. He groaned lifting the weight of the trunk with his legs. Back straight and eyes focused on the door, he made his way out to the coach.

"Ladies, shall we?"

The three of them exited to the waiting coach. Annette looked over her shoulder at Pang. She waved and held eye contact. Pang smiled, returned the wave, and set about sweeping the floor behind the bar. Annette made one last look around the inn. She took a deep breath and turned for the door.

When she reached the coach, Cynthia was already seated inside. Drake stood at the step and extended his hand to her.

"May I help you Miss Armtrove?"

"Thank you, sir," said Annette. Her auburn hair flashed in the bright sunlight before she disappeared into the shade of the coach.

Drake placed his left foot in the stirrup and swung up atop his mount. He lifted his hand skyward and threw it forward in a rapid motion. "Move out," carried down the small alleyway. The lone rider and coach disappeared to the main thoroughfare of Portsmouth.

From the shadows, the man in the rich brown cloak watched this small entourage exit from the confines of the alley. He rolled his thin black mustache between his index finger and thumb. His chapped lips broke open a little wider as they lifted into a full smile. Carlos had found what he had been seeking.

"This is not so bad," said Cynthia. She looked across the coach to engage Annette.

"Remember, Drake said this was the easy part," said Annette. She brought her gaze back into the confines of the coach.

"What crop do you think they have planted in these fields?" Cynthia's tone was light.

"Barley, perhaps?" said Annette. "Never been much on plant life you know. It's gorgeous though. Look how it stretches out over the rolling hills."

"I love the glow of the sun reflecting off its tops. It moves in time with the wind. Shimmering, is the word I'm looking for. It shimmers."

"Like the sea," said Annette. Her voice was as distant as her thoughts. She closed her eyes. Between the movement of the coach and waves of barley, Annette was upon the ocean once again. She could visualize Captain Darroch standing on the aft rail of *Comet*. He would be staring at her balancing a tray for Calder. She smiled.

The coach slowed, and Annette opened her eyes. Drake rode up along the coach window, his horse matched the pace of the team pulling their carriage.

"I trust everything is fine, ladies?" said Drake. He tipped his hat toward Cynthia.

"Yes, it's been a pleasant ride up from Portsmouth," said Cynthia.

"Well, we are almost to the inn. I'll get us a couple of rooms and we'll meet our escort in the morning."

Drake spurred his mount and trotted ahead of the coach. Annette looked over at Cynthia.

"Don't forget your assignment here," she said.

"Annette, I think I know how to keep the right honorable Earl occupied." They both giggled.

The coach stopped outside an inn just off the turnpike. The sound of laughter bubbled from the open windows. The footman opened the door and helped each of them out of the coach. He pointed to the back of the carriage.

"Do you ladies need both trunks?"

"Just this one," said Annette pointing at the four satchels strapped securely to the back of the carriage.

"This one, please," added Cynthia.

The Footman nodded. The two women followed Drake up to the desk at the front of the inn. They drew long stares from the men drinking in the adjacent room. Annette listened to the discussion between Drake and the desk clerk.

"Sir, that is correct. I have only the one room remaining."

"I've got two women traveling with me. Can't you find something else?"

"Sir, the room has a very large bed. I'll have the upstairs maid add a sleeping partition. We do this all the time."

Drake looked over his shoulder at Cynthia. She shrugged her ivory shoulders and smiled.

"I'll take it. Are you still serving dinner?"

"Yes, sir. In that room over there. I must say we are more than a little crowded."

Drake turned around and pulled the two women close. "Look ladies, it seems we will all be sharing a bed tonight. Let's get dinner before we retire upstairs. They will need some time to put the sleeping partitions up and prepare the room."

Annette worked to hold a disarming smile. *It be funny how that all worked out. Just the one bed and all. I wonder, did he have this planned all along?*

After dinner Annette followed Cynthia and Drake to the room. The two of them walked arm-in-arm down the hallway. She could feel her stomach tighten as they neared the doorway. On entering the chamber, she found her trunk positioned at the foot of the bed. A six-inch-high wooden board had been placed down the center of the bed. The maid had a cloth curtain suspended from a rope and it overlapped the sleeping partition.

"You two ladies prepare for bed. I'll join you in a minute," said Drake. He exited the room.

Annette lifted the top of her trunk. Without looking at Cynthia, she asked, "What side do you want?"

"I thought we would share a side."

"You don't really think that's what Drake has in mind do you?"

Cynthia exhaled. "No, I guess not."

Drake returned to find the chamber dark. He dropped his clothes and slid into bed. The mattress shook as he settled between the sheets. The sleeping partition clanked against both the head and foot boards. His hands explored the female flesh at his side. The sound of a single slap echoed within the room.

Thank God he guessed right. Annette breathed a sigh of relief.

"What are you doing?" whispered Cynthia. No response.

"Wait."

"Ouch."

The rocking of the bed was felt through the partition. Annette turned away from the motion on the other side of the curtain. *Are we ever going to get some sleep?* This thought dominated Annette's consciousness for the remainder of the night.

The sounding of the rooster signaled the start of a new day on the road north. Drake leaped from bed. He quickly dressed as if to outpace the cold that surrounded his body.

"Let's go ladies. We have many a mile to cover today," said Drake. Annette found the volume of his words annoying.

Annette stumbled out of bed. Her frame was stooped, and arms extended. She worked to dress and maintain some level of

51

demeanor amid the chaos of their bed chamber. Looking over at Cynthia she didn't feel so bad.

"You look terrible," commented Annette.

"Well, I didn't get a wink of sleep. Drake, he's out of the room isn't he?"

"Yes."

"He wouldn't let up last night. I never realized his level of stamina was so high. He just wouldn't keep his hands off me."

"Well then, consider you earned your pay last night. He can't keep it up forever. No man can. Even God rested on the seventh day."

"I don't think I can take five more nights like that Annette." They both giggled.

The morning routine that would dominate their travels took shape here in Reading. Cold breakfast for the ladies. The footman would load the trunks, while the coachman harnessed the team and inspected the carriage. The military escort rode up and dismounted. The Lieutenant in charge would confer with Drake to formulate plans for the day's march.

The two ladies departed the inn to embark for the continuation of their travels. As they approached the carriage, Drake signaled them to come closer.

"Miss Armtrove and Miss Maitland, this is Lieutenant Guthrie. He is our escort commander," said Drake.

The Lieutenant leaned forward and took Cynthia's hand kissing the back. He repeated the performance with Annette. However, with her he lingered with his clasp longer than protocol would have required. He stared into her green eyes unwavering. His smile was more than polite.

"Ladies if you would mount up, I have to talk with the good Lieutenant for a moment before our departure," said Drake.

Annette and Cynthia sat in the front and back seat respectively. They exchanged looks born more from boredom than friendship.

"Are you afraid the Lieutenant might show more than appropriate affection for you?" asked Cynthia.

Annette smiled. She lifted her dress along her leg revealing first the white of her silk stockings and then a leather sheath strapped to her upper thigh. The handle of a blade rode above the leather.

"That's William's dirk," said Cynthia.

Annette nodded. She lowered her dress and placed a single finger to her lips. "Shh . . . it's a secret," replied Annette. It was Cynthia's turn to nod.

As the gentlemen conferred, Annette watched a group of hens peck at the hard ground. The uneven rhythm of their efforts was hypnotizing. Their necks would bounce in pursuit of earthly delights unseen just below the surface. The rapid approach of a cock sent this flock scurrying in disorder. The sudden fluttering of wings and shrill screeching of these fowl startled the horses. They bolted down the lane with the coach in tow.

The coachman looked over at his footman eyes wide. "Hey," was all he could yell as the carriage bounced away.

Annette landed on the coach floor. Cynthia fell on top of her. The two ladies were now getting shaken in all directions as the horses accelerated.

"Damn," said Drake. "Lieutenant let's go!"

The two men grabbed their horses and took off after the carriage. The pounding of hooves in pursuit rang down the lane. These two riders leaned out low over their saddles. Drake shifted his weight rapidly forward and back adjusting to the quick cadence of his steeds' stride. His heels wrapped around the flanks of the animal beneath him as he fought to maintain speed and hold on. He looked up, the coach appeared bigger. He could hear the heavy breathing of the Lieutenant's mount just behind him.

"Come on," yelled Drake.

Cynthia struggled unsuccessfully to regain her seat. She could hear Drake's words.

"Drake," Cynthia yelled. "Help, Drake."

The dust from the carriage now lifted from the roadway into Drake's lungs. He coughed, looked away, and coughed again. *Closer now, keep going.* Cynthia's cries resonated in his brain.

Guthrie maneuvered his steed around Drake and closed on the coach. His horse was just enough faster that it paralleled the runaway carriage. Cynthia got just a glimpse of the uniform now adjacent to them.

"Help," she yelled again. "The brake. Get the brake."

Guthrie looked into the coach to see the jumble of lace and petticoats bouncing between the seats and floor. His eyes focused on the driver's seat and the long handle of the brake. He spurred his horse yet again.

"Yahh," rang out from Guthrie. "Come on boy, just a little closer."

He reached for the brake handle. His horse slowed, just a little and he fell back. He tried again, same result. One more attempt, he leaned closer to the carriage. Stretching to full length, he fell from the saddle. The wheel of the coach rolled over his hand and just missed his head. Drake's horse leaped over the Lieutenant and almost dumped him from the saddle in the process. Drake looked over his shoulder and saw Guthrie roll away. He came to a stop, unmoving.

"Damn," slipped from Drake's lips.

Guthrie's horse ran alongside Drake. The chase continued.

Cries for help resonated from the coach. The carriage moved unabated down the lane. Its speed seemed to increase with every furlong.

Drake now closed on the coach. He could see the tangle of auburn hair that must have been Annette. The rest of her body was covered by Cynthia. Everything else in the coach was a blur of defused colors and shapes. He spurred his horse again. He was just unable to close the final distance to the brake handle.

"That's enough," said Annette. "Get the hell off of me."

She pushed Cynthia off her back and worked to get her knees back on the coach seat. Holding tight to the window frame, she pulled half her body out from the protection of the coach. She hung in the breeze, her hair whipping her face. Annette grabbed the brass cargo rack atop the roof. Holding fast there, she was able to extend her long limb to reach the brake handle. She pulled back, but was unable to apply enough force to stop the carriage. It did slow.

Drake now could ride ahead and grab the horse team. He pulled back on their reins to first slow, and then stop the coach. The dust cloud that had been trailing the rig now swirled around them.

"Are you alright?" asked Drake. He lifted Annette through the window and slid her down his body to the ground. She stood close to him for a moment shaking. Looking up at him she smiled, felt her lips fall, and then smiled again.

"I be just fine. What took you so long?" said Annette. She backed away from Drake. Her hands worked to smooth her dress and regain something of a normal appearance. Her hair flew off in all directions completely teased by the wind.

The rest of the escort rode up. The Coachman and Footman rode tandem at the back of the column. The Lieutenant approached and dismounted.

"How's the hand Lieutenant?" asked Drake.

"The hand is fine. The ego is well bruised I fear."

Cynthia dismounted the coach and embraced Drake.

"I knew you were in a hurry to cover miles today, Earl. I had no idea that would be the way we would be doing it," said Annette.

Laughing Drake replied, "Yes indeed. We are off to a good start. We'd better keep at it if we're going to get to our tavern tonight.

The ladies waited until the coachman was seated before they re-entered the carriage. The escort mounted and stood in a column of twos on each side of the road. Guthrie looked over at Drake.

"Orders, sir?"

"You're with me. Place two scouts to ride ahead, four soldiers with me in front of the coach and the remaining four follow behind," said Drake. The confidence had returned to his voice.

The column fanned out along the lane. Trees overhung the path and shaded part of the journey. They continued on their way north. All be it at a more subdued pace than the morning's dash.

*****

The dust of the trail carried behind the column as they climbed slowly up a long grade several hours out of Newcastle. The sweat of the carriage team horses filled the mid-morning air. Their coats glistened, reflecting the morning light. The constant presence of large flies tormented the driver more than the rays of the sun. He would work his hand on one side of his face only to have these annoying insects attack the other.

"Did you sleep well last night?" asked Cynthia. She had grown fatigued of the passing scenery and decided to engage Annette.

"Yes. Thank you for asking. Since we left Northampton, I've seen fewer folks on the road. The inns have been more than accommodating and not having to share a room with the Earl has done wonders for my rest," said Annette. She paused, returned her gaze across the coach at Cynthia. "Of course, maybe it's just I'm so tired I could be falling asleep anywhere."

Drake rode up alongside the carriage. He leaned forward to make eye contact with Cynthia. The fog from the horse's breath in the early morning, had given way to the rhythm of the mount's

56

breathing as he labored up the hill with the Earl. Drake tipped his hat in Cynthia's direction.

"Good morning my dear," said Drake. He briefly glanced in Annette's direction. "Annette, good morning."

"Drake, good morning to you as well," said Annette. Both ladies now stared at this rider alongside their coach. "I trust the road finds the right honorable Earl von Hunter in good spirits?"

"Yes, indeed Miss Armtrove, since we are going to be somewhat more formal are we, the trip is going as well as one would expect," said Drake.

"How far out of Newcastle are we?" asked Cynthia. She twirled a long black curl of her hair in one hand. This drew Drake attention back to her.

"I would say, something on the order of eight miles," replied Drake. His hand and reins bounced in time with his horse's stride as his upper body rocked in the saddle. "I know that because we are reaching the end of the turnpike. I fear the ride will be much rougher on the trails and dirt paths ahead ladies."

This polite conversation was broken by the sound of four pistol shots up the road. The wood covered nature of the path at this point obscured what was in front of the column. Drake looked in vain down the road.

"Lieutenant, the scouts?" asked Drake.

"Nothing sir. They would ride back if they could."

"Lieutenant Guthrie, you and your four men are with me. You other four, surround and defend the coach," commanded Drake. He spurred his mount and rode full tilt ahead of the carriage. The Lieutenant and his men rode behind as they chased Drake's red cape down the lane into the unknown.

The carriage came to a stop. Annette stuck her head out of the window and struggled to see ahead. Her attention was captivated by a small dust cloud that followed the riders down the trail until they rode out of sight. The driver pulled back on the coach brake and held firm the reins. When he saw Annette half out of the window, he turned toward her.

"We'll hold here Mistress. Until the Earl can sort things out ahead, it makes sense to stay out of the fray," said the coachman. He turned away from Annette. His eyes straining to detect any sign of what was ahead down the lane.

Annette pulled herself back within the coach.

"Could you see anything?" asked Cynthia.

"No, but we have a rider on each corner of the carriage. Like a box around us," replied Annette. "Any highwayman would have to get through them to reach you my dear." Annette pulled her dress and underlying petticoats aside revealing the long athletic form of her legs incased in white silk stockings. She pulled William's dirk from its sheath. She spun it around by the handle and held the blade in a combative grip. "And me, they would have to get through me as well."

The sound of gunfire down the road renewed. A bird briefly cried from the trees around them. It was an eerie and unnerving calm that took hold of the coach occupants. The two ladies stared at each other. Annette watched Cynthia's black eyes tighten. She held a finger to her lips, and said, "Shh—" They both strained to listen. The faint sound of steel-on-steel reverberated through the woods.

"That can't be good," whispered Annette.

The slap of horse flesh against the carriage shook the coach and tossed about the two ladies. Annette gasped as one of the escorts rolled from his horse to the ground. The guard behind them was now engaged with his saber against a figure dressed in plain brown cloth. His opponent wore a black slouch hat, its brim was bent downward covering his eyes. She watched as the blades flashed in the light that filtered through the trees. She thought it odd how mounted sword play was so different from what she knew aboard ship. No side-to-side or low-to-high strikes were possible with a thousand pounds of animal strapped between your legs. The rider could only execute straight ahead and overhead thrusts. These ad hoc moves were often thrown off-balance as the rider attempted to stay in the saddle.

The escort on the ground recovered his stance. With saber drawn, his back was against the carriage, directly below Annette's window. The highwayman that had charged him and knocked him aside, now closed on his steed to finish the task. He swung down upon the escort. The escort raised his blade in an attempt to block the attack. The momentum and height of the attacker added such force to the blow that the highwayman's blade buckled the defender's arm and hit home on his neck. The blood splattered up on Annette, casting red dots of death on her cheek and dress. She tightened the grip on her dirk.

The coachman and footman both jumped from the carriage. They ran away from the fight around their vehicle and headed into the dense woods. Neither of them looked over their shoulder as they abandoned their passengers to their fate.

The sound of steel-on-steel subsided. An odd quiet filled the forest around the coach. No birds or sounds of any kind. One of the victorious highwaymen pushed his hand against the coach door securing it shut. He studied the passengers inside. His lips drew back revealing a smile of darkened teeth. The stubble on his face, coupled with the smell of unwashed flesh, made it clear he had been among the woods for a long time.

"James, look what we've be finding here," said the figure with the black slouch hat. "It seems a couple of ladies from court have decided to join us." He laughed in a manner that reflected not humor, but the arrogance of control. James stood back from the coach and held a pistol on the passengers inside. James licked his lips and the same slanted smile soon occupied his expression.

"Ladies, out here?" asked James.

"Aye, my lad. They be pretty ones too."

Out of the corner of her eye, Annette saw Drake maneuvering around toward the back of the carriage. She looked across at

Cynthia. Her traveling companion's eyes had widened, and her lips pushed together with such force the wrinkles around her mouth magnified. The highwayman reached into the coach and brushed the blood drops along Annette face. He smeared the red liquid around her cheek giving the appearance of heightened blush. His hand rested on the coach window. He pulled up the step to get a better view of the passengers.

Annette slid the dirk against the side of the seat to hide it from the inquisitive man in the slouch hat. As he looked in, Annette pulled her dress and petticoat back once again up to the knee. Her calf and ankle now exposed, drew the highwayman's full attention.

"James, have you ever been with a lady of the court before?" The highwayman asked.

"No, but I be willing to give it try."

Cynthia began to shake. The tremble in her lip reverberated down the length of her body. Annette loosened, and then tightened, her grip on the dirk.

"Red, I think I be liking what I see. Now it's time you and I have a little dance," said the man in the slouch hat. His exuberance was reflected in this tone.

"I think not," yelled Drake stepping from behind the coach with two pistols at the ready.

Annette drove the dirk into the hand of the man in the slouch hat pinning it to the window frame.

"Bitch," was all the man in the slouch hat could muster as he dangled with his hand pierced like a side of beef.

James' mouth fell open. He spun toward this new threat holding both pistols waist high. Drake's first shot cut James down in the middle of his turn. The force of the ball drove him back. His knees buckled as he collapsed to the red dirt of the road. Drake raised his pistol at the man in the slouch hat. His only defense was to hold the flat of his hand toward the Earl.

"Sir, I beg—"

The shot rang in Cynthia's ears causing her to jerk uncontrollably. The ball traveled clean to split the top jaw of the man in the slouch hat just below his nose. Once again, a splattering of blood was cast on Annette. She smiled and nodded toward Drake. The man fell toward the ground. His body weight pulled his hand through the sharp edge of the dirk, splitting it in half from the palm up.

Drake surveyed his handy work. "Humph," was the only sound he made while approaching the coach. He tucked his pistols in his belt and pulled a handkerchief from his pocket. He handed it to Annette. He eyed the dirk still driven into the coach window frame.

"Here you are my dear. It seems you might want to freshen up a bit," said Drake. As she took the cloth from his hand, he tapped the dirk a few times. "Just where did this thing come from?"

"I always carry one," said Annette. She worked to remove the red blood spatter from her face. "A girl can never be too careful in traveling these back roads, or so I've been told."

"Or so you've been told," replied Drake.

Lieutenant Guthrie rode back from the ambush site with two of his men. The Coachman and his Footman emerged from the tree line. Drake took a quick count.

"Lieutenant, any other survivors up forward?" asked Drake.

"No, sir."

"Damn, this is all we have left. We had better press on, before any more of this little band descend upon us."

"Sir, what about the dead?"

"We'll report the attack to the Magistrate up ahead. Let him deal with policing up this mess. He should have had a better handle on these brigands anyway."

Annette strained to pull the dirk from the window frame. It refused to budge. Drake stepped over.

"Would you like a little help with that thing?" he asked.

Annette nodded. He pulled up on the handle. It didn't move. He pulled again. This time his knuckles turned white, his cheeks bulged, and a guttural sound escaped his throat.

"Just how hard did you plant this thing?"

"I think the power of fright, might have been moving my hand here," said Annette in a soft voice.

On the third attempt the blade broke free from the window frame. Drake handed the dirk back to Annette.

"Thank you for your help," said Annette in a whisper.

The last day on the trail arrived more uneventful than this morning in the woods. As the column, now much reduced in length, reached the last high ground before the castle it paused for the horses to rest. The sun dipped behind the high ground to the west. It sent shades of red and orange across the sky and water until it was difficult to tell where the heavens ended, and the realm of Neptune began. The darkness of the surrounding high ground framed the two domains and accented the fact that they had reached the highlands. Annette and Cynthia dismounted from the coach to stretch their legs. They walked a few yards and stood overlooking their future home.

The grey walls of Eilean Donan rose on a small island and reflected on the still waters of the three lochs that converged around her. A light smoke rose above the brown tile roof of the main building. The stone walls stood as silent sentinels to the strength of this fortress long a bastion amid the rough and tumble clans of Scotland.

"This place has long been a strategic point in the north," said Drake. "It sits at the convergence of Loch Duich, Loch Long and Loch Alsh. Any movement from the Minch would have to pass this way if they wanted to move inland. The fortress has stood for over a hundred years. You ladies will be safe enough here."

Cynthia moved into the shelter of Drake's arms. She looked up at him, holding her gaze until he lowered his head and made eye contact.

"I'll always feel safe in your arms, Drake," she said.

Drake took just a little deeper breath. His chest rose a bit further out. He nodded.

"What are you going to do first, when you get settled, Annette?" asked Cynthia.

"The first thing I be doing is writing William a letter and tell him what a safe journey I had on my way to Eilean Donan castle," said Annette.

The three of them exchanged glances. The corners of Annette's mouth edged up. Then a loud deep laugher followed by all three.

Chapter 4 Court Conundrum

A small unassuming fishing boat landed on the wharf of Vigo, Spain. Few would have guessed that its length and design would have been robust enough to transit the choppy waters of Biscay Bay or the English Channel. The tattered nature of her sails and faded paint were evidence that the craft had traveled well beyond the fishing grounds adjacent to the Spanish coast. A lone figure, wearing a dark brown cloak, disembarked on the stone pier. This garment bounced along with his purposeful, if somewhat hobbled, stride as the solitary bent-over figure hurried toward the bastion of Fort Castro.

Lady Ernesta Rainerio sat in the reception room of the fort. Holding a crystal wine glass to her lips, she sipped a rich red port in the vain hope that the intoxicating liquid would help her relax. She had eagerly awaited news from the north and now it appeared her agent of investigation had returned. A loud knock on the door drew her gaze upward.

"Yes," Ernesta enquired.

"Lady Rainerio, I have a Carlos Andres here to see you. Shall I admit him?" asked the guard. His voice was broken, reflecting his tension when dealing with those of superior station.

"Yes, if you would be so kind."

Carlos push open the door and strolled into the room. His posture straightened in the presence of Lady Rainerio. Lifting both hands, he threw back his hood revealing his face and locking eyes with Ernesta. His cheeks were hollow and the thin black mustache along his lip appeared as if drawn on with a pencil.

"Carlos, you've grown a mustache," she said. Pointing toward the guard, she added, "Thank you. You are dismissed." The sentry retreated from the room and secured the solid oak door behind him.

"Is that port?" asked Carlos.

64

"Yes, would you like some?"

"May I?" he asked, while pointing to the chair next to Ernesta.

"Yes, of course. Please have a seat."

Carlos poured himself a glass of wine and removed his cloak. He hung the distinctive brown garment over the back of his chair as he settled into the wicker form that embraced him. Carlos took a long sip of port. His eyes widened, and one corner of his mouth turned up.

"Augh. Now I've been waiting for that for over a month now. The English hold to their beer. Terrible stuff but it does serve a purpose."

"What would that be?" asked Ernesta.

"That dark ale will loosen the tightest tongue of an English man or legs of their ladies. Most useful for collecting information, my lady."

"Collecting other conquests as well, from the sound of it."

Carlos twisted his thin black mustache between his thumb and index finger. He set the glass of wine down on a small table between the two chairs and crossed his legs. He leaned back in his chair.

"Ernesta, I have the information you asked me to get," said Carlos. His voice rang confident and almost proud.

"Do tell. What have you learned?"

"I traveled to Portsmouth as directed. I was able to find the Red Fox Inn. It was buried in the tangled streets and back alleys of the port, but I asked a local sailor who was only too happy to show me the way. It took me a week, but I finally saw the redhead of whom you spoke."

"Annette?"

"The very same. I hung in the alleyway listening to the passersby, always learning more about her routine, what she likes, and her mode of dress. I followed her when she shopped, noted who she talked with, and hell, I can even tell from what window she empties her chamber pot."

"All very interesting, but not very useful. Where can she be taken for our purpose?"

"The British have moved the fleet to anchor. She did not return to *Comet*."

"Then she and William are separated?"

"Exactly. He is aboard the ship with the Marines."

"Perfect."

"Oh, but it gets even better. I saw her leave in the company of another man. Found out he is Earl von Hunter. They are heading to a remote castle in Scotland called Eilean Donan."

"Scotland?"

"Yes, my lady," replied Carlos. He leaned close to Ernesta.

"We have allies in that God forsaken place. The Jacobite, perhaps—"

"I'm already on it my Lady. I've made contact with a local Jacobite leader that is willing to support us, surrender the castle and its occupants, if we help them gain independence from the English. You can secure Annette and make Captain Darroch come to you."

"How long are they planning to remain there?"

"That's the best part, my Lady. I heard the Earl say, for the duration. As long as the conflict between our two nations is active, they plan to stay distant from the English Channel."

"You know we are not at war with the English. At least not as of yet."

"No, but it is only a matter of time. Once the Royal Conundrum is resolved, all hell will break loose in the Mediterranean Sea."

"Royal Conundrum?"

"Yes, my Lady. Between the death of Louis the Fourteenth, and the war between Austria and the Ottomans, both those royal houses are paralyzed into inaction. We have a free hand to retake what was taken from us."

"I see. Let's let this play out. Perhaps England will attempt to go it alone. In which case, we may be able to strike north and secure our prize."

"Yes, my Lady. How shall I proceed?" asked Carlos. He took another long sip of port while awaiting a response.

Ernesta stood and walked toward the long and narrow window on the west wall of the chamber. She looked out into the harbor. A few warships swung at anchor, while cargo ships struggled to load and unload their wares along the wharf. Carlos continued to work his glass of port, consuming more than half its contents as Ernesta formulated her plan. She took a deep breath and turned back toward Carlos.

"Carlos, I want you to take a few weeks here to refresh and prepare. I fear the task ahead will be the most challenging I've ever assigned you," said Ernesta. A short pause and then she continued. "Go to Scotland. Align with the Jacobite as needed. Promise them anything you must, but you must gain their allegiance. Once they have committed to selling out Eilean Donan, let me know. Send a messenger. I want you to stay on scene and personally oversee the activities there. I trust this task to no one else. Let me know when I should go north. I will be the one to place that whore in chains." Her volume increased as she spoke. "Annette has stood between me and the love of my life. She will stand no more! Is that clear?"

Carlos stood and bowed toward Ernesta. His arm spread away from his body. On finishing this formal gesture, he straightened up and looked her in the eye.

"My Lady, I'm but yours to command. However, these tasks require financing. I fear my purse has run as dry as my wine glass."

Ernesta walked over and took hold of the bottle of port. She aligned the neck of the bottle with Carlos' wine glass. Tilting the back of the bottle skyward she drained the bottle until his glass was full. She untied a small pouch from around her waist and shook it. The metallic sound of coins clanking together resonated in the room. She handed the bag to him. He took hold of it with both hands.

"This will keep you going for now. If you require more, you need only to ask. However, ask only for what you need." Her eyes tighten on him as she spoke.

"Yes, my Lady."

"Let me know when you are five days from sailing. That's all, you are dismissed," said Ernesta. She walked again toward the window and extended her view to the sea.

*****

On board HMS *Comet*, Captain Calder stared at the dinner plate before him. The lone eye of a fish head returned his stare. He poked at the carcass flaking some the meat from its well-cooked body. The corners of his mouth turned down. The smell from this dish only seemed to confirm the isolation imposed by the surrounding sea as the ship swung at anchor.

"Fish," said Calder. His tone reflected the level of disgust the menu had generated. "Another night at anchor and we have fish. Yet again, fish." He spoke loud enough to ensure his new cook heard him.

Captain Darroch could feel the Captain's stare hold upon him. He took another full bite of the dead mackerel and looked over at his boss.

"This is your fault Marine," said Calder. His tone was accusing and condescending.

"Sir?" queried Darroch in response.

"If you had not told Annette to head off to Scotland, I'd be dining on something else tonight. She never, ever, gave me fish in port."

Lieutenant Martino sat across from the Marine and smiled at the dressing down his counterpart was enduring. He rested his knife and fork on the edge of his china plate.

"Sir, perhaps one of the new men have unseen culinary talents. Shall I survey the new recruits to find out?" asked Martino. He dabbed his mouth with his napkin as he spoke.

"That is an excellent idea, Charles. Make it so."

Martino flashed a subdued smirk in Darroch's direction. The Marine pretended not to notice and turned toward the head of the table.

"Sir does the Captain have any idea how long *Comet* will remain at anchor?" asked Darroch.

"I just returned from the Admiralty this afternoon, and the short answer is no. The timing of the Spanish advance in Sardinia has thrown everyone, or all nations, into chaos. Prince Eugene of Savoy and the Austrians are bogged down in the Balkans fighting the damn Ottoman Empire. He has made it very clear to the Admiralty that he does not want to expand the war to Italy. The French contingent is outraged, but with the central government still in turmoil on the loss of Louis the Fourteenth, they seem unlikely to engage," said Calder. He paused to take a sip of wine.

"How did we ever get to this point?" asked Darroch.

"I used to think one war in a generation was enough. Now, I'm not so sure. Remember, at the close of the War of Spanish Succession, England took the position that we would accept Philip, duke of Anjou, as King Philip the fifth of Spain on one condition."

"And what was that?" asked Martino.

"We, England, demanded that he be removed from the French line of succession. Our role is to balance power on the continent. We can never see Spain and France united against us."

"So, now the Spanish feel they can undo the Treaty of Utrecht of 1713 and retake their lost possessions in Italy and the Low Countries? How did that chain of logic ever emerge?" asked Darroch.

69

"Interesting my Marine knows about the Treaty of Utrecht. Well, much more in play at court here than just diplomacy and treaty making. I fear the bed chamber is fully in play as well," said Calder. He smiled when all eyes at the table turned his way.

"Bed chamber? How so?" asked Doctor La Roch.

"Oh, so the good Doctor is awake down there at the end of the table. I thought a little bedroom banter would perk you up. The main architect for retaking the Mediterranean Islands is an Italian Cardinal. The Steward Archbishop of Piacenza."

"Sir, you've got the church and bedroom in the same discussion. How did that align?" asked Lieutenant Laurant scratching his head.

"Because Lieutenant, it was Italian Archbishop Giulio Alberoni that arranged the marriage of the twenty-one-year-old Elisabeth Farnese to Philip the Fifth. He is now the personal advisor to the new queen. It is through her sexual aggression with the King that has sparked the Italian ambitions we see manifested in the Mediterranean today. You might say she has a lot more than command of the King's ear," Said Calder. A faint smile crossed his lips for the first time since the fish was placed before him. "Alberoni was the one, I learned when we were repairing *Comet* in Vigo, which has pushed to build fifty ships of the line in 1718. Think about what that could mean to the balance of power in the Mediterranean Sea," said Calder. He paused and poked his fish once again trying to gain the courage to take another bite. He settled for another sip of wine instead.

All eyes around the tabled exchanged glances. They collectively pondered the possibilities, but no one wanted to speak of them aloud. Calder set his wine glass down.

"Oh, but I've not even got to the good part," said Calder.

"The good part, sir?" said Martino.

"Indeed, the Russians just sent ships from both Riga and St. Petersburg to sea. They now dominate the Baltic and show no

70

signs of letting up. I have to give credit to Peter the First, he knows how to use sea-power."

"So, what does the Admiralty intend, sir?" asked Darroch.

They are discussing splitting the fleet and sending part of it to the Baltic and the balance to the Mediterranean."

"I vote for the Mediterranean. It's too damn cold in the Baltic," said Doc La Roch.

"Noted Doctor. A good call, if it were our call to make," said Calder. He shifted in his chair. "I discussed this very subject with Admiral Sir George Byng, none the less. He was tight lipped and refused to make any promises. However, I do think I was able to sway his thinking by pointing out that *Comet* and crew were the last ship to call in Spanish waters. We have some insight as to their thinking. When you add our experience in the New World, both ashore and afloat, he seemed impressed in what we could add to a southern expedition against the Iberian Peninsula.

"Sir, if we split our strength, will we have enough force to dominate on both seas?" asked Darroch.

"Why is it my Marine always asks me these hard questions on strategy? Naval strategy at that," said Calder. He pointed skyward to pause the discussion. Took a bite of fish and washed it down with a long sip of wine. He fought to not frown as the after taste of this combination assaulted his senses.

Darroch waited, smiled, and thought, *he's buying time to contemplate a response.*

"Well Captain Darroch, let me see if I can explain this to a landsman. As long as we match up one-to-one on both bodies of water, we'll be alright. However, we have to turn the tables in the Mediterranean Sea before the Spanish building program is in high gear. Once those fifty odd ships hit the water, they may in fact be able to edge us out in a slugfest. I don't like the odds should *Comet* have to join the battle in a line ahead formation and

71

slug it out with a larger, more heavily gunned, ship." Calder pushed his dinner plate away.

"Sir, may I change the topic a bit?" asked Martino.

"Yes, Lieutenant, what's on your mind?"

"Admiralty regulations, sir."

"Well then, not a common topic of table top discussion. What seems to spark your interest in admiralty regulations, Lieutenant?"

"Sir, since we have been called to anchor the number of bumboat sellers of wares and whores have all but taken over the crew's deck. As I checked spaces below decks yesterday, I all but fell over a couple engaged in all manner of indecent activity. They would have offended even the most robust of sensibilities."

"What sort of offensive wares are being sold Lieutenant?"

"Alcohol, sir. Whisky and rum are more common than water on the crew deck. It appears to breakdown the men's discipline, sir. The crew is more drunk than awake. They could never answer the call to duty."

"And what pray tell, would you suggest we do about these abominations below deck?"

"Sir," said Martino. He exhaled a large breath. "We must remove all spirits from the deck. Then the whores must be shown the beach. Clear the decks, sir. That is the only answer."

"Lieutenant Martino, what becomes of a man that is not allowed to interact with those of the fairer sex?'

"That sir, is not my concern."

"No, I'm sure it isn't. If you allow the desire and natural lust of the crew to build, without any prospect of release, they will explode in a manner no captain can tolerate. The buggering of boys spreads. Fights dominate otherwise meaningless disagreements. Order breaks down faster than what is our current situation. Until we have a mission Lieutenant, those whores serve as an important distraction to the tedium and boredom that dominate the consciousness of the crew."

Martino stared at Calder wide eyed. He opened his mouth but remained silent.

"How many other ships here at anchor have the same population of females eager to serve the fleet?"

"Sir, I know of none that do not," replied Martino. He stiffened his upper lip.

"So, perhaps there is a reason for that?" said Calder. He signaled for the dinner plates to be removed. "Until we leave anchor, the women stay if it serves the interest of the crew."

"Aye, sir," replied Martino.

"Don't smile down there Doctor. I would never expect to find my officers in the company of bumboat women. Not proper or consistent with your station I would say," said Calder. His eyes traveled around the table to gauge the level of understanding of his comment.

The cook came to clear the plates. Looking at the Captain's plate he frowned.

"The Captain didn't like the fish?" asked the Cook.

"No. As a rule, fish is only palatable when underway. Never serve fish in port, is that clear?"

"Yes, sir. Would I be able to get a pass to go ashore and resupply the Captain's mess?"

"Yes. Make it so. If anyone questions your mission, have them see me direct. I would be more than happy to make it clear.

Captain Darroch had almost cleared the great cabin before he heard Captain Calder say, "Marine, this is your fault. I hope you realize that?"

"Yes, sir. Never let Annette off the ship. The Captain has made himself perfectly clear."

They both smiled. Calder waved his hand to move Darroch along.

Captain Calder stood and walked over to an aft cabin window. The spectacle of the fleet around him at anchor gave some measure of relief. Security in numbers, perhaps. Each ship bounced on the light chop of the bay pulling against its rode. The strain on each cable measured by its angle of descent into the dark waters of the bay. Crewmen wondered idle on deck. Their heads down, thoughts internalized. Smoke rose from the stacks of numerous cooking fires that fed the fleet. These generated a light haze that hung above the tall masts of the ships. The sails were tied tight along their horizontal spars, keeping in check the potential power of the wind.

He pulled a shilling from his pocket. *Do we head north to the Baltic or south to the Mediterranean? That's a coin toss either way. If the King's head, we go north. On the coat of arms, we head south.* Calder threw the coin on the chart table. It bounced and rolled to a stop adjacent to his chair. He walked back to his chair and studied the silver coin.

"Conundrum solved," he said aloud.

*****

Bright banners from each region of Spain hung from the walls of the Grand Hall in Madrid. The thick stone walls from which they were suspended, helped mitigate the summer heat. Forty courtiers gathered in the hall. They clustered in small groups consistent with the prescribed social standing and region. Most of those in attendance were men. A few women were scattered in this elite mixing. They were there due to individual ability or social position. Both the men and women wore black costumes. The color reflected the collective mood within the room.

Ernesta held her father's arm as they made their way through the crowd of nobility. She turned away when the prince tried to catch her eye. Her rebuff of his advance had weighed heavy on the status of the family name. She wished to avoid reopening any such uncomfortable dialogue. Her auburn hair was covered with a black vail, which extended well down her back. The dark tone of her dress accented the ivory white hue of her skin.

The confused light conversation of the court fell silent. Everyone turned toward the center of the room. King Philip moved with Queen Elisabeth Farnese hanging on his arm making their entrance. The age difference between these two was pronounced, but their stride and mannerisms meshed with seamless perfection. Everyone turned in their direction. The men bowed forward, while the women curtsied. Without command, the crowd formed into a semicircle around this couple. The Queen released her husband's arm and began to circulate through the assemblage.

"Ladies and gentlemen of the court, I think you all know why I have called this meeting. Our efforts in Sardinia are proceeding as planned. So, decisions as to what to do next compels us to consider the possibilities," said Philip. He walked from side-to-side seeking to gain eye contact with his guests. "I would invite the Marquis of Lede forward to illuminate us as to the situation of our campaign."

"My King, thank you. Ladies and Gentlemen, our soldiers have won two key victories in as few months since landing on the Island of Sardinia. We have secured a bridgehead at Cagliari. Resistance to our advance is light to non-existent. We have taken the city of Oristano, leaving only Sassari on the northern tip of the Island out of our control."

A light applause echoed beneath the regional banners. The Marquis raised his hands to silence the crowd. He took a step toward his audience.

"Please, let me add the conduct of our soldiers has been beyond reproach. Everywhere on the Island they have been greeted by the locals as liberating heroes. I would say we will be able to conclude this campaign within a month. The question becomes, then what?"

The crowd remained quiet. Input, while invited, was not welcome. Those were the rules of court life.

"I have proposed to the King to lead an army to conquer Sicily," said the Marquis.

Audible gasps were heard across the Great Hall. Ladies covered their half open mouths. Some of the men coughed for the sole purpose of breaking the tempo of the announcement.

"Hear me. We have ruled that Island for almost two hundred years. It shall be ours, yet again. It is only fitting, that what was taken from us by force of arms, shall be returned to us by force of arms. I see no reason the expedition to Sicily will not go as well as our effort in Sardinia," said the Marquis. The corners of his mouth turned down as the rumpling within the crowd increased in volume.

"If you have a point to discuss, do so now. Let no citizen of Spain hold their tongue on this matter," said Philip.

Rainerio let loose of Ernesta. He moved to the front of the circle. His path cleared as courtesans stood aside unable to carry the mantle of opposition to this planned attack. Briefly, he looked back at his daughter. Then he cleared his throat.

"My most honorable Marquis, I personally appreciate the self-sacrifice you are proposing here. Your leadership in battle is unquestioned. However, we are not the first people to propose expanding a conflict into Sicily before concluding operations nearer to home. The Athenian General Alcibiades initiated such a move in 418 BC during the Peloponnesian War. His efforts led to a protracted conflict and the ruination of that once prosperous Greek city state. We must not follow the same path to defeat," said Rainerio.

"I hear the points being made. I'm not without concern as to their validity or consequence. But, I do know that nothing is gained without risk. Now is our time to risk, conquer, and regain what they have taken from us. If we take Sicily, the road to Italy is open," said the Marquis.

Queen Elisabeth smiled on the mention of her home country.

He continued, "Complete redemption is ours for the asking."

The muffled applause returned to the hall. Elisabeth continued to work her way through the crowd. Her eyes moved in a deliberate search pattern. Scanning left, then right, slowly and with precision.

"What say you, Rainerio?" asked the Marquis.

"Everyone here knows I stand with the Crown. I will follow the King in both conduct and conscious. He need only say the word."

"I say we go," announced the King. Philip's hand raised well above his head wrapped in a tight fist.

"Here, here!" Rang out from the crowd. The applause exceeded the polite refrain recorded earlier. Behind the King a drumbeat rose above the intensity of the courtiers challenging them to increase the volume of their support. They accepted the contest and soon their collective efforts drowned out the drummer.

Ernesta felt an arm reach along her back. Looking back, she found Queen Elisabeth pulling her close, hip-to-hip.

"My dear Ernesta, you are looking well," said her majesty.

"Queen Farnese, you honor me by addressing one so humble in the familiar."

"Address me as Elisabeth. We are almost the same age. I need to understand something," said the Queen in a whisper. Holding firm to Ernesta's hip she ran her free hand down the length of this courtier's smooth belly. She patted lightly just below her belt.

"Tell me, dear, how is it you refused the offer of marriage to the honorable Prince on the grounds of having your virtue forced and yet I find your belly as smooth as any virgin maid?"

"I fear I lost the child while horse riding in the hills above Vigo, Elisabeth. Tragic, no?" whispered back Ernesta.

"Tragic indeed, but for whom? The Prince has suffered many a night coping with the loss of his betrothed. You should have honored the wishes of your parents. It was your duty to do so, and you failed. Failed the most fundamental obligation of any woman of means. It is not your decision who you may, or may not, marry. That is a privilege bestowed upon you by your entry into the ruling elite." The Queen lowered her hand just a little and pressed with decidedly more force. Ernesta's lips tightened under the pressure.

"Do you think it appropriate for the Prince, potential future king, to marry one that has been violated?" asked Ernesta.

"My dear, we have already made arrangements for the Prince to marry one far more appropriate than you. I just wonder if you, and your family, should remain within our circle."

"Do not hold my family in any way accountable for my actions. What I have done, was done by me and by me alone."

"Oh, of that I'm sure Ernesta. But I still wonder. If I pressed between your legs with my fingers, right here and right now, would the floor run red with the blood of a virgin? My guess is it would. I don't believe in mystical Marines, raping our ladies of the court." Elisabeth's hand settled lower into Ernesta's crotch. The muscles in Elisabeth's arm tightened forcing her fingers forward.

"But my Queen, you were not there," said Ernesta. Her mouth fell open in response to the Queen's assault. "You did not suffer the press of his flesh, hungry with desire, against the nakedness of my virtue."

"Lift your dress Ernesta. By order of your Queen, I command you to lift your dress," said the Queen. Her tone remained a whisper. "I will have my answer and know the truth of this matter."

"I shall not."

"You shall not defy the royal order of your Queen."

"I will not lift my dress in front of this court to satisfy some idle curiosity born of the most vindictive and vicious gossip that has gripped the soul of this ruling elite."

"Then you will retire with me to a chamber, where I may learn with my own eyes the truth or lies of your presentation before this court. It has become a matter of honor."

"As you wish, my Queen."

The two women turned from the assembly and walked out the back door. Only an occasional glance followed them as they made their exit. Elisabeth held firm to Ernesta's belt to control her pace. They both smiled when presentations were sent in their direction.

The guard on the other side of the door, popped to the position of attention as the Queen went by with her charge closely controlled. The awkward gait of these two women stumbling down the hall as they pushed and pulled against each other caused the guard to smile.

The Queen twisted Ernesta through the door to a room far from the prying eyes of the court. She turned the key in the lock and then placed the key down the front of her dress. The cold steel on her breast caused the Queen to shutter.

"Alright then, you have your privacy. Lift your dress," said the Queen repeating her royal command.

"I shall not."

"What?"

"Nothing good can come of this investigation. If I am, as I have said, then your curiosity will not have been consistent with your royal standing. On the other hand, if your penetration causes me to bleed upon the floor I will have sacrificed my virginity on a whim. Your whim. You will have desecrated one of the most holy aspects of womanhood. For what?"

Elisabeth's eyes widened. She slumped about the shoulders.

"It is not my custom to have my requests denied. You present me with a most unusual conundrum, my dear." The Queen leaned against the door and wiped her hands together.

"My Queen, it is not my purpose to cause you the least grief or mental anguish. But I will not have my body or soul violated yet again."

"Placing virginity aside, why did you not want to marry the Prince?"

79

"I love another. I would, and will not, live without him."

"Does he know?"

"Of course not."

"So sad," said the Queen. She stood firm with both feet on the ground.

"That he does not know?"

"No, that I did not have the courage to refuse my betrothal."

"What? He's the King. No one could refuse the King."

"And yet, you found it in your heart to refuse one who would be king."

"I did, but that's different."

"Only different in time my dear. Please know, you have my respect for your decision. In the end, our Prince will marry and produce a child to assume the thrown. Given the recent War of Secession, I think you can see why that is so important to Spain."

"Yes, my Queen."

"Come now, please address me as Elisabeth. I need to learn from your strength. I'm sure you can, in turn, benefit from my patronage."

"And what price this patronage?"

"I think you know, Ernesta."

"To remain deaf, dumb, and blind to this entire incident?"

"Of course."

"Done. We shall talk of it no more," said Ernesta. She curtsied in the direction of the Queen.

"Now then, shall we rejoin the discussion? Hopefully, we are not at war with all of Italy at this point." They both laughed.

The Queen struggled with the lock. The door squeaked on its hinges as it swung slowly open. They departed the room arm-in-arm.

"When do I get to meet this gentleman of yours?" asked the Queen.

"I don't know, it's complicated."

"Why is that, Ernesta?"

80

"He's English. A Royal Marine in fact."

"What is it about impossible my dear, that you don't seem to understand?"

"Impossible, only makes life interesting," said Ernesta. Her smile returned.

Chapter 5 Highland Fling

A small fishing boat struggled on an angry sea to make headway against the wind. The sails flapped overhead, only to fill unexpectedly with the sound of a sudden pop. The snap in the sails would pull the boat along for a short sprit only to be followed by the roll of the surrounding swell that once again dumped the air from the canvas. The oppressive sound of sails flapping uncontrollably returned once again. This process was repeated with the passing of each torturous minute.

Carlos sat at the bow. He used a small bucket to bail the ever-present water from the bottom of the boat over the side. The leather of his shoes was soaked through, chilling his feet. His normally olive skin was now pale as the essence of his body and his mind struggled to contend with each rise and fall of the boat on successive waves. He paused from his chore, leaned over the side of the boat, and vomited the contents of his stomach into the sea. The crew at the back of the boat tightened their face muscles at the scene of his discomfort.

"Are you alright, sir?" said the man at the tiller.

Carlos used his cloak to wipe the foul-smelling residue from his face. He shook his head toward his inquisitor.

"No. I don't think I can keep this up much longer. I've not been able to hold food for four days now. Can't sleep, either. How much farther?" Carlos leaned across the rail as he finished his response.

"The Outer Hebribes will provide some relief from the swell, once we get a little farther north. We should be in the Minch, that's the waters between the Islands and Scotland, in a day. You'll be fine once we get there."

"I pray God will call his faithful servant to his side before then. I don't think I can take another day out here."

The three-man crew of the small craft exchanged smiles. Carlos returned his head over the gunwales. The dry heaves that followed were more painful than the previous loss of fluid from his system. He pulled his body back in the boat. Looking aft, his expression was compressed and twisted.

"Sir, everyone here has been through this in the past. I need you to bail. I can't afford to let the water build any more within the boat."

Carlos nodded and continued to work the bucket to move bilge water over the side. His hands shook as he emptied the bottom of the boat. His pale fingers turned a light blue color. He pulled his hood up over his head. This blocked the wind, and for one brief moment Carlos almost felt as if he would survive the journey.

In the dark depths of the night, Carlos was unable to see the waves approach. He could no longer anticipate their influence in tossing the craft. He could only react to unpredictable motion that unhinged his stomach and disrupted his sense of balance. Sleep was impossible. Fatigue commanded the deepest parts of his soul. His mind wondered down twisted dull paths of despair. He thought, *God, take me now. Do not punish your servant in this manner for another minute, let alone another hour. Call me up from this place to be at your side. Let me cast away the things of the body, that my soul may be refreshed and renewed in the name and promise of your son.*

The sun broke upon the surface of the Mitch and the reflection hit home on Carlos. The swell had given way to waters less tangled and confused. He opened his eyes slowly. The realization that he was still within the world of man, caused his mouth to turn sharply down.

"I see you're awake. The worst of the journey is now behind us. I was sure we were going to fling you out of the boat at one point last night. That's Skye Island on our starboard side. It won't be long before we make the turn south to enter the Inner Sound. Just beyond that—"

"Eilean Donan?" asked Carlos.

"Yes, very good. Eilean Donan it is. I think we'll land south of there. Should give you a chance to gauge the castle for yourself."

"How long?"

"Oh, we're still a good full day out. The winds seem steady and that should help."

"What do we have left to eat?" asked Carlos. His empty stomach grumbled so loud the rest of the crew looked his way.

"I've got some salted herring in that tub. Good stuff. My wife prepared it with family seasoning. Try some."

Carlos picked and pulled on the fish flesh gleaning what he could. After days of not being able to hold his food down, his body screamed for any form of nourishment. His lips smacked together making a puffing sound. He didn't care. Manners fell aside to the needs of survival.

"Try some of that whiskey in the jug. My own brew. These folks call it the water of life for a reason, you know."

Carlos curled the jug over his forearm and let the mouth of the container settle against his lips. The amber liquid trickled down into his mouth. He could feel the burn all the way down his throat and into the middle of his chest. The warmth of the drink provided his first bulwark against the cold damp air that surrounded him, and from which the open boat offered no escape. For the first time in a week, a smile slowly lifted upon his face.

"Damn, herring and whiskey to break the evening fast, by God we'll make a Scotsman of you yet, Spaniard," said the man at the tiller. The other two crewman laughed at this comment.

"Do you know who we'll be meeting with when we land?" Asked Carlos. It was the first time in days he was able to think about what was ahead.

"Yes. Yes, I do. The other reason we want to get south of the castle, is to linkup with Odhran MacLead."

"Who?"

"Odhran MacLead. He's a Clan Chief and you damn well better treat him like royalty, else you might come back missing a body part or two."

"A good man?" asked Carlos. The color started to return to his skin.

"The best. He's very much against anything English. Once you tell him your plan, you'll have a friend for life."

"Very good. I look forward to embracing his support, for life."

Unheard by Carlos the man at the tiller whispered, "Aye, let's be hoping it's a long life then."

*****

On the ramparts of Eilean Donan a lone sentry paced along a well-worn path. The fall winds blew in over the water carrying a chill that penetrated the thick wool cape he wore over one shoulder. His gaze drifted on the small wavelets that churned in the late afternoon sun. The reflecting dots of light danced like diamonds cast before the wind. It was difficult to make out the exact shape of a small boat that mixed within this shimmering reflection. By its size alone it was clearly not a warship, or threat to the sturdy stone walls that had held attackers at bay for over a hundred years. It was no different than the numerous other small craft that wondered along the Scottish lochs seeking to pull a living from the sea beneath bare green hills that framed the confines of these disjointed bodies of water.

The soldier's relief approached and presented arms. The off-going watch returned the honors as dictated by military protocol. Through watery eyes, the off-going soldier smiled.

"Thank you for being on time," he said. He pulled his cloak higher.

"Not like I be having a choice here, you know. Damn, the witch of the North is in full breath today. Has it been this cold all day?"

"Yes. I found if you stay near the wall you can break some of the force of the gale."

"Do you have anything else to report, before I be assuming the watch?"

"Nothing. However, I did see the string quartet arrive. Must be one big party planned for the evening."

"I take it you be going then?" The sentry smiled as he spoke.

They both laughed before parting ways. The changing of the castle guard was complete. The night approached, and with it came the heightened sense of danger. For of all those things, often unseen in the darkness, few would bode well for the realm of man.

Annette and Cynthia prepared for the welcoming gala planned in honor of Earl von Hunter's arrival to Eilean Donan. Annette positioned herself behind Cynthia with corset in hand. Cynthia held the front of the garment against her stomach, while Annette attended to the lacing at the back. She pulled and weaved the lacing with a speed bore of repetition.

"That's about got it I think," said Annette.

"Tighter, Annette."

"Are you sure?"

"Oh, I'm sure. I want to look nice for Drake. He's only seen me on the road now for the better part of a month. I want this to be a vision he holds in his memory."

Annette worked to further draw the lacing together. The accent of Cynthia's hour glass shape cut like crystal. With her figure wrapped in the latest London fashion, her movements flowed as the dress bounced in time with each step. Yellow ribbon framed the multiple layers of satin and lace that circled her body below the waist. The soft rustle of unseen petticoats announced her arrival. Cynthia spun quickly in front of the mirror watching the bottom of her dress elevate and then settle once again.

"Gorgeous," said Annette.

"Let's get you ready," Replied Cynthia. "Corset first."

"I have to get my shoes, then we can be doing the lacing."

With roles now reversed, the two ladies finished preparations for the evening. By the standards set at court, their makeup would have been considered light. Still, the pale shade of white dominated their complexion. They made no attempt to powder their hair for this dinner party. Annette's auburn mane stood in sharp contrast to the raven black locks of Cynthia. They each wore their hair piled high above their head, with a single long curl trailing down toward bare shoulders. With lips painted rose red, they invited the attention of their male counterparts at this stylized gathering.

Cynthia turned to exit the chamber. Annette scurried back and picked up two objects from the dressing table.

"Cynthia, wait," said Annette.

Cynthia eased about and faced her colleague.

"You mustn't forget this," added Annette. She extended a folded fan toward Cynthia. They both giggled with an air of innocence long distant from their age or life experience.

"Oh, yes. The fan-dance. Always in style, when flirtations are to be extended," said Cynthia.

She took the fan and opened it with a pop. Lifting the fan to cover her mouth and nose, she tilted her head forward toward Annette. Staring over the top of the fan, she locked eyes with Annette. Cynthia worked the fan back and forth a few times with short rapid strokes, while batting her eyelids in time with the fan's movement.

"Oh, that's good," said Annette.

"You think so?"

"Yes, the Earl doesn't even stand a chance tonight."

"One would hope not. But then, we don't really know who else will be attending the dinner tonight do we? Maybe he has been keeping some hearty Scottish lass up here for his amusement. He certainly could afford such distractions," said Cynthia. She closed and lowered the fan, revealing the tension in her facial muscles. The edges of her mouth were turned down.

"Don't frown my dear. It's not becoming," said Annette. She reached out with one hand and lifted Cynthia's chin. "With that dress, you can compete with anyone. You know what the Earl likes . . . on the dance floor. You need only be keeping him amused and the rest will take care of itself."

"You're right. I also know how to occupy his interest off the dance floor as well." Again, the giggling returned to fill the chamber.

A knock on the door signaled they were no longer alone. Annette walked over and opened the door. She found Drake and an unknown man in uniform on the other side.

"Ladies, good evening to you both," said Drake. He walked into their chamber with the soldier marching dutifully one pace behind. Drake's eyes focused on Cynthia. "We are here to escort you lovelies to dinner."

Cynthia opened her fan and shielded her face. The movement was graceful and unrehearsed. Without removing his eyes from Cynthia, Drake continued.

"Lady Armtrove, may I introduce Captain Aaron MacPherson. He commands the guard here at Eilean Donan. He's a good chap to know. Plus, I know your preference for a man in uniform," said Drake smiling.

Annette ran her stare of this soldier from head to toe. Her ability to size up a man in a single glance was well known within the walls of the Red Fox Inn. The greens and dark blues of his tartan kilt crisscrossed forming the customary plaid. A few lines of white thread highlighted the pattern. His high socks held just below his knee and extended down to highly polished black shoes that shown like mirrors. The high collar of his coat forced his head to remain erect. The solid red of his coat held a single medal that swung on a dark blue ribbon. Brown hair and blue eyes pulled Annette's attention to the chiseled chin and cheek bones of his sturdy face.

Annette curtsied deep with head forward. She lost eye contact with her escort for a moment. As she started to stand, she found the Captain's large hand extended to assist. The support rendered was strong and firm. She easily returned to an upright posture.

"Why thank you, Sir. A true gentleman. Most refined for these northern parts, or so I've been told."

"Well Lady Armtrove, you'll find we aren't all half-naked highlanders running wild through the heather up here. A few of us even use silverware when dining and not our hands," said the Captain.

Annette laughed, a smile grew upon her face directed toward the powerful frame of the man in uniform. She pointed to his legs.

"Half-naked or not, I do like the kilt, sir. Your knees draw one's attention."

"Please address me as Aaron, my Lady. I hope to get to know you much better this evening."

"Aye, and Aaron, please call me Annette. The title of Lady can seem somewhat overstuffed."

Annette looked over to find Cynthia returning her stare with head tilted to one side and eyes wide.

"Ladies, shall we?" said Drake. He swept his hand toward the door. Drake extended his elbow toward Cynthia and she took hold.

"Annette, would you do me the honor?" said Aaron. He lifted his elbow in her direction.

"The honor, sir, is mine," replied Annette. She wrapped her hand through the nook of his arm. Annette maneuvered her body next to his, legs touching, but unseen beneath her dress.

The two couples walked down the long hall toward the main dining room. They moved down the spiral staircase with each escort steadying their lady, as they fought to control their dresses and not get tangled on the descent.

Attendants opened the large double doors to the Grand Hall. Entering they found over twenty guests talking and mingling around a long table. The setting on this occasion was designed to impress as much as to be functional. Three forks were aligned on one side of the china plate, while a knife and spoon stood guard on the other side. A dessert spoon held muster at the top of the plate. Crystal glasses stood ready to receive wine and water. A large fireplace was fully aglow, casting both light and heat through the room.

The head waiter tapped his wooden staff on the marble floor. It resonated across the room and drew everyone's attention in his direction.

"Lady Armtrove and Captain MacPherson," he announced. They walked into the room hovering at the side. The guests would dip their heads toward them as they went by.

The wooden staff struck the floor yet again.

"Lady Maitland and the right honorable Earl von Hunter," he said.

A light applause filled the room. A few wine glasses were raised in their direction.

"How do we know where to sit?" whispered Annette to Aaron.

"Just follow me. I was told where earlier this morning."

She tightened her grip on his arm. He widened his smile in response. The thumping of the wooden staff echoed one more time.

"Ladies and Gentlemen, your host for this evening, the most honorable Lord Seaforth."

The elderly gentleman entered the room unescorted. His dress was more English than Scottish, lacking the traditional highland kilt or accoutrements. Everyone turned in his direction and rendered honors. He took his position at the head of the table and everyone took their seats. The quartet filled the room with the latest chamber music. Their volume was low enough so as to not encumber the conversation around the table.

Annette was seated away from the head of the table and the main fireplace. She looked down the long row of guests to find Cynthia next to Drake and only a few seats from Lord Seaforth. She couldn't tell what they were discussing, but judging from the smile on her face, it was welcome news. When Cynthia laughed it carried all the way to Annette.

Being distant from the fire, Annette felt the full chill of the Scottish fall. Goosebumps formed on her shoulders, as the cold hung heavy in the damp air. She shuttered uncontrollably. She rubbed her hands over her arms to generate enough friction to mitigate some of the chill.

"Are you alright, Annette?" asked Aaron leaning close to her ear. The sound of heavy rain echoed above them on the roof.

"Yes, Aaron. I be just a little cold. I'm still getting used to the highland climate."

"Oh, you have not embraced our liquid sunshine as of yet?"

Annette looked over at her escort and smiled. The two were close, and his attention focused on her comfort. She in turn focused on the blue of his eyes. They were clear, familiar, and reassuring. He similarly was drawn to the green of her eyes, more radiant than the hue of the hills that surrounded them. The server stepped between them breaking the implied intimacy of the moment. She straightened up and joined in the other guests in the robust consumption of the evening meal.

The banquet before them was amble in its portions. Lamb was sliced in thick slabs. The steam rose from each piece as it was cut beside the table and placed directly on the plate. Potatoes filled most of the rest of the plate. This heavy combination ensured no one would leave the table hungry. Fruit and wine completed the feast. Constant conversation bubbled around the table making it difficult to engage anyone not directly adjacent.

As the remaining food was cleared, couples formed up to dance. Two lines faced each other with the men on one side and the women on the other. They would swirl across the center, exchange a quick embrace, and return to their starting position. Cynthia and Drake were one of the first couples to engage in this post dining entertainment.

"Annette, shall we?" asked Aaron.

She nodded. "I'll do anything to warm up," she said.

He helped her uncoil her dress from the chair and table. Arm-in-arm they soon joined the motion around the room. Annette watched out of the corner of her eye, as Drake and Cynthia exited the hall. His arm wrapped around her waist, while she was hanging about this chest. The tone and volume of Cynthia's laugh made Annette wonder, *too much drink perhaps. I hope she knows what she is doing. I'm sure the Earl knows what he wants to do.* They disappeared, and Annette was left with Aaron to complete the evening.

Drake and Cynthia entered his room. She looked around and took measure of his accommodations.

"Drake, your room is larger than the space Annette and I have to share."

"Well, yes. Being an Earl has certain privileges. So, does being an Earl's Lady, my dear."

He walked her over to the bed. While she began to unlace her dress, he dropped the curtains encircling the four-post bed.

"Would you undo by back?" asked Cynthia. Her voice reflected a slight flutter. Her pulse quickened.

"Yes, my dear."

Drake moved behind her. He ran his hand over her bare shoulders and squeezed them. Cynthia rolled her head back toward him smiling. Moving down to the center of the corset, he pulled the lacing out to its full length and untied the knot. In a measured cadence, he worked each pull to separate the ribbed panels that had held the object of his burning desire. The constraining device fell free and she dropped her dressing gown to the floor. She turned around to find Drake naked before her.

The two embraced, the full length of their skin melting into the warmth of the other.

"You're chilled my dear. This way, join me," said Drake.

He pulled her onto the bed, now surrounded by the thick cloth curtains. They worked themselves under the blankets to gain some protection against the chill of the Scottish Highlands. Their passion provided all the heat required to fend-off the cold of the night. Cynthia willingly subjected herself to each of the Earl's whims. Her touch, squeeze, and lick became the vehicles of his burning lust that found release in this chamber so distant from his Southampton estate. At length this couple settled into a dance, a rhythm, as sensual as life itself. He forced his weight upon her, rocking in a manner she found undeniably exciting. Her breathing accelerated, her mouth fell half open, and the edges of her eyes tightened and released as pleasure rippled through her. Cynthia reached around his back, dragging the full extent of her finger nails over his bare skin.

Through the intimate contact, Cynthia thought, *this is what I want. An Earl in my bed and a title to my name. Damn he's good to me. Perhaps, I've finally got a man able, and willing, to take care of me. He could . . . uah, uah, oh!*

Her moans filled Drake's ears. He pushed on. The warmth of her body, the softness of her touch, and her enthusiasm to please, left Drake defenseless. As he struggled to extend the moment, he thought, *this is what I want. A mistress to please me. Perhaps, a mother to an heir, a son. This tight ass whore doesn't even know . . . oh, that's it.*

The shaking of the bed subsided. The rate of the breathing behind the curtains slowed. Silence filled the large room once more. Drake stoked her face with the edge of his fingertips. He did so lightly, smoothly, with affection.

"Stay with me tonight," whispered Drake trying to let Cynthia enjoy the quiet warmth of his embrace. "Stay with me always."

"Drake I'm yours whenever you need me. Ask, and I will come. Smile, and I will laugh. Rest in my arms, and I shall sing you a lullaby," said Cynthia. Her voice muted beneath the covers.

Drake closed his eyes with his arm wrapped fully around Cynthia. The corners of his mouth edged up into a smile concealed within the darkness. He thought, *I've got her.*

Cynthia relaxed into his embrace. Rested, satisfied, and content. She thought, *I've got him.*

"It seems the Earl and your friend have made their exit," Said Arron.

"Yes, it does," said Annette. "The men be dancing with themselves now. Perhaps, it's time for me to retire for the evening."

"That's the Highland Fling, Annette. Sometimes it's better to dance than freeze," said Aaron. He chuckled as he spoke.

"Aye, I get that part."

"Do you want to try?"

"No, sir."

"Let me walk you back to your chamber then," said Aaron. He smiled and pointed to the door.

Annette nodded. Aaron extended his elbow and Annette took hold. The two of them departed as if they were a royal couple on parade. On reaching the stairs Annette struggled to lift her dress and better negotiate the spiral steps. She made it almost to the top before stepping on her dress and falling.

Aaron caught her and pulled her up. They were close now, eyes locked together, lips but a whisper apart. He leaned in closing his eyes. Annette mimicked his advance. The resulting kiss was both passionate and abridged. Annette put her hand on his chest and pressed firm. They both straightened up and continued to the top of the stairs.

"Annette, I know you felt something just then," said Aaron.

"Aye, that be true. I'm not here in the Highlands looking to fall in love."

"Why is it you talk like a sailor?"

"Perhaps because until a short while ago, I was the cook for a ship's captain. Sailed to the Americas and back, I did."

"Well if you can be stolen away from the sea, perhaps your heart can be stolen away as well."

She smiled, but shook her head. Annette opened her fan and sought refuge behind its arching shape. Her green eyes stared just over the top of the deployed blades.

"Your gestures tell me no, but that kiss, that kiss said yes. A loud yes at that."

"Captain MacPherson, I be thanking you for escorting me to the banquet. I really enjoyed the dancing. I best be saying goodnight."

The Captain leaned in to kiss Annette, but the fan remained raised. A defense against his advance. He straightened up and pulled away from her.

"How long will you be staying with us Lady Armtrove?"

"For the duration, sir."

"Well then, goodnight," said Aaron.

He turned away and walked down the hall. Annette stood almost paralyzed by his abrupt departure. She studied his stride as he marched, tall, and deliberate off into the night.

Annette thought, *I'll bet that son of a bitch thinks he can have me at his beckon call.*

Aaron reflected as he walked away, *the duration is a long time. She'll come to me. They always do.*

Annette entered her chamber. She wasn't that surprised that Cynthia had not returned since her exit with the Earl. Peeling off her clothes, she stood with only her dressing gown at the edge of the bed. Lifting the covers, Annette slid between the sheets finding little comfort there. She was cold, lonely, and afraid. She closed her eyes, and thought *William, my love, you should have never sent me away.* A lone tear ran down her cheek, settling in the soft cotton of her garment.

*****

A fishing boat stroked ashore on the banks of Loch Duich below Eilean Donan castle. Carlos pulled the hood of his cloak up over his head. He swung his heels across the gunwales and stood on dry land, or something close to it, for the first time in over two weeks. He let out a long sigh.

"By the powers of providence, I've made it. Thank you, Lord," Carlos said.

"This way, sir," said the boat captain.

The two men walked inland across the bog. While they were no longer on the ocean, they weren't exactly on dry land as well. Carlos' wet shoes sank ankle deep in back mucky soil as he pushed along the trail. Looking ahead he could make out a cluster of thirty to forty houses. Smoke rose from most of the dwellings, adding to the combined mist and haze that hung along the high ground. Rough rock walls circled around the exterior of the dwellings. Moss grew low on these stones blending the structure with the adjacent turf. The roofs were a combination of sod and thatch. His military eye couldn't help but notice how walls connected these structures within, or around, the village forming a strong and defensible position.

Walking through a burnt wooden gate placed them on the main village thoroughfare. He studied the faces of the people he passed. Dirty face boys battled with wooden swords adjacent to their dwellings. Girls carried firewood or water to their mothers. Most of the women stood around cooking fires stirring unknown brews within blackened iron pots. Smiles revealed darkened or missing teeth. Yet, it was those smiles that dominated the scene. Everywhere he looked, he was greeted with a welcoming nod or grin. Carlos didn't have time to ponder the contrast between the cold embrace of poverty and the apparent warmth of the people.

"Carlos, this is the Chief's house. Let me make the formal introduction. I think you've already been told not to cross their leader if you want to keep all your body parts," cautioned the boat captain.

Carlos smiled unconvinced of the reported dangers within the house before him. He bent down, entering the low-slung stone enclosure.

"Chief MacLead, it has been a long time my friend," said the boat captain. The two men threw their arms around each other slapping their backs. The sound of this embrace rang within the dim lit room. "Let me introduce Carlos Andres, from the Spanish Court. I believe you two have business."

"Aye, we do. Carlos it is good you have made your way across the waters to us. Please call be Odhran."

"Odhran, this meeting is perhaps too long overdue, sir. I believe we share a common interest that we could pursue," said Carlos. He stared at the long knife Odlran twirled in one hand.

"Aye, so I've been told. Is it true you come here to oppose the English?"

"Our two countries are not currently at war, but all signs point in that direction. Should conflict come, it is perhaps in the interest of both our people to combine efforts and remove English rule from this region."

"What struck you most when you walked through our village?"

"No men. I didn't see any men. No fathers, husbands, or elders."

"You sir, have a very good eye. Most of my men are pressed to English service. Some in the army or at sea. Others in the fields to tend crops. Those that oppose this labor, end up in the dungeon Eilean Donan or elsewhere. The end of a rope holds the future of any man unwilling to comply with their edicts. So, tell me what you can do for my poor clan?"

"If war comes, I will ensure Spanish troops arrive here and take Eilean Donan."

"How many?"

"How many what?" asked Carlos.

"Troops, man. What size of an army can you guarantee?"

"Perhaps as many as five thousand."

Odhran straightened up. His aged shoulders pulled back. He shook his head and re-engaged his guest with tightened eyes.

"Aye, five thousand would be about right. If you agree to attack or reduce the castle, I'll find a way to get your men inside the walls without a shot being fired."

"How can you promise that?"

"I've already got men inside the place. Most of the heavy lifting it takes to run a castle are done by my crew. It would be nothing to coordinate a surprise attack and take the bastion."

"Then why, pray tell, have you not thrown off the yoke of English tyranny to date?"

"I think you already be knowing the answer to that question. No troops. My men are kept dispersed and separated. We can't mass to take the garrison. Their Captain of the Guard is a mean, sadistic, son of a bitch. He uses random acts of force among the people to keep us off guard and unable to work together. But, five thousand Spanish regular troops. Aye, that's a force that could take the castle and more important—"

"What could be more important than control of the fortress?"

"Such a force could defeat the counterattack that would surely follow. Reprisals against uprisings are never pretty. I fear this small, and humble village, would bare the blunt of force directed against any Highland move for freedom. Know, we have tried before to cast the British out, but no move for independence has ever been successful. Nor do I believe any independence movement will be victorious against the strongest empire of the world," said Odhron. His tone was somber and downcast.

"Let me stay within your village. I will work to bring enough force here to defeat the English and return your lands. Nothing can be lost by planning such a move. If providence provides the opportunity, we'll be ready."

Odhran threw his knife past Carlos' head and directly into the wooden door. The blade struck home point first and waivered on impact. Carlos' eyes widened. Odhran smiled for the first time since their introductions.

"It will be done. You'll stay in my house tonight and we'll talk more of this in the morning."

Carlos nodded. His head swiveled left and right unsure of what protocol demanded next.

"Shana," yelled Odhron. "Shana, your presence please."

A tall young lady entered the room. Her long blonde hair extended to her waist. She wore animal skins to buffer against the ever present cold. Without any makeup, her appearance was less defined than the ladies at court. Yet, her lean facial features, coupled with high cheek bones, gave her a beauty that could not be masked amid the poverty of the village.

"Carlos, this is my daughter Shana. She will see to your sleeping arrangements for the evening. Rest my friend, we have much to discuss," said Odhran.

Carlos stood. Shana extended her hand securing his. The two made for the door, the knife was still embedded in its planking, and paused. The boat captain grabbed Carlos' arm and whispered in his ear.

"Some of the customs of these folks stand in sharp contrast to those found at your court. Only take was is offered, and never refuse an offering," said the boat captain. He released Carlos arm smiling. The grin slanted on his face indicated a level of understanding as to what was ahead that Carlos didn't comprehend.

Carlos and Shana moved within the dim of the dwelling. She showed him to a door. Casting it open they both went inside.

"This is my room. You'll be staying here tonight," said Shana. Her voice was low and steady.

Looking around Carlos noted a small table with a single chair. Some papers were jumbled on the desktop. One candle provided the only light. A small slit allowed air to circulate in the confines of the stone enclosure. The weight of a book, open to some unknown page, kept the papers in position. The room had no bed. In one corner a mat of straw was covered with animal skins and a blanket. Carlos scratched the back of his head. He looked back a Shana.

"Where will you be staying tonight, my dear," he asked.

Shana dropped her animal skins off her shoulders and let them settle to the floor. She pulled loose the lacing on the front of her dress. Tilting her head forward, she held eye contact with the Spaniard.

"Here," came her reply. "You do not object, I hope."

"No, Shana. Honored in fact."

Carlos nervously twisted his thin black mustache. Watching Shana he thought, *somehow, I don't think this is what Lady Ernesta had in mind when she sent me to Scotland."*

Shana slid beneath the blankets, leaving little time for the cold air to settle on her pale skin.

"Carlos, are you going to join me?" she asked.

"Are you offering, my dear?"

"Yes, of course," said Shana. Her smile was illuminated by the lone candle in the room.

"Then who am I to refuse," said Carlos. The words of the boat captain echoed in his ears.

Chapter 6 Virgin of Vigo

Dust chased the hooves of the Adjutant's horse as he galloped up the trail. He pulled hard on the reins of the beast to halt its advance. A soldier grabbed and controlled the mount. The Adjutant swung down from the saddle. His stride was awkward from the trail as he approached the Militia Commander. Unlike his dust coved uniform, his salute was crisp.

"Sir, a message from Prince Eugene," he said.

"Let me see what you've got here," said the Commander.

He pealed back the wax seal of the documents and unfolded the correspondence. His eyes tightened as he read the text. He paused, lowered the paper, and then raised it to read it again. His lips moved as he reviewed the text. The Adjutant studied these movements, trying to get some read as to the nature of the message he had just delivered.

"What does it say, sir," asked the Adjutant.

"It says, we will not receive any reinforcements to defend the Island."

"Well we can't hold with what we have. When do we embark, sir?"

"We don't. We are to hold to, let me see if I can get this right," said the Commander. He raised the letter once again. He scanned down the page until he found the words he was looking for. His head recoiled just a little from the text. "to the last round, man, and essence of our military virtue to ensure the honor and glory of the regiment."

"Nice words," replied the Adjutant.

"When you sit at higher headquarters you have both the time and distance to write such horse dung. Time, because those officers don't have real responsibility. Distance, because they are removed from the human contact of the soldiers they are about to send to their deaths."

"What are your plans, sir?" The junior officer removed his hat and wiped his brow.

"We hold here. Sassari is our final stand on Sardinia. Once it is over, our presence on this Island will end. Please ride out and tell the unit commanders my decision. We stand here."

"Yes, sir," rang from the Adjutant's lips. His salute, just as crisp as the first one, snapped up and down to mark his exit. Dust once again chased his horse as he sped along his way.

The Militia Commander walked to a viewing point on a small rise outside of Sassari. He pulled his spyglass out and scanned down the three lines of soldiers that defined his defense of the city. Their off-white uniforms, topped with black tri-corner hats, were aligned with precision. Two regimental standards waved defiantly in the wind. He nodded in self-congratulations as he reviewed the deployment of his men. He thought, *here, we stand here. For King and country, Sassari will be the turning point. To hell with reinforcements, who could carry a wall such as this?*

The sound of drums was faint at first. From beyond the distant ridge, its methodical beat grew in volume. Dust then rose skyward announcing the Spanish arrival well before their green uniforms came into view. The Militia Commander's attention was now fully focused on the unseen threat gathering just over the rise. His horse jostled beneath him as the opposing army appeared to lift from the ground, like departed souls rising from the grave.

The first block of the advancing green columns deployed on line overlapping the width of the defender's line. The second block followed and matched the deployment size of the first. Row, after row, of green uniforms marched in step to the sound of the marshal cadence that now filled the low ground between them. The beat of the drum, accented with the shrill tone of the fife, dominated the movements of the Spanish.

"We appear to be outnumbered two-to-one, sir," said the Commander's aide.

"More like three-to-one, I fear," replied the Commander. He collapsed his spyglass with a force indicating he had seen enough. He rode down the battle line, addressing each of his few cannon crews.

"Men, it would appear they hold the advantage in number of cannons today. Grapeshot only. Wait till the muskets let loose. Then add your grape to rip their lines apart," yelled the Commander from his horse.

The cannon crews responded with a yell. Some lifted their hats upward. Shot and shell were shuffled aside. Deadly grapeshot was readied at each gun.

The pace of the Spanish advance never slowed during their initial deployment. Cannon crews struggled to get into firing position ahead of the pending contact between opposing infantry formations. The slap of leather against horse flesh reinforced the importance of getting these guns into the battle. The shouts and commands of the cannon crews were clearly audible to the defending Savoy line. The defenders looked left and right. The pending threat was evident as the sun reflected off the brass cannon tubes now only a few hundred yards away.

The crack of a thunderous explosion signaled the start of the artillery duel. Given the orders to hold for grapeshot, the exchange was one sided and favored the Spanish. The first-round shot fell short of the defending line. The iron ball bounced along the ground tearing a hole in the neatly formed ranks of off-white uniforms. Bodies were tossed aside. Blood, mixed with detached limbs, spattered the clean marshal appearance of the infantry. The carnage inflicted by this solid shot was violent but limited. Those in the path of the rolling iron were dismembered in a painful manner. The second volley of cannon fire sailed overhead. The whoosh of the cannon ball passing overhead sent fear spreading within the ranks.

The Militia Commander spurred his horse along the back of the line. He reflected on the opening of the cannonade, *first round to the devil, second round to the heavens, damn. The next rounds will strike home. They have the range now. Their troops, one hundred yards distant and closing.*

The Spanish artillery was now effective in finding the battle line. Round after round bounced across the turf and collided with the stoic infantry arrayed like bowling pins to be knocked down. Occasionally, a round would hit home on a defending artillery piece and shatter brass and wood. The loss of this potential firepower was not missed by the Militia Commander.

The Spanish infantry stopped at fifty yards, leveled their muskets and fired. The dense smoke of this discharge obscured the carnage inflected from this disciplined volley. Ten percent casualties, the highest loss inflicted at this stage of the battle, dropped to the red clay of Sardinia. All along the line of green uniforms bayonets leveled and the Spanish continued their grinding advance toward the defending line. They made no attempt to reload. This was the assault and it was the assault that would, according to doctrine, carry the day.

The Militia Commander watched, and waited, as his battle line straightened up following the combination of fire and lead cast into his soldiers. Unit leaders yelled commands above the rhythmic pounding of advancing boots. Muskets leveled toward the advancing troops.

"Fire, fire at will," yelled the Militia Commander.

The response was immediate. Flame and fire lit across the length of the defensive line. Green uniforms crumbled before the conflagration of musket balls that tore into flesh and bone. Screams echoed in the afternoon air, but on they came. Muskets were reloaded by trembling hands. Defenders strained to focus on ramming the combination of musket ball, gunpowder, and wadding into a compact lethal mass at the bottom of the barrel. Every time their gaze looked into the low ground to their front, they were confronted with the green uniformed mass getting closer one pace at a time.

The lull in defensive fire did not last long. Grapeshot from the cannons soon followed. The whistling of chain, iron balls, and random lead screeched toward the advancing line. Unlike solid shot that bounded through the formation, grapeshot impacted full force on the leading edge of the formation. It dropped a number of soldiers across the frontage of impact. Sheets of red blanketed the Spanish as blood ran freely from the newly induced wounds. Amid the carnage, on came the mass of green uniforms.

"Again, lads, fire. Take them now, fire," commanded the Militia Commander.

With muskets reloaded, one more volley was poured into the attacking formations. They waivered, but then pressed on bolstered by the second regimental line behind them. Fresh and unencumbered by losses, these soldiers ran into the melee.

The once solid blocks of off-white and green uniforms now defused into numerous mixed patterns as troops pushed into hand-to-hand combat. The Militia Commander hacked downward from his mount on the numerous foes around him. Bayonets locked with each other until the more proficient combatant stood victorious with his blade thrust into the mass of his opponent's body. The screaming and guttural sounds of the fight carried to the ears of the Militia Commander. He fought from the embattled center of the line, desperate to hold here and not fall back into the city.

It started as a trickle. A few troops in off-white, turned and ran toward Sassari. Heads along the defensive line began to look over their shoulders. The hostile press to their front seemed too much for their limited numbers to readdress. The Militia Commander watched in horror, as the left side of the center gave way. A large group of soldiers took flight. He rode in their direction to stem the tide of this unwanted ebbing. His presence was ignored by wide eye soldiers seeking the protection of the rear.

"Stand with me men. For King and country, stand with me," said the Militia Commander.

His plea was loud but irrelevant. The green tide now pressed against them with unwavering momentum. He never saw the bayonet that pierced his leg and unhorsed him from the saddle. His horse spun around and kicked him in the side of the head with his hooves. Rearing up on two legs for a moment, the horse dropped to all four and followed the retreating army into Sassari.

A Lieutenant lowered his sword to the Commander's neck. The press of this edged weapon communicated his fate. Looking up, he saw a smile cross the face of his opponent.

"You, sir, are my prisoner. Do you yield?" said the Lieutenant.

"I yield, Lieutenant. Would you be so kind as to take me to your commander?"

"No need, sir. Our general is here," said the Lieutenant. He pointed toward a figure approaching on horseback. "On your feet, sir."

The Militia Commander struggled to get to his feet. Both hands were holding to his leg wound. It was only by this constant pressure that the wound did not bleed out. The profuse ringing in his head was more a function of his horse's impact to the head, than the bayonet that had unhorsed him.

"Marquis of Lede, at your service, sir."

"Sir, I'm in command of the remaining forces on this Island. I fear at this point I must yield, sir." He let loose his wound with one hand and lifted his sword toward the man that had defeated him on the field of battle.

"Am I to understand, you just surrendered all forces on the Island, sir?"

"Yes, we surrender."

"And you as their commander, surrender without condition. Is that correct?"

"Yes, sir."

"Very well then. Lieutenant, see to the immediate medical attention for his man and all the wounded we are able to help."

"Yes, sir," said the Lieutenant. His salute held all the pop of a new cadet.

"We will do all in our power to ease the suffering of your men. You have fought well and with honor. It is with honor you shall now be treated, sir."

The Militia Commander raised his arm in a ragged salute. He had been bested and now recovery was his only thought. He turned toward the city and followed the trail of broken bodies in off-white uniforms toward the city center. He paused before entering the city at the broken body of a soldier.

"Did you know him, sir?" asked his captor.

"Yes, he was my adjutant. I shall be at a lost without his service."

"Terrible cost, sir. You will have to notify his family?" His captor extended sincere regret.

"No, I think not. He's my son."

*****

The church was lined with Spain's ruling elite. No one would miss this event or be called for showing a lack of support to the ruling family. Maximo and Ernesta Rainerio sat in the middle of this august group. Not quite at the side of the royal family, but well forward of the on-lookers at the back of the church. The Prince stood at the altar. His hands held firm behind his back limiting the release of any nervous energy. His lips were tight, compressed, and pale. The arch of his nose dominated his face and made it appear out of proportion to the other features around it, except his ears. They hung heavy on each side of his skull making his head appear round.

Ernesta studied his appearance and mannerisms. She let out a long sigh. Her mind raced, *that could have been my husband. Better to die alone and penniless than to sleep with that clambering to ride above you. How could the Queen ever question my motivation for my little ruse to derail an unwanted betrothal? I think in the end she came to understand the forces at play here. Ah, the bride.*

The music announced the bride's entrance down the aisle. Ernesta turned to view the Prince's half-sister for the first time. They had never been formally introduced and studying her appearance it became clear why this creature had been hidden away in the south. Her black hair was streaked with premature grey that foretold a haggard future. She walked with a slight limp, perhaps one leg was a little shorter than the other. Her eyes were small and located too close. This beady eyed gaze was questioning and penetrating without speaking a word. She walked with her shoulders rolled forward and bent. This added to an already diminutive stature. Her father looked over at her.

"I shudder to think of the children, these two will—""

Ernesta shook her head, silencing her father. Looking around she noticed several sets of eyes had fallen on them as he started to speak.

The mass, and the ceremony that followed, were conducted in Latin. Few assembled spoke the language, so everyone kept looking around to see when to stand, kneel, or pray. Smiles began to randomly appear as the scene progressed. Ernesta waved her fan to gain some relief from the ever-present heat generated by the large crowd. She couldn't help but think, *this must be the ugliest royal couple to ever be wed within the Catholic Church. In some ways, they deserve each other.*

Ernesta shifted in her seat, she silently prayed, "Thank you lord for the many blessings you have bestowed upon me and my humble home. Please bring William back to me. In one piece if you can, but broken if you must. Amen."

The ceremony concluded, and everyone filed out into the courtyard to greet the couple. The catering of food and wine left nothing to chance. Certainly, cost was not an obstacle. Ernesta circulated through the crowd on her father's arm. They smiled and nodded to each courtier they passed. The cool November air in the courtyard encouraged the crowd to extend their stay and the quality of the wine enhanced their discussion.

"May I borrow your daughter, Maximo?" asked a voice from behind the pair.

Turning Maximo's mouth opened first to an oval and then he replied. "My Queen, I'm honored. Yes, Ernesta and your majesty, I bid you ado." He moved out of ear shot but hovered within eye contact of the two women.

Ernesta turned toward the Queen and curtsied deep. Rising she said, "Your majesty, so good to see you again. I hope the court at Madrid is treating you well."

"The court," she laughed. "They treat me just fine. It's all a big game. They tell me what they think I want to hear, and I pretend to be amazed by their divine counsel. Which is why I wanted to talk with you my dear."

"I don't think I can provide any insight into the inner workings or issues that command the court, my Lady."

"Exactly, which makes your opinion fresh and most welcome. Have you heard of the situation on Sardinia?"

"Only what I heard months ago. We landed and took about half the island back. Up to Oristano, I think."

"Yes, but they now control all of Sardinia and are moving on."

"On to where? Are they still thinking of Sicily after my father's warning?" asked Ernesta. Her tone had tightened.

The Queen took Ernesta's hand and guided her away from the eyes within the courtyard. She whispered, "Yes, the next invasion is Sicily. The Marquis of Lede is talking of no less than thirty thousand men. As you may have guessed, that is a sizeable force."

"And who has aligned against us?"

"When Philip claimed the French throne in the event of the death of the infant Louis, he generated opposition to us in France. None other than Louis the Fourteenth's nephew, the Duke of

Orleans sought to align with England and the Dutch Republic. They are calling themselves the Triple Alliance."

"And what of Austria and Savoy?" asked Ernesta. Her curiosity rose to the political intrigued of these combinations. Her eyes widened as she listened to the Queen.

"Well, the Austrians remain locked in conflict with the Ottoman Empire. Savoy on the other hand is difficult to read. Why did they not send reinforcements to defend Sardinia? I'm betting they are looking one step ahead. A conflict with Austria perhaps. They are, and will remain, a wild card. What do you think, my dear?"

"We are acting just a little too passive for my liking. Right now, we are striking at shadows. None of the powers of the Triple Alliance are in direct conflict with us in Sardinia. Nor would I feel that they will oppose us when we move on Sicily. But, when they move, how do we approach the conflict, strategically?"

"What do you mean?' asked the Queen. Her cheeks tightened into a slanted smile.

"If we act defensively, then we would only strike in response to the countermoves they make in the Mediterranean Sea or against Spain directly. On the other hand, if we act offensively then we would strike at their home land. Most likely that would mean a move against France or England."

The Queen let loose of Ernesta's hand for a moment and faced away. She rubbed her chin. She turned back around with such speed it surprised Ernesta.

"We lack the numbers to invade either France or England," said the Queen. Her tone had grown cold and stern.

"True. However, in the case of the English, they have a large population that resists the crown."

"The Jacobite?"

"Exactly, if we gain their support, the numbers of a smaller raiding force could be magnified tenfold. Five thousand could become fifty thousand, and in their backyard. They would have to react to our move. Spain would set the pace of the engagement. We would not have to respond to their actions," said Ernesta. She looked at the Queen's expression trying to gain some insight as to how her words were received.

"Ernesta, I've listened to generals and admirals talk for hours. None has detailed anything as simple and direct as this. I like the idea of taking the campaign to them. Making them react to us and not the other way around."

Ernesta curtsied deep, and said, "I hope I've been of some service my Queen."

"Rest assured my dear that is in fact the case. We will talk more of these matters, but for now, we should return to the celebration of the day," said the Queen. Her majesty started to walk away but paused. Turning over her shoulder, she added, "You need to wish the Prince and his new bride all the best. It is the proper thing to do. You don't have to feel it in your heart, but you do have to say it to him personally."

Again, Ernesta found her knees bent as the Queen made her exit. She took a quick spin through the courtyard. Locating the newlywed couple, she approached. She had to stand in line to greet the couple.

"Your most honorable Prince, and his lovely bride, it is an honor to wish the two of you all the best and most happiness in your new life together," said Ernesta. She added to what seemed like an endless stream of curtsies and presentations.

"Thank you Ernesta. I was a little worried you would hold a grudge for not going through with the arrangement of our parents," said the Prince.

"It has been difficult to come to grips with my reality, but I will adjust."

"So, I see. I fear I must pass you along my dear. More guests to greet."

Ernesta moved down the line. She smiled and pouted, but inside her level of excitement was unparalleled. She thought, *I can't hardly believe it. I've ditched the pig prince, gotten in good with the queen, and still have time to get William back. If I'm unable to secure Annette, perhaps, I can find another way to influence William back into my arms.*

"Ernesta, are you ready to depart. We have a long ride back to the coast starting tomorrow. I would at least like to start fresh," said her father.

"Yes, sir. I'm ready for the road. Let's depart before more difficulties consume us."

"It may be too late for that, my dear."

"What do you mean father?"

They both walked toward the courtyard exit. He once again extended his arm to her.

"I've had someone inquire as to your marital status," said her father.

"And whom might that be father?"

"The Harbor Master of Vigo," he said. They locked eyes.

"Father, the Harbor Master, really? He must be at least in his late forties."

"More like early fifties my dear. He wants you and is willing to accept you regardless of the nature of your virginity. He made it very clear, he didn't have to marry the Virgin of Vigo."

"Father, just once can't a young lady of the court marry whom she wants?"

"Sounds a lot like pure chaos to me, but it's the start of a new century. Maybe it is time for women to exercise more control in their affairs. To make enlightened choices as to who they marry. How many children they have. Even perhaps, what type of government they support. No, this is all silly talk. Let's focus on what is possible and not deal in things that can never be."

"Yes, father," said Ernesta smiling. They left the gathering and headed home.

Two months passed since the royal wedding, and Ernesta and her father found themselves on the road once again. The trip to Cadez had strained the family budget, but the potential return in business appeared worth the reward. The team of horses pulled the coach along at an even canter across the difficult roads of the Spanish countryside.

"There's always something special about a journey's end," said Ernesta. The coach bounced over a large stone that always seemed to be directly ahead.

"Yes, my daughter. I've worked hard to secure our hacienda, but I wonder sometimes," said Maximo.

"Wonder what father?"

"If you feel your upbringing complete without a mother in your life?"

"I have never wanted for anything father. You have given me all I could ask. I suppose I'll always think about what it would have been like to have her in my life, but you have never left a gap in my heart. She gave all when I was born. It must have been hard for you to watch her choose between her life and mine."

Maximo shifted in his seat. His grip on the coach window tightened and then relaxed. He looked out the window toward their house down the trail.

"Every decision your mother made was painful. How she bore-up under such stress is beyond me. She was a woman of character. Christina will live in our hearts, always."

"Yes, father . . . always."

The sun hung low in the west. The heat of the day slowly surrendered to the cool of the late winter evening. Yellow and orange combined as if on an artist palette, covering the sky with brilliant hues seen only in that mixing bowl of the heavens at dawn and dusk. The divide between night and day transitioned in a manner that neither the day or night could recognize or claim as their own. It was a time when people would stop and embrace the moment. To put aside those things of routine and just look, enjoy, and think. As with all transitions, it was a time when reflection could command clarity.

Ernesta fell silent and just stared out the coach window. Her thoughts hurried back to what she had heard at court. Thoughts of her time with William randomly flashed across her canvas. *Would she see William again? To be held in his arms. I've surrendered a kingdom and title of queen for his touch. I must command his love, as he commands my heart.*

The coach lurched to a stop. The constant clanking of wooden wheels over rough ground gave way to the heavy breathing of the horses. Maximo pushed the small coach door open and stepped to the ground of his hacienda. He lifted his hand toward the coach.

"May I help you Ernesta?"

"Thank you, father," said Ernesta. She reached out and took his hand. Pulling her dress through the narrows of the coach door, it flowed around her as she dismounted.

Pili Tonia's mother approached at a quick trot. She waved her hand toward Ernesta in time with the waddle of her oversized frame. Her breathing was heavy.

"Mistress Ernesta, Pili is in labor and has asked you be at her side on your return," she said.

"How long?'

"She has been at it for nine hours now. The mid-wife said long labors are common for first born."

"But she's not due yet."

"I know, mistress. I'm worried. Pili has asked for you. Only you. Please hurry, it will be comforting for her to know you have returned in time."

Ernesta lifted her dress off the ground with one hand on either side of her body. She moved across the courtyard to the room where Pili would deliver her child. The rustling of her dress announced her presence to her hand maiden.

Pili lay on her bed. Her knees were pulled up and legs held apart by the mid-wife. Ernesta hurried to her side, partly to comfort her servant and partly to avoid the view below her waist. Pili's cotton dressing gown was covered in sweat. The moisture pooled on her chest, brow, and neck. She had labored through the day and now the evening was providing some small measure of relief. Her breathing was shallow, rapid, and uncontrolled.

"Thank God . . . you're here. I was afraid . . . you would," said Pili. She paused and snapped her lips together. The lines around her eyes deepened as the contractions took hold over her body once again. No control, no relief, just deep muscle spasms that took control of her reality inducing pain throughout her body. She wanted to push the child from her and transition him into the world of light.

"Not yet. Don't push. We're close now, little one," said the mid-wife.

Pili tossed her head from side to side. Her body told her to push, but the mid-wife was directing her to wait. The conflict held her captive to the pain. Her breathing returned to rapid panting as she grabbed Ernesta's arm. Her fingers dug into Ernesta's flesh, perhaps a subconscious effort to let her experience some of the joy of child birth. She pulled her mistress to her and whispered in her ear.

"You did this to me. You sent me to his bed. I did what you asked, and now—"

Pili gripped Ernesta's arm with the same painful lock she held before. Ernesta's mouth turned down as the finger nails of her servant deformed her skin. She looked down at the mid-wife.

"How much longer now?" asked Ernesta.

"We are close. The head is beginning to crown. It will be time to push now. No holding back, Pili. On the next—"

"Augh," rang out from Pili. She let loose of Ernesta and grabbed both knees with her hands. This time the pain had purpose, she pushed and pushed hard. This action gave her focus. The end of the task was in sight. Hope returned to her consciousness. But, not done yet.

"How much longer?" she asked. It was more a plea than an inquiry.

"A few more and we'll be done here. On each contraction, you've got to push. Just like the last one. That was good, I think the child is ready now," said the mid-wife. Her tone was measured, unexcited, and calm.

"The child's ready now. Well, I've been ready for—"

"Yes, push. I think I can see—"

The sound of a child crying announced to the world that Pili was a mother. Somewhere, on a distant wave, a new father was unaware of his change in status. The skilled hands of the mid-wife pulled, cut, and wrapped the child with speed and precision any military man would have found impressive.

"What is it?" asked Ernesta

"It's a human soul delivered by the grace of God," said the mid-wife smiling. "Oh, you mean is it a boy or a girl. It's a strong, healthy, baby boy my dear. A big one too."

The mid-wife handed the child to Pili. She pushed back the blanket around his face to study closed eyes and tightened lips. She started to sob.

"A son," said Ernesta. Her mind wondered, *William's son. Perhaps Annette is no longer needed to bring him back to me. I have his son. His flesh and blood. Is that enough?*

"Oh, there it is," said the mid-wife. "That's one nasty flow, my dear." She set about her final task of cleaning the afterbirth from Pili's legs and body. The clothes were soiled with the blood from the birthing.

"May I hold him?" asked Ernesta. She picked up the child without waiting for Pili to acknowledge her question.

116

Pili's fatigued eyes squinted at Ernesta as she held the child close, rocking the infant. The edges of her mouth turned down, not from the pain of labor but from the unseen trials her child might have to endure. She had been held in Williams embrace. In the dark of the night, she had felt him ride beneath her skin to heights of pleasure they each enjoyed. She birthed his child. Now it fell to her to protect this new soul cast into a difficult and chaotic world. She reached up to take the child back from her boss.

Ernesta turned away from the out stretched arms.

"In a minute," said Ernesta. "Just let me hold him a little longer."

The child was sleeping. Silent. Unware of the conflict building around him.

"I have to record a name for public records," said the mid-wife.

"William," said Ernesta. "Have you ever heard such a lovely name? Willian shall be your name, and your destiny, my little one."

The mid-wife looked over at Pili with quill in hand.

"William, madam. William Christopher Tonia will do just fine," said Pili.

The mid-wife scribbled across two pieces of parchment. She placed one on the table next to the bed. The other she secured in her bag. She covered up Pili and pushed the edges of the blankets around her. She walked around the other side of the bed and took the child from Ernesta.

"Time to let mother and child sleep now, my dear. It's been a long day for both. Come now, let them be," said the mid-wife.

"Yes, of course. Let them be, for now," said Ernesta. She blew out the flame from a whale oil lamp and let the dark shades of night envelop the room. They made their exit and slowly shut the door behind them.

*****

The cold of the Scottish winter night chilled the room. Annette pulled her shawl higher across her shoulders to defend against the cold. Her stare on Cynthia was as cool as the air in their chamber.

"How long has it been since your last flow?" asked Annette.

"I think about eight weeks or so," replied Cynthia.

"Child, you're pregnant for sure. Does the Earl be a knowing?"

"No. I couldn't tell him. He might throw me out."

"Tell him or not, your belly will be announcing the news soon enough. You can't be wearing those tight dresses much longer and will have to shift the hem line upward to tent the growth within."

"I can do that."

"No, you need to let the all mighty Earl von Hunter know he has a child on the way. He can't be turning you out. It is his doing as well. I'm reasonably sure he enjoyed the acts that brought you to this condition. How long have you two been at this?"

"Almost every night since we got here to Eilean Donan. It's not like it has been a chore. I'm sure we both enjoyed the ride," said Cynthia. She smiled as thought of romantic nights briefly filled her imagination.

"Aye, that would be doing it. Look, you have to tell him. You might well be surprised by his response. I doubt the Earl wants a bastard child chasing his name any more than you want to try and raise this child without the support he could offer."

"He loves me you know."

"He does? Well that be reassuring. A child conceived in love, deserves loving parents and the support to prosper. You're the mother, only you can secure that for the child. You have to confront Drake."

"I'm scared."

118

"If you can't do it, I will," said Annette. The force of her words made Cynthia recoil.

"You wouldn't dare."

"How long have you known me?"

"Oh, God, you would dare. Annette, please let me handle this in my way."

"Sure, but your way had damn well better include letting the right honorable Earl know he is a father. He has family responsibilities and commitments. We are not talking about a consensual romp in the sheets anymore. We're talking about a child."

Cynthia lowered her head. She nodded and looked up.

"Annette, I'll tell him," said Cynthia. Her voice almost a whisper.

"When?"

"Soon."

"How soon?"

"Next week."

Annette's stare tightened. The bright green of her eyes flared hotter than the sun. She focused this heat on Cynthia. She watched as Cynthia lowered her head once again.

"I'll tell him tonight."

"Good choice. Tonight, it is," said Annette. She leaned back in her chair. "Cynthia, you know whatever Drake may do, the Red Fox Inn is, and will always be, your home."

Cynthia smiled. She looked over at Annette and nodded.

Chapter 7 July's Judgement

An early spring was not the only surprise that fell upon the Highlands of Scotland. Cynthia lay next to drake within the darkness of their curtained bed. She ran her hand down his back. He stirred in the silence of the morning. Pulling her head just above his ear, her black hair fell across the side of Drake's face. Even in the dark she could see him smile.

"Drake," said Cynthia. Her voice low and soft.

"Yes, my dear."

"I have to tell you something."

Drake turned toward her and placed his hand on her naked hip. His thumb rubbed along the smooth flesh.

"What?"

"Drake, I carry your child. I'm pregnant by you."

"How do you know?"

"It has been two months since my, since my—"

"Your last flow?"

"Yes. I'm sure it's your child Drake. I've not been with another."

He moved his hand down from her hip to cover her belly. He spread his fingers wide across her slight bump. His touch was light but deliberate, firm, and reassuring.

"Well, I hope you haven't been with another. I never gave you time for any of that, now did I?"

Cynthia shook her head.

"Cynthia, you have just made me a very happy man."

Her eyes widened, and her head recoiled to this unexpected comment.

He added, "Is it a boy or a girl?"

Cynthia giggled, and said, "Drake you can't tell until they join us in the world. That's when we will know for sure."

"If you would honor me, I want your hand in marriage. This will not be a bastard child, is that clear," said Drake. His military command tone had returned.

"Wait, what?"

"Marry me. I think it only right for my child, he or she, be in the kingdom of God and my house. A bastard would be cast out from both."

"When can I give you an answer?"

"Before my hand releases from your belly would be nice," said Drake. He deliberately lightened the press against her skin.

"Yes, yes, of course I'll marry you. What girl wouldn't?"

What girl wouldn't indeed? They all would like a piece of me, or at least my standing. Before a new marriage can begin, an old childless union must end. Complicated. These thoughts ran through Drake's skull as he struggled to find a plan that would allow him to claim this child as a potential heir.

He slid his hand from her belly, around behind her, and pressed her ass hard against his lower body. He lightly patted her buttock.

That's an odd gesture, thought Cynthia. *Does he think he owns my ass now because I carry his child within?*

"Cynthia, I'm glad you shared this with me. I was going to tell you, I have to return to my estate in Southampton to conclude some affairs down south. You know the road and how long things take. However, if I leave soon, I'll be able to make it down to my estate, conclude my business, and be back here well before the child is born. I should have told you sooner, but I was afraid you might tire of waiting and forsake me for another."

Drake sprang from the bed. Cynthia lifted up on one elbow and watched him get dressed. He hurried along with an energy found from new purpose and the prospect of new life. She reflected as she watched, *it may well be a long way from your estate to the castle Eilean Donan in Scotland, but my journey from the Red Fox Inn to your bed can only be measured in uncountable miles.*

The wife of an Earl how can that even be possible? I've never heard of an entertainer advancing within the social ladder like that. Yet, here I am. In his bed chamber. With his child growing in my belly. I have what he wants, and he has what I need. Perhaps a perfect match.

As he started for the door, he turned back toward her. "Cynthia, please do not discuss our plans for union with anyone until I return. I want to make the announcement at a formal Highland gathering here at Eilean Donan. Can you do that for me?"

"Even Annette?"

"Yes, my love. Even Annette will have to wait to hear the news with the rest of Highland society," replied Drake. He strapped his Dirk to his side.

"Drake, as you command," said Cynthia. This comment drew a wide smile from Drake.

He walked down the passageway toward the dining hall. He approached Annette, who stood hovering at the fruits arrayed on the breakfast table.

"Good morning to you, Earl," said Annette. Her tone was respectful and even.

"Annette, top of the morning to you as well." A short silence filled the space between them.

"Annette have you heard the news from Cynthia?" asked the Earl. He was perhaps the worst keeper of his own secrets.

"And what news would that be?" said Annette. She lowered her green eyes in the Earl's direction.

"That Cynthia is with child," said Drake. The edges of his mouth had lifted into a full smile. His tone was upbeat.

"Oh my," said Annette. Her mouth opened to a wide circle. "What does the Earl be thinking about that?"

"I'm excited. I've always thought I'd sort of be a good father. Now, amid the heather of Scotland, I'll find out."

122

"It's not a trial run in the northern part of the country or something like that you know. It's a commitment to the mother and child until he is an adult. That's like eighteen or twenty years. Are you excited about a commitment like that?

"Annette, I'm sure of one thing."

"And what would that be, the right honorable Earl von Hunter?"

"I love Cynthia, and I will surprise even you with my level of commitment. Let's just leave it like that, shall we?"

"We shall, sir. Yes, we shall indeed," replied Annette. Her mouth fell half open as she reflected on the conversation. She studied the Earl as he directed his staff to ready his mount for the ride ahead. Her thoughts wondered in his presence, *I hope to hell that son of bitch returns. If he leaves Cynthia hanging, I'll kill him myself. Perhaps an early spring is a sign of the warmth about to enter all our lives. William, I need you. God, please bring me my love.*

*****

The shadow of Gibraltar highlighted the rock's sheer solid face. Captain Darroch had to squint through the early afternoon haze to get a glimpse of the monolith's distinctive shape. The wind beat upon the surface of the narrow sea, forcing white caps to dance along its surface. Sergeant Worth joined his commander at the railing. His sharp salute broke Darroch's thoughts and shifted his attention back aboard *Comet*.

"An impressive sight, wouldn't you say Sergeant Worth?" asked Darroch.

"Yes, sir. Of course, it looks much more refined then when I landed on it fourteen years ago."

"You were part of the assault force in 1704?"

"Yes, sir. We sailed in a combined English-Dutch squadron under the command of the very same Admiral Byng that is running this force," said Worth. He pointed toward the small town at the base of the rock. "We had twenty-two ships pound

123

that hunk of rock for days before we went ashore. Good fight that one."

"Indeed. Good thing your crew was able to take it. That choke point between the Atlantic and Mediterranean is one of the strategic keys to worldwide commerce. Thank God England controls it," said Darroch.

"I don't know about all this strategy stuff, sir. I'm just glad to get underway and off anchor. I found the bumboat women and their rum to be more than a little distracting for the crew. All that time at anchor made the winter drag on. However, the Marines are back in their shipboard routine. They are ready now, sir." Sergeant Worth smiled as he rubbed the hilt of his saber with the palm of his hand.

"The warmer climate of the Mediterranean, coupled with the onset of summer, should thaw even the most chilled bone among us," said Darroch.

"What does the Captain think we'll be doing moving forward?"

"The Spanish have taken Sardinia. We don't know what they are planning next. They could expand their presence back onto the Italian Peninsula or Sicily. My guess is we are here to deter such a move."

"Deterrence, sir. Sounds like a lot of sailing in circles to me."

Darroch nodded. He looked off to the starboard side of the ship. The ships-of-the-line were sailing in column well ahead of the beam. The northwest wind had pushed them all over on a slight list toward the African Coast. The surface swell was high enough to rock each ship fore and aft as the wind pushed them ahead into the chop. Their flags and pennants beat overhead, snapping in the breeze. *Comet* held position to the north side of this formation covering the Spanish side of the line as it sailed through the Gibraltar Straight.

"Sloop approaching on the starboard quarter, prepare to receive," said Lieutenant Laurant.

"Aye, aye, sir," replied Midshipman Rutwell.

The young lad moved over to the ladder adjacent to the starboard quarter.

"Chief White, lower a line as they come along side," he said.

"Aye, sir."

"Lieutenant Laurant, she's a currier boat. I need a runner," yelled Rutwell.

Laurant waved in acknowledgement. A new seaman ran from the command deck to join Rutwell. He carried a bucket on a rope. He slipped on the wet deck as he approached the Midshipman.

The boat eased alongside *Comet* and secured the line to its bow. The coxswain let out the boom to parallel the ships rate of advance. The bucket was lowered away and hauled back to the main deck in short order. The coxswain held his hand alongside his mouth.

"A message from the Admiral for your Captain," he yelled.

Lieutenant Laurant heard the coxswain and turned toward Captain Darroch.

"A message from Admiral Byng aboard *Barfleur*. This should prove interesting," said Laurant.

"*Barfleur*, that's a ninety-gun ship," said Darroch.

"She's rated at ninety guns, Marine. I'll bet Captain Saunders has squeezed a few more on deck somewhere. He loves his firepower."

Laurant looked at the letter. The words, "For Captain Calder's eyes only" limited his options.

"Take this to the captain's cabin. Wait and see if he has any instructions for the Officer of the Deck."

"Aye, aye, sir," said the runner.

In observing this scene unfold, Captain Darroch thought, *what the hell could that be about. The fleet is hours away from shifting course or formation. We'll have to clear the straight before we maneuver. The Spanish Fleet is still in the middle of the*

Mediterranean, so we can't be clearing for action. Odd, just very odd."

The runner returned to the command deck. His breathing was heavy and labored. He put his hands on his knees for a second to catch his breath.

"Out with it, man. What does Captain Calder want?" asked Laurant.

"Sir, you are to turn over the deck to Midshipman Rutwell. Captain Calder would like to see Captain Darroch, Lieutenant Martino, and yourself in his cabin immediately," panted the runner.

Laurant and Darroch exchanged stares.

"I'll get Charles and meet you at the captain's cabin. Please wait until the three of us can enter together," said Laurant.

"Aye," said Darroch.

Damn it's dark down here after standing on deck, thought Darroch as he waited in the passageway outside the captain's cabin. A single flame from a whale oil lamp flickered amidships turning aside the darkness with limited results. The joints of the wood planking creaked around him as *Comet* beat into the swell. This background noise was drowned out by the clip-clop of wooden soled shoes on the deck. Two silhouettes approached down the passageway.

"Charles, David, are you ready?" asked Darroch.

They both nodded. The Marine knocked on the hatch.

"Request permission to enter the captain's cabin?"

"Granted."

The three middle grade officers entered the domain of their boss. They found Calder already seated at the head of the table. Two charts were spread across its flat surface. The Captain's fingers were tapping the table in quick time. His chin rested in the palm of his other hand. He straightened up and folded his arms in front of his chest as his officers entered the cabin.

126

"Gentlemen, please take a seat. We have new developments to contend with here," said Calder.

As the officers took their seats, Darroch studied the charts. His mind raced, *Central Mediterranean and the Island of Sicily. Target. Sicily must be their next move. If I recall my history from the Peloponnesian war, that means Syracuse, Palermo, or Messina are targets.* Captain Darroch pulled his green notebook from his coat pocket.

"Gentleman, I guess by now you know the Spanish are following up their attack on Sardinia with an invasion of Sicily. They are closer and already on the move. It is unlikely we can intercept them at this time. I would like to get everyone's read as to where you think they will strike first and why," said Calder. "Lieutenant Martino, what do you think?"

Charles ran his hand across the chart several times. He smoothed its rough edges and measured a few distances on the scale. Turning away from his contemporaries, he focused on Calder.

"Sir, they will strike Syracuse. It is the largest port. It was a historical target during the Greek wars. The rode stays and anchorages are good. Yes, sir. Syracuse is the target. We'll be able to intercept their fleet there if *Comet* sets course toward the south side of the Island."

"Thank you, Charles. David your thoughts?"

"Sir, I say they will head for and defeat the garrison at Messina. The straight is narrow and controls traffic flowing near Italy going both north to south or east to west. Controlling the central Mediterranean is best accomplished with this straight in hand."

"Marine, you're our resident landsman, what are you thinking?"

"Sir, they will not want to sail into the teeth of any defense. Palermo is the best shot. It is an open city. The defenders know the port of Syracuse and straight are key. This will compel their defense to concentrate in these two areas. Palermo commands the north coast. It could provide a base of operations for striking out at either Messina or Syracuse."

"Do you three bastards ever agree on anything?" asked Calder. His tapping of the table top resumed. "No, I didn't say that. Well, I appreciate your input. You all brought out good points and some I didn't consider in a quick look at the campaign. This is, after all, why you have a council of war."

"It might help if we knew our mission, sir," said Darroch.

"*Comet* is to sail ahead of the main body, locate the Spanish navy, report back and if directed engage. I guess it's important to add, England and the Triple Alliance are not at war with anyone at this point." Calder's tapping on the table halted.

"What about the Austrians, sir?" asked Darroch.

"That Marine, is an excellent question. I've heard of talks to end their current conflict with the Ottoman, but until that shakes out they are on the sidelines. Damn it. We need their troops if we are going to turn this around on the land. How many Marines total in the squadron?"

"Not more than a few thousand, sir," said Darroch.

"The Admiralty is confident they left Sardinia with upward of thirty thousand."

"Well, we're good, but not against that many. Sir, we can strike and raid the coast at any selected point. We can't stand against them toe-to-toe in open combat. It's a numbers issue at this point." Darroch rolled his shoulders when he finished.

"Thank you Captain Darroch, I understand," said Calder. He looked around the table to gain eye contact. Moving his hand along the Sicily chart, he explained his intent. "Here is what *Comet* will do. I'll sail along the northern coast of the Island. That way we can cover the approaches to Palermo and Messina at the same time. With two of three under our contact, we should have a good chance to locate the Spanish fleet. Questions?"

"Any changes for the Officer of the Deck, sir?" asked Laurant.

"Yes, of course. We are breaking formation and pulling out ahead of the fleet. Let's get studding sails flying soonest and see if we can gain a few knots to out distance the battle line."

The sound of wood scraping against wood echoed through the cabin as chairs were pushed away from the chart table. Calder looked toward his galley half expecting Annette to emerge and offer him a glass of wine. His moment of reflection was shattered when his unshaven steward stuck his head from around the corner.

"Does the Captain need anything?" he asked.

"No thank you. Carry on."

Alone in his cabin, he looked aft through the stern windows. *Comet's* wake rolled away in white foam that spread across the surface of the sea and faded from view. He thought, *not at war with Spain, but no peace either. Halfway between cold iron and hot war. Damn the indecision. Just what the hell I'm going to do if the threat of force is extended by the Dons. Make contact and report. Not much of a mission for a warship.*

*****

Captain Calder walked up the command deck and received a salute from Lieutenant Martino.

"Officer of the Deck, report," he said.

"Sir, we are clearing Cape Gallo. Palermo is just around the peninsula. I've had no sign of Spanish activity since I assumed the watch. Our speed, with the studding sails flying, has been steady at eight knots. We lost contact with the main body several days ago and haven't had any messages from them since. At our current speed, I'm not sure a currier boat can even catchup with us," said Martino.

"Noted Lieutenant."

Calder walked over to the starboard side railing. He extended his spyglass and looked along the shore line from the cape eastward. The bay before Palermo was clear of Spanish ships. But, in the distance a plume of smoke rose above the horizon.

"Lieutenant, do you make that out as smoke in the distance?"

"Yes, sir. Something is alight out there."

"Palermo, perhaps?"

"Could be, sir. The position and distance would be about right for that to be the case."

"Lieutenant, it would appear we are not alone out here."

"Sir?"

"That bay I thought was clear has a small boat in it. The crew is now making sail."

"Direction, sir"

"Directly for us, of course,' said Calder. His voice seemed calm.

"Spanish, sir"

"That's what the yellow and red flag would seem to indicate, Lieutenant. Still too far to tell for sure." Calder looked into the rigging to ensure the Union Jack was flying.

The small boat tacked back and forth, beating up to a point directly in *Comet's* path. An officer in the back looked up to the command deck to hail the approaching ship.

"English, you are entering an area under the control of the Spanish navy. What are your intentions?"

"We are at peace with Spain, sir. We have demonstrated no hostile act. Our intent is to parallel the coast to Messina," yelled Calder. He held his gaze on this small boat challenging his warship. A moment of silence followed.

"Proceed at your own risk. Our navy is conducting landings in this area and will defend itself if necessary."

Calder waved toward the small craft. Captain Darroch climbed the ladder up one level to the command deck. Calder smiled but turned his attention to the Officer of the Deck.

"Lieutenant Martino, I want *Comet* to continue to press along the coast," said Calder.

"Aye, aye, sir," replied Martino.

"It would appear Captain Darroch, that your assessment of the landing site was correct," said Calder. "The smoke plume confirms Palermo as the landing point. Officer of the Deck, can we get closer to see the landing?"

"Sir, it would be good if we could confirm numbers, uniforms, and such," said Darroch.

"Aye, aye, sir," replied Martino.

At the end of the day, *Comet* was within five miles of the Spanish landing. Darroch strained to see events ashore through his spyglass.

"What do you see, Marine?" asked Calder.

"As near as I can make out, the city is in Spanish control. Yellow and red flags are flying from above the port area. We'd have to get closer to be sure, but those appear to be Spanish."

"What else?"

"For me, it is interesting to see two columns of soldiers in green uniforms marching in different directions. One is moving along the coast and the other is heading inland. I would say that confirms the battle for Palermo is over."

"Sir, I know the events ashore are interesting, but you really need to see this," said Martino.

Calder and the Marine walked to the other side of the ship and scanned the horizon.

"Yes, that would be their fleet. Did you get a count?" asked Calder.

"I've got them at over thirty ships, sir."

"Damn. How many are warships?'

"More than twenty, sir."

"Officer of the Deck, bring us about. I've got to get his information back to Admiral Byng. He's sailing into a trap, outnumbered."

"Aye, aye, sir," acknowledge Martino. "We'll have to tack and beat back and forth given the wind direction, sir."

"Do it, man. We've not a minute to lose," said Calder. His voice tightened as he spoke.

"Sir, it will take all night to work our way to the main body. We won't be able to exchange signals until daylight tomorrow."

"That will work, Charles. It will have to work."

*****

"I've lost track of time, what's the date?" asked the Austrian Ambassador in a whisper.

"Sir, it's 21 July 1718," replied his aide.

"I know the year damn it. I'm not that far gone."

"Yes, sir."

"Gentlemen, we have an agreement. At the bequest of his majesty, I sign this Treaty of Passarowitz to end all hostilities between my country and our neighbors to the south. May the Ottoman Empire and people of Austria move forward on a path of non-aggression toward each other and with reverence toward our unique differences and beliefs," said the Austrian Ambassador. He raised his champagne glass toward the diplomats assembled and moved it across his chest. The moist bounce of the bubbles fell upon his hand and tickled his nose when he sipped the beverage. A light applause drifted through the room.

Heads appeared to nod, and smiles were exchanged between two peoples that only days before were doing all in their power to kill those across the room. The Ambassador signed and dated the document of intense attention before retreating to a corner of the room with his aide. He took his underling's upper arm and turned him away from the guests.

"Get a rider to deliver the sealed documents on my desk to the Royal Court. It is critical that the Emperor knows he is now able to enter into the alliance," said the Ambassador. Again, his words were spoken in hushed tones.

"Which alliance, sir."

"The one with England, France, and the Dutch. The Quadruple alliance my good friend. Its sole object will be to turn back the Spanish and prevent them from uniting with the French against us."

"Why now? We just concluded one war."

"Right, with the Ottoman's out of the picture we can send an army to reverse our recent loss of Sicily to the Spanish. I fear July's judgement will not be kind to them."

"Does the alliance mean all four nations will go to war with Spain?"

"No. It doesn't matter. The English are in. Once they control the sea, we can put an army ashore in Sicily and retake the place. I leave it to England and fate to convince the French and Dutch to join the battle."

"I see, sir. If you'll excuse me, I will secure the services of a rider."

"Yes, by all means. Carry on."

*****

The lone rider paced his mount up the long arching estate entrance near Southampton. Weeks on the road had taken their toll on this traveler. His head was downward cast to either the miles behind him or the miles ahead. His expression gave little in the way of foreshadowing as to the direction of his melancholy mood. Drake dismounted and handed his horse over to the stable boy. The young lad's enthusiasm to help his boss induced a slight awkwardness to his efforts. It was Sunday and only minimum estate staff were on-hand.

Drake walked up the stairs to the second floor. The wrinkles around his face reflected the twisted nature of his thoughts. His boots left dirt marks on the smooth marble.

"Drake, you're back. Wonderful," said Rachel. Her rosy cheeks bounced as she spoke.

"Yes, Rachel. I have a few things to take care of before I return to the militia up north."

"Is everything progressing in Scotland as you planned, dear?"

"Yes, I think our troops have been able to convince the Jacobite elements among us to stay low and not interfere with the plans of King and court. How are thing here with the estate?"

"Well, let me tell you. The estate manager has been keeping everything in order. Of course, we haven't been doing any entertaining in your absence. I sort of miss that."

"Do you have any regrets? About us, I mean."

Rachel's mood shifted. The edges of her mouth turned down. She lifted her arms akimbo.

"Is your dower demeanor reflecting a lack of an heir again?"

"Yes, my time in Scotland had forced me to face my own mortality. I can't let the family line end here. Without someone to pass this estate to, I feel small before all those family portraits that hang in the long hallway. They stretch back several generations. To end the Hunter name here, with me, is painful."

"Drake, this is silly talk. We have tried to have children. Tried hard when we were both a little younger," said Rachel. She covered her mouth and giggled. Looking back at Drake her tone grew increasingly stern. "I know you want a child. My dear, you will have to let this obsession pass from your thoughts. I'm too old at this point, let it go."

The two of them approached the spiral stair case and paused. Drake hung his head. His eyes were distant. Rachel turned and placed her hand on his chest.

"It will be alright, dear. I'm sorry children didn't work out for us," she said.

"So am I," Drake mumbled.

Drake shoved Rachel with both hands. She tumbled head over heels down the stair case. The smacking sound of her skull impacting the marble resonated off each step and back to where Drake was standing at the top of the stairs. She impacted the iron railing at the bottom slicing her head open. The pool of crimson blood collected around her torso. Like a pebble cast into still water, the ring of blood expanded outward around her. Rachel's twisted limbs and body lay motionless. Her chest expansions were unseen from Drake's perch.

He waited, watching, and listening. He took one step away from the stairwell, his eyes still locked on the scene below. She looked no different than when he had watched her sleeping by his side for over sixteen years. He retreated one additional step, still observing like a silent sentinel. Mist formed in his eyes, blurring his vision. He listened, his hearing was still sharp.

Footsteps, damn. The realization that someone was approaching demanded action. Drake retreated to his bedroom and removed his coat and shirt.

"Mistress, mistress," called out her attendant. "Help, someone help."

Drake ran from his room bare chested to the top of the stairs.

"What happened," he yelled. He ran down the staircase.

"She must have fallen, sir. I found her like this."

"Go get the doctor."

"Yes, sir."

The servant exited the foray. Drake held his hand atop her mouth and nose. *No breathing,* he thought. A smile briefly lifted on his face.

He whispered, "Business complete."

Chapter 8 Poseidon Paradox

Two land masses converged to form narrows between the Italian Peninsula and the Island of Sicily. Vertical walls lifted from the sea on each side of these constricted waters, limiting maneuver options for approaching ships. The water lightened in color as the influence of the approaching shallows held sway. *Comet* steered a southerly course directly toward this passage. The Greeks, Romans, and Venetians had all glided along these waters in search of their destinies. Now the Royal Navy surged ahead into an uncertain future.

A long boat pulled up to *Comet*. The side boys mustered on the main deck made it clear the ship's skipper was returning from his conference with the Admiral. The Bosun's pipe sounded the return of Captain Calder. The rhythm of the notes was well known to the crew.

"Comet, arriving," said Lieutenant Laurant. His voice was elevated so the crew would be clear their boss was aboard. He joined the side boys in a hand salute. Calder returned the honors with a crisp movement of his hand to the brim of his hat. As Calder cleared the two rows of side boys, Lieutenant Laurant joined him at the centerline of the ship.

"How did it go over on the flagship, sir?" Laurant Asked.

"The *Barfleur* remains shipshape as always. Admiral Byng was in rare form. His animated gestures reflected the excitement in his mood. I really don't think he can wait to make contact with the Spanish."

"Do we know what we are up against?"

"Hell, we don't even know if they have received the Quadruple Alliance's ultimatum yet."

"Then we are not at war?"

"Not so far as the diplomats are concerned. However, we do have orders to engage if they demonstrate any hostile intentions."

"Hostile intentions, what does that mean, sir?"

"Lieutenant, I'm not sure I can give a direct answer to that question. One thing you'll learn about being a captain at sea, not all situations are defined in Royal Navy regulations. The book, you might say, is missing a few pages at times," said Calder. He motioned for the Lieutenant to walk with him up to the command deck.

Laurant positioned himself one step behind and to the left of Calder as they moved aft. Sailors rendered courtesies toward these two blue uniforms as they went by. They would stand, bow slightly forward toward the officers, and touch their knuckles against their brow. Otherwise the crew was too consumed with the routine of sailing *Comet* to pay much attention to the discussion between them.

"What is our role, sir?"

"*Comet* will sail ahead of the battle line and prevent any smaller ship from interfering with their progress. Admiral Byng will be a few nautical miles behind us. It will be easy to see any change in direction from *Barfleur's* flag signals. Anyway, with forty guns, *Comet* will be able to standup to anything but their battle line."

"Course, sir?"

"Lieutenant Laurant, please keep us two miles off the coast of Sicily as we continue south," said Calder. He raised his arm and pointed toward the brown coastline ahead.

"That will allow us to maneuver seaward or pin them to the coast as needed on contact," said Laurant.

Calder looked over at his Lieutenant. Locking eyes with him, he smiled. He made a fist chest high and gave it a few shallow pumps. "Exactly, Lieutenant Laurant. We'll make a fighting captain out of you yet." Calder turned and headed toward the ladder. Over his shoulder he said, "Keep me advised of any contact, or wind change, as we clear the Messina Straight."

"Aye, aye, sir."

Midshipman Rutwell walked aside Laurant on the command deck. They both looked ahead to the narrows. Rutwell raised his spyglass and scanned the coastline.

"Anything interesting, Mister Rutwell?" Laurant's inquiry didn't surprise the young Midshipman.

"No, sir. Not a sign of any military movement. I've got a couple of donkey carts heading toward the port town, but nothing that would constitute a threat to *Comet.*"

"Very well. Into the narrows it is," said Laurant. He paused and turned to look aft.

The long boat had disappeared back across the white capped waters toward the battle line. The ships leaned with the wind at a uniform angle. Flags carried leeward, as the wind continued to build from the northwest. The Admiral's pennant flew from the main mast of the lead ship. It meandered in slow twisted strokes as it reflected each shift in wind aloft. Laurant motioned for Rutwell to join him on the aft rail.

"Take a good look, Mister Rutwell," said Laurant. Both officers lifted their spyglass to their eye. "That's what sea-power looks like. English ships of the line, battle ready, sailing to impose the King's will at the discretion of their captains. I hope to captain one of those ships someday."

"As do I, sir."

"A long journey for both of us, I fear."

"Do you know any of those ships, sir?"

"Well, let's see. Of course, the flagship is *Barfleur.* She sails at the head of the column. Behind her I think it might be *Breda,* followed by *Burford,* and perhaps *Essex* further aft. They all carry at least seventy guns. Let's count: one, two, three . . ." Laurant's lips continued to move but his count fell silent. He lowered his spyglass and looked over at Rutwell. "I hold at least twenty ships with more cannon than *Comet.*"

"Damn, sir," said Rutwell. His voice tightened as his spoke.

"Damn, sir, indeed, Mister Rutwell. Damn sir, indeed."

The next day the sun rose over the Mediterranean Sea, its rays illuminated the slopes of Mount Etna. Clouds hovered atop the volcano. The shoreline was bare of vegetation. Long shadows were cast by rocks and gullies that broke the otherwise smooth terrain. Captain Calder climbed on the command deck and turned his collar up against the morning chill.

"Status, Lieutenant Martino?" Calder looked south over a wind chopped sea as he spoke.

"Sir, we have cleared the straight and are continuing on the southerly course as ordered. The battle line has held position astern. We have had no signals from the flagship."

"Very well, Lieutenant Martino."

Calder looked over at Midshipman Dugins. The lad stood next to the helmsman, keeping an eye on the compass. The Captain squinted, as he looked his subordinate over.

"Mister Dugins," said Calder.

"Yes, sir," said Dugins. The Midshipman turned to face the skipper.

"What in God's name is that on your face?"

"Make-up, sir. I've found it helps prevent sunburn."

Calder glanced over at Martino. He returned his stare to Dugins.

"Very well. It gives you a ghostly appearance. If we ever get boarded again, you'll scare the Spanish to death. That's for sure." Calder pressed his lips together and exited the command deck.

Mount Etna faded astern as the day wore on. The sun continued toward its zenith, increasing the temperature as it made the deliberate ascent. The morning dew evaporated leaving the wooden deck and railing dry and rough to the touch. Chief White sat on the main deck with his back resting against a pile of coiled rope. His head nodded in time with the rolling of the ship. Between the heat and rocking on deck, the Chief's eyelids lowered but didn't quite close. His state of semi-consciousness was ripped to full alert by the cry from the lookout on the main mast.

"Sail, ho. Sail on the horizon. Dead ahead."

Lieutenant Martino moved to the port side. He studied the scene ahead with his spyglass. He slowly lowered the long tube, holding it diagonally across his undefined chest. Looking down to the main deck, he said, "Chief White, please inform Captain Calder we have sails on the horizon."

"Aye, aye, sir." Chief White struck below in search of the Captain.

"Mister Dugins, what can you make out in the distance?" Martino motioned for the Midshipman to join him. He placed his hand on the young lad's shoulder and pointed to the south with the spyglass.

Dugins scanned the horizon. He could feel Martino rub his shoulder but ignored the light pressure and peered out across the waters.

"Sir, it looks like the land ends ahead."

"Yes, that would be Cape Passaro. Sails man, what of the ships?"

"Too many to count. Must be around forty or fifty out there. Some are ships of the line, that's for sure. Three masts and multiple gun decks. Yes, sir. Ships of the line."

Calder's heavy footsteps announced his return to the command deck ahead of his question.

"What do you have Lieutenant Martino?" Calder was still buttoning his coat as he spoke.

"Just the Spanish fleet, sir."

"How many?"

"All of them, sir."

"Numbers, man."

"About fifty, sir."

Calder lifted his spyglass and studied the scene ahead. Lowering the glass, he asked, "Do you notice anything unusual about their fleet, Lieutenant?"

Martino raised his spyglass upward and assumed a position akin to the Captain. They both rocked in time with *Comet* holding their lenses as steady as possible. Martino looked at the Spanish fleet. His mind raced. *About fifty ships. Some, many in fact, ships of the line. Too large a force for Comet to deal with. Just what the hell is Calder driving at here?*

"Sir, I believe my report is accurate. Nothing additional to add," said Martino. His tone was firm, if not condescending.

"Formation Lieutenant. They are not in line ahead or column. The entire Spanish fleet is scattered."

Martino returned his gaze south. Nodding he said, "Yes, sir. No formation."

"Did you signal contact to the flagship?"

"No, sir. I assume they can see them."

"Don't"

"Don't what?"

"Don't assume they can see anything. Fighting instructions, Lieutenant. When the enemy is sighted, the ship in contact will . . ." Calder waited for Martino to respond.

"Will notify the Senior Officer Afloat that contact has been established," said Martino. His tone fell off as he spoke.

"That's right. Excellent. Make it so."

"Aye, aye, sir."

Martino moved over to the railing between the command deck and the main deck below. Gripping the rail, he leaned over to establish eye contact with Chief White.

"Chief White, the contact signal if you would."

The Chief acknowledged the order and ran back to the Bosun Locker. Two other sailors secured a main mast halyard on the leeward side and lowered it to hack on the contact pennant. The three of them fumbled over the line until the cloth was attached.

They now pulled hand-over-hand to lift the pennant skyward. This signal was soon mirrored on *Barfluer*.

"Orders, sir?" Martino asked.

"Continue to press forward, Lieutenant," said Calder. He looked over his shoulder to see if the flagship had raised any signals to change the fighting instructions. "Admiral Byng has the contact signal. He'll let us know if we need to engage or not. My guess is they are having an interesting discussion right now on the command deck as to whether, or not, this fleet disposition constitutes hostile intent."

"Sir, the watch relief is about due. Should we rotate personnel, or beat to quarters?" Martino asked.

"Given the wind, how long do you think it will be until we make contact with the Spanish?"

"Sir, given the distance, it could be hours. However, we do command the weather gauge, so we should be able to control the approach and engagement. At least in the opening rounds."

Calder rubbed his chin. He looked out over the fleet ahead, and then back to the English battle line astern.

"Let's rotate the watch, Lieutenant. I'll need you topside for the ship handling during any battle. Even if you can get a few hours of rest, you'll be better off than continuing on watch until this battle is resolved."

"Aye, sir."

Lieutenant Laurant and Midshipman Rutwell were on deck at the appointed time. The entire British fleet continued to press forward in battle formation. As the distance between the two fleets tightened, signals rose and fell on the yardarms of the Spanish ships. Calder remained on the command deck, studying the disposition of the opposing fleet. It took another two hours until the intent behind the flag signals was evident. The mass of Spanish ships, which had been sailing without any form, broke into two separate groups.

"Sir, you should come take a look at this," said Lieutenant Laurant.

"Aye, the smaller ships and merchant fleet are making a run for the coast. The rest are forming into a battle line," said Calder. The Captain looked to the flagship. He didn't need a code book to decipher the flags now being lifted.

"What does that signal mean, sir?" Midshipman Rutwell's inquiry was directed to Lieutenant Laurant.

"That, my good man, is the signal to engage by ship," said Calder tapping the spyglass against his leg.

"Are we giving the merchant fleet chase, sir?"

"No. Those duties fall to HMS *Canterbury* and crew. We continue as planned."

"Who has *Canterbury, sir?*" Laurant asked.

"That would be Captain Walton. He'll chase them down."

Silence gripped the command deck. The Helmsman gripped the wheel so tight his knuckles turned white. Calder looked toward Chief White, "Could we get the drummer topside, Chief?"

"Aye, sir. Right away."

It didn't take long for the Marine Detachment drummer to reach his assigned position. Captain Darroch was right beside him. All eyes now focused on Captain Calder.

Calder paced behind the Officer of the Deck. He lifted the spyglass to rest over his left shoulder. The tapping of his wooden sole shoes resonating on the deck became predictable. His uniform cadence could have been used to predict longitude. He stopped, placed arms akimbo, and said, "All hands, beat to quarters."

The drummer's rhythm set the stage for the crew. Sailors, in all states of dress, hustled across the main deck. On the gun deck, the two Midshipman took up Gun Battery officer duties on the port and starboard sides. Cannons were rolled back, loaded, and rolled out through open gun ports. Sasha ran gunpower bags up to each crew as the loading process proceeded. The younger "powder monkeys" struggled to keep pace. Her black hair bounced amid the grey light of the gun deck.

Lieutenant Martino reached the command deck. He rubbed his eyes in the bright afternoon haze. A huge yawn accompanied him from his stateroom below decks.

"I hope we didn't interfere with your beauty sleep, Lieutenant," said Calder. His tone was light.

"No, sir. I live for this. Let's get at these Spanish," said Martino. His tone was rested and deliberate. "Shall we engage, sir?"

"We have to wait on the signal from the flagship."

"Sir, *Comet* is better suited to make for their merchant ships. Prize money, sir!"

"Not our instructions, Lieutenant. Hold your course."

"Aye, sir." Martino let out a long breath.

"Sir, their larger ships of the line are forming up," said Darroch.

"That's going to be a lot of firepower, sir," said Sergeant Worth.

"A lot compared to what?" Darroch's interest had been perked.

"Compared to land combat, sir."

"How so?"

"An artillery battery ashore occupies a hundred yards. That's maybe a cannon every thirty feet. The navy has their cannon spaced every ten feet or so. If that wasn't bad enough, they tend to have larger caliber guns that can throw more lead. To make matters even worse, they can stack their firepower vertically on each successive deck. Three decks for a ship of the line, well you get the idea."

"Yes, Sergeant Worth. We get the idea. Thank you for that insightful commentary."

"Sir, seriously, it will be hell if *Comet* has to go against a ship of the line. Perhaps, Lieutenant Martino has a point here."

"Not our instructions, Sergeant Worth. We hold the van. Clear the way for the main battle line."

"Aye, sir. I know. God help us."

"See Lieutenant Martino, the Admiral has our line up wind of the Spanish. We can control the rate of closure," said Calder. The Captain pointed over to the Spanish ships struggling to form into a proper battle line.

"Yes, sir. So, I see. One thing, however."

"What would that be?"

"Unless the wind shifts, the head of our column will impact several ships short of their van. The back of our battle line will be out of contact."

Calder looked up into the rigging. He studied the flags to gauge the wind direction. The angle of the flags, when compared to the mast, indicated a relative wind speed of fifteen knots. Staring back at the English column, his jaw dropped.

"Damn," escaped Calder before he realized what he said.

"Why is that an issue?" asked the Marine.

"Because Captain Darroch, the Spanish van can fall back and double up on our flagship easier than our rear can beat-up wind to close the gap. The Admiral will be fighting outnumbered."

"Sir, we are ahead of both battle lines. *Comet* can still break contact and steer toward the merchant fleet along the coast. We'll clean them out, sir," said Martino. His expression was upbeat.

Calder returned to pacing the command deck. He paused looked back over the aft end of the ship straining to see if any signal from the flagship would relieve him of his instructions. No change. The British battle line pressed ahead. The Spanish line, while still unorganized, was beginning to take shape.

"No, gentlemen, our task is here," said Calder. His tone was deep. The flesh of his face had turned to stone. No emotion visible to the crew. "We are to clear the way for the battle line. I

145

intend to fall back and not allow the Spanish van to wrap back upon the Admiral."

"Sir, that's madness. The intent of our instructions is to clear the way of small ships, not fight as part of the battle line," protested Martino.

"True enough, but now the threat has changed. The intent remains. I will not allow the flagship to go down without at least giving this fight a try. If we can hold the first two ships of their van at bay, it will be an even matchup for the rest of the line."

Sergeant Worth looked up into the rigging. Unseen by the officers, he crossed himself to beckon divine protection.

"Two ships of the line, seventy guns each. That's a hundred and forty guns against our forty. Sir, if you can get us close, we'll board and even things up somewhat," said Darroch.

"I appreciate your support here Marine, but if we grapple with one ship the other will be free to fall back on the van. No, we need to take one out of action before we surrender our maneuverability."

"Sir, perhaps we could ask the Admiral to dispatch *Comet* to the pursuit force," said Martino. The pitch in his voice increased.

"No, Lieutenant. We fight here. Back wind the foresail and let's fall back alongside the Spanish van. I want you to keep *Comet* between the flagship and the first two ships of the Spanish van."

"Aye, sir." Martino hung his head between his shoulders and moved up to the railing looking over the main deck. Fifty pairs of eyes stared back at him, waiting. The mumbling on the main deck could be heard up on the command deck.

"All right you sons of bitches fall in and make ready. We've got fighting to do," said Chief White. His abrupt instructions silenced the crew.

Lieutenant Martino cleared his throat. He tightened his grip on the railing.

"Chief White, back wind the royals and topgallants on the foresail."

"Aye, sir," said Chief White. He eased about and faced the crew. "You heard the Lieutenant. Let's go, get up into the tops. Move."

His last word was met with a scurry of bare feet shuffling across the wooden deck. The rope ladders were soon occupied with sailors moving skyward one unsteady step at a time. They twisted against the ropes. The muscles in their arms strained to overcome the force of gravity that desperately strived to pull them down. The mast captain now took control of these ragged souls to shift sheet lines and ease the sails to back wind and slow the ship.

Captain Darroch looked aft from the command deck. The Spanish line lacked the geometric precision of the British formation, but it was functional as a combat alignment. Admiral Byng was using his upwind position to close the distance on his opponent. The Spanish crews hustled from tops, to the deck, and back skyward. Atop the rigging, sails rose and fell, but the net effect of these efforts had little influence on the overall rate of closure between the two fleets.

"How far now, Captain?" said Sergeant Worth. His voice cracked when he asked the question.

Captain Darroch looked over at his leading Sergeant. He noticed this Marines' eyes were just a little wider than his normal stone-cold appearance. He swayed on the rolling deck to hold a rigid position of attention. Darroch looked out at the two Spanish ships in the van of their column. He held his middle three fingers up and they covered the length of the enemy warship. *Rule of thumb, three fingers covering a ship of the line is about six hundred yards.* He tapped his saber to the deck.

"Sergeant Worth, I make us at still over six hundred yards to contact. Stand by."

"Aye, sir. Standing by."

The flags aloft pointed directly toward the Spanish line. The white caps slapped the side of *Comet*, nudging her toward the impending cannonade. Calder walked over to the starboard railing. He gripped the polished wood with both hands. He studied the leading two ships in the Spanish van. Their loose order of battle made it difficult to read their pending intent. He pulled himself toward the rail, and then pushed away. He locked eyes with Lieutenant Martino.

"Officer of the Deck, what is your read on the intent of the Spanish van?" said Calder. His tone was direct.

"Sir, they will fall back and crush us. After that, I would assume they will continue back and rake the flagship. I fear the Admiral has placed us too far astern of the enemy column," said Charles. His tone matched the intensity of Calder's question.

"Very well. Let's ease to starboard one point. I need to keep between those two ships and the flag."

"Aye, aye, sir," said Martino. His tone was an uncustomary surrender to the authority of the ship's captain.

"Can you see them?" asked Dugins. His words flowed as rapid as his pulse. His position on the port side of the gun deck, coupled with the limited light below decks, kept him in the dark as to the unfolding events.

"Yes, Brice. The van is a little ahead and the main battle line remains somewhat astern. We're still too far away to open, but *Comet* is closing," said Rutwell. He pulled his head back inboard from the gun port and looked across at his midshipman peer.

"Thank you, Mr. Rutwell. I can't see a bloody thing on this side."

"Just be ready. If the enemy maneuvers, or if Calder brings us through the wind, you'll get a better view of the action than you ever wanted."

"I know. That's my fear."

The gun captain next to Dugins smiled on overhearing this exchange. Sasha pushed two young boys forward with their

148

gunpowder charges. Silence dominated the deck. Cannon crews gripped their instruments of destruction. Fingers tapped against ram rods or otherwise struggled to remain idle.

"Sir, come take a look," said Lieutenant Martino. He raised his spyglass to view the Spanish van.

Calder mirrored the Lieutenant's stance. The two officers gazed at the enemy ships leading their column. The sun's reflected light shifted, changing the color of their sails from shadow to bright white. The rate of closure between the two ships of the Spanish van and *Comet* increased.

"Sir, they're turning back on us," said Martino.

"Us, and the head of our column," said Calder.

The Lieutenant lowered his spyglass and looked across the main deck.

"Orders, sir?"

"Steady as she goes, Lieutenant. Stay between them and the flagship. I'll fight the rest of the ship. Just keep me in their path."

"Aye, aye, sir," said Martino. He swallowed hard after he spoke.

"Range, two hundred yards. Wait for the command, lads," said Rutwell. His voice reverberated down the length of the gun deck. Looking out the gun port, he added, "Three."

"Sir?" asked his nearest gun captain.

"Three decks, lad. Our two opponents each have three decks of guns."

"Damn it. What are we supposed to do, sir?"

"Fire faster is a good start." Rutwell looked over to find one corner of his gun captain's mouth elevated. "We'll aim at their lower decks first. That's where the heavier guns are located. Take them out, and it's a fare fight."

The gun captain nodded. He pulled on the cannon's outhaul line.

"Hold lads. We're at one hundred yards. Let's get within fifty. Keep your sights low," said Rutwell. He yelled as loud as he could. *That just might be the last command I issue. Once the shooting starts, they won't hear squat.* Looking down the starboard gun battery, he watched as gun captains gave their elevation blocks another tap or two.

The sequential roar of the Spanish opening cannonade rippled down the length of *Comet.* Their top two gun decks tended to impact into the rigging. Sails were holed. Canvas was no match to the penetrating power of solid shot passing through them at high velocity. Topside, sailors watched as rigging strained or buckled, on impact. A spar on the fore mast was blown from its bindings and fell to the deck. The impact instantly killed a tar holding station near the forecastle.

Solid shot from the twenty-four inch heavy guns on the bottom deck of the Spanish gallon impacted *Comet's* gun deck. The gun port cover, and part of the hull, above the number eight gun were blown back, scattering wood splitters and debris across the full length of the deck. Ten sailors from the cannon crew were blown back to the port side. One was decapitated, and two others died from blunt force trauma inflicted from wood fragments. Blood ran on the deck as the wounded moved away from the point of hull penetration. Those sailors on the port side, went to assist their counterparts in clearing the area.

"Dugins, the number eight gun is intact. Get me a gun crew over on this side, now!" screamed Rutwell. He had to redirect his attention out the gun port to gage the distance between the two ships.

Dugins squatted behind his number ten gun. His knees were on the deck. Both hands rested on the cannon barrel. Only his wide-eyed face looked over the top of the brass cannon. His eyes flashed between the wounded of the number eight cannon crew and Midshipman Rutwell.

Rutwell look across from his position to see his counterpart cowering behind the cannon. He yelled, "Dugins, I've got to open fire with all cannons. Get me a crew on number eight, now!" The range was down to sixty yards.

Sasha ran to where Dugins squatted. Her black hair bounced around her face. Pointing forward she said, "Mister Dugins, would you be getting a crew on the number eight cannon. I haven't been running powder up from the magazine to see the damn thing sit idle."

Dugins stood. He opened his mouth to give a command, but nothing came out. He shook his head.

Sasha grabbed him by the crotch. She squeezed hard until Dugins faced her direct. Letting go of him, she pointed forward. "You've got a set, now use them. Put a cannon crew on number eight." She turned away from the Midshipman and grabbed two powder monkeys and said. "You two, with me. We'll have to get more powder up here once we fire." The three of them dropped through a hatch and disappeared below decks.

Dugins looked down his gun line to find no one would face him. He yelled, "Port side, number eight cannon crew. Move over and assume the starboard number eight. Now, damn it." His lips flattened from the pain emanating from his groin. He rubbed that area to gain some measure of relief from the throbbing.

The sailors dashed over to the other side of the ship. They looked back to see Mister Rutwell raising his arm. The range between the two ships was under fifty yards.

"Fire," said Rutwell. "Let them have it, lads."

The cannons rippled from the fore to aft. The impacts on the Spanish hull were heard on the gun deck as well as topside. At short range, the impact of shot and shell was dramatic. The lowered deck of the first ship in the Spanish van was silenced. The moans of sailors echoed across the waves. The water between the two ships was soon littered with debris from both sides. Sailors that had gone over the side on impact, now clung to the floating twisted mess that bobbed along the sea's surface.

"That's good. Don't give them time to recover, lads. Reload and fire," said Rutwell.

Dugins stood behind the aft mast on the gun deck, observing both sides. His crew was out of the fight for now, but he didn't want to be engaged by Sasha yet again. He held both hands behind his back, while attempting to be seen by his cannon battery.

"Fire," said Rutwell. Once again, his voice was clearly heard across the gun deck.

Cannons rippled again down the line. The English had loaded, fired, and prepared to fire yet again faster than the Spanish. Sasha and her powder monkeys were moving from cannon to cannon, replenishing the gunpowder at each weapon. She gave Mister Dugins a stern stare while passing on her replenishment rounds. He looked away before eye contact was established.

The weight of the second Spanish broadside was noticeably reduced. The effects of battle damage, coupled with the downwind smoke obscuration, limited the ability of the Spanish to engage *Comet*. The smaller ship was gaining the upper hand. Rutwell placed the next three broadsides across the water before the Spanish could respond.

"That's faster than they drilled, Captain," said the Marine. He stood adjacent to his boss so as to be heard amid the dim of battle.

"Much so, Captain Darroch. Much so."

"Perhaps we should come about and give the portside cannons a chance, sir?" said Martino.

"Not yet, Lieutenant. We are pounding this ship. His counterpart has not fallen back in support. Until he does so, let's continue to hole this ship until she sinks."

"Aye, sir." Martino directed his attention to the British column astern.

"There, sir. Look!" said Darroch. He pointed over to the Spanish ship. "She is fading toward her line, sir."

"Yes indeed, Marine. Let's see what the other ship in the van will do."

They both now joined Martino in looking aft at the battle unfolding between the two lines of ships. Column order had broken down, and ships were now seeking individual engagements. The random flash of cannon would illuminate the building smoke clouds in shades of red and orange. The smoke would carry on the wind and cover the Spanish fleet. The surface of the water was littered with floating objects of all descriptions. Long spars from shattered masts, still draped with canvas, moved amid broken sections of hull. Small boats moved between the flash of flame and flight of iron overhead, attempting to pull sailors from the water.

"What do you think Lieutenant Martino?" asked Calder. He lowered his spyglass.

The Lieutenant lowered his spyglass, turned around to face his boss, smiling he said, "Sir, we've got them. I counted six colors struck from Spanish ships. I'm sure more will fall before this day is done."

"Why?"

"Sir?"

"Why do you think we won this round?"

"Firepower, sir. Our rate of fire was faster. We hit home more often on their hulls. The damage inflected was more direct and severe. Oh, and the weather gauge. That allowed us to control the timing of the engagement and forced their gunners to have to look through our smoke to engage."

"Well, said."

"Sir, the other Spanish ship is breaking contact," said the aft mast lookout.

The crew on the command deck watched, as the other Spanish galleon pulled back along the broken line and headed for the coast. The distance between the two ships began to increase.

"Sir, Admiral Byng is flying a new signal from the flagship," said Calder. His comment drew the full attention of the watch team.

"So, I see, Captain Calder. Do you know what it means?'

"Well, a white square on a blue background, no sir. Can't say as I can read the signal book. Never needed to do so on land," said Darroch. His tone fell off as he spoke.

"Pursuit, gentlemen. The fleet has been ordered into a general pursuit. I'd say we have a full rout here today."

"Should we chase down the other ship in the van, sir?" asked the Marine.

"Oh, hell no. The flagship is no longer threatened. I think we'll follow Lieutenant Martino's idea at this point. Let's head for the transports and smaller ships along the shore. Maybe we can scoop-up some loot for the crew."

Martino smiled. He looked over at Darroch. His bearing stiffened, and his nose elevated toward the rigging. He turned away from the Marine and directed his attention to the Captain. "Sir, recommend we ease *Comet* through the wind and head due west. Perhaps we can catch a ship or two before they clear the cape," said Martino.

"Make it so, Lieutenant."

Calder walked back and stood next to his Marine. He directed him to face away from the rest of the crew on the command deck. He pointed back toward the high ground around Mount Etna.

"Captain Darroch, the Royal Navy now controls the waters around Sicily. That is, until the Spanish send another fleet in our direction. We don't know what, if anything, the Spanish were able to land on the island before we got here. If you were going to land on Sicily, where would you try to hold?"

"You mean after I lost total control of the waters around the island?"

"Yes, exactly."

"I would contest the Straight of Messina. It's the only point where land forces can influence seaward events. Just a guess, sir."

"Well, Captain Darroch, a guess is all we've got at this point. I'll let the Admiral know. I'm sure he will have a captain's call here shortly."

Chapter 9 Damn Straight

"Well?" asked Hunter. He paced outside his bed chamber. The scuffing of his shoes on the stone floors echoed in the hallway.

"You'll know, Earl," said Annette. She sat in a straight back wooden chair, rocking her posture from side to side to gain a measure of relief from its stiffness.

"How?"

"If the child is healthy, you'll hear it cry. If not, then I fear it will have entered this world only to be passing on to the next."

Hunter took a deep breath. He turned his back to Annette and studied the scene depicted on a tapestry hung on the castle wall. The picture showed a highland hunt from an earlier age. The fact that the hunting party was mounted on horses, indicated they were from the ruling elite. He gripped his hands behind his back. His focus left him oblivious to the increased activity entering and leaving the bed chamber.

Annette stood when she heard the first cry emanate from behind the heavy wooden door. She moved next to the door and listened. Hunter joined her. The two of them looked at each other and smiled. The door to the bedroom opened a few inches.

"It's a boy," said the chamber maid. She ducked back inside.

Hunter stood to his full height. Taking a deep breath, he nodded.

"A boy," said Hunter. "An heir. Excellent." He looked Annette in the eye. "I hope you're as happy about all this as I am?'

"I be happy for both you and Cynthia."

"Well, I sort of owe a measure of thanks to you."

Annette's cheeks drew taut. One side of her mouth rose. She blinked a few times.

"How so, Earl?" asked Annette. Her tone was reserved.

"This all started at your establishment. I still recall the details of the engaging night I twirled Cynthia across the dance floor of the Red Fox Inn. She in turned twirled me through the night upstairs."

A second cry was heard in the chamber. Annette and the Earl looked at each other wide eyed. They both directed their attention to the door when it opened a few inches.

"Twins. It's a girl," said the chamber maid. Her smile lit up the dim passageway. "Cynthia is doing well. You can enter."

Drake Hunter entered the chamber. Annette followed one step behind. She looked beyond his back to see how Cynthia was doing. The fatigued smile on her face needed no explanation. She held a child in each arm. The chamber maid patted the sweat from her brow and adjusted the covers around the new mother. The curtains around the bed waved, as a gust of cool fall air carried through the chamber.

Drake stared at his two children. He stroked Cynthia's face. Silence filled the space between those in the room. Outside, the wind increased in volume announcing a change in seasons was approaching the highlands. Annette could only smile at the platonic scene.

"I think you two be needing a moment alone," said Annette. I'll be in my chamber if you need anything." She turned and walked into the long hallway.

Annette stopped at the tapestry of the hunting party. She studied the detail of the needle work that brought the realistic scene to life. The men in combative poses were riding ahead on their horses. They were followed by the women riding sidesaddle with long trailing garments that were carried in the wind. *Not very practical for hunting, but fashionable none the less.*

She turned her back on the needle point and walked across the hall to a narrow window. It opened up on the waters of the Inner Sound. Grey clouds hurried on the wind over water just as grey.

The granite stones of the castle walls only added to the grey of the scene and her mood. For one brief moment, she imagined a white sail cutting across the monotone grey of the choppy sea. Not a sail, but a white cap in the distance. Then the brightness faded from her vision.

"William, come back to me my love," she said in a muffled tone. The whisper was not audible to the passersby eager to view the new line of inheritance in Hunter's bed chamber. Her eyes filled with moisture. She closed her eyes to the scene across the bay forcing a lone tear to travel down her cheek.

*****

The knock on Lieutenant Martino's stateroom hatch was firm.

"Request permission to come aboard," said Dugins.

"Enter," said Martino. It was a request he had been anticipating.

"Sir, Midshipman Dugins reporting as ordered."

"Yes, Mister Dugins, I heard you had a little trouble during the engagement on the gun deck." Martino moved over and locked his hatch. Dugins held the position of attention with his eyes straight ahead.

"No trouble, sir."

"I heard from the crew that you froze when the first solid shot penetrated the hull."

"Well . . . yes, sir. I was scared as hell. We had dead bodies cast about and blood everywhere."

"Ok, let's work on that shall we. Remove your coat and blouse."

Dugins complied with the instructions. He folded the garments and placed them on a chair adjacent to the table on which he had lay prostrate during instruction.

"Put this on," said Martino. His tone was commanding. He handed the lad a binding with two panels and scrambled lacing.

"A corset, sir. Why?"

"It will help you control your breathing. We will do some battle stress drills. Next time the ship is penetrated, it will be no big deal."

Dugins held the garment to his stomach. Martino moved behind him and pulled the lacing firm. Then he exerted more force to draw the panels closer. The Midshipman's cheeks tightened as his ribs were compressed.

"How does that feel, Mister Dugins?"

"A little uncomfortable, sir. I can hardly breathe."

"Good. Now remove your trousers and put this on."

Dugins lowered his trousers to the deck and stepped out of them. He took the garment from Martino and lifted it to the light. The soft and smooth feel of its silk stood in sharp contrast to the wool of his uniform. The shallow nature of his breathing caused his vision to blur for a moment. He struggled to think, *a slip? What the heck.* He pulled the fabric up to his waist and tied it into place.

"Assume the position for instruction," said Martino.

Dugins bent over the table, as he had done many times in the past, and spread his arms across its polished wooden surface. He could feel the weight of Martino's hand pressing down on the small of his back.

"Sir, I can understand the corset is to help control my breathing, but I don't understand the purpose of the slip."

"The slip is for my pleasure, Mistress Dugins. Not yours."

Martino flipped the slip up and over Dugins back. It covered his head, leaving him in darkness. Martino's full body weight was now upon him. Between the constricting design of the corset, and the weight of the lieutenant on his back, he could hardly breathe. The pain of penetration rippled through him, as Martino sought to pleasure himself. Dugins' vision narrowed in the darkness. At last he found some measure of escape, he fainted.

"Get up and get dressed, Mister Dugins. We have watch in one bell," said Martino. His tone was level as if nothing had transpired.

Dugins unlaced the damp garments and let them fall to the deck. His stance was somewhat bent over as he dressed.

"Straighten up, Lad. We have to take command of the ship for the next watch. Can't have the crew thinking their officers are too depressed to execute their duty."

"Duty, sir. Was it duty that compelled your actions here?"

"No, Mister Dugins. When you accepted my sponsorship, you became mine. You serve me as I see fit and how I see fit. Is that clear?"

"Yes, sir."

"In return, I shall ensure you're promoted. When you are a lieutenant you can tutor your midshipman as you wish. We have all gone through this. Don't think that you are somehow special in that regard. My guess is this little exercise will harden you to the challenges ahead."

Dugins sobbed as he tied his shoes.

"Control your emotions, Mister Dugins. It is the first requirement of an officer to be above the common whims of the masses. Once you master your emotions, you'll be able to master this ship."

Dugins stood at the position of attention. His back ramrod straight. His lips flat and eyes looking unblinking forward.

"Mister Dugins, you are dismissed," said Martino.

"Aye, aye, sir."

Martino watched as the Midshipman eased about and departed his stateroom. The corners of his mouth edged upward. Nodding he whispered, "Excellent."

Midshipman Dugins looked down the dim passageway toward the captain's cabin. The sound of laugher of the assembled dinner party could be heard beyond the hatch. He frowned, as he thought, *no one can ever know about what happened tonight. I would never recover my reputation if this got out. No one would ever believe Lieutenant Martino, a member of the ruling elite, was a bugger of boys. What price, this promotion?*

Calder drew his spoon across the steaming hot soup before him. He blew on the hot liquid dissipating some of the heat. He sipped the soup and the smell of its rich vegetable broth filled his nostrils. He tapped his empty spoon against the side of the soup bowl. All eyes at the table turned in his direction as the sound resonated within the confines of the cabin.

"Gentlemen, I need to get your assessment as to the battle damage *Comet* sustained in the last fight," said Calder. He looked over at Lieutenant Laurant.

"Sir, the rigging is in bad shape. We lost a spar on the forward mast and two on the main. Our canvas looks more like Swiss cheese than sail. The hull was penetrated at four points. The gun deck, near top side, and two down in the cargo hold. It's the latter that have me concerned, sir. Sure, the shoring is holding for now, but a storm or another engagement and I can't ensure water tight integrity. I've got the Bosun working repairs, but I fear we don't have the material or tools to return the ship to full fighting trim," said Laurant. He lowered his eyes when he finished.

"That's worse than you first reported, Lieutenant Laurant."

"Yes, sir. It most certainly is worse, but it reflects my personal investigation below decks."

"Doctor, what of the Reaper's tally?"

"Sir, sick bay is full and will be for some time to come. We had seventeen killed. I'm still treating thirty-eight wounded. Twelve are serious at this point, sir. I fear most of the others can return to some duty in a week or two," said Doc La Roch. He wiped his mouth with his napkin.

"Marine, how did your crew do?"

"Sir, we never fired a shot. Not much of a fight from my perspective. No loss to report, sir."

"Well that's good. I have a special mission for you and the detachment," said Calder. His focus shifted to the only red uniform at the table. "The Austrians are going to send a landing force to Sicily. They have requested assistance in landing and amphibious operations. The Admiral offered your services up before I could comment. I fear having a positive reputation can swing like a two-edged blade."

"Aye, sir. What do we know about this plan?" asked Darroch. His napkin wiped across his brow.

"Not that much, Captain Darroch," replied Calder. His hand tapped on the table a few times before he continued. "They tell us six thousand troops just embarked at Naples. They will be off the coast of Sicily in two days. *Comet* is to sail north and link-up with them. That will give you a day to advise them as to landing technique and time tables."

"A full day. Sir, that's not enough time to do much."

"I know. I tried to explain that to the Admiral's staff but got nowhere. What I can tell you, is we will put them ashore at a point the Spanish are not defending. It's the best hope to get their feet dry at this point."

*****

Captain Darroch's red uniform stood out on the white sands of the beach, as the columns of grey and white Austrian uniforms marched past him. He motioned with his arm to keep the soldiers moving inland and away from the beach. A colonel from the allied landing force approached. Darroch broke his routine of directing the beach traffic and saluted.

"It seems to be going as planned, sir," said Darroch. He dropped his salute and stepped closer to the colonel.

"Yes indeed, Captain. Your help in organizing the landing boats is a key part of all this you know."

"Thank you, sir. Any word on the Spanish response to our landing?"

"Why don't you ask them yourself?"

162

"Sir?"

"We have spotted the yellow uniforms of Spanish dragoons just up the road. Both sides are forming for battle. I would expect them to attack in less than an hour. How many Marines can you muster, Captain Darroch?"

"Sir, I can put thirty in the line. You need only ask."

"Your command will not contest such a request?"

"Sir, I was told to support your attack in any manner I could. My Marines stand ready, sir."

"Excellent, I have a special mission for your highly trained strike troops. You will guard the general's staff."

"Aye, sir," said Darroch. His shoulders slumped just a touch. His lips tightened, as he thought, *guard duty, great. Is that all they think we're good for. How am I going to get these Marines into the battle? They didn't come here to look pretty on the beach.*

"Take your Marines over to that hill top. Link up with the general's honor guard. They will provide additional direction."

The short march to the General's Command Post felt like one of the longest Captain Darroch had ever experienced. Sergeant Worth could only smile at the Captain's predicament. On reaching the elevated position, Darroch waved his hand for Worth to join him.

"Sergeant Worth, deploy the detachment in two ranks on the forward slope. Defensive positions for now. Let's see how all this plays out, shall we."

"Aye, aye, sir," said Worth. His salute was crisp, and his actions were immediate. His coarse commands rang in Darroch's ears as he walked over to report to the General's Chief of Staff.

"Sir, the Marines are in position as requested," said Darroch. He saluted and held his hand against the brim of his hat until the Chief of Staff acknowledged his comment.

"Very good, Marine. As you can see, we are about to launch into the attack here. This landing caught them by surprise. They have only been able to throw forward a thin line of dragoons in our path. We should be able to break the siege of Messina in an hour." The Chief's voice rang with a sense of confidence.

Captain Darroch lowered his salute but remained silent. He extended his spyglass to full length and scanned the approaches along the coast road. His tactical instincts took over, as he thought, *narrow coastal plain, one road, and not much room to maneuver. They might only have a regiment of dragoons now, but the Austrians will be hard pressed to gain any advantage on this terrain.*

The first wave of white uniforms flowed over the broken ground directly at the thin yellow line of dismounted dragoons. At this distance, Darroch could just barely hear the shouts and commands along the battle line. The smoke from musket fire soon obscured his vision. He lowered his spyglass, only to find the General's staff had done the same.

Then movement amid the smoke of battle. Soldiers retreated in battle order, firing as they fell back. The Austrians were in retreat.

"Look, they are reforming for another attack," said the Chief of Staff. All spyglasses at the command post were raised in unison. Darroch redirected his stare to the battle line.

The Mediterranean Sea wind pushed the smoke of battle inland. As it thinned, the silhouettes of soldiers in formation were visible. Long lines of men shuffled, adjusted their alignment, and assumed the precise geometric appearance developed from long hours on the drill fields of their homeland. The defending line, although diminished, had held. This thin barrier of yellow uniforms stood defiantly atop a small ridge, barring any advance toward Messina. A dust cloud behind the dragoons carried aloft, announced the movement of troops on the coast road.

Darroch strained to determine what was lifting the dust skyward behind the defending line. Shapes were too difficult to read. The Marine watched as the cloud closed on the battlefield, he thought, *given their speed of advance, they have to be mounted troops. More dragoons, no doubt. Reinforcements. We've lost the element of surprise. This is going to be a hard fight.*

Once again, the Austrian line advanced. Muskets leveled forward, with bayonets gleaming in the sunlight. They stopped fifty yards short of the Spanish. Muskets were shouldered and fired. This drew a like response from the defenders. The grey Austrian line surged forward at the double. The cries of men in battle drifted on the wind back to the command post. Gunpowder smoke enveloped the scene, obscuring the viciousness of the melee from the staff. The clatter of steel on steel rang on the valley floor.

Senior staff officers lowered their spyglasses and mumbled between themselves. Some pointed to the scene below, while others shook their heads. Notes were scrawled on parchment and handed to aids that stood nearby. Sergeant Worth joined Captain Darroch. He watched intently as the Austrian staff attempted to appear engaged.

The smirk on Sergeant Worth's face was difficult to conceal.

"What is it, Sergeant Worth?" said Darroch. He could read the level of skepticism in his subordinate.

"You see all that activity by the staff behind you, sir?"

"Yes."

"Well, it won't change a damn thing for those poor bastards on the valley floor. Sure, they will all get their medals, but it's the poor son of bitch down there that will determine the outcome," said Worth. He pointed toward the battle line.

Darroch silently nodded.

They both watched as the Austrian assault wavered and returned to their starting position. Darroch viewed the valley with his spyglass.

"Damn it," he exclaimed.

"What is it, sir?" said Worth.

"Look, the color of the defending line is changing. I've got green uniforms aligning on the seaward side of the line. That means another regiment of dragoons has, in all likelihood, joined the battle. They're going to have to assault again. This is turning into a bloody slugfest."

"Yea, soldier's blood," said Worth. The frown on his face reinforced his normally truculent bearing. "Sir, I'd better check on the Marines. By your leave, sir."

"Carry on, Sergeant Worth."

Darroch watched as Worth moved down the hill to the Marine line. He could hear the Sergeant yell something, but the words were unclear. The formation tightened, and the line straightened. The Captain could well guess the nature of the message his Sergeant had delivered.

Cannon fire boomed in the valley. Shot and shell raked the Spanish dragoons. Dust and smoke scattered on the breeze, as the impacts of the artillery fell in and around the defenders. Darroch studied the assault columns below forming into the shape of three long boxes. Austrian and regimental colors flew at the front of each formation. These proud ensigns snapped in the wind causing their standard holders to struggle to hold them vertically aloft. He blinked as his eyes strained to focus on the pending attack. A lone saber in the front of the allied formation rose, and then flashed with reflected sunlight as it was lowered to signal the assault. All three columns stepped off as one. The distant sound of drums marked the marshal cadence. The front two ranks lowered their muskets to present their bayonets toward the defending line. Soldiers behind the leading edge of the assault, marched with muskets held straight up and down at their sides. The vertical reach of the weapons, coupled with their oversized head gear, made them appear taller.

"An impressive sight, wouldn't you say Captain," said an Austrian staff officer.

Darroch lowered his spyglass. He looked this senior officer in the eye. His brow was wrinkled, and eyes squinted in the afternoon sun. "Sir, they are very impressive to look at. Let's see if they can carry the line," said Darroch. His tone was even.

Musket volleys were exchanged. The leading edge of the assault formation appeared to crumble under the discharge of hot lead. Where yellow and green uniforms had stood shoulder to shoulder, gaps began to appear.

"We've got them now, English," said the Austrian staff officer.

"Not yet, sir. Look on their left flank. Inland, away from the sea."

Both officers focused their spyglasses along the high ground guarding the allied inland flank. Three lines of infantry, all wearing green, broke through the smoke and dust that had concealed their approach. Darroch looked over at the staff officer, the Austrian's mouth had fallen wide open.

"Flanked. We've been flanked. You'll excuse me Marine."

Darroch nodded. He rolled his shoulders. The relief of tension in his frame was fleeting. The Marine returned his spyglass to his eye and studied the unfolding tactical situation as best he could through the fog of war.

The sound of muskets in battle faded. They were replaced by the clash of steel against steel. The shouts of men emanated from the smoke and haze. Two languages, unrecognizable to Darroch or each other, left their orators compelled to use the universal language of violence to communicate. These were desperate voices of unseen soldiers, locked in a death struggle not visible to the staff officers on the hill.

The neat columns of white and grey uniforms, that only moments before had marched proudly forward beneath their colors, now fell back toward the general's command post. Darroch lowered his spyglass to find Sergeant Worth looking over his shoulder at him. The Sergeant shook his head.

The Marine Captain felt a hand on his back. He turned to find the senior staff officer once again at this side.

"The assault has failed," said the staff officer. This voice was short of breath and choppy. "Your Marines are to hold them off until we can get the command back to the Milazzo Peninsula. The narrows of that land mass, coupled with the old fortress, will allow us to hold them at bay."

"Well, at least the Royal Navy will be able to add its firepower to the defense of the Peninsula. That must count for something."

The two exchanged salutes. Darroch moved down the hill to join Sergeant Worth and his Marines.

"Sir, this doesn't look all that good to this Sergeant's old eyes," said Worth. He pushed his hat back on his head.

"No, it doesn't. The Austrians are falling back to the Milazzo Peninsula. We're to conduct a rear-guard action and slow the pursuit."

"Slow the pursuit, now is it. Thirty Marines to hold off the entire Spanish army so these Austrians can set-up at Milazzo. Sir, you can hold a front of twenty yards. No more."

"Noted. Let's move them back to the narrows of the valley road. That way it will be difficult for the Spanish to get around our flanks. You know, like the Spartans at Thermopylae."

"Sir, the Captain does know what happened to the Spartans there."

"Yes, Sergeant. We all know. Now, move them out. Form in two ranks on the road and prepare to execute a firing withdrawal."

"Aye, aye, sir. I hate withdraws. However, if you have to move backward, using musket fire is the only way to go."

The Marines formed in two ranks on the coastal road, with the high ground on their right and the sea on their left. The Austrians flowed by the Marines heading for the peninsula. With their heads cast downward, they refused to make eye contact.

Sergeant Worth moved through the ranks checking, and rechecking, the musket of each Marine.

"Withdrawing fire, prepare," said Darroch. His voice carried above the sound of the waves lapping against the shoreline. He looked over his shoulder and noted the Austrians were still taking up defensive position. "Looks like we'll have to hold the Spanish at bay, while our allies prepare to defend."

"Aye, sir. We'll hold the Dons while we fall back. Just watch, sir. This ought to be fun."

"Looks like we'll be having fun in short order. Here they come!"

The crush of green uniforms filled the road. Dust rose over the rear of the column, making it impossible to tell how many soldiers were on the move toward the thin red line. Darroch took a deep breath.

"Make ready," commanded Darroch.

The Marines pulled the hammers of their muskets to the rear. They locked home with a distinctive click. The front rank kneeled into a firing position. Weapons were held at a forty-five degree angle.

"Present."

Muskets leveled toward the approaching Spanish. The support of resting the weapon on their leg steadied their aim. The black dots of their musket bores were now visible to their attackers.

"Fire!"

Smoke lifted up along the length of the line. The sound of musket balls slamming home into soldiers and their kit was audible. Bodies fell backward under the force of this impact. Wherever a gap formed, a soldier marching one rank behind moved forward to take their place. Without commands, the kneeling Marines now stood. They stepped back through those behind them and started to reload their weapons. Those that had been in the second rank, were now the front rank. They kneeled, leveled, and fired all without command. Again, the Spanish line wavered under the weight of lead thrown in their direction.

The advance of the green line pressed ahead. Stepping on their fallen comrades, the Spanish continued the attack. Another Marine volley, and the green line halted. Commands in Spanish now echoed along the beach. Muskets leveled toward the red uniforms. The smoke from the firing line was visible to the Marines before they heard the distinctive pop of the musket balls passing overhead.

Four Marines fell along the two firing lines. Three were dead on impact, while the other was wounded in the arm. Sergeant Worth stepped forward, grabbed the fallen Marine by his leather belt, and pulled him back behind the firing line. The Marines let loose another volley before the Spanish could reload.

"Sir, are those our Marines," asked Lieutenant Laurant on the command deck.

Calder scanned the shore with his spyglass. Lowering the instrument from his eye. He nodded.

"Yes, indeed. Only one military unit ashore is wearing red. Can you get us closer? Cannon range perhaps?"

"Aye, aye, sir." Laurant looked over at Midshipman Rutwell and then back to Chief White.

"Helmsman, ease three points to starboard. Let's parallel the shore. Mister Rutwell, attend to our cannon battery, if you please."

"Aye, aye, sir."

The next Spanish volley dropped three more Marines. Both Darroch and Worth pulled the wounded back. They encouraged the firing line to increase the pace of each volley.

"Sir, seven out of thirty, the firing line is thinning out. I don't think we can hold here much longer," said Worth.

"I need to keep the Spanish at arm's length until the defense is set. Hold what you've got."

"Sir, seaward. Is that *Comet*?"

"Yes, by God. Yes it is," said Darroch. He lifted and waved his hat over his head. Hoping to get their attention, he yelled. "Over here. We need cannon fire, over here."

Judging by the gold braid, Rutwell could assume the Marine on the beach waving like a mad man must be Darroch. He pulled his head back aboard and looked down the firing line.

"Lads, it seems our good Captain of Marines requires a little assistance. Let's say we give it to him and flatten a few Spanish," yelled Rutwell.

The cannon crew gave three quick, "Hurrahs."

The seaward cannon fire impacted the beach and ran down the length of the Spanish line at a right angle. This enfilade fire sliced through men and equipment with deadly effectiveness. The Spanish line wavered and fell away from the Peninsula. Another broadside from *Comet* opened the distance between the two ground combatants.

"Sergeant Worth, this is our chance. Back to Milazzo, on the double," said Darroch. His head swiveled between the Austrian defenses and the position of his Spanish attackers.

Sergeant Worth rattled off a series of commands that would have confused anyone not trained in the subtleties of land combat. The red uniforms shifted from line to column and oriented away from the Spanish.

"Detachment, double time, march," said Sergeant Worth. He ran alongside the column controlling the speed of the retrograde. A Marine helped each of their wounded counterparts stumble along as best they could back to the safety of the fortress.

Calder studied the events ashore through his spyglass. When the last of the red uniforms closed on the narrows of the peninsula, he moved next to Lieutenant Laurant.

"Officer of the Deck, bring *Comet* around to the other side of the Peninsula. Then lower boats and let's get our Marines back aboard," said Calder.

"Aye, aye, sir."

The last of the long boats approached *Comet*. The light was fading, and events ashore had settled into a stalemated siege of the Milazzo Peninsula. Captain Darroch let out a long sigh as he pulled himself up on the main deck. His eyes widened when he saw Captain Calder waiting for him.

"Sir, all Marines returned aboard. Mission complete," said Darroch saluting.

Calder threw a quick salute. He paused. Rubbing the back of his neck, he looked the Marine Captain in the eyes.

"Losses?"

"Five killed and two wounded. It would have been much worse, if *Comet* didn't open fire when you did, sir."

"Your welcome. Get your men below. I would think food and rest are in order for a job well done."

"What's next for *Comet* and crew, sir?"

"Well Captain Darroch, *Comet* stands detached from the fleet. We have clearance to sail to Gibraltar for repairs. Given the pounding we took from those two Spanish ships of the line, I think we are due a port period to fix our more problematic wounds. I'll see about getting your Detachment some replacements from the garrison at Gibraltar."

"Thank you, sir."

"Well, I've learned one thing about having Marines around."

"What's that, sir?"

"When you need them, you need as many as you can get. I'm sure this war is not over. Also, I'm sure *Comet* will see more action before all this is done. Captain Darroch, you've earned your shillings this week, strike below and see to your Marines."

"Captain Calder, sir," said Laurant pointing toward *Barfleur*. "Flag signal from Admiral Byng, sir."

Calder studied the flags through his spyglass. He lowered the glass and rubbed his chin.

"Bring me the signal book, Bosun."

The Bosun carried a large book over to his boss. Calder thumbed through the pages. He handed the book back and returned his stare to Admiral Byng's flagship.

"What is it, sir," said Laurant. His tone was inquisitive.

"What it is Lieutenant, is the Spanish have taken Messina. That damn straight controls our movement north and south. Things could get interesting in this campaign going forward."

"Aye, sir. What does it mean for *Comet?*"

"Not much. We stand detached and are to proceed independently as instructed. But not to Gibraltar as I thought."

"Where to now, sir?"

"Home, Lieutenant. We are ordered to head to Portsmouth. Make repairs and await additional instructions. Sorry lads, I fear *Comet* is out of action for a while."

All eyes on the command deck turned toward Calder on the mention of Portsmouth. A smile gripped the Bosun. Feet shuffled as the reality of a homeward course set-in with the sailors on deck.

"Lieutenant Laurant, I didn't mean to disrupt the focus of your watch team. Keep them at it. You had better steer a westerly course tonight, Lieutenant. I'll be in my cabin if you need anything."

Rutwell joined Laurant as the two of them watched the Captain depart the command deck.

"Well, Mister Rutwell, what plans do you have on our return to Portsmouth?"

"Sir, when I get back I want to visit a young lady that works at the Red Fox Inn."

"Midshipman Rutwell no women, worthy of the title Lady, work at the Red Fox Inn."

"Sir, Pang runs the place in Annette's absence. I've sort of committed to her. You know, to see how things go."

Laurant let out a long breath. He scratched the back of his head. He raised a finger skyward as if to reinforce a point, but

173

froze and remained silent. Lowering his hand, he looked Rutwell in the eye, and said, "Pang is like the ocean. Many men have ridden atop her, but none have tamed her or know the secrets of her depths. She is a beauty, can't be denying that. Trust, can you claim you trust her?"

Rutwell stared back unblinking. He lowered his gaze to the deck and then returned the intensity of Laurant's gaze. A calm washed over him. His smile widened larger than the Messina Straight.

"Yes, sir. I can trust her. She has never pretended to be something she is not. That took courage. Yes, I trust her."

Laurant looked over the aft railing, and said, "God, it's good to be young. I hope this works out for you Mister Rutwell. By the force of providence, I hope this works."

Chapter 10 Counter Conspiracy

The winter air chilled the crew on the command deck. Coats and scarfs were inadequate to fend off the combined effects of wind and cold. Dugins stomped his feet on the deck and rubbed his hands together. The fog of his breath carried away from his mouth as he blew into his cupped hands. Calder approached the Officer of the Deck and pointed to the buildings on the starboard side of *Comet*.

"We have been cleared direct to dry-dock, Lieutenant Martino. Take her in," said Calder.

"Aye, aye, sir," replied the Lieutenant. He took a couple of steps toward the Captain and lowered his volume. "Sir, do you think the officers will be able to break away at Christmas?"

"That is tradition. We'll see how the work can be divided so the ship is ready. I don't have orders yet, but I'm reasonably sure the Dock Master will want us out as soon as possible."

"Sir, look to port," said Dugins. His voice was elevated and pulsated with anticipation.

Signal rockets flew up from three ships swinging on anchor. They hoisted their battle standard on the main mast. The wind blew them straight away from the ships. Bells from the church broke the calm of the winter day. The three officers on the command deck watched as a boat rowed alongside. The coxswain in the back pumped the tiller a few times as he approached. He cupped his hand around his mouth and looked up toward Captain Calder.

"War! France has declared war on Spain. It's official, sir. We're at war with the Spanish," said the coxswain.

"Imagine that, gentlemen, England is at war," said Calder smiling. He looked back at his assembled officers.

"Shocking," said Martino.

"Stunning," said Dugins.

"Thank you for the news. Always difficult to keep up with current events when you're under sail you know," said Calder. He waved to the boat crew as they rowed toward the fleet to pass the word.

"Do you think it will impact Comet, sir," said Dugins.

"Yes, I would not make plans for Christmas just yet. I'm sure the Admiralty will want us to turn our repairs quickly. Every hull on the water will now be more important than ever," replied Calder. His jaw set firm against his upper lip.

Martino lowered his head and turned away. He walked over to the aft railing and stood in silence. He did take notice of the flag signals waved from the Dock Master.

"Lieutenant, please respond to the Dock Master. We need to get Comet secured, if we could."

Martino nodded. He straightened up and walked back the center line of the command deck. His orders followed with nautical efficiency, as he brought the ship into the confines of the dock. Lines were passed across from the shore and the ship was positioned under the watchful eye of the yard foreman. The squeaking sound of the pumps resonated into the night as the water level in the dock lowered. It would take a full day before Comet was left dry on the hard stand of the Portsmouth yard.

Calder stared at the rest of the Royal Navy swinging at anchor in the sound. Crews were working to ready their ships for the challenges of combat. Lines were tarred and run aloft. Sails hacked on spars. On the command deck he walked from side to side, watching the walls of the dry dock rise above the main deck as Comet settled in.

"A bloody fine way to start a war," said Calder to himself.

*****

The gathering at the Spanish court radiated proper etiquette and decorum. The ladies hovered on one side of the room and cast glances above their fans to the gentlemen across the way. An occasional nod signaled an advance well received, while an abrupt break in eye contact indicated the flirtation was not complete or well accepted. The rustle of the elaborate gowns signaled the expense of the garment and perhaps the patron's potential power. The gentlemen carried swords of light construction and ornate embellishments, making them more status symbols than instruments of death. The courtiers whispered in rapid, but low, tones. The constant buzz within the room reflected a sense of nervous excitement.

Queen Elisabeth stood radiant in a black dress trimmed with gold lace. The low cut of the garment's front and back revealed the youthful exuberance of her figure. Her matching black fan allowed her to cover, or unveil, her enticing form as she wished. The attention she commanded from across the room made the King smile. He knew she was the envy of many of those gathered. A powerful token to be played at court with proper timing. She moved through the women at court, courteous to all, but seeking out one person in particular.

Ernesta curtsied as the Queen approached. She held the dip until Elisabeth signaled with her fan for her to stand.

"Your highness, it is a privilege to see you again," said Ernesta. "Are the rumors true?"

"Yes, my dear. I fear France is massing on our northern border. My generals tell me by the spring both the Basque and Catalonia regions are subject to invasion," said the Queen. She took Ernesta by the arm and turned her away from the other courtiers. They cleared a path, curtsied deep, and avoided eye contact as the two women walked by.

"The generals must believe they can muster a solid defense?"

"With part of our army trapped by the Royal Navy on Sicily, and the English able to use the sea to pressure our coast, I'm not sure that is true."

"I believe you know what I think Spain should do at this point," said Ernesta.

"Refresh my memory, dear."

"We can no longer just wait, and react, to the moves of the coalition building against us. England, Austria, and now France all stand arrayed in opposition to our claiming back our territory," said Ernesta. She pulled close to whisper in the Queen's ear. "We must carry the war to England. Make them defend their northern provinces in Scotland. That will draw their sea-power away from us and we can fight each alliance member in turn."

"I don't see how we can launch an attack on England, when we lack the ground strength to defend the northern border or the ships to carry such an army."

"The army is already there, your highness."

The Queen pulled away from Ernesta. She faced her directly and her eyes tightened. "Explain."

"The Jacobite are no friend to the English crown. If we sent a few ships with a modest landing force, they would rally to the cause of their own independence. This would force England to pull their fleet and army from the Mediterranean. We could crack the alliance."

"How do you know this, my dear?"

"Does her Majesty remember Carlos Andres? He has been in service to our family for some time now. You may have seen him with our carriage when we visited Madrid?"

"No, Dear. I fear with so many coming and going from court your coachman escapes me."

"Well, he is in Scotland. I get communiques from him every few weeks. He has a very good read on the Jacobite. We should move against England before the French can strike across the Pyrenees Mountains."

"Just where would such a force land?"

"On the west coast of Scotland. We can side step the Royal Navy in the channel. Once the landing is complete, the ships would return before English ships can stop us."

"What pray tell do you mean by us, my dear?"

"Yes, I will sail with them to ensure your interests are well represented. I will not fail you, your Highness."

"I see. Just where on the west coast would you propose to land?"

"We will take the castle at Eilean Donan. It sits on the confluence of three lochs and controls the waterborne movement along the western coast. It would serve as the ideal base of operations for a Jacobite uprising," said Ernesta. She smiled, feeling her plan was gaining favor with the Queen. Her heart rate increased when she saw the Queen nodding with each word.

"I will carry your plan to Cardinal Alberoni. I fear he, and the court, would not listen to a young lady on such military matters. Especially, one as pretty as you, my dear. Beauty can be its own curse. However, the Cardinal has the King's ear on these marshal matters. He may well be the man we need to pull the Duke of Ormonde in on such an expedition. A wide net cast, has a better chance to catch the sea's bounty."

"Do you think the court will consider this idea?"

"Ernesta, the court hangs on every word the King utters. In the dark of the evening, when I hold his line of succession between my sharpened fingernails, he hangs on every whisper I make. I will present your plan at a time, and in a manner, that will give it the best chance of acceptance." She tapped her red filed fingernails against the black wood of her fan. The sound filled the momentary silence between them.

The King began his walk across the hall. It was the signal for the genders at court to mix. As he approached, the Queen spoke rapidly to Ernesta. "I will send you a letter with all the details of what is agreed to. It will have instructions for you as to where to go, and what to expect." The Queen's smile widened as the King drew near. They both raised their fans above their lips and waved a few rapid strokes. They each curtsied as he came within ear shot.

"So, ladies, what have you been discussing so intently over here?" asked the King. His eyes flashed back and forth between Elisabeth and Ernesta.

"We have been discussing the ramification of France joining the war against us," said the Queen. She batted her eyes at her husband.

"Oh, really," said the King. His eyes widened, and his lips flattened. "What impact do you ladies think it will mean? This change in the balance of power and all."

The Queen lowered her fan. She looked briefly over at Ernesta, before reengaging the King.

"We are very concerned on whether, or not, the court will have access to the latest Paris fashions. It could be devastating to our social season, you know," said Elisabeth. She smiled as she took the King's arm, assuming a position at his side.

The King began to laugh. The volume was muted, and he covered his mouth, shielding his emotions from the court. As they walked away, the Queen looked over her shoulder and winked at Ernesta.

Ernesta thought, *well then, the seed is planted. Perhaps it will bloom, and I will capture Annette before another season passes. William will be mine, forever.*

*****

The sound of footsteps reflected on the tile walkway and bounced off the walls of the enclosed courtyard. Pili Tonia balanced her child in one arm while controlling the flow of her dress with the other. Her eyes were focused forward as she scurried on her rounds. Ahead, her mistress sat in the shade of an olive tree. The early air of March was temperate. She noticed how relaxed Ernesta appeared in the confines of her father's estate.

"Mistress Rainerio, you have two letters from court. They have the Queen's seal, Mistress," said Pili. She took shallow breaths to recover from the exertion of her hurried pace.

"Let me take a look then," said Ernesta. She pointed to the chair across from her and waited for Pili to take a seat. Pili rocked the child as Ernesta pealed open the correspondence.

A wide smile took command of Ernesta's expression as she worked her way down the page. Her eyes widened as she reached the bottom of the letter.

"Is it good news, Ernesta?" asked Pili.

"Yes. I need you to pack my things for a long trip. It appears I will be heading north into a colder climate, so ensure my wardrobe reflects the same," said Ernesta. She rocked in her chair. Lowering the letter, she looked over at Pili.

"Where are you heading, Mistress?"

"Can't discuss that right now. I should be gone a month or two. Perhaps, just perhaps, this trip will put me a position to bring your child's father here to Vigo."

"William?"

"Yes. Captain William Darroch, here. First, I need to complete this little mission up north. Then I'll control my competition for his affections. When I get done with her, no man will want her."

Pili shuttered as Ernesta spoke. She locked eyes with her Mistress, and thought, *she must never know how I feel about William. I'm the only one here that has ever taken him into their bed. I would do so again, anytime he called. If Ernesta knew that, she would have me eliminated, just like Annette.* Pili looked down at her child and rocked him slowly.

"Does your father know?"

"Know what?" said Maximo as he approached the two women, having caught just the end of their conversation.

"Father, there you are. I was just getting ready to come see you."

"Yes, yes, what news from court?"

"I have been instructed by the Queen to represent her on a mission to Scotland. It seems she found out our servant, Carlos, is in communication with the Jacobite leadership. I'm to go there and help set up an uprising in the highlands. The hope is this disturbance will pull England's attention away from the Mediterranean."

"When did all this come about?"

"Just now, I have a letter of transit from the Queen, plus her personal instructions. I will depart for Cadiz in the morning."

"No, my daughter. Scotland is too wild and fearsome a place. It's not civilized. I love you too much to see you exposed to such danger. I'll talk with the King and put all this silliness to rest."

Pili looked from Maximo to Ernesta and back. Her child wiggled in her arms as the volume of the discussion rose.

"Father, I have told the Queen I would accept this task. To maneuver behind her would cause both of us to lose face. You will, on this occasion, stand aside. I rarely ask for such consideration, but now I must demand it."

Maximo let out a long breath. He kneeled next to his daughter. Taking her hand, he stroked the back of her ivory white skin.

"I would be crushed if anything happened to you, my daughter. I think you know that. Since your mother's departure, you have been, and remain, my entire world."

"Nothing will happen, Father. I will sail with the fleet, complete my task, and return on the first ship. That, I promise you."

"As you wish, Ernesta," said Maximo. "I do not want to talk of this again." He stood and walked out of the courtyard.

Ernesta looked over at Pili and her child. Her stare intensified. The muscles on her cheeks tightened. She nodded toward her chamber maid to exit.

"Pili, you had better get packing. I leave in the morning."

Pili faithfully nodded. In silence, she rose and departed with her child bouncing on her hip.

The next week found Ernesta looking out her coach window as she neared her destination. The port city of Cadiz was alive with movement under the warm Atlantic sun. Barrels and crates were lifted on block and tackle to the decks of Spanish warships. Long lines of uniformed men stood at various points waiting to embark on the numerous transports that jostled for dock space along the wharf. She noticed a man on a black stallion, giving directions and lifting his hand to every compass point as he spoke.

"Coachman, over there. Take me to the man over there," said Ernesta. Her voice was rough with dust from the trip south.

The man on horseback rode alongside the coach as it approached. He looked through the window. He tipped his hat forward and smiled.

"You must be the Lady Rainerio. Earl Marischal, George Keith if you please, at your service madam. I was told by the Queen you would be in attendance. Do you have her letter?"

Ernesta handed him the letter of instruction. He scanned down the length of the paper. He nodded.

"Written in the Queen's own hand. I would recognize that script anywhere. Impressive. Are you traveling alone, or do you have a lady in waiting or handmaid?"

"Alone Mister Keith."

"I've got three hundred Marines and six thousand troops embarking today. I fear you will have to share space on a ship with one of these rabbles. Do you have a preference?"

"I've always had good luck with Marines in the past. I shall sail with them," said Ernesta giggling. Her light response, caused Keith to raise one eyebrow.

"Well then, you and I will be sharing the captain's cabin on that ship over there. By sharing, I mean they will rig a canvas partition so we each may enjoy some element of privacy in the cramped conditions aboard."

"Mister Keith, how is it this expedition was put together in such a rapid manner?"

"Well madam, it seems the Irish exile, the Duke of Ormonde, has lent extensive support to our efforts. He wants to see King

George the First replaced with James Stuart. I would think his sponsorship will be instrumental in pulling in Jacobite support once we land. I understand you have a spy at Eilean Donan?"

"Yes, my last correspondence with him indicated he can get us into the fortress without a shot being fired. He has contacts within the walls ready, and able, to assist. They will follow you, sir."

"So, what is your interest in this matter, madam?"

"I'm here to represent the interests of the Queen. Additionally, I'm to take a certain redheaded woman hostage and return her to Spain. She figures as a bargaining chip in the potential negotiations between our two countries."

"A redhead, by God the whole of Scotland is filled with redheads. How will you know her?"

"We have met before. I will know her," said Ernesta. Her shift in tone was aggressive. The Earl leaned away from the coach in his saddle.

"Lady Rainerio, this is not my business and I apologize if I might have intruded. But know this, I will bring Scotland to flames. The revolt is all that matters to me. If I can assist in your kidnapping, I would be honored to do so. The uprising is, and remains, my overriding interest."

Keith reached into the coach and took Ernesta's hand. He lifted it to his lips and kissed the back.

"I shall see you aboard, my Lady."

He spun his horse away from the coach and proceeded toward the waterfront. Ernesta lifted her fan across her face and waived it a few times. She looked up at the sun and thought, *it must be these southern latitudes, this coach is getting damn hot.*

The ship rode with a starboard list as the fleet beat its way north along the Spanish west coast. Ernesta looked in the mirror and struggled to lace her corset and dress. She thought that perhaps she should have brought Pili along to assist her with these mundane tasks. Keith had invited her to share dinner on his side of the cabin canvas and she knew her status as a lady of the court demanded a certain level of appearance.

"May I join you?" asked Ernesta. She wrapped her knuckles on the bulkhead to announce her appearance.

"Yes. Come in. Please join me at the table."

He rose and walked behind her to assist with the chair. As she sat, he hovered over her and ran his hands along the length of her bare shoulders. His hands were smooth, and Ernesta thought, *a gentleman. Royal upbringing, refreshing.*

The two shared dinner and small talk as the level in the wine bottle slowly lowered. Wax from the lone candle pooled around its brass holder as the hours ticked by with seeming ease. The flame provided just enough light to illuminate their expressions as they locked eyes across the table. Laughter and light conversation accompanied proper decorum as topics ranged from the pending operations to past court intrigue.

Ernesta's eyes widened when she felt his silk covered foot sneak beneath her dress and rub along the back of her calf. She smiled and set her fork on the plate.

"Mister Keith, it has been a refreshing evening. Your company has proven to be a welcome surprise on this voyage. I fear the toil of the day has left me to retire to my chamber."

Keith rose to help her once again with her chair. Looking down she noted both his shoes were removed. They both stood. The ship rolled hard to starboard throwing the two them against the bulkhead. Keith took advantage of this unexpected turn of events to secure her in his embrace. His arms wrapped tight around her waist, pulling Ernesta against him. She turned her cheek to him, avoiding the carnal intent of his advance. His lips demanded skin, and he kissed the soft nakedness of her shoulders. The flash of light through the aft windows briefly illuminated the great cabin. The crash of thunder broke the mood as quickly as it had started.

"The storm. The storm is upon us," said Keith.

He released Ernesta and exited the cabin in such a rush he left his shoes on the cabin floor. The lighting and thunder continued to dominate the scene in the cabin. The steward struggled to remove the dinnerware amid the violent rolling action of the ship. The mournful sound of the ship's beams straining against the wind and waves filled Ernesta's ears. Her stomach became more unsettled then the surrounding sea.

Looking aft through the cabin window, she struggled to peer through the darkness. The thunderbolt's flash would light-up the seas revealing white foam carried aloft by the wind. Its swirling mist obscuring her view aft before settling once again on the ocean's surface. Between the brilliant flashes, the stern lamps of the surrounding ships were faintly visible. She clutched her stomach, sure the sickness would envelop her at any moment. Every muscle in her body fatigued as she struggled to hold on to the rolling and pitching space around her.

One by one, the stern lamps of the fleet disappeared. These small pin points of light vanished between the rise and fall of each swell. Over the course of the night, few would return. As the thunder abated, an uneasy darkness covered the ship. At last, Ernesta was able to return to her swinging bed. She found that by closing her eyes the apparent motion of the ship would subside. Sleep became a welcome refuge from the violence of the storm.

"Lady Rainerio, I must speak with you," said Keith. His voice penetrated the canvas screen between them.

Ernesta rose and walked over to the screen. The morning's light flowed through the aft windows of the great cabin. With her head held down, she pulled back the canvas to find Keith fully dressed and eager to engage her. He stared at her. Wearing only her dressing gown, the curve of her form was not difficult to imagine. The garment clung to her upper body accentuating each protrusion, before falling straight away to just below her knees.

"You must excuse me, Lady Rainerio. I'm not used to having women on my ship. Especially one as lovely as yourself."

"I hope that's not why you chose to wake me."

"No, my Lady. We have lost the fleet in the storm. I fear we are alone. I wanted to inform you the ship's captain is recommending we turn back to Spain or—"

"Or what?" interrupted Ernesta.

"Or we wait until the rest of the fleet is found."

"How many Marines remain in our company?"

"Three hundred. I fear that is not enough to take on the northern English armies."

"Of course not. However, they are more than enough to support the Jacobite rebellion. That is why we are here. We will continue. The Queen's mission is not yet compromised, and it is by her command you will continue."

Keith's mouth opened. He took a step away from the canvas curtain. Ernesta followed him into his space. She pointed north. He nodded.

Turning away to exit the cabin, he said, "I hope you know a single ship does have much of a chance against the Royal Navy."

"Mister Keith, a single ship will never draw the attention of the Royal Navy. Just get me close to the north side of Syke Island on the Little Mitch. My agent will be there. If he can't get us into Eilean Donan without an assault, then we'll retire. But, if we can take that bastion, the rebellion will expand."

In the days that followed, Ernesta heard the sound of the anchor falling away at the bow. Looking in the mirror, she adjusted the alignment of her dress and pushed her hair a little higher on her head. She walked up the command deck to see what was going on. The dim light below deck mirrored the dark grey day that surrounded her topside. The seas were flat. The green of Syke Island stood a few hundred yards off their starboard side. She took a deep breath of the clear air above deck. The smell of the land, and its vegetation filled her senses. She noticed the ship was not flying any colors to mark their nationality.

"Good morning, Lady Rainerio," said Keith. He pointed to the Island. "Syke Island, as you requested. I hope this is your contact in the approaching boat."

Ernesta turned to see Carlos waiving rapidly above his head. She instinctively returned the gesture.

"Yes, that's him. Please bring him aboard."

Carlos walked on the command deck and bowed deep before Ernesta. His hat and arms carried away from his body. His sword bounced against his leg when he stood up.

"My Lady, all is in preparation. When will the rest of the fleet be here?" said Carlos.

Keith cleared his throat. Ernesta frowned toward him.

"Carlos, this is it. I've got three hundred Marines aboard. Can you get us behind the walls without a fight?"

"Yes. All can be made ready in a day. You'll have to attack at dawn. Have your boats come ashore on the landward side of the castle island. That's were our man at the gate will let you in. The garrison is about one hundred and twenty-five. They can hold the walls, but once you're inside your numbers will hold sway."

They both looked over at Keith. He nodded his concurrence.

*****

Cynthia walked to the edge of her bed chamber looking out into the courtyard below. She held her young boy in her arms and rocked him. His mood rested uneasy. She pulled back her dressing gown to expose her breast to the child. He suckled contently, safe within his mother's arms. She looked across to see her daughter asleep in the crib.

The light glow of sunrise lifted the veil of night in slow deliberate strides. A glimpse, a shadow perhaps, moved on the grounds below. In his feeding exuberance, her son bit down on her bare nipple.

"Ouch," said Cynthia. "You are the devil, aren't you?"

She stroked the side of his cheek, settling the child. He continued to draw nourishment from his mother's body. She more securely covered him in his blanket to guard against the predawn chill.

Drawing near the window she held her eyes steady to view into the twilight scene. Three figures rushed across the grounds to the castle keep.

Turning away, she thought, *odd, why would Captain MacPherson drill his soldiers at this hour?* The stillness of the bed chamber stood in contrast to the scene below.

Looking back into the courtyard, ten figures clad in uniforms unknown to her ran toward the main house. She looked up on the walls, more soldiers were moving along the ramparts from one guard position to the next. She looked over at the bed.

"Drake, we're under attack. Men are inside the walls."

"What?" said Drake. He struggled to lift his body up on his elbows.

"Come look, soldiers on the walls."

Drake threw back the blankets and stumbled over to the window. He rubbed his eyes and peered into the soft light building on the grounds below.

"Damn," he whispered.

He dressed and pulled his sword around his waist. The door to their chamber was thrown open. Four men in Spanish uniforms and battle regalia pushed their way inside. Drake drew his sword and took a position between Cynthia and the intruders.

The first attacker rushed directly at Drake. He sidestepped the attack and thrust his blade in the man's side as he moved by. The Spaniard took one more step and collapsed. Drake sliced the air with his sword from side to side. The whooshing sound filled the chamber as he did so.

The second attacker raised his blade to the on-guard position. He took one step forward and slid his trailing foot up behind him into his original stance. He continued to shorten the distance between himself and Drake using this stylized technique. Drake reached out and touched his attacker's blade. Noting his response, he beat parried his opponents lunge and rolled his blade across the direction of his attacker's advance sending his blade upward. The exposed torso of his opponent was an easy target. Pulling his elbow back to his chest, he then extended the point of his saber directly into his attacker's heart. The sound of his gasp was loud enough to suck the air out of the room.

Drake lifted his boot to the man's chest and pushed him off his sword. The third attacker followed close on the heels of the second. Drake only had time to drop to his knees spin around and slice his saber across the thighs of this attacker. He crumbled forward on his knees. Drake stood and thrust his blade into the man's neck.

Before he could extract his weapon the forth attacker thrust his sword into Drake's side. He grabbed the weapon to slow its penetration. His hand oozed blood turning his night shirt crimson red at the point of the wound. Cynthia's scream woke both her children. Crying and confusion filled the room. The attacker twisted the blade in Drake's side. His face tightened as he spit blood.

Two more attackers entered the room. On observing Drake's resistance, the next attacker lifted his sword above his head and struck directly down on Drake's shoulders. The blade sliced through his collarbone and the force of the strike carried three inches down into his chest. His shoulder eased away from his spine, widening the gap and increasing the loss of blood. His hand slackened, and the soldier with his blade in Drake's side, pushed it deeper into his frame. He collapsed to the floor.

The soldier pulled his blade from Drake's spent body and walked over to Cynthia. He dropped his weapon and grabbed her child from her arms. He walked to the window and pushed the child out. The scream fell silent when the sound of her child's impact on the stones of the courtyard reached the upper story.

190

Cynthia's mouth fell open. The second soldier now pulled the crying child from the crib and she found the same fate as her brother.

The two men looked at Cynthia, then at each other. They grinned in anticipation. Walking back from the window, the soldier struck Cynthia across the face. She fell to her knees. He followed this abrupt blow with a kick to her head. She collapsed to the cold floor. The sound of her dressing gown being ripped from her body filled the room. The men picked her up from the floor and spread her across the bed. Cynthia struggled to get up, only to find a fist once again impacting her face. Blood flowed from her nose. She could feel the weight of her attacker ride up on her. Pressing, pumping, and penetrating her body, the men took turns with her. When they let up for a moment, she sighed. Then they turned her over, violating her in a manner she had never experienced. She surrendered all resistance, all feeling. Cynthia just wanted it to end. She sobbed in near silence, as the men around her laughed.

Annette had heard the scuffling in the hallway. She went to the door and looked down the passageway. "Soldiers," she whispered. She shut the door but failed to slide the bolt home before an attacker pushed against its solid oak. The door slid back enough to prevent the locking mechanism from engaging. She pushed back to hold the opening shut. The sound of a second soldier on the other side was audible. She felt her feet slide back a few inches.

The door swung open as the force of three soldiers overcame Annette's failed attempt to hold them at bay. She was knocked to the ground. Her saber was only a few feet away. She crawled on the ground toward her weapon, and extended her arm reaching for the blade. A boot fell home on her hand, smashing it to the wood floor.

"Not so fast, lassie," said the Spaniard. "Swords aren't proper toys for young ladies."

191

"Take her to the Queen's agent," said a Sergeant.

"Yes, Sergeant."

They dragged Annette out of the room, with a soldier on each side of her. They pulled her along quickly, so she couldn't get her feet underneath her to stand. Her knees scuffed along the stone floor. Her mouth twisted with each impact down the passage. They yanked her half way down the corridor, until a backlit figure stood before them.

"Is this the redheaded bitch you're looking for, my Lady?"

"Yes, this is the one. Chain her and take her back to the ship."

"Yes, my Lady."

Annette struggled to see the figure in silhouette, but she was unable to determine who it was. The voice, however, it was familiar.

"Oh, one more thing boys. If I find she has been violated, I will take from you something you value. Something you find . . . pleasurable. Without getting too specific, all I can tell you is its removal will be painful and permanent. So, no side stops along the way. Am I clear?"

"Yes, my lady," said the soldiers in unison. They both swallowed hard in speculation of the threat.

The metallic sound of the lock clicking home on Annette's chains echoed in the hall. She looked down at the iron that now encased her wrists and shook her head. Her auburn hair fell around her cheeks, obscuring her face. Shackles, linked by chain, hobbled her feet. The weight of the chains that connected the two constraints painfully pulled her shoulders downward.

The two soldiers lifted her over the gunwales of the boat. They forced her to sit in the wet and damp of the floor boards. She looked up to see the stone walls of Eilean Donan fade in the mist, until the tones of grey blended and the castle disappeared from view. A light rain fell on her as she listened to the rhythm of the oars pull the boat toward a lone ship at anchor in the loch.

The dark hull of the Spanish galleon cast a long shadow over the approaching boat.

Annette thought, *what just happened? Who the hell are these people? I have never feared going to sea in the past, but a darkness commands this ship.*

Chapter 11 Irish Sea

"Charles," said Captain Darroch. His tone was unusually tentative.

"Yes."

"Do you notice something strange in the dock yard here?"

"You mean the water level."

"Yes. It's been on the rise now for ten minutes. Any idea why?"

"Not a clue, but here comes Captain Calder from the Dock Master's Office. Perhaps he'll have some idea."

The Bosun's pipe called out in its traditional sing sound manner, as salutes were exchanged, and Calder was welcomed back aboard his ship. Martino motioned for the Captain to join him. Darroch hovered near the two men, eager to glean any information he could.

"Sir, the dry dock is not so dry at this point. Any orders, sir?" asked Martino shifting the Officer of the Deck spyglass under his arm.

"Yes, Lieutenant Martino," replied Calder. His bearing was somber. "A change in mission indeed."

"Sir, we still have work to do here in the yards. Can't the Admiralty see fit to let us finish before throwing us back into the fight?"

"The Admiralty could, but I fear the Spanish can't."

"Sir?"

"A Spanish force has landed in Scotland. They seem intent on stirring up a rebellion in the north. Not bad strategy, if I do say so myself. We hit them hard off Sicily, now they are trying to backdoor our campaign and divide the coalition."

"Where in Scotland did they land, sir?" asked Darroch. The Marine now stepped into the tight circle formed by these three officers.

"Eilean Donan, on Loch Duich in Kintail. Do you know of it, Captain Darroch?"

Darroch's cheeks lost all color. His mouth pressed into a flat line. The Marine blinked and stretched his neck to the side and back.

"Yes, sir. I'm very familiar with the location. That's where your cook is sitting out this conflict."

"Annette?"

"Yes, sir. She left for Eilean Donan when the recall signal sounded in Portsmouth. Well, that's not entirely fair. I told her to go there to get away from any Spanish threat along the channel."

"Oh brilliant, Marine. When was the last time you heard from her?"

"More than two weeks ago. Everything up north was fine at that point. She was riding out the conflict in comfort and enjoying Scottish hospitality. She didn't much care for the climate, if I recall correctly."

"Damn it, man. I don't need a weather report. We may well have to pull her out of this mess. The Jacobite have set up a base of operations in the castle and are threatening the entire west coast of Scotland."

"What is *Comet* instructed to do, Captain?" said Martino. He spoke without emotion.

"The ship is one of five to be dispatched to suppress this uprising," said Calder. He pointed toward the few other ships remaining at anchor in the Portsmouth Sound. "I'm to report to Captain Chester Boyle on HMS *Worchester*. Good man, we've worked together before."

"What is this makeshift squadron supposed to do, sir?" asked Darroch.

"We are to blockade the Spanish occupied coast. Prevent any reinforcement or supplies from reaching the rebel base," said Calder. He straightened up and turned toward Darroch. He placed his hand on the Marine's shoulder. Locking eyes, he continued, "If possible, we are to take Eilean Donan and prevent it from being used by the Jacobite." He paused and turned away from Darroch. "If we can't take the stronghold, we are to bombard it into submission."

"And what of the loyalists inside the castle?" said Darroch, his voice cracked as he spoke.

"You mean Annette, don't you?"

"Yes, sir."

"Captain Darroch, if we can't seize the strong hold, the squadron will bombard it into submission. Those are the Admiralties instructions."

"To hell with the Admiralty. We have to protect the loyal English caught in this unfortunate change of events."

"Damn it, man. You misspeak, sir. Our orders from the Admiralty are clear. I strongly recommend you reconsider your words, Captain Darroch."

William glanced over at a smirking Martino. The Lieutenant rocked back and forth on his heels. He held his tongue, more than happy to be an observer of the verbal sparring between the ship's captain and the Marine. Darroch lowered his gaze to the deck.

"Aye, aye, sir. What can I do to help?"

"Do you know anything militarily about Eilean Donan?"

"Sir, let me check my other notebooks. I was there a while back and may have recorded some observations that can assist in taking down the bastion."

Calder nodded. "Now that sounds more like my Marine Detachment Commander. Get at it man."

Martino and Calder were left topside as the Marine went below. The Lieutenant stopped rocking and slid his left foot forward. He grabbed the lapel of his uniform with is right hand. Looking Calder in the eye, he asked, "Sir, orders for the Officer of the Deck?"

"Get with Lieutenant Laurant and compile a list of repair work that remains pending. Divide it up into tasks we can complete underway, and those that must be accomplished dockside. Then confer with Laurant as to which division on *Comet* is responsible for task execution. Ensure he provides me the list at the Eight O'Clock reports this evening."

"Aye, aye, sir. Any idea when I, I mean we, will fight the ship to victory again?"

"Lieutenant, just worry about getting me that list first. It will be days before *Comet* will be in contact. One step at a time, shall we."

"Yes, sir."

"The first thing we need to do is make ready for the Irish Sea. The wind and waves of that small body of water can turn witching wicked without warning. Make all preparations for getting underway."

"Aye, aye, sir."

Below decks, Captain Darroch shuffled through the pages of his little green notebooks. He strained to read his scrawled handwriting by candlelight. The wax from the candle dripped onto the exposed flesh of his hand. His mind was too focused to register the burning pain that should have been self-evident.

"That's not it," Darroch whispered to himself. He cast the book on his bunk and pulled another from the shelf above his small writing desk.

"No," reverberated in a low tone as another journal took flight toward his bed.

"Eilean Donan, here it is," said the Marine in a low voice. He thumbed selected pages back and forth studying the lines written several years ago. His mind struggled to recall the tactical significance of the words.

He read aloud, "Eilean Donan sits on an Island that is unapproachable but by sea. Only a Marine assault, taken on all sides of the fortress simultaneously, will carry the position."

He paused and stared at the candle on his desk. Reaching for his quill, he dipped it in the ink well. He underlined the word "simultaneously" and set the book aside. Pulling a paper from his drawer, he wrote at the top: mission, stated tasks, and implied tasks. He glanced at the wooden beams above his head before writing out his thoughts. He would run through several more pages, and the candle would burn down into its holder, before he finished his planning. He blew lightly across the last page to dry the newly inked words.

He took a deep breath and closed his eyes. His mind wondered uncontrolled, and came to rest on a vision of Annette. The auburn hue of her hair, the rounded curve of her hip, and the smooth touch of her legs. He could imagine her on his bed, eyes locked on him, but head tilted forward and slightly down. Smiling, inviting, with her tongue dragging across moistened lips. The corners of his mouth edged up.

"Sir, the Captain would like to see you in his cabin," said the voice outside his stateroom door. The reverberating knock on his hatch had broken his train of thought. Its harsh tone had brought him back to the maritime world of *Comet*.

"I'll be right there."

He gathered his notes. Darroch held the papers so as to not smear the fresh ink. He smiled, and thought, *at least I know what the hell I'm fighting for. Let them try and stop me.*

*****

The long faces seated around the oak table were as grey as the stone walls surrounding them. The leadership of the Spanish expedition gathered to discuss their options now that it was clear the rest of the six-thousand-man army would not be joining them at Eilean Donan. Two of the Jacobite clan leaders had joined the gathering to represent their kin.

"We have three hundred Spanish Marines camped outside the castle walls. How many clansmen have joined our uprising?"

asked Keith. His eyes traveled around the table reading the faces that stared intently back.

The clan leader with the long beard leaned forward. He said, "Clan Mackenzie, Clan MacRae, and Clan MacGregor are all with us. Some, perhaps more, than others."

"What is your strength, sir? How many men can you put in the field?" Keith continued to probe.

"We are glad to have our Spanish allies with us, but you told us six thousand would be showing up. As you say, we've only counted a few hundred. It's not the inspiring sight we would be hoping for."

"Numbers aside, these are elite troops. They are prepared to stand side-by-side with your clansmen."

"The men have lost confidence in you, sir," said the Marquis of Tullibardine. He held his stare on Keith to study his response.

Keith tossed his hands upward. He shook his head. Looking back at the Marquis, he said, "Very well, I resign my command. I will retain control of the ships, less, the one that sailed yesterday with the Queen's agent. I wish you luck with this rabble, sir. I stand relieved."

The Marquis smiled. He pointed over to the clan leader once again.

Clearing his throat, he asked, "To the point, sir. How many men can you muster?"

"The clans stand ready with fifteen hundred. Ready to march against these English."

"Fifteen hundred, you say. We can put almost two thousand combined in the field. It is key that we strike before the English can react and muster their forces against us. I need recommendations as to where we should move."

Keith stood and walked away from the table. All eyes followed him in a moment of silence as he left the room. The only sound in the chamber was the click-clack of his wooden heels on the stone floor.

"Well then, I ask again, where should we strike?" said the Marquis.

The two clan leaders conferred in whispered tones. Their hands gesturing with a rapidity consistent with the building tension around the table. The one with the long beard turned toward the Spanish leadership and smiled.

"Inverness, sir. Aye, that should be our target." He stroked his long beard after speaking.

"Why Inverness?" The tone of the Marquis indicated he was less than convinced.

"Inverness sits at the northern end of Loch Ness. We can control the southern end here at Eilean Donan. We can divide the highlands from the lowlands and split the English into two. Inverness is also the seat of English power in the north. Break it, and we'll be buying time to rally more of the clans. The best way to add strength to our rebellion is through victory. Gain a win there, and more clans will rally to the cause. I think it be clear, no one wants to join a losing fight."

"What is the strength of the English garrison at Inverness?" Asked the Marquis. He leaned back in his chair. He touched his fingertips together.

"We don't be knowing that. Reports indicate that the garrison is being reinforced from Edinburgh. Their strength is growing each day. If we want to attack, the time to move is upon us. What say you?"

"Are the garrison troops local militia or regulars?" asked the Marquis. His pose remained unchanged as he spoke.

"Aye, they be English regulars. Redcoats, with some cannon. It be true, this is not the time for those faint of heart. We attack, or we'll go back to the Highland way of war."

"And what pray tell would that be?"

"Hit them in the field. Hurt them where they stand. Return to the hills and never allow your men to stand toe-to-toe against the

English. Best to be above ground at the end of battle than below. Aye, that's the Highland way."

"Hit and run than?"

"I prefer to think of it as hit and maneuver, sir."

"I will take all this under advisement, gentlemen," said the Marquis. "We will attack, or wage hit and maneuver tactics as our two options. I must say, I'm not keen on lining up the clansmen against English regulars. For, while victory would rally the clans, defeat would end this effort prematurely. What I can tell you for sure, I intend to leave forty to fifty men here at Eilean Donan. This castle will serve as our base of operations and fallback position. The rest of the army will get to the field where it will be more difficult to pin us down or corner us into battle on terms not to our liking."

The council of war broke up and departed the hall. The Marquis and his leading officer moved over to the fireplace. Warming themselves, the Marquis watched as the Highlanders departed.

"Look at those scruffy Scotsmen," said the Marquis in hushed tones. He pointed at them as they reached the exit. "Their shoes are worn leather, shirts in need of patching, and the smell of them could turn your stomach. This is our great northern rebellion?" He leaned against the fireplace and locked eyes with his counterpart.

"Sir, they are despondent," said his leading officer. "Think on it, sir. They were told six thousand regular Spanish troops would join their cause. They got three hundred. I think we were lucky to get the fifteen hundred we did."

"Yes, my friend, you may well be right. Spain's interest is to draw out the rebellion as long as possible. Keep the English distracted here, that's the name of the game. We need not go out in a flash of glory against English regulars and cannon. I will not march to Inverness."

"Gentlemen, a glass of wine perhaps?" asked the servant balancing a tray.

Each of them took a glass. They waited until the servant had retreated from the fireplace.

"Sir, to the Highland way of war," said the leading officer.

"Indeed, to the Highland way of war," said the Marquis.

The sharp ringing sound of wine glasses colliding echoed above the crackling of the fire. It was only a toast. However, it was a toast that would chart the campaign's path beneath the grey Scottish skies.

*****

Captain Darroch watched his boss pull the full extent of his large frame up the ladder of HMS *Worcester*. Open ocean transfers of personnel were always tricky, this one had proven no less so. The surrounding swell lifted the long boat up, and it nearly impacted Calder's feet. He hastened his pace up the ladder. William looked out at the sea, he saw no relief in sight as waves and wind cut the surface of the water in random torrents of white foams and chop.

"Up you go, sir," said the coxswain. His body rocked side-to-side.

Darroch looked back at the sailor's white knuckled hand on the tiller. This death grip was the only means the coxswain had to steady himself on the rough sea. The Marine nodded. He reached out and took hold of the ladder. It was his turn for a white-knuckle ride. The long boat fell from beneath his feet, as the swell receded taking his footing from under him. William scrambled up the side of the ship knowing that the swell would reverse its movement returning the long boat upward. He didn't want to get slammed between the side of the ship and the boat.

On reaching the main deck, Calder signaled for him to join a small group of naval officers at the main mast. He walked over, saluted, and studied the faces around him. *Strangers,* he thought.

"Captain Darroch, this is Captain Boyle. He is our squadron commander for this expedition," said Calder.

"My pleasure, sir," said Darroch shaking Boyle's hand.

Boyle cupped his hand downward and signaled for an officer in a red coat to join the circle.

"Captain Darroch, let me introduce my Marine Detachment Commander, Captain Riddell."

The two Marines nodded toward each other. Their bearing was stiff, formal, and guarded.

"Yes, I know of Captain Darroch's exploits. Haven't seen you since I instructed you at basic. You appear to have done well," said Riddell. His tone was just a little condescending.

"So, Captain Riddell, you are the senior Marine?" asked Boyle.

"Guilty as charged, sir."

"Well then, here is what we'll do. Captain Calder, you take control of HMS *Adventure*, that's Captain McCarthy commanding, and patrol off Syke Island to enforce the blockade. I'll proceed forward with HMS *Enterprise* and HMS *Flamborough* to capture or reduce Eilean Donan. Captain Darroch, you will transfer your Marines to my ship. I'll need every one of you if we are to assault that place."

Darroch looked back at Calder. His boss nodded. He returned his gaze to Boyle and Riddell.

"Aye, aye, sir," said Darroch.

"It's settled then. I'll let the two Marines develop a plan for assault. Captain Calder, you and Captain McCarthy formulate the details of the blockade. I'll work with the other captains on a plan to reduce Eilean Donan by bombardment," said Boyle. His tone was gruff.

Darroch studied the expression of the naval officers that surrounded him. He thought, *too many smiles. This is not some yacht club sail. Too many damn smiles.*

Riddell walked with Darroch over to the stern of the poop deck. They could watch the two groups of naval officers planning on the deck below. Judging by the waving of hands and broken dialogue, the plans were solidifying.

"Captain Darroch, what are your thoughts on assaulting the castle?" asked Riddell.

William pulled the pages he had prepared from his coat. "These are my first thoughts on the matter, sir." He handed the plan to Riddell. "It has however, been over a year since I visited Eilean Donan."

Riddell lifted his eyes from the text. "You've been inside the castle?"

"Yes. I made notes at the time. That plan reflects my observations then and what I think we can do."

Riddell returned his attention to the pages. His lips moved as he read the words. At length, he snapped his fingers against the paper. The noise popped in William's ears.

"This is excellent. I must have taught you damn well all those years ago. I clearly can pull the theme of a simultaneous assault on all walls from your plan. How did you reach that conclusion?"

The ramparts connect each side of the bastion. If we only attack one side, the garrison will shift troops from wall to wall as needed. A small company would be able to hold at bay a much larger force. But, if we hit all walls together, they would need several hundred men to man the ramparts."

"How many Marines can you bring over from *Comet*?"

"Thirty-four, counting myself."

"I'll add fifty, plus any sailors I can organize into an assault party. That's over a hundred. Do you think we'll have enough?"

"Close. I know what the walls could hold. The issue is what will they hold?"

"Garrison size?"

"Exactly."

The two Marines studied the sketch of Eilean Donan. Darroch traced his finger along the walls as he talked.

"Let me take the east side. The main gate and tower are there," said Darroch. He tapped his finger on the sketch. "That way we'll put a good part of our force, under one command that has worked with these folks, against their strength."

"That's good. I'll take the south and west walls. We'll leave the naval landing crew on the north. That will put them under the guns of the fleet. In short, that's the most cannon support possible."

"Aye, that's true. Do we have enough boats to land on all sides at the same time?"

"Damn good question. Let me get with Captain Boyle and see what his thoughts are."

"Right. You might want to suggest we take in tow the boats from *Comet and Adventure*. Less those they need for blockade, of course."

"Of course," said Riddell. "This is good work Captain Darroch. Thank you."

Darroch looked below as his counterpart disappeared amid the mass of blue uniforms on the main deck. He watched as Captain Boyle slapped his Marine on the back.

You're welcome, thought Darroch studying the scene.

A few days later, Sergeant Worth had to push his way to the hand-rail on HMS *Worcester*. He elbowed by the collection of observers to Captain Darroch's side. All eyes settled in on a lone boat, under a white flag, approaching Eilean Donan on the north side. The three ships of the Royal Navy swung on anchor and dominated the loch. The boat's oars cast out ripples as the crew pulled across the smooth morning waters.

"What seems so damn interesting, Captain?" asked Worth. His untiring tone was too loud for the quiet of the still morning air.

"Our boat is about to parley with the castle for their surrender," said Darroch in a whisper. "It should be interesting to see what terms they demand in their response."

A lone puff of smoke rose from the rampart of Eilean Donan. The sharp report of a cannon soon followed. The round shot from the cannon appeared to drift in slow motion toward the long boat. All eyes were fixated on its smooth arching trajectory over the water. It landed short and to the right of the coxswain. The splash of impact cast water up and soaked the boat crew with icy loch water. He shoved the tiller over to the right and the long boat circled around to the left. The crew was now pulling on oars at a frantic pace. The once long, smooth, and steady strokes of the oarsmen, were now rapid short choppy pulls. The panicked cadence of the coxswain could be heard on the main deck of *Worcester*.

"It would seem we have their reply, Captain."

"Aye, that be true. Ready the Marines, Sergeant. My guess is this will have to be settled at the end of a bayonet."

"Aye, aye, sir," said Sergeant Worth smiling. He turned and headed below deck.

"Fire," rang from the command deck. This order was relayed down the gun deck. One of the officer's commands were broken and scratchy as he yelled. Darroch couldn't help but think, *a novice. We all have to start at some point.*

The cannonade from HMS *Worcester, HMS Enterprise,* and HMS *Flamborough* broke the calm of the morning. Iron balls were thrown against the castle walls pounding stone into dust. The rigidity of the walls held the damage to small holes equal to the size of the projectile. The ships pockmarked the structure, but they were unable to collapse it.

A knock on Captain Boyle's cabin hatch announced the arrival of his messenger. "Enter," rang from his lips.

The messenger entered his cabin and centered himself on Boyle's desk. The Captain took a long sip of tea, as he pushed his breakfast plate aside. He took the folded paper and spread it across his desk. He traced his finger down the page. When he reached the bottom, he turned to look out the aft end of the ship.

His cabin shook, as it did every time the rear most cannon on the gun deck fired, and this broke his train of thought. Turning back to the messenger, he tapped the top of the desk a few times with his knuckles.

"We have reports of rebel supplies located in a house farther up the loch," said Boyle. "Dispatch *Enterprise* from the firing line to investigate. If we can't break them with cannon fire, perhaps we can capture their supplies and force capitulation. Go now, make it happen."

The cannonade was slow, but deliberate, throughout the day. That evening, long boats pulled over to the flagship for a council of war. The fading light brought a welcome pause to the ears of all those gathered on the north side of the castle. Riddell studied the rampart of Eilean Donan with his spyglass.

"What are you looking for?" asked Darroch.

"A white flag."

"Not likely. Those Spanish and their clan supporters have no place to run. They have to fight it out. I think we both know the assault will fall to us."

Riddell collapsed his spyglass. He nodded in agreement.

"Let's join the council, shall we?"

The two Marines marched off in step to join the sailors assembled on the main deck. Their joint military bearing drew a couple of muffled laughs from the officers of the wardroom.

"Looks like you lobsters are about to earn your pay," said one lieutenant. His smile indicated the degree to which his comments were playful banter. Both Marines frowned in his direction.

"Gentlemen, it appears they're not going to throw down to our cannons alone. Marines, I look to you to put this flag on that keep," said Boyle. He lifted the English flag skyward. He handed the ensign to Captain Riddell. "What have you two come up with for an assault plan?"

Boyle handed him the notes Darroch had crafted. The Navy Captain scanned down the document. "Say, these are really good. You two did this in short order. Impressive."

"Thank you, sir," said Riddell. He tucked the flag under his left arm.

Darroch flattened his lips together and drew a hard stare on his counterpart. He could see beads of sweat form on Riddell's brow. All eyes now turned on this Royal Marine Captain clutching the flag and hopes of the expeditionary force.

"Please brief us on what has to be done to make this assault happen," said Boyle.

"Yes, I would very much like to know, Captain Riddell," said Darroch. A smile slowly bubbled up on his face, as an odd silence gripped the main deck.

"Well then, Captain Darroch, you put most of this together, would you do us the honor of sharing your approach here?"

"Yes, but first, I need the crew of *Enterprise* to update us on their raid up the loch."

"We found the gunpowder storehouse. It was just upstream about a mile. The garrison won't be getting any supplies, or reinforcements, from there anytime soon," said the Captain from *Enterprise.*

"Excellent, sir. That should help make our efforts tomorrow simpler. Gentlemen, I'll need a bombardment on these three sides of the castle. It is unlikely the ships will be able to maneuver at low tide to gain firing positions on the southern shore, so keep focused on the north and west sides," said Darroch.

He held the attention of those assembled discussing the details of the assault plan. Silence dominated the briefing. Noticeably absent from the background noise were the random coughs that inevitably disrupted these meetings. Questions from the ship captains were few as the council of war concluded. An element of sadness swept over Captain Darroch as he watched the blue uniforms depart HMS *Worcester*. Leaning over the side railing, he straightened up when a hand came to rest on his shoulder. He turned to find Captain Boyle.

"Good brief, Marine. Just so you know, it is clear in my mind who authored this attack plan. I hope you're up to leading your part of the assault," said Boyle.

"Yes, sir. I have my own reasons for taking down Eilean Donan. I will not fail you, sir."

"Of that I'm certain," quipped Boyle. He rubbed his chin while holding a stare on Darroch. "Just don't let yourself down, lad. It is not lost on your navy captains that you have elected to take on the most difficult part of the assault. I'll get as much firepower on the walls as *Worcester* is capable of sending, but that east side is going to be difficult to align on given the shallows of Loch Duich."

On the morning of the assault, the sun took its own slow measure to climb above the hills east of Eilean Donan. The bastion had remained darkened throughout the night, making the sunrise the first illumination of its grey stone walls. Sergeant Worth and Captain Darroch stood on the ship's railing, studying the fortress. Their Marines were in formation behind them. Three ranks, straight and aligned with precision.

"The east side you say, sir," said Sergeant Worth to Captain Darroch. His tone while respectful, was none the less questioning.

"Yes, Sergeant. Our detachment is solely responsible for the assault on the east gate."

"Does the Captain really hate me that much?"

"Sergeant?"

"The Captain wants me to assault a thirty foot plus wall, defended by two guard towers, and do so with little to no support from the navy's cannonade."

Darroch didn't reply. He held his stare on Worth, showing no emotion.

"Aye, the Captain must be hating me that much," said Worth. He grinned before turning away from Darroch.

HMS *Worcester* fired the first shot of the assault preparation. The crack of the cannon forced the water fowl on the loch to take flight. Their arching path away from the castle stood in sharp contrast to the defenders within the thick stone walls of the fortress. A random cannon or two attempted to return fire, but each shot only subjected the position to intense counter fire. The guns within the fort fell silent.

On the water the cannonade continued with full intensity. Each ship positioned to engage part of the castle. In the stillness of the morning, cannon smoke hung in the air. It drifted slowly and obscured Eilean Donan as the bombardment continued. This masking of the fleet allowed the boats to position alongside the ships. The shouts of coxswains up to the crew on deck indicated that the loading for the assault had begun.

"Sergeant Worth, put them over the side," said Darroch. He pointed to the side away from the castle.

Worth's lips tightened when he nodded his acknowledgement to Darroch. Without a word, he waved the First Squad to the railing. One-by-one, the Marines scaled down the side and took their position in the boat. The Sergeant stepped in front of Darroch as he approached the rail.

"Sir, it's my place to take the first wave ashore. I would be honored to have the Captain in the second wave. That's the only way I know you'll get these knuckleheads to follow me in," said Worth. He pulled his belt somewhat higher around his waist.

"I know Sergeant Worth, but I wouldn't ask you to do anything I'm not willing to do. I'll take the first wave this time around."

Sergeant Worth looked down at the deck. He rubbed the back of his neck. Placing his arms akimbo, he asked, "Sir, this wouldn't have anything to do with a certain redhead and former cook on *Comet* would it?"

"You figured that out, did you," said Darroch smiling.

"Aye, sir. I'll bring the second wave ashore. Just don't be doing anything silly and getting yourself killed. It's too damn hard to get replacements in time of war. You know?"

"Sound tactical advice as always, Sergeant. Your concerns are noted for the record. I'll see you on the ramparts. Just don't shoot any red uniforms when you get there."

"Aye, sir. The thought never occurred to me." Worth watched as his Captain went hand-over-hand down the side. He whispered, "Good luck, sir."

Flame and iron continued to pound the castle as sailors pulled the boats near the fortress isle of Eilean Donan. Then as quickly as the bombardment started, silence fell upon the waters of Loch Duich. The long boats came aground one right after the other. Marines and sailors moved against the fortress walls. Only random musket shots attempted to deter their advance.

Corporal O'Keefe used his powerful frame to throw a grappling hook up and over the guard tower wall. He tested the rope and was about ready to start his ascent, when Darroch took the line from him.

"Follow me up once I reach the top. Your squad will take this tower and open the main gate," said Darroch.

O'Keefe could only nod, as he watched his boss climb upward. He motioned for the rest of the squad to get their grappling hooks up on the walls. When one of the attempts failed to reach the top of the wall, he walked over and took the line from the Marine. He cast the hook effortlessly up and over the wall.

"Like that, get it," he yelled. "Now get going. First Squad, let's go. I don't want to leave the Captain alone at the top. Move!"

Darroch rolled across the top of the wall and landed on his butt. The stone of the rampart bruised both his bottom and ego. He stood and drew this sword and pistol. He stepped over a dead Spaniard as he started down the walkway toward the tower door. His pace quickened. The tower door flew open and a soldier in an off-white uniform took a position defiantly in front of the Marine.

The Spaniard lifted his sword to the on-guard position. His trailing hand assumed a pose above his head. Darroch leveled his pistol and fired. The smoke cleared, and the defender remained untouched. He thought, *I missed. Marines don't miss. Shit, here he comes.*

The Spaniard lunged at Darroch. He beat parried the attack to the side. His opponent spun around and sliced overhead to force his blade from high to low at the Marine. Darroch lifted his sword upward parallel to his shoulders and intercepted the downward blow. The force of the attack caused him to step aside, unable to counter the attack with strength alone. The two exchanged rapid strikes, engaging their opponent's blade while looking for any sign of weakness. The Spaniard thrust low, retreated, and then quickly lunged forward with a horizontal head high thrust. Darroch ducked to the side, but not in time. The blade cut across the leather neck piece of his collar. The sword edge cut the leather, but it failed to penetrate to flesh. The Marine stepped into his attacker and pushed him back along the rampart.

Both combatants assumed on-guard positions. Eyes focused on each other with heads held slightly forward. Darroch could feel his breathing was rapid and uncontrolled. He loosened and then tightened his grip on the sword handle. He took a deep breath, it didn't slow his breathing. The Spaniard leaned forward and thrust toward Darroch's torso. The Marine dropped to his knee, spun low and sliced his blade across the inner thigh of his opponent. The Spaniard dropped his blade and rolled to the rampart grabbing his leg.

Corporal O'Keefe cleared the top of the wall in time to see the duel between his Captain and Spaniard end. When both his feet were secure on the wall, he unslung his musket.

"Would the Captain be needing any assistance, sir?" asked O'Keefe.

"No, you're a little late. Watch this one, would you?"

"Aye, sir."

Darroch looked around the castle while reloading his pistol. The walls were now topped with red and white uniforms from the fleet. Resistance had been lighter than thought. The rest of the First Squad now stood with him, victorious on the rampart.

"Corporal O'Keefe, let's get this gate open, shall we," said Darroch.

"Aye, sir. It would be a pleasure."

Darroch led the Marines down the tower stairwell. O'Keefe took several Marines and opened the gate. Sergeant Worth walked into the courtyard with head held high. The Marines flowed around him as they began searching the castle and rounding up any prisoners. He walked over toward his boss.

"Sergeant Worth, so glad you could join us," said Darroch.

"Aye, sir. Better to walk through the gate than drag these old bones over the wall. Did the Captain have fun scaling the walls?"

"Too much fun to be getting paid for it. The view up there is one of the benefits. Too bad you missed it."

"I'll pass, sir. Looks like we have things well in hand here. Perhaps the Captain should address that issue over there," said Worth. He pointed toward a hooded figure kneeling over two small white crosses in the courtyard.

Darroch squinted at the figure. He couldn't tell who it was, but he was sure it was a woman. He approached slowly, studying this person with each step. Yet, something about her was in fact very familiar. She heard his footsteps behind her and stood to face him. She cast back the hood, revealing long locks of black hair.

"Cynthia?" Darroch asked. His tone was welcoming and low.

She fell upon him sobbing. Her arms draped around the Marine, as if embracing the past to deny a dreadful future.

"William, you've come. Thank God, you've come," said Cynthia struggling to get the words out between her crying.

"Where is Annette?"

She looked up at him with bloodshot eyes. She shrugged her shoulders. "I don't know. They took her."

"Who took her?"

"I don't know, Spanish or Jacobite, I guess. They stormed the castle and they took her."

"Are you alright?"

"They killed my two children and Drake," said Cynthia pointing to the marked graves. "Then they raped me."

"Do you want to return to Portsmouth?'

"Yes."

"Do you need some time to gather your baggage?"

"No. A few papers and personal things perhaps, nothing more. I have nothing here, no baggage, no husband, and no family. Nothing. Just get me the hell out of this awful place. For the love of God William, get me home."

Chapter 12 Scottish Turf

The halls of Eilean Donan reverberated with the sound of barrels being rolled along beneath the ornate tapestries and paintings that adorned the walls. Marines and sailors pushed and pulled these bulky objects under the watchful eye of the HMS *Worcester* First Lieutenant. His experience in civil construction, prior to his entry into the Royal Navy, made him uniquely qualified to direct the project. Captain Darroch stood next to Captain Boyle, the pair watched the progress of the crew's efforts.

"Sir, do you think it wise to bring down the castle walls?" asked Darroch.

"My good Captain, this is one of those things I don't have to think about too much. I have orders from the Admiralty. I will defer the thinking to them on this," said Boyle. His posture stiffened. "The squadron is to prevent Eilean Donan from becoming a base of rebel operations, blockade the west coast, and support operations to put down this damn uprising. My First Lieutenant tells me he needs twenty-seven or so barrels of gunpowder to drop the walls. Should make for a fine show."

Darroch nodded. A messenger approached and saluted Captain Boyle.

"Sir, message from General Wightman," said the soldier. He bowed slightly forward as he handed the Captain the letter.

Boyle ran his thumb under the wax seal and popped the parchment open. Captain Darroch stared at his new boss, watching intently for any shift in mood as he read the correspondence. Boyle lowed the letter and tucked it into a pouch on his belt.

"Where is General Wightman located now?" asked Boyle.

"Sir, I left him in Inverness. He planned to move south and should be on the march by now."

"That confirms what the letter said." Turning to Darroch he added, "Marine, the general plans to engage the rabble that escaped our assault. Would you like to get in on that action?'

"Yes, sir," said Darroch. "The Captain must have read my mind. I still have a score to settle with these Spanish."

Turning back to the messenger, he said, "Let the General know we have received his letter and will comply with the intent to support his operations. Additionally, let him know I have a Marine Detachment of . . ." He looked over at Darroch. The Marine flashed ten fingers up three times. "With thirty men shadowing the rebel force that left Eilean Donan yesterday. They will maintain contact and provide information upon link-up. Any questions?"

"No, sir," said the messenger. He saluted and retreated down the corridor dodging casks of gunpowder that now lined selected points.

"Captain Darroch, don't let any personal vendettas interfere with your mission. You are to follow and report. Do not engage, except for self-defense. Is that clear?"

"Yes, sir. Very clear."

"One more thing Marine before I let you go. I hesitate to share this with you, but the war with Spain is widening. In April, yes, I know word travels slowly, the Duke of Berwick invaded the Western Basque districts. France is carrying the war to Spanish soil. You and your Marines will be needed for future operations, so don't do something foolish."

"Aye, aye, sir. Did the letter give any details on how the campaign in Spain is progressing?"

"Very limited reporting. It seems they have encountered light resistance, but the army is suffering from sickness. They wanted to know how we were doing at these latitudes. This just gives me a chance to write another report. Charming."

Darroch returned to the courtyard to find his Marines cleaning weapons, sleeping, and drinking something that resembled tea. He saw his counterpart from HMS *Worchester* and approached.

"How is Captain Boyle doing?" asked Riddell. "Are you done sucking up to my boss yet?"

Darroch frowned. "He got a change in orders. I've got to follow the Jacobite inland and report to the army marching out of Inverness. I find myself in the unfortunate position of having to ask a favor."

Riddell straightened up. He flashed a crooked smile, anticipating that rendering a favor would enhance his power when dealing with Captain Darroch. He crossed his arms over this chest.

"A favor, what would that be?"

Darroch signaled for Cynthia to join them. She walked over with her head held slightly forward and down. She stopped a few paces away from the Marines and curtsied. Standing up, she pulled her apron higher around her waist. Her coal black eyes focused on Captain Riddell. He returned the stare, unblinking, but kept an ear for what Darroch had to say.

"This is Cynthia, she has been stranded her by the unfortunate turn of events. Her husband and family were killed when the Jacobite took this castle. I'm looking to secure her passage back to Portsmouth," said Darroch.

"Portsmouth, I have no idea when *Worchester* will ply those waters."

"I know. However, *Comet* is due back in the yards to finish some work. If you could see her safely to my ship, I would be in your debt."

Riddell eyed the woman before him. He lowered his stare from her eyes, followed the curve of her neck down, until the roundness of her form dominated his consciousness. His lips parted in contemplation.

"Yes, Captain Darroch. I will take your charge and see her safely to *Comet*. We will settle this debt on our next encounter," said Riddell. He tipped his hat toward Cynthia and walked back toward the guard tower.

"Did you see the way he looked at me?" asked Cynthia.

"Cynthia, he is a gentleman. As long as he believes you are a lady, he will not make any unwarranted advances. I believe you know how to conduct yourself."

"I've had over a year of practice, Captain Darroch. I'll be as prim and proper as any of those tight tail ladies everyone wants to sip tea with, but no one will pillow," said Cynthia. She smiled for the first time since Darroch had seen her at Eilean Donan.

She moved back to the graves of her two children. Standing in the cool Scottish breeze, her dress carried on the wind sending a snapping sound to ring in her ears. Cynthia pulled her shawl higher across her shoulders. She stared at the freshly turned earth below her feet. The image of children at play, on the water, and at her and Drake's side rippled through her mind like the wavelets of a stone cast into the loch. She whispered something, crossed herself, and walked away. Darroch studied her exit, Cynthia never looked back. She never would allow herself the self-denigrating pleasure of such torment.

"Sir, the Detachment is ready to march," said Sergeant Worth.

"Aye, then. Move them out. I want to take the first halt on the hill overlooking the castle."

"Sir?"

"This place is going to be blown sky high this afternoon. I just think the Marines will enjoy the show."

"Aye, aye, sir," said Worth. He couldn't help but smile.

The sound of battle accoutrements bouncing against the side of the Marines spread along the column of men as they marched up hill. The length of their stride shortened as the steepness of the grade increased. The leather soles of those at the back of the column tended to slip on the ground broken by those marching ahead. Breathing within the formation became noticeably loud. The cool of the highland air refreshed them as they marched. Stopping at the top of the hill the Marines looked back on the castle below.

"Sergeant, I think we've been at sea too long if it takes only half a mile to wind the detachment," said Darroch. He dropped his pack to the ground as he sat.

"Aye, sir. It will not be long before the Marines gain their stride. How long does the Captain plan on staying here?"

"Until I see that damn place blown apart."

"It should be soon, sir. The last of the long boats has returned to the ships."

The grey of the clouds hung low on the ramparts of the castle. The water reflected the same monochromatic tones of grey as the sky. The black smoke from the main building grew in volume as it bellowed out of the windows, only to be carried quickly off by the ever-present wind. The low hum of the Marine conversations competed with the whistle of the wind providing the background noise of the scene.

This jumbled hum was replaced with the sudden crack of the first explosion. Well positioned barrels of gunpowder were ignited in turn, sending flame and smoke skyward. Silence fell on the Marines watching the carnage below. An occasional yell broke the thunder clap, as Marines randomly cheered at the destruction of the fortress they had fought to secure. The skyline of Eilean Donan changed from fine lines of pristine architecture to a jagged saw cut of broken stone and splintered beams. Debris were cast skyward and carried out away from the Island fortress. A large stone landed twenty feet behind Sergeant Worth.

"Sir, I think we might have been a little closer than we realized when we stopped," said Worth. His tone was unaccustomedly rapid.

Darroch swallowed deep and then nodded.

"Get them up, Sergeant Worth. We need to close on the band of Jacobite that left here a few days ago." Pointing to the wide swath of broken grass and ground, he added, "I don't think it will be that hard to track them across the bog."

"Aye, sir." Worth waved his hand to reform the column. Marines slowly stood to their feet and lifted packs across their backs. "Scouts out, let's go Marines, we've got an enemy ahead and the sea behind us. Couldn't ask for more."

Once again, the rhythm of the march found its own melody. Feet pounded against the ground, combat kit bounced against their sides, and the sloshing of soft ground underfoot pulled against their progress. Thirty Marines were on the move. What was ahead, remained a mystery. But between the weight of their pack, musket, and other kit, few in the column pondered the possibilities. The fatigue of the march now dominated all those in the column. All, that is, but one. Captain Darroch paused at the side of the trail, pulled his spyglass to full length, and scanned the rolling hills to their front.

*****

"Sir, scouts coming in," said Sergeant Worth. He pointed down the trail.

The figure of a lone Marine running at port arms was illuminated by the morning light. His sling bounced along as he double timed down the path. His red uniform stood out in sharp contrast to the earthen tones around him.

"What have you got?" asked Worth. Captain Darroch was adjacent, waiting to hear the reply.

"Sergeant, I've got 'me. Their setting up on five hills to our front. They're putting up a barricade across the road where if narrows against a spur from the high ground," said the Marine.

"How many?" asked Darroch, unable to keep silent at this point.

"Not sure, sir. I would guess at least one thousand."

"Any Spanish?"

"Yes, sir."

"How many?"

"Looks like about one in five are in Spanish colors. The rest are clansmen. Judging from the various tartans, could be four or five separate clans in the gap."

Sergeant Worth looked over at Captain Darroch. He tilted his head forward.

"Sir, you're not thinking of . . ." said Worth.

"Of course not. Let's develop as much information about the position as we can. Then, when we join forces with the Inverness garrison, we can work out a plan of attack. We can't be much more than ten miles from Eilean Donan," said Darroch.

"I make it a little more than that, but the Captain's point is well taken. Perhaps they just decided this was their best place to defend."

"The other factor is maybe they have spotted the garrison from Inverness. That would mean they are closer than we thought, and we don't have much time for reconnaissance."

"Orders, sir?"

"Look, you and I will climb up on the high ground over there," said Darroch pointing to his left. "Have the squad leaders rest and prepare the men while holding here. The trick will be getting around these clans and linking up with the northern force unseen. Not sure how, or if, we'll pull that off."

Sergeant Worth pointed at the scout. "You're now the Captain's runner. Go down to the Detachment and brief them to get ready. The Captain and I will be down shortly. Once you see they are making ready, take another Marine and see if you can locate a bypass around the barricade so we can linkup with the force from the north."

"Aye, aye, sir," rolled from the Marines' lips. He turned around and headed down the hill.

Captain Darroch couldn't help but notice the nautical terms, so far from the ocean, seemed a little out of place. The two Marines

221

worked their way up the side of the hill. Approaching the topographical crest of the hill, they both lowered to the ground and crawled forward. Darroch pulled his spyglass out once again to scan the area ahead.

"What do you see, captain?" whispered Worth.

"Well I have to give them credit. They picked a solid chokepoint to defend. Looks like we have the Spanish uniforms on the top front slope in the center. Based on their frontage, maybe two hundred. Below them, on the barricades, are the Jacobite Scots. I can't tell how many Scots; their damn open order is too hard to figure numbers. But we have another problem."

"What's that, sir?"

"I've got a dust cloud to the north."

"On the road?"

"Yes, indeed."

"That should be our government forces."

"I fear you're correct. We have to get our folks on the road now, if we're going to intercept them before they reach the barricade. Slide back."

The two of them reversed down the hill. With the hill between them and the Jacobite, they broke into a run. Fighting to maintain their balance on the wet grass, and given the slope of the hill, they quickly descended to the Marine position.

Sergeant Worth thought, *I'm getting too damn old to be running through the heather chasing raggedy ass Scotsmen.* He huffed and puffed as they closed on the other Marines.

Captain Darroch signaled his runner to join him. The Marines jogged over to his position and saluted.

"Did you find a way around the Jacobite barricade?" asked Darroch.

"Yes, sir. The draw on the right drops and goes all the way back to the north. It should intercept the road at some point."

"Did you send someone to check it out?"

"No, sir. Didn't have time. I thought—"

Darroch waved his hand to silence the Marine. He looked over at Sergeant Worth. His chest rose and fell taking in deep breaths as he tried to recover his wind from the sprint down the hill. The Sergeant was bent over and placed his hands on his knees. He didn't say anything, he knew the Captain would have to make the most important decision to date.

"Okay, we either sit out the fight or risk getting lost in the draw attempting to reconnect with the garrison from Inverness," said Darroch. He watched Worth nod but remain silent. The Sergeant looked down at the ground, avoiding eye contact.

"Sir, what should I tell the Detachment?" asked his runner.

"We move, and we move out, now. Let's get up the draw and see if we can contact our crew before the Jacobite find out we're here."

"Aye, sir."

The drainage through the draw had exposed many rocks and boulders in the now dry stream bed. The Marines stumbled and strained to make their way unseen to the north. Some Marines cursed as they fell forward. Bodies bumped into each other as the rate of march slowed, sped-up, and then ground to a halt only to resume on the run.

Captain Darroch reached behind to pull a Marine over a boulder, when he heard a voice above him.

"Halt, who goes there?"

"Captain Darroch, Royal Marine, from HMS *Comet*. I have scouting information on the Jacobite position just ahead."

"Up here, sir."

Darroch was lifted out of the draw by two of his Marines. Looking around he realized he was on the road about half a mile from the Jacobite barricade. He waved for the other Marines to join him on the road.

"Whom do I have the honor of addressing?" said Darroch.

"Sir, Subaltern Bastide, of Montague's Regiment. I'm sure my commander will want to know what you've learned of the enemy position."

The two officers moved up the column to find both General Wightman and the Regimental Commander on horseback. Darroch saluted the General.

"Sir, Captain Darroch reporting. I've—"

"Darroch, I'll be damned. My messenger said you would be joining us. Couldn't think of how that would happen. But here you are. What did you learn of the enemy, my good man?"

"The Jacobite have a barricade across the road. The Spanish are the only regulars in sight. They are holding the high ground in the center. The clans are blocking the low ground on each side," said Darroch. He had to force himself to speak slower than normal.

"I see," said Wightman. He signaled for his regimental commanders to join him. "Glad you got here when you did, Marine. We would have marched right in there amongst them. Would have been a pretty parade, but not much of a fight, I fear."

The commanders gathered around their general. Pointing toward the high ground Wightman spoke, "It would seem this Marine here has given us some very important information. I want to push on the clans in the low ground to the left and right of where the Spanish are defending. Those regulars will hold firm, but if we break the clans on the flanks, we should be able to carry the position. What say you, Clayton."

"Yes, sir. It will take the better part of the afternoon to get into position against their southern side. Once there, we'll take them, Sir," said Clayton. His horse stepped sideways and lifted up.

"Very good. Harrison and Montague, you'll press the other side. Where is my Mortar Battery commander?"

"Here, sir."

224

"Oh, good. You'll cover the whole of the line with fire. However, I don't want the Spanish to move. Pin them first and foremost, so the rest of the plan can develop. What say you?"

"Yes, sir."

The command group talked and discussed plans until three O'clock. The troops began to maneuver and align in their attack positions. The broken nature of the terrain made it difficult to dress the ranks with the degree of precision normally found on the drill fields of England. The Mortar Battery set up on the road. They could see the choke point ahead and aim as needed to engage the high ground, left flank, or right flank.

Captain Darroch looked at his watch, five O'clock. The first rounds from the mortar tubes arched upward toward the southern side of the barricade. The heavy thud of the impact, followed by the muffled thunder, announced the start of the pre-assault bombardment. White smoke rose from the impact. The haze hung in the late afternoon air. The breeze had long since settled down for the night. The crisp crack of the mortar tube sent more rounds arching high into the air. They impacted amid the center of the Jacobite right wing. A few screams followed. Those sounds served to acknowledge that those on the receiving end of the bombardment were unable to influence the traumatic events that surrounded them.

General Wightman arched his back a little taller in the saddle. Looking to his left, he waved his hand forward. The mortar fire now shifted to the high ground and north side of the barricade. The pounding sound of rounds impacting the ground reverberated in the narrows of the gap. Clayton acknowledged the General's signal and started his advance.

The British leveled their muskets and marched toward the rebel position. The cold steel of their bayonets led the tip of the formation. The men followed their officers who marched to their front with sword in hand, held straight up and down. The drums pounded out an unthinking cadence, as the men stepped in time to the beat. Perfect thirty-inch steps, sixty steps to the minute. Left, right, and left; forward moved the line of battle. A mass of red uniforms, linked by discipline and hours of practice, continued the attack. Their heads remained steady, not bouncing, as they glided forward.

Ahead of the British advance stood one hundred and fifty men of Clan Murray. This was the spot where the Marquess of Tullamarine had elected to make his stand. The men in tartan gripped a wide assortment of weapons. Muskets were held by most, but some were limited to edged weapons including long swords and the poleaxe. The spacing between the ranks was more random than their British counterparts. But the barricade to their front could hold sway, forgiving many of their inadequacies in the execution of the formalized style of European land warfare.

Muskets leveled across the top of the earth and logs piled before the Scotsmen. "Fire," rang out along the line as muskets discharged a wall of lead toward the British formation. Smoke blinded both sides from assessing the results of this musket fire. The sound of impact gave some sense of the ballistic result. A heavy thud resulted when a lead ball impacted flesh and the liquid rich material expanded and burst from the rapid attenuation of kinetic energy into the body. A metallic pinging sound indicated equipment had been struck. The deformation of combat kit, while often not fatal, could degrade an opponent's ability to fight. The yells or screams of men provided solid evidence that the victim was wounded, but not fatally. This could in fact be better than a kill, as now additional soldiers had to remove the wounded from the battlefield.

General Wightman scanned his left flank. His spyglass moved from right to left and back. Finally, he studied the mortar impacts landing among the Spanish on the hill top.

"I can't tell a bloody thing over there with Clayton," said Wightman.

"Give it a second, sir. Once the smoke clears—" Darroch stopped in the middle of his sentence.

A sudden burst of musket fire resonated between the hills.

"There, sir," said Darroch. He pointed to the red line of men stalled in front of the barricade. "They returned fire. They stopped the advance to exchange volleys."

"Damn it. Stop playing with the firing line and close," said Wightman. His comment only falling on Darroch's ears and not influencing the action.

Each side exchanged volleys yet again. Smoke lay as thick as freshly picked cotton, obscuring the battle along this key flank. The white veil was slow to surrender its secrets. The constant thumping of mortars harassed the Spanish and north side of the gap. The rattle of musket fire soon gave way to the shouts of men. Shouts of close combat. Screams echoed from the confines of the gap. The two sides were in melee now. Only one would command atop the barricade. The General stood in his stirrups forcing any bit of altitude he could muster to get a glimpse of the action. The uncertainty of the outcome made the General shrug his shoulders.

"What do you think, Marine?" said the General.

"There, sir. Look there," replied Darroch pointing to the southern flank.

Row after row of red uniforms rolled up and over the barricade. The glint of bayonet would flash for just a moment, as the troops pushed up and over this obstacle. The General sat in the saddle and slapped his knee.

"Clayton did it. He has dislodged that flank. Now the other side," said Wightman.

He looked back over his shoulder and signaled Harrison's and Monique's regiments forward on the right flank. The mortar battery now concentrated their fire on the high ground. The Spanish drew the whole of their attention. Rounds impacted on them with a slow but consistent cadence.

The two English regiments pushed forward. Captain Darroch looked through his spyglass trying to track the attack to his direct front. The lines of red snaked along the hill side paralleling the uneven nature of the ground. Rock outcroppings stood like small fortresses on the open slopes. The clansmen fired from concealed positions that offered solid cover from musket fire. They slowed or stopped the English advance to their front, as the rest of the battle line pushed forward. When they realized the enemy was behind them, they would break and run. These men would stream back up the hill, one or two at a time, to avoid capture. He could see sergeants at the back of the English formations use their pikes in a vain effort to keep the ranks aligned. Yet, the red coats pushed forward. Without reinforcements, those in tartan fell back.

The Spanish now stood alone atop the high ground. The disciplined defensive line of regular troops sustained a level of musket fire equal to the task of holding the attacking English at bay. Three times the soldiers in red formed one hundred yards downhill from the men in light grey. The marshal cadence of drums rose on the hilltop, as the English marched forward. Their posture was straight up, eyes unblinking, with muskets lowered forward. The pressure to stay shoulder-to-shoulder and in formation, removed the need for the troops to think as they neared the hostile position ahead. When the advancing ranks were fifty yards from the top, the line would burst like a late afternoon thunderstorm in summer. This deluge of lead, instead of water, thinned the ranks of red. Voices, coupled with confusion, stalled the upward push. Smoke obscured the British briefly, until the wind carried their protection away.

With the defenders now insight, the British returned fire. The rumble of muskets flowed down the line rippling in rapid succession as each weapon was discharged. Flame and smoke poured forth sending a twirling lead ball in a direction generally toward the opposing line. With the forward progress of the attack stalled on the steep slope, officers ordered the troops to withdraw. Wounded were pull back down the hill and out of the line of fire. Ranks were readdressed and tightened to replace the holes where once the living held sway. Flag signals flashed back and forth, their meaning soon apparent to the defenders on the high ground.

Mortar rounds impacted on, and near, the top of the hill. Shell fragments from these weapons scattered in all directions. Flesh offered little resistance as this hot iron cut through muscle in abrupt slices. Unlike the smooth cuts of meat offered at the wardroom table, these carvings were rough and uneven. This made closing the wound in the field very difficult. Blood flowed freely from the wounds inflicted by this distant weapon. Spanish officers glanced from left to right. The clans had taken to the hills, they were alone. Without artillery, they were unable to influence the action with firepower. Their attention was drawn back down the hill. Rows of men, clad in red, started toward them yet again. This bloody dance would continue to the rhythm of Mars. Rapid pounding echoed in the heart of those compelled to move into the maelstroms of hot lead and cold steel.

"Despots," was clearly heard across the narrows of the valley.

"Navel," followed quickly in cadence.

"Fuego," needed no interpretation as the muskets opened with clouds of smoke once again covering the hill side.

The English moved away from the heights. By late afternoon the men in red on the low ground had outflanked the enemy on the hill to their front. Captain Darroch watched through his spyglass as the Spanish retreated up the hill.

"The Spanish are pulling back, sir," said Darroch. He pointed with his spyglass fully extended in the direction of the high ground.

"Yes, so I see. Very good. We'll keep pressure on them. Let's see where this leads," said the General. The General pulled on the reins of his horse and spun him away. He started toward the swirling cluster of flags that marked Colonel Harrison's command post.

With sunrise, came the sight the English has been waiting to see. White flags waved from the hill. The Spanish, without clan support, decided they had enough. Darroch followed General Wightman up the hill to accept their surrender. He wrote in his notebook selected points of the battle. He was eager to record the details of this hard-fought victory. After discussions, signing a few documents, and the traditional marshal formalities of defeat, the Spanish stacked their muskets one last time and fell into a column. They were now prisoners of war, on a distant field of battle, far from home. Their eyes stared out beyond the horizon, unfocused, fearing the pending internment.

Captain Darroch walked along the line of prisoners. Not sure what he was looking for, his eyes darted from one man to the next. So many faces of strangers. Yet, in their uniforms and bearing, there was something familiar about these men. Their bearing would have passed on the finest drill fields of Europe. Their uniforms, while dirty and sweat soaked, were cut in the style known across the continent. Darroch froze. This Spaniard was known to him.

"Carlos, it has been a long time," said Darroch.

Carlos looked up. The fatigue in his eyes was evident in the early morning light. He stood and pulled the front of his uniform down.

"Captain Darroch, Royal Marines, I'll be damned. By what force of providence are you here on this battlefield so distant from your maritime home on *Comet*?

"I have been chasing after my Captain's former cook. She's a red head, last seen at Eilean Donan castle. Do you have any insight as to where she ended up?"

"If I knew, why would I tell you? Once my acquaintance, now my enemy. I think these are not the terms for exchanging information. Are they?"

Captain Darroch drove his shoe into Carlos' crotch with such force, he doubled over unable to breathe. The Marine grabbed his ear and squeezed as hard as he could. He lifted Carlos' head back up to look him directly in the eye. The twisted lines on Carlos' face reflected a new level of pain.

"Listen to me you worthless piece of bull dung, tell me where she is, or I'll use my dirk to slice the pain inflicted by my shoe clean off your disgusting body."

Carlos shook, he knew these were not idle words.

"Annette was taken by my Mistress back to Spain. She is being held hostage."

"How do you know her name?"

"My Mistress had me follow her here when *Comet* sailed from Spain. First to Portsmouth, and then here, to this god forsaken place."

"Who is your Mistress?"

"You would know her as the Lady Ernesta Rainerio of the Spanish Court."

"Why was she taken?"

"My Lady demands you come to take her place in exchange for her release."

"Oh, really? Where did they take Annette?"

"The plan was to take her to the dungeon at Fort Castro."

"In Vigo?"

"Yes. That was the plan. I can't tell you if that's what happened. I have not heard from Spain since the fighting moved here to Scotland."

"What do you know of the Fort?"

"Nothing, I promise. I was never cast into that awful place. But this I do know, no one that enters the dungeon there ever comes out. I fear you will have to negotiate with Ernesta for her release."

Darroch threw him back to the ground. Carlos looked down avoiding eye contact.

"Sir, do you want to pull this one out for special treatment?" said the guard.

"No, he'll go into interment with the rest. Have you seen the general?"

The guard pointed down the hill. Darroch turned his back on Carlos and started down the hill. Carlos yelled after him, but his words were not audible. Darroch didn't look back but continued on his course. Approaching the general he saluted.

"Well Captain Darroch, I must thank you for the information you provided. I think we have turned back the Spanish support for the rebellion. Subduing the clans will, as always, take some time but we'll bring them back in the fold eventually. We always do."

"Yes, sir. I need to get my Marines back to the ship. Request, you cut us back to HMS *Comet*."

"Of course, I detach you immediately for duties to be assigned by the Commanding Officer of HMS *Comet*. Carry on Captain Darroch. Good luck, wherever this crazy war may take you."

Darroch started down the hill to join the Marines below. The steep grade of the slope pulled each step with increased force that rippled through his body as he walked. He could feel the tension in his frame build. His fist tightened around the webbing of his backpack. His mind reflected on Carlos's words, *no one ever comes out of the Fort Castro dungeon. Damn it. We'll just have to see about that. Ernesta, how can such evil lay below beauty that is so commanding?*

Chapter 13 Dungeon's Depths

The full warmth of the summer sun returned to Vigo. Donkeys stood motionless in the street. Their tails fell limp behind them unable to challenge the buzzing of flies that circled around them in search of fluids. The afternoon siesta stretched well beyond the noon hour. Animals and man alike drifted to any shade that cast its cooling powers across the streets and alleyways of the city. Flowers that yesterday stood bright and tall, found their pedals wrinkled and withered. The blue shutters of upper story windows stood wide open, desperate to capture any faint breeze that was cast their way.

Ernesta sat in her favorite wicker chair, fanning her body with the flat of her fan. Although she was wearing only a light cotton dressing gown, the heat built around her. Looking out her window, she tracked the heat waves rising above the red tile roofs in uneven wavy lines that oscillated in time with each other. They made the trees in the distance appear to dance as their distorted images moved side-to-side. Small droplets of perspiration formed on her brow and arms. However, it didn't pool into drops large enough to fall along her cheeks or neck. She stood when Pili entered the room.

"Pili, it's time to visit the dungeon, help me get dressed," said Ernesta. Her voice rang with the air of aloofness common to ladies at court.

"Yes, my lady," said Pili. "Would my lady be wearing flats or heels today?"

"Heels, of course. We mustn't let the dress drag in the mud of the dungeon. I choose to stay above the muck."

Pili helped guide her silk stockings into position and tie them emplace with a ribbon. The shoes followed and Ernesta did a quick pivot in front of the mirror. A smile crossed her face.

Moving over to Ernesta's dresser draw, Pili pulled a corset from its resting place. She flexed the whale bone lined garment back and forth and loosened the laces that joined the two panels. Ernesta lifted her arms away from her sides. Pili slid the corset around her mistress and waited for her to fasten the front. Ernesta held the front while Pili worked to tighten and smooth the lacing. Then alternating top to bottom, and back, Pili worked the laces and tightened them until she reached the center.

"Tighter," said Ernesta. "We want to look royal for our very special house guest." She giggled at her own joke.

Pili let out a shallow sigh. Wrapping the lacing around her hand, she lifted a knee into the small of Ernesta's back and pulled. Ernesta wiggled as the full effect of the garment's constricting design engaged around her. She studied her figure in the mirror. She pushed her hands along the narrow smooth contours of her figure.

"Yes, that's better. Let's see Annette compete with this, shall we?" She once again spun around in front of the mirror. Ernesta paused to study the manner in which the corset accented the roundness of her bottom. Nodding, she said, "What man could resist that?"

Pili patted her behind, and said, "Yes, very nice. Now let's add a bumper for more shape, shall we?'

Before Ernesta could reply, Pili hung the padding around her and tied it in front. The dress followed and was lowered over the undergarments. The result was a tight waist, accented with a roundness that flared away from her hips. The low cut of the front allowed the dark grey of the dress to highlight her ivory white skin. Pili stood behind her patron and tied a black choker in position around her neck. The lines of this accessory framed her face and the efforts Pili had made to complete her hair and makeup before the dressing began.

Pili stepped back to admire her handy work. A warmth overtook her when Ernesta smiled at the reflection in the mirror.

Her lady was pleased with the result, and she had made the transformation possible.

"Something else, Pili. I need just a little more. What would you recommend? Jewels, perhaps?" said Ernesta. Her tone was reflective and soft.

"No, my lady. Overdone for the darkness of the dungeon. You want to blend into the dim recesses of that place. I would recommend a head scarf."

"A common head scarf?"

"Not common, my lady. Nothing you do is common. This one would do nicely."

Pili lifted a finely crafted black piece of cloth. The wide nature of the stiches made the fabric appear transparent. Its dark color fell across the white of Ernesta's skin and blended with the dark grey of her dress. The pale features of her face stood out against the darkness around her.

"Not common at all," said Ernesta.

The two women headed out of the hacienda toward Fort Carlos. Ernesta's heels clicked along the cobble stones, while Pili's leather soles whispered as they scuffed across the smooth rocks. The two guards exchanged glances as the women approached.

"We don't get many women visitors, do we," said the Corporal of the Guard.

"Hell, we don't get many visitors at all," replied his counterpart.

Ernesta paused at the guard shack. She held up a letter from the Fort Castro Commander.

"I'm here to see Annette Armtrove, the prisoner taken in Scotland," said Ernesta.

The Corporal took the document and scanned down its length. He looked at Ernesta and then over to Pili. Returning the letter, he said, "Do both of you wish to see the prisoner?'

"Yes," said Ernesta. Her tone crisp and direct.

The Corporal lifted a set of keys on a large brass ring. They made a metallic clinking sound as he picked them up. He pointed down the dark passageway.

"Private, I'll show these two ladies the prisoner. You hold here," said the Corporal.

The three of them started down the passageway. The private locked eyes on the back of Ernesta as she went by. He was enchanted by the sway of her hips, a sight not often seen in the stone-cold confines of the dungeon.

He thought, *now that is a sight for the lonely. One would like to ride that for pleasure's sake.* He bit down on his glove. Shaking his head, he assumed the position of attention and redirected his focus to the duties of the guard.

Annette sat in the confines of her cell. The heat of the day failed to penetrate the lower levels of the dungeon. With no windows to know the time of day, light was limited to the torches carried by the guards as they made their rounds. The wet of the dirt floor seeped through her dress adding to her discomfort. The only sounds that emanated from the other side of her iron door were the constant coughing of prisoners and an occasional scream of agony. No one could long occupy that dim, damp, and dour environment, without descending into the depths of depression. The verbal outburst was the only release a prisoner could control, when freedom was held under lock and key.

She wasn't sure in the darkness, but Annette had calculated that her cell must have been about ten feet by ten feet in size. She had a chamber pot to defecate in at one corner. On the other side of the cell, was a small layer of straw to sleep on. One blanket, still dirty from the filth of the last occupant, provided the only shield against the ever-present chill. The smell of her own feces and unwashed body provided a constant assault to her sense of smell.

Annette struggled to stand. The chains that constrained her on the day of her capture, remained locked. The weight of this iron, coupled with their rather short length, prevented her from standing fully erect. The constant pull of her shoulders inward made any movement painful. The expression on her face tightened as Annette started her daily routine.

She counted the steps down one side of her cell. One, two, three, four, and five. Turn, and one, two, three, four, and five. The clinking sounds of chain echo up from under her dress as she turned to reverse the truncated route. The sound of her breathing dominated the cell walls. She could hear Midshipman Rutwell's voice in her imagination, "Again, yet again." She continued to make her way around the cell. As she forced herself to walk in this small space, Annette thought, *I've got to keep moving. I can't let these bastards win. I will not idle away in this hole in the ground. Movement is the key. Keep moving, Annette.*

Annette lost track of the number of trips she had completed in the confines of her cell. She sat down on the straw. Leaning back against the cold stone walls, she could feel the moisture dampen her garment. She ran her hand down the side of her body. It bumped along the ribs that were now pronounced and stuck out from her side. The softness of her form had once commanded men to stare and long to touch her feminine shape. Annette's dirty skin barely covered the hardness of her skeleton.

Hunger tugged constantly on her consciousness. The dull pain pulled her stomach tight. It felt like a stick poking her from the inside out. Always there, never leaving. Annette ran her hand across her stomach and rocked for a moment to ease the pull of gripping desperation. She waited in silence for the highlight of her day. A flickering light in the hallway outside her door, announced her daily meal was just on the other side.

The door opened. The guard didn't say a word. He pulled the chamber pot from the corner and emptied it in a container he pulled down the hall. After returning the pot, he slid a tray of food toward Annette. He hovered over her for just a moment. She took no notice of his lustful stare. It was difficult for Annette to think anyone would take notice of her in this emaciated condition. He turned and continued on his rounds. The sound of iron slamming home, indicated that the bolt was once again secure, and Annette remained trapped.

She pulled the plate close in the darkness. Annette could tell it was a meat sauce spread on rice. The bread pulsated when she picked it up. She thought, *weevils perhaps? I don't care, I'm eating them as well. Cold food, cold floor, cold walls, and no human contact. Cold.* She lifted the cup and smelled the contents. *Great, stale water. How can you mess up water?* She forced herself to swallow the fluid and wash down the disgusting food scraps that the Spanish tried to pass off as a meal.

Annette could feel her stomach rumble, like a drum pounding out a rapid beat. She doubled over on the floor and let the pain wash over her. Dragging her chains, she crawled over to the chamber pot. Using her sense of touch, she guided the pot below her chin. Her stomach rejected the contents she had forced down. Vomiting into the pot forced her to taste again the foul substances, yet again doubling the torment of the meal. She wiped the residue from her mouth on the bottom of her dress.

The torch light appeared again in the hallway. Annette slid back across the floor to the straw of her sleeping area. She sat on the blanket to gain some measure of insulation from the cold stone floor.

"She's in this cell, my lady," said the Corporal.

The door swung open. Annette had to squint to help her eyes adjust to the brightness of the torch light. She could see three people enter her cell. Crowded for a ten by ten foot space. As her eyes focused, she could tell two of them were women. The Guard handed the torch to Ernesta. She moved closer to Annette, the light now illuminating both women.

Pili had never seen these two together, and now in the dull light of the cell her eyes flashed back and forth between her Mistress and Annette. The contrast was striking. One was well fed and clothed in the finest fashions. Her bearing upright, noble, and clean. The other was crunched over in the dirt, filthy, and dressed in aging clothes on the edge of becoming rags. However, for all the obvious differences, something appeared to link the two women. Both were lean and athletic. The auburn main atop their heads each reflected the torch light with the same radiance. Their facial structures were similar. Pili blinked twice as she studied these two. Her mouth fell open, but she remained silent.

"Unchain her," said Ernesta. She motioned the Corporal forward.

The guard pushed the various keys around the brass loop of the ring. They clinked into place as they fell from the top of the arch to the bottom. He tried one key to unshackle her wrists. It was the wrong one. He flipped through several more and tried again. He twisted the lock, jiggled the key, and twisted again. It opened. The heavy bar fell to the floor. Annette was able to roll her shoulders back for the first time in weeks.

"Now the leg irons," said Ernesta.

"Could you lift your dress a little," said the Corporal.

Annette pulled her hem above the leg irons. The guard repeated the process, trying several keys before at last her feet were unencumbered. Picking up the shackles, the Corporal made his way out of the cell. He stood at the door eager to see how this dialogue would unfold.

"So, you have survived your stay so far. I hope none of my guards has found their way beneath your dress, my dear," said Ernesta. Her tone was sarcastic. She smiled when Annette shook her head in the negative. "It would seem Captain Darroch has no interest in finding his way there as well. He has not made any advance on your behalf. Until he does so, you will stay here."

"He'll come. I hope for your sake you're gone before he arrives. He will not take kindly to the torment you have put me through," said Annette. Her voice was soft but firm.

"Oh, my dear. I don't think he will be reaching these shores any time soon. Spain just won a fabulous victory in Sicily. It seems your Austrian Count Cluade Florimond de Mercy was roundly defeated at Francavilla. Your allies attacked us in three columns. They fell upon the city three times. Each attack was turned away. While your army did gain some advantage on the other flank, I fear our artillery inflicted such damage, they were forced to withdraw. England is losing this war and will suffer, as you have suffered.

"No, William will come for me."

"Sorry my dear, but he has already left you behind. I have his child," said Ernesta. She turned toward Pili. "Isn't that right?"

"Yes, Mistress. He is a year and a half old this month," said Pili in a low tone.

Annette was running the math in her head. *Eighteen months, plus nine, would be twenty-seven months ago. That would be –.*

"That's right, he was unfaithful to you on his first visit to Vigo. My guess is it was not his last. You can't possibly think he will risk himself to get you out of here," said Ernesta. The volume of her voice was increasing.

"I don't believe you," snapped Annette.

"Believe what you want, bitch. You're nothing more than a fun ride on a rough road. William loves me. He told me so, two years ago. He would be in my bed right now if it weren't for this damn war."

Annette remained silent. She didn't doubt William's affections, but it was clear any statement she made would only be thrown back at her. Her green eyes, now burning with hate, locked on Ernesta.

Lady Rainerio couldn't hold that gaze. She handed the torch to Pili and moved next to Annette. The back of her hand flew across Annette's cheek, forcing her head to snap away. The Corporal's shoulders cringed when he heard the slap.

"Don't you ever look at me like that, bitch. I'm the Lady Ernesta Rainerio of Vigo. Council to the Queen and member of the Royal Court at Madrid. The ruling family values my guidance, and I would not be looking so indignant at me or my handmaiden. Just be glad I haven't opened you up as a play thing for the guards. I'm sure at least one of them might find you modestly amusing."

Annette held her gaze downward, avoiding eye contact. She lightly rubbed the side of her face. She made sure not to nod or otherwise show any sign of weakness.

"Annette this is your life now. Until William is at my side you will be here. My advice is for you to make the most of it. If you're a good girl, we shall not chain you again. But I think you know, one misstep or insult, and I'll place you back in irons so fast you won't know what the hell happened," said Ernesta.

Ernesta lifted each side of her dress and spun around on her heels to exit. She paused at the iron cell door. Looking down at Annette, she smiled. The Corporal moved forward and took hold of the door.

"Is that all, my lady?" he asked.

"Yes, that will do for now. I plan on a weekly visit, so make sure all your guards understand my special instructions for this one."

"Yes, madam. Leave the redhead alone or face a punishment that is both painful and permanent. It didn't take much to read between the lines on that one, my lady."

He pushed against the full weight of the door to ease it shut. It creaked on rusty hinges as it slammed home. The tone sent a shiver down Annette's spine. The bolt slid home with a distinctive thud. The sound of keys bouncing off each other, sounded like chimes in the wind. The click of the lock being secured ended the visit between these two women. The dim of the dungeon returned as the limited light of the torch made its way down the corridor.

Annette sat alone in the dark once more. The tingling in her face was a reminder of the slap delivered by the back of Ernesta's hand. She tried to sob, but her eyes wouldn't water. Taking a deep breath, Annette looked up into the dark of the ceiling. Her mind raced, *William, stay distant. Nothing good can result from your coming here. That woman will never release me, I'm seen as too much of a threat to her possession of your soul.*

*****

"Welcome back aboard, Captain Darroch. The ship has not been the same without you lobsters about on deck," said Bosun McKay. He pointed aft and added, "I believe the merchandise you ordered is in your stateroom."

"Merchandise?"

"Well, if you don't know, a surprise then," said McKay smiling. He pulled his pipe from his pocket to end the conversation and not give away too much.

William looked around the main deck. He saw Sergeant Worth with a small group of Marines near the main mast. He walked over to their location. His stride was purposeful and deliberate. The Marines stood on his approach and the Sergeant saluted.

"Good morning, sir. What can I be helping the Captain with now that we are all back aboard *Comet*?" said Sergeant Worth. His salute was crisp and did not waiver until his boss returned the greeting.

"Sergeant Worth, I see the Marines will need a little reminder on shipboard protocol. Please ensure the gear is stowed, and the berthing area is ready for sea," said Darroch.

"Aye, aye, sir. Where shall I tell the Marines we be going, sir?"

"Portsmouth. We are leaving the blockade and going back to finish our yard work."

Sergeant Worth closed the discussion with another salute. He eased about and pulled the advanced party of the embarking

Marines together. He spoke in a low voice that the Captain couldn't discern. Given the amount of activity by the men in red, his instructions must have been effective.

William left them in his wake and returned to his stateroom. He checked the door handle, more out of force of habit, than any conscious decision. He was surprised when the knob turned freely. He pushed open the door and got a bigger surprise. His bed was occupied. The long black hair that flowed from under the covers could only belong to one person.

"Cynthia, I see our good friend Captain Riddell was true to his word and got you back to *Comet*."

Cynthia tossed back the covers and cast her legs over the edge of the bunk. Her dressing gown was untied at the top, it fell to one side of her body exposing the roundness of her shoulder. The black locks of her hair hung on either side of her face, accenting the olive tone of her skin. Her mouth opened into a wide yawn, as she wiped the sleep from her eyes.

"Nice digs, William. Thank you for putting me up for the return voyage," said Cynthia. Her mind was beginning to engage now that the blood was pulsing through her veins.

"I trust Captain Riddell treated you well?"

"Well, yes. It is amazing the difference in how folks treat you when they think you're from the ruling elite. I never had to open a door. They stumbled over themselves to get me in your stateroom. I found it all a little too stiff and formal. Not one of those gentlemen even attempted to put a hand on me. I had to inspect my reflection in the mirror to ensure I hadn't grown a wart on my nose or something. It was almost boring, actually."

William softly laughed at this comment. He fell silent when Cynthia stood in the confines of his cabin and pressed her half naked body against him.

"You know, William . . . I've always wondered what it would be like if you and I—"

"Cynthia," said William. His pitch elevated as he drew out her name longer than normal speech would require.

"William," replied Cynthia using the same octave and tone.

She reached her hand under the strap of his backpack and pushed it aside. It settled to the deck with a thud. Lowering her forehead Cynthia stared from under her brow and locked the dark pools of her eyes on the Marine. His blue eyes returned the stare. William was frozen, unsure as to how to respond. Her hand traveled down the expanse of his chest to wrestle with the locking device of his belt. She tugged on the belt until the latch popped free and the belt joined his pack. Looking down below his waist, Cynthia smiled as she noted his reaction to her advance.

"You know, William, I've always wanted to get you alone. Away from the prying eyes of Annette. Now, it is just the two of us. I know from our distant dance, you have wondered as well. What if? You and I, alone but together. Free to do as we please. No commitment or purpose, just two souls exploring all passion has to offer. Now, here we are. Annette need never know. I promise you, I'll never share what happens here with anyone."

Cynthia crossed her hand over her chest. Then she lowered the back of her hand down William's stomach to entice and arouse the most primitive instincts within him. The pressure against her hand indicated in this she was successful.

"Cynthia, bless you, but I fear I would know. I would have to carry that secret. It is a burden I'm unable to tote. You know from our past, I hold you above all others at the Red Fox Inn. Perhaps, someday this is meant to be, but not today. I have to find a way to get Annette away from those damn Spanish. I need your help to do it," said William. His tone softened as he spoke.

Leaning his cheek against the side of Cynthia's face, he let out a long breath. She lifted her hands from his waist and pulled them around his neck. Her lips aligned next to his ear.

"Then kiss me deep. Give me a sensation to remember this moment. If you can let me go, I'll stand as a second to Annette.

I'll do so willingly, and in anticipation," said Cynthia in a low whisper.

William slid his lips atop hers. He found her mouth open and receptive to the thrust of his tongue. They engaged in a long, wet, kiss. Both of them were unaware of their surroundings as these moist body parts pressed against each other finding pleasure in the exchange. This peaceful interlude stood in sharp contrast to the violence they had each witnessed. The duration of this passion would have continued, but a light rapping on the door broke the moment.

They didn't know how long the knocking had been going on, but they separated, each holding eye contact. Cynthia reached for a shawl and drew it up over her shoulders. William pulled on the front of his coat straightening his uniform.

"Yes, what is it?" said William in his best military voice.

"Sir, Petty Officer Burgess. The Captain would like to see you."

"Thank you, Petty Officer. Please inform the Captain I will be right with him."

"Aye, sir."

William looked back at Cynthia. She shrugged her shoulders and smiled.

"Thank you, for the moment. This is how I want to remember you. When we both explored the possibilities," said Cynthia. Her tone was reflective. "I was serious, if we can't get Annette back, I'm here for you. You must know that."

"I've always known that," said William. A smile returned to his face.

Willian stepped out of the stateroom and departed down the passageway. The clip-clop of his wooden soles on the deck grew faint as Cynthia listened to his departure. She lay back on the bed and stared up at the beams that ran athwart ships in the stateroom overhead. She thought, *he wants me. He has always wanted me. God, to have his touch, if only for a moment, is to know what passion's potential can bring. How can I work to free Annette, when failure to rescue her will fulfill my deepest desires? He must know I love him and have since our first dance at the Red Fox Inn. That seems like such a long time ago, and yet I know the day, the dress I wore, and the color of his eyes when first they locked on me. Why is this so? Perhaps some desires are best locked away, held distant, and kept hidden from our daily intercourse. Perhaps, so.*

Chapter 14 The Bastard

"Come on William, you can do it," said Ernesta facing the child and Pili. Her voice was high pitched and singsong in its tone. She sat on the floor ten steps distant.

The child's eyes flashed toward Ernesta. His response to her voice was immediate. He stretched out one hand in her direction but held a firm grip on Pili's coat sleeve. A small stagger step toward her ladyship, but he did not release hold of his mother.

"Come on, then," Ernesta continued. Her smile was welcoming. The fingers on her outstretched arms curled toward her, as if to pull the child across the tile floor of the hacienda.

William released his trailing hand from his mother's arm. He wobbled on his own struggling to stand. He weaved toward Ernesta and then back toward Pili, before straitening up. He looked back at Pili, then toward Ernesta. The giggling that flowed from his lips made both the women chuckle. He took a few steps toward Ernesta, leaning forward in her direction, he accelerated. Then William slowed and straightened up again. He was about half way between the two ladies. He looked once again back at Pili. He mimicked her chuckling.

Turning back toward Ernesta, he raised his arms chest high on each side of his small squatty body. His weaving steadied. William's bare feet slapped along the tile floor, as he continued to her ladyship. His cheeks tightened on approaching the end of his journey. He fell into Ernesta's lap and gazed up at her.

"Momma," said William in the stuttered rhythm only toddlers command.

Ernesta's eyes widened. She hugged the child and looked over at Pili.

"Did you hear that?" Ernesta said. "He spoke his first word."

Pili eyes tightened on Ernesta. Her giggling halted abruptly.

"I heard," she said. "He should have said that to me. I am, after all, his mother."

"Oh, my dear, let's not get too testy here. Think about what is best for the child. With him, I can secure Captain Darroch. He could have a proper home with both a father and a mother. He wouldn't have to be a bastard child, cast out by the church. What could you possibly offer?"

"I'm his mother!" Pili explained. Her voice elevated for the first time to her mistress.

"Only because I sent you to Captain Darroch's bed. He only slept with you because he thought Ernesta had joined him in the cool of that night. His body may have contacted yours, but his mind was holding my image. I'm the one in his thoughts. My figure is etched in the deepest parts of his subconscious. When he calls out to fulfill the lustful yearning of his passion, it is Ernesta that plays forth from his lips . . . not Pili."

"You may well capture the mind of that Marine. But know this, when he whispered grateful words in the depths of our embrace, his body was enjoying my moistness, touch, and smell. His ears were held captive by my moans of pleasure and shortness of breath. You can never love him in that manner, and you can never have my child."

Ernesta stood holding young William away from Pili. Her bare shoulder pointing at her servant as if to check any advance. She noticed Pili's chest rise and fall more rapidly than only a moment before.

"You seem upset, my dear," said Ernesta, in a cavalier voice devoid of emotion.

Pili exhaled through her teeth, now snarling at her lady. The guttural noise that spit from behind her teeth was not a growl, but it communicated her displeasure none the less.

"My child, if you please, my Lady," said Pili. She held out her arms to receive the child.

"I please not. You are to go to your room and not emerge until you can conduct yourself in a more appropriate manner."

Pili didn't move. Her eyes widened, as her reach remained extended toward Ernesta.

"Do I need to call the guard?"

Pili lowered her arms. She bowed forward slightly, and said, "No, my Lady. The guard will not be necessary. But you know in your heart . . . the child is mine. William is my flesh and blood, and all the fantasizing of families yet to be will not change that. As long as I can breathe, I will never surrender my right as a mother to claim him."

"As long as you can breathe, an interesting choice of words my dear. Words I would not throw about foolishly. You serve me. You will always serve me, until such time as I determine otherwise. That is the way of things, and you damn well know it to be so."

Pili turned away from her Lady. She took a few steps toward the door, when her child's voice rang in her ears.

"Momma," said William.

Pili looked over her shoulder to find the child gazing, unblinking, up at Ernesta. Her Lady softly touched him on the lips. Wiggling her finger across his lips, she made soft cooing sounds. The child smiled and giggled. Ernesta looked over at Pili and gave a slanted smile. Pili turned away. Lifting her dress on each side, she hurried down the corridor. Her sobs echoed above the sound of her footsteps on the tile.

"Don't worry, little one," said Ernesta in a soft whisper. "Mommy will never let the mean servant lady do any harm to you. Your father will join us soon, and we'll all be one big family. He will teach you to ride, and hunt, and how to handle a sword. Your place among the ruling elite of Spain is secure. The minstrels will sing songs about your exploits on both sides of the Atlantic. That is your destiny, and no one shall stand between what is supposed to be and this path ahead."

Ernesta looked down the hallway to ensure Pili had done as instructed. She swayed from side to side with the child cradled in her arms. William rested comfortably against her bosom. His eyes slowly fell shut.

The rhythmic sway of her frame continued, as she thought, *as long as she has a breath. Well that can be truncated on my command. Before Captain Darroch arrives, she will have to go. But who, and how? These are things best left to those that are skilled in such matters. However, they would have to secure such an action in silence."*

Ernesta lowered the sleeping child into his crib. She moved over to the door.

"Guard," she said. Her tone was whisper soft.

"Yes, my Lady," replied the guard in an equally soft tone.

"Send for Ildefonso Tacito."

"Are you sure, my Lady?" said the guard. His eyes widened on the mention of Ildefonso's name.

Silence filled the space between. It was clear Ernesta was rethinking her comment. She nodded.

"Yes, I'm sure. Your concern is appreciated, but the task I have for him is well beyond what I can ask of any of my Household Guard. It has nothing to do with your capabilities, but then, I think you know that."

"Yes, my Lady," said the Guard. He started to turn away but paused. Looking back, he said, "Have I ever questioned my Lady in the past?"

"No, can't say as if I ever recall such a comment," said Ernesta. Her lips tightened. She thought, *"Really, now what? I've had enough opposition to my plans today."*

"Your guard will always stand with you, my Lady. But to bring Ildefonso into this house, is to invite all manner of treachery and cost. I fear the price he may extract, will exceed what you and your father can bare," said the guard. He avoided making eye contact as he spoke.

"Thank you for your concern. You have always served me well, and I would expect that to be so in the future. As for cost, on some matters . . . cost is not a concern. This happens to be one of those affairs. We shall speak of it no more. If I find you have discussed this matter with my father, I will be unable to gracefully return the loyalty you have extended now and in the past."

The guard nodded and made a rapid exit from her chamber.

Her mind wandered, *Carlos was good. A true champion of the court. Eldefonso is better. He is an assassin of the finest measure. Swift, sure, and unflinching, he'll dispose of Pili and bend William's father to my will. His reputation with the female courtiers, makes me blush just thinking of it. Yes, Eldefonso, he is just what I need to complete my plan.*

*****

The wind held steady from the northeast. *Comet* rolled with the swell against the constant whine of the wind through the rigging. It was mere background noise at this point of the cruise. Each sailor on deck knew from the direction of the sun, *Comet* was heading home. Portsmouth was only days ahead. The prospects of the bumboats coming along side at anchor with ready and willing women made many of the men smile. Perhaps, some old acquaintances would be renewed, and other new ones formed.

Bosun McKay roamed the deck with a scowl fouler than his normal truculent mood. He knew what the sailors were thinking, and he had been around long enough to appreciate the danger inherent in not manning your station with the keenest of mind and attention to duty. Midshipman Rutwell saw the temperament of McKay and let his curiosity get the better of his judgement.

"Is something the matter, Bosun?" asked Rutwell. His tone was too fresh for the state of sea that tossed the crew about.

"I hate this part of the voyage, Midshipman Rutwell. The men are all distracted and bad things inevitably happen."

"Even when only a few days out of port?"

"Especially when only a few days out of port. Most of these lads can only think about the pleasure of those damn Bumboat women. They have saved their pay, and these whores are only too happy to help them part from their coinage."

"Isn't that a transaction as old as men at sea? At least that's what I've been told."

"Aye, that be true. I'm less worried about the exchange, than I am about the lack of attention these sailors are paying to their duties. Especially, those that head aloft. I've seen more than one lad fall from the tops not more than a day away from port. The impact on deck, will split open a skull like a melon. That's why I always call these knuckleheads 'Skulls.' I would hope they pay a little more attention to the fragile orb atop their shoulders than to the distractions from their duty. I'll be needing your help Mister Rutwell, if we're to get all these lads home to Portsmouth."

"How so?"

"When you see me point to a lad, that means he is slacking off. You need to call him out, and I'll cane him across his backside. It only takes a few of those to keep everyone's attention. You'll see."

"Why can't you just give him a good whack?"

"Sir, only an officer can dish-out corporal punishment. As a midshipman, that's clearly in your power. I fear too many a Bosun in the past has placed hands on lads that didn't deserve such treatment. But, with you and me working together, we'll get this crew home, sir."

Midshipman Rutwell nodded. This alliance drew a smile from the Bosun. Both men walked the deck paying increased attention to any sailor not attending to his task with the appropriate sense of urgency or rigor.

In the great cabin, Captain Calder studied the papers before him. Lieutenants Martino and Luarant sat in silence watching their boss. They each sat with their backs straight and arms folded on the felt covered table top. Calder lowered the parchment and looked over the top of his spectacles.

"I fear we are at an impasse, gentlemen. These are the only two candidates you feel confident to bring forward for the lieutenant's exam?" said Calder, his tone was rigid.

They both nodded.

"I see. Well, they are both good chaps and *Comet* will be hard pressed to replace them should they pass the exam and be commissioned as Royal Navy lieutenants. I think you both know, I can only submit one name for consideration. Given this is time of war, I'm sure the lad will be picked up and reassigned once the results are known."

Martino and Luarant exchanged brief stares. The Captain cleared his throat.

"Let's see, Lieutenant Luarant, you are advocating for Mister Rutwell correct?"

"Yes, sir."

"And Lieutenant Martino, you are in turn advocating for Mister Dugins, is that correct?"

"Yes, sir."

"So, Lieutenant Laurant, tell me why I should risk my professional reputation placing the young Mister Rutwell up for advancement?"

"Sir, Midshipman Rutwell has demonstrated both a willingness, and ability, to learn the ship and her crew. Given we are at war, sir, his prowess with the saber has proven itself in combat. His willingness to lead from the front, commands the highest respect from the men. I have watched him in our boarding actions kill in close combat with a degree of precision few of his years could muster. His seamanship is first rate. He took us into Brest, anchoring the ship in position. He never sleeps or dodges duty when on watch," said Luarant. He paused and looked over at the skipper.

"Sir, if I may," said Martino. "Rutwell's said reported prowess with the blade has come mostly on land when under the tutelage of our Marine Detachment Commander. Marines tend to be nothing more than braggarts. They self-inflate their accomplishments and those of their underlings for self-aggrandizement. Sir, this is an examination for Royal Navy lieutenant, we should pay little attention to the non-nautical achievements in considering this matter." Martino broke eye contact with the skipper and looked over at Laurant to find him staring with twisted rage. This response caused Charles to smile.

Calder looked over at Laurant, and said, "Well?"

"Sir, Mister Rutwell is not only accomplished on land. He has shown all proclivity to attend to duties as Officer of the Watch. I have overseen his development on the command deck and can speak to this at length if needed."

"Not at this time. Charles, why do you feel Mister Dugins is ready for this examination?"

"Sir, I have personally seen to his development during this voyage. I have ridden this young lad hard and at times well into the night. He has been most receptive of my instruction and we have penetrated into a wide range of nautical topics from the bottom up. I have personally found his efforts in this endeavor most satisfying. On watch, his navigation skills are evident. He has piloted *Comet* by dead reckoning with a degree of precision that exceeds the excepted bounds of the technique. He has a firm grasp of the influence of wind and tide on the maneuvering of the ship. His knowledge of the signal book is first rate. He's ready, sir."

"Lieutenant Laurant, your observations on Mister Dugins?" said Calder.

"Sir, I have no ill will toward Mister Dugins," said Laurant. "He is developing in a fine manner and Lieutenant Martino's efforts are evident in his growth. However, he does not command the respect of *Comet's* crew. I fear the men would place him over the side at the first opportunity in the dark of night."

"Thank you Lieutenant Luarant for your observation, but I am reminded that this is not a popularity contest. If it were, your counterpart here would still be a midshipman," said Calder. This drew a stern look from Lieutenant Martino. Calder continued, "We are looking for those best suited to operate as a junior lieutenant, on one of his majesty's ships in time of war. In this case, I'm afraid it may well be a dead heat. These two are different. They each have strengths and weaknesses, unique to the experiences they have had under my command. I don't often do this, since it goes against standing protocol, but it is my intent to advance both these names forward to the Admiral's Flag Lieutenant for consideration. He will use these recommendations to advance both or narrow the field."

"The Flag Lieutenant, sir. Isn't that Lieutenant Pennycock?" said Martino.

"One in the same, Lieutenant. While I've had words with him in the past, he has the Admiral's ear and has been aboard *Comet* enough to make a sound recommendation. We'll let the matter rest with him, shall we?"

"Yes, sir. Sounds fair to me," said Martino. His smile widened. He thought to himself, *Basil Pennycock, he owes me. I think it's about time I cash in. Hate to lose Dugins, however. Good lad. Can't say as I've ever found one so eager for personal instruction and willing to accept all manner of humiliation at the hands of his seniors. With what I have against him, he could never oppose me in a pinch.*

Lieutenant Laurant looked over at Martino, and thought, *that bastard.*

*****

A tall gentleman, escorted by a servant, walked down the interior court yard of Maximo Rainerio's hacienda. His gait glided across the red tile with an ease and smoothness common to

255

the Royal Court in Madrid. His black hair was pulled back behind his head in a short pony tail and not in keeping with the accepted styles of the day. His thick dark eyebrows, like his thin mustache and goatee, were shaved and plucked to perfection. Knee high cavalier boots of brown leather tapped along the tile in time with his stride. His short riding cape carried behind him as he walked. His sword bounced against his hip. On closer inspection, it was clear this blade was combat capable and not for decoration. A short dagger was suspended across from the sword on his belt. The jewels encrusted on this fighting instrument reflected both wealth and power. His brown eyes, while shaded by his wide brim hat sporting a long ostrich feather, sparkled with a sober intensity born of a man on a mission.

The servant stopped outside Ernesta's door. He knocked hard twice on the firm oak panels.

"My Lady, I have the right honorable Viscount Ildefonso Tacito here to see you."

"Show him in."

The door swung open. The servant hovered by the portal holding the door for this guest. Idlefonso entered and removed his hat. Sweeping the ornate headgear to one side, he bowed forward toward Ernesta.

She stood, and her black dress extended behind her. The waist of the garment had been tightened and accentuated the flow of the dress from her hips to the floor. The cut of her sleeves fell above her elbow, while the plunging neckline revealed the ivory white skin of her rounded forms. She waved her hand for the servant to depart. Closing the door limited the light in the room to the narrow windows along one wall.

Ildefonso stepped forward and lifted Ernesta's hand to his lips. The kiss was within court customs, but the separation between these two would have drawn intervention from a chaperone were one present. Of course, they were alone, and no such interruption was forthcoming. Ildefonso lifted his eyes from her hand, and they came to rest on the shadow between her well rounded forms supported and shaped by her corset.

"Your Lady has requested my attendance. I have traveled from Madrid to fulfill your desires," said Ildefonso. His brown eyes continued up to lock in the deep blue pools of Ernesta's eyes.

"I have a job for you," she said. Her cheeks ran flush, as her body and mind reacted to the closeness and innuendo of his words.

"Let me guess, my Lady. A jilted lover, persistent rogue, or rival for your father's inheritance needs to be dealt with in a manner that removes them as a distraction?" He lowered her hand but slid half a step closer.

"No, nothing so mischievous. I have a servant girl that needs to be disposed of, without question or comment."

"I see. That is certainly well within my skill set, my Lady. Is this servant located on the grounds here?"

"Yes," said Ernesta. She thought to take a half step away from him, but her feet refused to move. She popped open the fan looped around her wrist and pumped it a few times sending a light breeze across both their faces.

"Are you prepared, and able, to pay from my unique services?"

"Yes, name your price."

"My Lady, I'm a rich man. I do not value your money." His eyes fell again to the low cut of her dress.

"What then?"

"The rumor at court is that news of your recent pregnancy was a ruse, used only to escape the betrothal arranged by your father. The general opinion is you remain a virgin. The cost is that you allow me to explore that possibility in a manner I find pleasurable," said Ildefonso. The back of his hand now traced down between her rounded forms. This area commanded his attention. "So, soft, Ernesta." He whispered. His olive skin stood in sharp contrast to the pale hue he now embraced.

257

Ernesta closed her eyes. Tilting her head back, she traveled her hands behind his neck and pulled into his embrace. She could feel the moistness of his kiss on her mouth. She did her best to feign that the experience was pleasurable. His hands worked behind her back, unseen, to unlace the dress and under garments that stood in his way. She reached above her head and removed the hair pins and terraria that had supported her locks atop her scalp. Her auburn hair fell below her shoulders, as her dress descended to the floor. Ernesta had to fight not to laugh when his sword clattered to the floor with a ruckus inconsistent with the romantic mood he was trying so hard to create.

He lifted her in his arms. His stare focused on her eyes as he carried her to the bed. Ernesta closed her eyes and leaned her head back unsupported. It bounced with each of his steps.

Her mind raced, *surrender. Complete and utter surrender. This damn well better be worth it.*

For one that established a reputation at court as a skillful lover, Ernesta was unimpressed with what followed from Ildefonso in the dark. His polished façade was replaced by rough and unpleasant advances. His fingers pushed and pinched her a manner that was neither sensuous nor stimulating. She had witnessed riders more skillfully mount a horse, than the abruptness with which he jumped upon her and then dismounted. She did not find the way in which he ripped into her flesh to fulfill any of her intimate expectations.

When he fell from atop her, she bit the inside of her cheek to prevent from laughing. The smirk on her face would have given away her thoughts had it been visible, but in the darkness her expression remained masked. Her mind pondered, *well that was fast. A few quick humps and groans, that's it. That's all the great maiden killer of Madrid has to offer? No wonder he has to move from conquest, to conquest, who the hell would want a repeat performance like that? Who indeed?*

Ildefonso awoke to the sunlight cutting a narrow beam into Ernesta's bed chamber. As he got out of bed, he paused to inspect the sheets. The reddish hue announced that the rumors at court were correct. Ernesta had been a virgin all along, but a virgin no more. He thought, *another conquest for the court's most prolific lover. These ladies can't get enough of the great Ildefonso. How lucky this one was that I was her first. Who could possibly compete with that experience? Who indeed?*

Ernesta looked up at him as he dressed. He took his dagger in hand and held his sword to the side. He hovered alongside the bed.

"Where is this servant?"

Ernesta pointed to the room across the courtyard.

"What is her name?"

"Pili, she should still be in her chamber. You'll need to dispose of the body when you are done. I doubt anyone will be up at this hour."

"Of course, my lady. If you ever need my services in the future, you know how to get ahold of me."

"Same price?"

"Of course."

Ernesta smiled, she thought, *not likely. God, I hope I'm never this desperate again.*

Ildefonso walked across the court. He slowly pushed back the door. Looking inside he found Pili still in bed. The light cast through the doorway woke her.

"Who's there?" said Pili. She lifted up on her elbows.

"Pili?" he asked.

"Yes, who's there?"

Ildefonso set his sword belt down at the foot of her bed. He lowered his dagger next to her neck. The sharp point of the blade depressed her flesh.

"Be still and be quiet, or I'll slice your neck like a leg of lamb," said Ildefonso.

Pili's face tightened. She squinted her eyes to better see who was holding a blade to her throat. She felt the morning air cool against her skin as the covers to her bed were cast aside.

"This won't take long. Don't move bitch," said Ildefonso. His tone was curt but low.

True to his word, it didn't take long. As he finished yet another conquest, he pushed his dagger forward into her neck. Forcing the blade along the bottom of her jaw, he cut her wind pipe from side-to-side. Her mouth fell open as if to scream, but no sound was forth coming. Blood spit and splattered, as a low gurgling sound bubbled from Pili. Her eyes fell half closed. They were unseeing and blank. A full smile crossed Ildefonso's face, he thought, *more bloody sheets. I love my work.*

He wiped his blade on the bedding. He looked down at the terror gripped face of Pili. The lines on her face frozen in a twisted expression of surprise and pain. The blood within his body accelerated at the sight of this woman, helpless and powerless, to resist his dominating advance. He smiled thinking, *this was a good one. The shock of not understanding that she was about to be penetrated twice, powerful. Damn, I'm stiffing at just the thought of controlling her for my pleasure and purpose.*

Pili was wrapped in the sheets and carried to his horse. The clip-clop of hooves on the hard-red soil echoed in his ears as he rode away from the hacienda. The blood hue on the sheets continued to expand as he went. Ildefonso swatted at the flies that gathered around him in flight. They would land on the blood stains, hover, and then circle his head to return. When he reached a point about five miles away from the hacienda, he dismounted. Reaching in his saddlebag, he pulled a shovel from its strap.

"Now the real work begins," said Ildefonso to himself.

The sun was straight overhead when he first thrust the spade into the hard soil. The shock of impact rippled back through his arms. The blade sunk an inch into the dirt, before bouncing along the surface. He lifted the spade and reattacked the unyielding ground at his feet. Again, and again, this lonely effort continued. Sweat formed on his body. It provided little in the way of relief from the sun overhead. When the breeze would roll across the rocky scrub oak countryside, Ildefonso would stop, wipe his brow and then continue his efforts.

When he reached a depth of four feet, he looked over the side of the hole and found flies were now thick upon Pili's death shroud. He climbed out of the grave. He arched his shoulders back to pull some of the stress from his body. Dragging Pili along the ground, he rolled her limp corpse into the pit. He stood for a moment over her body but didn't really know why. It was something he always had done. Was it out of respect, or was it a gesture to celebrate his victory? Ildefonso didn't know. He let out a shallow sigh, and said, "I'm an assassin. That's what I do better than anyone else. If it means I can engage a lady or two at court, that's good by me. As for Ernesta, it was I that captured her virtue. I bled her in her own bed. Many wanted that honor, to include the future king." The volume of his voice was increasing. "But, no, it was I . . . Ildefonso. I was the first, and by God's own hand, I will be her last. I own that wench now. She will be mine."

Over a month had passed since Pili had disappeared from the hacienda unannounced. She had been replaced by a young country girl, which while somewhat awkward, was loyal to a fault. Camila lacked basic knowledge, but her willingness to learn was refreshing. Her short-cropped hair and freckled nose made her standout within the household.

Mystery and rumor followed Pili's departure. Some said she ran off with a sea captain to the Americas. Others, that she had fallen victim to wolves along the country roads. None of these tales were close to the truth, but then, the truth was too unreal as to be believable.

Ernesta sat at her breakfast table in the center of the interior courtyard. Her tea cooled, while she poked at her freshly sliced fruit. Her father looked across the table at her. The edges of his mouth turned down.

"Ernesta, are you feeling well?" said Maximo. He lowered his cup to the table.

"I haven't felt well for a few days father. If you'll excuse me?"

"Of course."

She walked back to her room with Camila close on her heels. She fell into her chair and pointed over toward her bed.

"Camila, my chamber pot. Bring me my chamber pot, quickly," said Ernesta.

Camila moved to her bed, lifted the covering, and pulled the brass pot from beneath. Holding it with her apron, she took it back to Ernesta.

"Here you are, my Lady," said Camila, always the dutiful servant.

Ernesta nodded, took the pot with both hands, and hung her head over the top. Vomit flowed from her mouth. It plopped into the bottom of the pot, making a slashing sound as the level rose in the container. Camila extended her apron, and Ernesta wiped her mouth clean. She handed the pot back to Camila.

"I don't know what's wrong with me," said Ernesta. She was not addressing Camila direct, but no one else was in the room.

"How long has it been since your last . . . flow, my Lady?"

"What, you don't think—" Ernesta paused. "How old are you?"

"Thirteen, my Lady," said Camila.

"At thirteen, what can you know of these things?"

"I have three older sisters, my Lady. Each has given birth. The eldest, three times. I have seen this before, my Lady."

"Are you suggesting I've committed sin?"

"No, my Lady."

"That's good, because I could have your head for it."

"How long?"

262

"Six weeks. Is that bad?" said Ernesta. The tone in her voice had grown passive.

"That depends, my Lady."

"Depends, what the hell does it depend on?" Ernesta's tone had grown more on edge.

A moment of silence passed between the two women.

"It depends on whether, or not, you would welcome a child into your life."

"A child, I already have a child."

"I do not believe that one's the limit, my Lady."

Even Ernesta had to chuckle at that comment. The mood between the two of them lightened. They each exchanged a shallow smile.

"How did your sisters know? I mean, know for sure they were with child," said Ernesta breaking the awkward silence.

"After six weeks, you should have a flow. If not a normal amount, some trace is always present," said Camila, speaking with the confidence of experience gained from watching her older sisters go through the process. She handed a handkerchief to Ernesta. "My Lady, wipe this around . . . well, around. It will tell the story better than I."

She took the handkerchief and cleared her throat. She stood and lifted her dress up around her hips. Running the cloth lightly over the exterior of her most intimate flesh, she pulled it up and inspected the handkerchief. Her mind raced, *white, no it can't be just white. There must be a trace of blood.* She thrust the handkerchief between her legs yet again. This time with more force. It went visibly inside her loins. On inspecting the cloth, her shoulders slumped. She dropped her dress and flopped back into the chair.

"It's white, my dear. No doubt about it . . . white as snow," said Ernesta. She stared out the narrow window.

"Congratulations, my Lady," said Camila. Her tone was so positive as to be disgusting to Ernesta's ears.

263

"Camila, my dear."

"Yes, my Lady."

"Would you excuse me a minute."

"Yes, my Lady."

Ernesta watched as her new handmaiden walked from the room. The spry thirteen-year old's flesh embodied a level of innocence she couldn't stomach right now. She lowered her hand over her belly. Without thinking, her fingers tightened into a fist. She hit herself hard above her crotch. She sobbed for a moment. The tears fell on her dress, darkening its already black satin color.

"How could I be so stupid," whispered Ernesta. "I could explain one child to William, but this, how in the hell do I explain this?" He will know I was untrue to him, mocking him, devoid of his touch. What story can I conceive to make him accept this?" She chuckled, "Conceive, good one Ernesta."

Looking out the narrow window, she took in the fresh morning light. She thought, *it's not fair. I had this all worked out. William would return to take his rightful place at the head of our family. Ildefonso, you fucking bastard, you did this me.*

Chapter 15 Portsmouth Plan

The Portsmouth bay burst at the seams with ships at anchor.
Merchant ships sat idle, but on charter to the King. The Royal
Navy dominated the hulls that responded to shifting wind
directions in unison. They would swing in wide arcs on the full
length of rode that ran out to submerged ground tackle. Small
wavelets rippled across the surface of the sound and lightly
lapped against the wooden hulls of his Majesty's fleet. Few
sailors were seen topside, but those on deck were constantly on
task varnishing wood, mending sails, and tending lines. The sky
was grey, but this hue did not reflect the mood of those rowing
ashore.

Captain Darroch sat near the back of *Comet's* long boat.
Lieutenant Martino was next to him, and both officers faced
rearward toward Captain Calder. The ship's Captain's attention
was steady and focused ahead on the wharf near the ship yard.
The Marine watched *Comet* grow smaller as the distance from
her increased. Her sails were rolled up and tied along horizontal
spars. She looked dirty and worn from the hard seas in and
around Scotland. Black streaks ran down her side from the
scuppers on the main deck, giving her a weeping appearance.
Between the rolling motion of the boat and the consistent rhythm
of the oars gliding on the water, Captain Darroch felt his eye lids
lower to half-mast. As they left *Comet* in their wake, another
boat pulled by them on an opposite tack.

The Marine looked across to see a bumboat pulling in *Comet's*
direction. The small craft was filled with women of all sizes and
shapes. Grey hair spilled from under a cotton bonnet on one
woman, betraying an older lady well beyond her prime. A
younger dark hair girl, with bones visible even at this distance,
looked to be no more than in her early teens. A brown jug
circulated around this cheerful mob, as they laughed and sang.

These were forced smiles, more the reflection of drink's consumption than the true temperament of this crew. Two heavy-set women rocked the boat when they moved together toward the side to get a look at *Comet's* long boat as it passed.

"Get back inboard," said the lady at the tiller of the bumboat. "You'll be putting us all in the bay. I'd have thought you two would know better. This isn't your first time out to anchor."

The two ladies sat back down giggling. The full influence of the rum numbing their minds.

"Captain Darrock," yelled a female voice from the passing boat. An upright blonde lass worked her hand from side-to-side trying to get his attention. The Marine returned the wave, unsure of who was on the receiving end.

"Friends of yours, Captain Darroch?" said Calder. His voice was level and his eyes remained focused ahead.

"Not sure, sir. Perhaps some of the girls from the Red Fox Inn. It's hard to say with any degree of certainty."

"Well, at least those lasses know what their getting themselves into by pulling out to the fleet," said Martino. He turned away from the scene to starboard. His lips turned downward. "It's not like they have been driven to sea by the press gang. These ladies at least go of their own free will. I can't say the same for all of the crew."

"Not sure if you can make that assessment, Lieutenant Martino," said Darroch. "They may not fall victim to the blunt end of a belaying pin, but they are pressed none the less. Poverty can be more forceful than any press gang. Hunger, can break your free will faster than force. Do you really think these girls, most of them are too young to be called women, subject themselves to the foulest perversions that haunt the darkest parts of a sailor's imagination because they find it pleasurable? No, I would say not. They have lost all means of support and are unable to sustain themselves without sponsorship. It is sad, sir. Very sad indeed."

The blonde turned away. She slumped back into the boat. The jug of rum found her, and she tilted in back for an extended swig.

The laugher of the bumboat faded as the two boats pulled in opposite directions. Portsmouth was ahead. The docks were crisscrossed with a flurry of activity. Cargo was run to the quay wall, awaiting movement to transfer barges. Gunpowder barrels stood under the watchful eye of Marine sentries. The red coats would pace from side-to-side holding their Brown Bess muskets over their shoulders. The scene reflected the full force of the destructive power waiting to be unleashed against England's foes.

"Ready alongside," said the Coxswain.

Two sailors on the wharf stood ready, but uninterested, to help tie the long boat up to the pier. Their hands were thrust deep in their pockets, reflecting an abridged level of enthusiasm. They kept their eyes on the coxswain, waiting for instructions.

"Oars up," said the coxswain. He pumped the tiller a few times to slow the boat. "Throw them those lines," soon followed. Hands sprung from pockets as the immediacy of the task, now commanded these two sailors into action. The bow and stern line were cleated off on the pier as the boat drifted to a stop.

The three officers stood atop the wharf. Each had a satchel at their side. They had prepared to stay a few days, but every sailor knew that a short stay could often be extended without warning. With the future course of the war uncertain, the proposed combined planning session between army and navy representatives took on increased importance.

"Captain Darroch, does that Red Fox Inn of your rent rooms?" said Captain Calder.

"Yes, sir. Not sure what their availability is, but they will rent them out on a not to interfere basis."

"Not to interfere with what?"

"Business, sir. The entertainment business. Of course, we just saw a bunch of the young lasses heading out to the fleet. It may well be that rooms are more than available at this point with the fleet at anchor."

"Well, let's find out, shall we?" said Calder. He lifted his satchel and pointed with his free hand for the Marine to take the lead.

William started up the well-worn track to his favorite establishment in Portsmouth. It was a route he could negotiate in his sleep. At times, he had done so in less than a sober state. On spying the inn's banner, with a red fox in full stride, he smiled.

"This way, gentlemen," said Darroch. His tone of voice reflected the eagerness of his mood.

The three officers entered the inn to find the main floor nearly deserted. A few merchant sailors sat at one table near the bar. The relaxed nature of the bearing indicated they had been there for some hours. Pang was wiping the surface of the bar, when she noticed William had returned. She didn't know one of the two men with him and remained guarded on her greeting.

"Gentlemen, welcome to the Red Fox Inn. What can I be getting you on this early afternoon?" said Pang. Her brown eyes traveled in turn to each of them.

"We are looking to secure a room for a few days," said William. His tone was equally guarded.

"Well, you're in luck. With the waterfront all but closed down, I've got two rooms available. The Captain can have the room down the hall on the left," said Pang. She looked over at this senior officer and his abundance of gold braid. "That's right across from my room. So, if you be needing anything, just knock." Pang winked at Calder, causing his cheeks to flush. "You other two will have to share a room. Let me show you the way."

The four of them made their way up the stairs with Pang in the lead. She made sure to accentuate the sway of her stride. This movement captured Lieutenant Martino's attention, as his head pivoted in time with her ascent. His stare was unblinking.

Captain Darroch watched his counterpart's actions and thought, *Charles, you don't even know what you're looking to get involved with my good man. You sir, had better tread lightly.*

With each officer assigned a room, Pang turned to Darroch and said, "If you gentlemen be needing anything else, the inn is more than willing to accommodate your request. I hope you'll be joining me at the bar for a pint." She smiled at each of them in turn. Her hand settled briefly on the forearm of Captain Calder. She walked away confident their eyes would follow her exit. Pang knew how to command rhythm and sway to gain and hold a patron's attention.

On her exit, the three of them hovered in the hall for a moment. Calder looked from side-to-side to ensure they were alone.

"Let's rally tomorrow on the main floor before we head out to the Admiralty Headquarters," said Calder. His voice was whisper low. "I will be very interested to see what Vice Admiral Mighels has to say on future operations. As a landsman, where do you think England will focus her strength, Captain Darroch?"

"We either go back to Scotland, on to the Mediterranean, or strike direct at the Spanish coast. Having worked with the Army General Staff, my guess is we'll be going to hit Spain direct. No more playing on the fringes. It's time to bring this damn war to an end, sir."

"We shall see, gentlemen. We shall see indeed. Good night to you," said Calder closing the discussion.

Darroch left Martino in the room and walked down the stairs. He noticed a few more merchant sailors had found tables on the first floor. He thought the activity below was a fraction of what he recalled in earlier times. Pang extended her arm with the fingers of the hand pointing down. Using a cupping motion, she signaled William as if to pull him to the bar. On reaching the base of the staircase, he eased toward the bar and moved to Pang.

269

He rested his foot on the step-board below and his elbows on the oak surface.

Pang reached out and stroked his hand. The words that flowed from her lips were predictable.

"Good evening, William," said Pang. Her voice was low, and she continued to stroke William's hand maximizing flesh contact.

"Pang, it has been awhile."

"Awhile indeed, William. Did you miss me?"

"I always miss you. Why would this time be any different?"

"If I can get a stand-in at the bar, can this be the night I finally convince you to come upstairs with me?"

"I don't think Midshipman Rutwell would be too happy about that. He is the one person on *Comet* I would not want to face with a saber in their hand. As always, I'll have to pass."

"And, as always, I have to ask."

They both laughed.

"Pang, I always enjoy our discussions because I don't have to pretend to be something I'm not and you feel the same. You know I find you exciting. I know this can never be—"

"Never?" said Pang. She dropped his hand and straightened up.

"I fear never. I respect both you and Michael too much."

"I know that. I always knew that," said Pang. Her voice remained soft. She leaned back on the bar and drew her fingers across Williams forearm. "What do you hear from Annette? She hasn't sent a letter from Scotland in several months now. So long, I've lost track."

"She is no longer in Scotland."

"What? Where the hell did she go that she couldn't tell me?"

"Hostage, damn it. The Spanish took her hostage."

Silence stood between them. Pang's mouth had cracked open. The white of her teeth was circled with the red of her painted lips. She blinked her brown eyes. They looked at William questioning. She gripped his hand, as if to hold him would secure the past.

"How long?"

"No one is sure. In fact, no one saw the Spanish take her. I heard it from a Spanish agent I met in Vigo when we stopped there after our Atlantic crossing," said Darroch. He let the air escape slowly from his lungs.

"What are you going to do to get her?"

"I have a plan."

"Damn it, William. The Duke of Medina Sidonia had a plan when he sailed the Spanish Armada up here to the channel over a hundred years ago. It didn't do him so well, now did it," said Pang. Her voice was pitchy. Her face tightened. For the first time since William knew her, he saw a small tremble in her lower lip. Uncontrolled, awkward, as it fluctuated up and down almost unnoticed.

"Pang, it will be alright. I can't tell you why, but it will be alright."

"I'm scared, William. For the first time, in a long time I'm scared. When Annette and I are at the Red Fox Inn, we are in control. The patrons may think they are selecting their partners, but it's the two of us that call the shots in this place. Now, she is kidnapped. Damn it."

"I'll get her back here, or die trying."

"Oh, that's much better. I lose the both of you. Good plan, William. For God's sake, I'm scared. You know I've seen lots of dung in my time, but this, for the first time scares me."

It was William's turn to take her hand and stroke her exposed flesh. She locked eyes with him.

"William."

"What?"

"Sleep with me tonight. No coupling just hold me. Reassure me, until the dawn. I will be better tomorrow," said Pang. "Please hold me in my bed. I do not want to be alone tonight."

271

He could see the lamp light reflect off the building moisture in her eyes.

He let go of her hand. William took in a deep breath. The kind of breath you take when preparing to dive underwater. The kind of breath when you know it might be your last.

"Pang, I would never trust myself to just lie in your bed and only hold you. Your beauty is elegant beyond compare. My feelings for Annette are rarely challenged. But, our history runs back well before the first time Annette and I took to that dance floor," said William. He pointed over the well-worn wooden floor, now vacant. He let loose her hand. "Don't ask me to do something that could forever change our relationship."

She gave him a shallow smile. Nodding she said, "You're right. Thank you."

William started up the stairs. He paused on the third step. Looking over at Pang, he made sure she was listening.

"Pang, I will make this right. I really do have a plan," said Captain Darroch. His tone was level. With a smile, he added, "Good evening."

*****

The sun's pounding summer rays only made the temperature in the Naval Imperial Staff meeting room more unbearable. Captain Darroch wiped his forehead several times to hold at bay the moisture that hovered there. General Temple gave him a nod when he stood to brief the campaign plan. The officers senior to the Marine began to mumble in a low chatter between each other. He could make out enough of this gossip to know these folks were trying to understand how a junior officer, such as Darroch, could gain favor of someone so senior and well connected.

He didn't realize the corners of his mouth had edged up into a smug smile. *Let them gossip,* he thought. *This conflict will be settled on the plains in Spain, not the hallways of this old rundown red brick building.*

General Temple talked, uninterrupted, for the next three hours. He did so without notes. He walked his hand across the map, and with force detailed the army's plan to take Vigo and Pontevedra on the west coast of Spain. This effort was to be launched simultaneously with the French attack descending from the north. Sailing schedules, troop deployment, and enemy strength were all dealt with in detail. Many of the words he used, were known to William. He had written much of the text many nights before at the Red Fox Inn planning conference. He knew the First Viscount of Chobham owed him a favor, and he intended to cash it in when closer to Annette.

Most of the details of this effort were not of interest to the Marine captain. However, he keyed in on two parts of the plan. The twin fortresses at Vigo of San Sebastian and Castro would be the objects of the attack. If he could align the assaults correctly, perhaps, Annette could be liberated in the process. Additionally, they would have to conduct a "press" to get the manpower needed to conduct this operation. Many of the ships that swung at anchor were shorthanded. Securing enough sailors to man them for combat would demand a press gang to round up seamen from the local pubs and inns. His thoughts drifted back to the idle merchantmen half asleep at the Red Fox Inn. He thought, *stand idle no more lads. King and country are about to come calling.*

He looked over at Calder as the pending operation was briefed. His boss was taking detailed notes. This was something Calder had not done in the past. Darroch's mind stopped wandering long enough for him to scribble a note in his green notebook.

"Captain Darroch, are you prepared to handle the press gang?" said Captain Calder.

"Yes, sir," said Darroch. "I couldn't help but notice the Captain took several notes this time around. Not something I've seen you do in the past, sir."

"This is one of the most complex operations I've ever heard. Too many moving parts. If one goes off the track, the rest will follow. I don't know what idiot came up with this, but for the sake of the King he should be shot," said Calder. He drew the attention of those in his immediate vicinity. He cleared his throat realizing he spoke just a little too loud.

"I don't know who the son-of-a-bitch is, but we'll run him out on a rail if we find him," said Darroch. He was careful to keep his volume in check.

"Finally, I would like to thank Captain Darroch, of the Royal Marines on HMS *Comet* for his assistance in pulling this plan together," said General Temple. He pointed in William's direction. Darroch could only nod in reply.

Calder turned and squinted a hard stare at Darroch, "Oh my God, you're a dead man Marine," said *Comet's* Captain.

William cringed. He knew the Captain always used the term "Marine" to address him when he was in a world of trouble.

The meeting broke up and small groups of officers formed to confer on details of the plan. Many discussions of how each could assist the other dominated this professional dialogue. The three officers from *Comet* stood in a tight circle aside from the rest.

"Any concerns in taking the advanced guard forward with the van of the fleet, Lieutenant Martino?" said Calder. He purposely turned a shoulder toward William.

"Sir, the chance to operate with a degree of independence can only serve to help *Comet*. The crew has been in the area before, and we're well suited to guide the rest of the fleet forward."

As Charles finished, Lieutenant Pennycock approached them. His stride was quick. He glanced over at Martino and the two of them exchanged a nod that was lost on Calder. Darroch picked up on this subtle communication and couldn't help but think, *these two bastards are up to something. When it comes to Martino, it's never something good.*

274

"Sir, may I address the Captain," said Pennycock. He held eye contact with Calder, but his tone was low and unobtrusive.

"Yes, Lieutenant Pennycock. It has been some time since I threw you out of my cabin in the Caribbean. No grudge on my part. Have you been well?"

"Yes, sir. Thank you for asking. I have news regarding the lieutenant examination."

"Go on."

"HMS *Comet* was the only ship to forward two nominations. After due consideration, the board decided to accept Midshipman Dugins for the exam. All members of the board were impressed with the qualification of both candidates. They explicitly asked me to ensure Midshipman Rutwell prepares for examination next year," said Pennycock.

He turned away slightly from Calder and smiled at Martino. Charles returned the facial gesture.

"Excellent," said Charles, in a whisper.

"Thank you for the update Lieutenant. I'll personally inform both candidates of the result," said Calder in his official sounding command voice.

The Marine crossed his arms over his chest. He let out a sigh but held his tongue. Martino flashed his eyes in his direction, only to turn them away as fast as he had engaged the Marine.

William felt the muscles in his face contract, he thought, *damn it. Rutwell never got a chance. The fix was in all along. One can never trust the ruling elite.*

*****

Captain Darroch looked along the red coats perfectly aligned on the quay wall. The morning air was thick with fog, not all that uncommon a sight along the Portsmouth estuary. He gazed out over the calm waters to the lightly manned ships swinging on anchor in the sound. He thought, *ships short of sailors, always bad for the Empire. Time to set that right. Separating seamen from their families without their consent is never a pleasant task.*

Only the command of the King justifies such action. Well, then, back at it.

Sergeant Worth approached his Captain. He saluted. The Sergeant held his hand against his hat until his boss acknowledged the greeting.

"Sir, the Marines are formed and ready. I have coordinated our efforts with the other detachments, so we don't all go looking in the same pubs or inns. Would the Captain like to lead the march today?" said Sergeant Worth.

"What's our quota?"

"Sixteen, sir."

"Do you have a like number of press papers?"

"Yes, sir. Right here in my pouch," said Worth. He patted a leather satchel on his side.

"Let me see one."

The Sergeant lifted the flap on his pouch and shuffled through the assortment of papers. He carefully pulled an off-white piece of parchment from those clustered in the pouch. Handing it to the Captain, he repeated his question."

"Sir, will the Captain be leading the press this morning?"

"No, Sergeant Worth. That honor will fall to you. I will take this one press order however. That means your quota is now down to fifteen."

"Very good, sir. Will the Captain be needing anything else?"

"Yes, have Corporal O'Keefe report to me with a private. That should be sufficient to fill this single quota."

"Aye, sir," said Sergeant Worth. He eased about and marched the detachment up into the narrow confines of Portsmouth. The early hour of the day found the alleyways and inns silent. The sound of leather soled shoes pounding in unison on the cobblestones cut through the quiet with a marshal rhythm. Those that had the presence of mind to stay ahead of the press scurried off deeper into the recesses of the city. The scream of a scrubwoman at the Blue Boer announced the press gang was on the move.

"Sir, Corporal O'Keefe and Private Gibsone reporting as ordered," said O'Keefe. The two exchanged salutes.

"Marines, we are in search of one key crewmember. His skills will be useful to us going forward. If you would, follow me," said Darroch.

The small band of Marines marched down the waterfront. The click-clack of their shoes on the cobblestone was muffled when contrasted with the pounding beat generated by the rest of the detachment. Darroch's eyes flashed from side to side.

"What is the Captain looking for, sir?" asked O'Keefe.

"I'll know when I see it," came the rapid reply.

Looking down a narrow alleyway, Captain Darroch squinted to better focus through the ever-present fog. He could not make out the words, but the shape of a long key suspended out from a store front provided compelling evidence, he had found what he was looking for.

"This way Marines," said Darroch.

The three of them moved into the tight enclosed alleyway. As they approach the key shaped sign, the words confirmed their quest. It read; "Lock Shop."

Two bells echoed across the ships at anchor. These were rendered not in unison but staggered as the watch waited on the Admiral's flagship to initiate the signal. It spread out from this point delayed by the reaction time of each watch team in turn to mimic the bells. The Marines pushed open the door to the shop.

The bell on the door, competed with those in the bay, to announce the entry of *Comet's* Marines. A man labored with a file under the limited light of a whale oil lamb to shape a small steel object. His bent over frame made him to be in his late forties. He didn't look up from his work. His focus remained unwavering. The file was pushed up along the steel, its scraping sound reverberated in the shop. The same sound echoed out as the file was pulled back toward him. He drew his finger across the new depression in the steel to confirm its depth and smoothness. He set the file down, pushed his spectacles atop his head, and looked up to address his visitors.

"May I help, you?" said the shop keeper.

"Yes, sir. Are you the proprietor of this shop?" asked Darroch. In his business-like Marine tone, that bordered on harsh.

"Yes. Yes, I am."

"I have a job that will require the expertise of the best lock picker in Portsmouth. Could be a hansom sum of shillings involved. Can you recommend anyone?"

The man at the desk looked up. He thought, *a hansom sum of shillings, could be pirate treasure. Maybe a prize ship was taken.* His eyes fell back to the Captain.

"Yes, if it's a lock that be needs picking, I'm you man."

"Are you qualified?"

"Sir, I've picked every lock known to man. I have a complete set of tools that will pick French, Spanish, or German locks with ease. Plus, I'm the only one that knows how they work. I've built them, so I know how to pick them."

"How do we know you in fact have these tools?"

The man stood and dropped to one knee. He pulled a couple of drawers at his desk open and pushed aside the tools hidden there. The metallic sound of instruments bumping into each other lifted above the counter. At last, he stood and unrolled a cloth organizer across the counter surface. Tools of all sizes and shapes were neatly stowed in the pockets and straps of his cloth.

"See here, this one is used for most locks. These others are for special ones, often built in France," said the man at the counter.

"Very good, sir. I didn't catch your name?" Captain Darroch said.

"Smyth, Edward Smyth to be exact."

"Well Mister Smyth, you are hereby pressed into service with the fleet by order of the King," said Darroch. He held up the press papers for the man to read.

"Some mistake, I think. Some mistake, indeed. I'm forty-seven years old and never served a day at sea in my life. I'm no sailor, sir."

"You were no sailor. Now, by order of the King, you work for me."

Corporal O'Keefe stood on one side of Mister Smyth, and the Private took up position on the other. Mister Smyth looked left and right. His jaw dropped.

"Sir, I must protest. You don't need any landsman aboard," said Smyth. His tone was defensive and choppy.

"You may be right, but I do have need of someone that can pick locks. My promise to you is this; get me through the locks and I'll get you home as fast as possible. On the ship, you'll work for me directly which means light duty. Fail me, and I'll cast you among the crew to fend for yourself. That means hard work aloft," said Darroch in a harsh voice.

"Look at these hands," said Smyth. He raised his thin fingers before the Captain. "Work aloft with these? That sir would be a death sentence."

"Then I suggest you deliver what you said you could do, pick the locks assigned and we'll have no trouble. Fail, and the Bosun will do with you what he pleases. Get your tools."

His frail hands shook as Smyth lifted his tools under his arm. The four men exited the door. Captain Darroch paused at the door. He pointed back to the latching mechanism. His hand turned, as if locking the latch. Mister Smyth studied the sign language.

"No need, Captain. I never lock the place," said Smyth smiling.

The two Marine guards chuckled. Darroch looked at him, his eyes widened.

"You never lock you own shop?"

"No, never do. Not likely for anyone to check ye old Lock Shop."

Darroch shrugged his shoulders. They marched back to *Comet* with a guard on each side of Smyth. They stopped at the base of the quay wall. Darroch put his hand on Smyth's frail shoulder.

"Look here, Mister Smyth. I'll do all I can to keep you out of the rest of the ship's routine, but you have to do what this Marine tells you. Is that clear?"

"Yes, I understand. Not too happy about any of this, but I understand."

"Corporal O'Keefe, when we get on deck take him to the Marine berthing area. Get him settled in and keep him out of sight."

"Aye, aye, sir," said the Corporal.

"Just what do you want me to unlock, anyway? Chests of pirate gold?" Asked Smyth.

"Something more valuable," replied Darroch.

Chapter 16 Castro Copperhead

Captain Darroch had not left his stateroom since *Comet* got underway two days ago. He studied the contents of his little green book while the ship sailed out of Portsmouth, passed the Isle of Wright, and along the southern English coast toward Falmouth. He had diagramed the forts at Vigo during his first visit. He knew well the ramparts of Fort Castro. However, the dungeon had escaped his detailed review. Now the grey stone walls of that citadel held Annette, and he was determined to reverse that chain of events and break the bonds of her captivity.

His finger traced along the worn yellow pages of the fort perimeter sketch. He struggled to read his own cryptic handwriting at one point of the fortress wall. The combination of thick and thin lines, coupled with blocks and diamonds, detailed the battlements of the bastion. Pulling the candle closer he deciphered the words, "Service Entrance." Closing his eyes, he let his head fall backward. *Why did I write that two years ago? My God, has it really been two years since Annette and I were together? Annette, that's it, that's where we drew supplies for Comet. From the service entrance. It was a small door leading to the general courtyard.* Darroch sat up and stared at the page. He tapped his finger against the worn pages of his book. "That's it. I'll gain access right here," said Darroch aloud. He folded the book closed with such force it made a distinctive thud.

The Marine walked down the dimly lit passageway. The thumping of the anchor cable over the hawse pipe confirmed *Comet* had reached the fleet rendezvous point. Walking up to the main deck he paused. He lifted his hand to shield the direct sunlight from obscuring his vision. Looking left and right, the full fleet was spread out at anchor before him. Warships, transports, and smaller sloops were all pulling against their rode in the shallows of Falmouth. The afternoon wind cut the waters of the bay into a light chop. The small white caps formed into random patterns. He took in a deep breath. The fresh smell of salt air was a pleasant change from the stale mix found below deck.

"Captain Darroch, a moment if I may," said Calder

"Yes, sir," said Darroch.

"I think you can see from the Admiral's flag signals, I've got a conference on his flagship."

Darroch looked toward the center of the ships at anchor. Returning his attention to his boss, he shuffled his feet.

"Aye, sir. Does the Captain need anything in preparation?" said Darroch. His tone was inquisitive.

"I need you to attend with me, man. The army will be there, and I need you to translate all that landsman talk into something understandable. Here is my boat alongside, now."

The men went over the side to the traditional sound of the Bosun's pipe whistling its high and low notes in a familiar rhythm.

"*Comet*, departing," said Midshipman Dugins as the Officer of the Deck.

The locus of small boats pulling in the direction of the flagship converged in a random manner. Each coxswain jockeyed for position alongside the ship's ladder to unload their passengers. Protocol dictated that only one ship's captain could board at a time. This lengthened the queue, delayed many of the boats to bounce along in the afternoon chop. Captain Darroch could feel his stomach start to churn and bubble from the resulting prolonged uncomfortable motion. Looking up at the mast of the flagship, it appeared to move left, then right, then back again.

"Captain Darroch, you don't look so well. Are you alright?" said Calder. He couldn't conceal a slight smirk.

"I'll be fine when we get to the big deck, sir," said Darroch.

The salvation of the flagship's main deck arrived just in time for the Marine. He faced into the prevailing wind and took a few deep breaths. His nerves and stomach settled, as a familiar voice engaged him from behind.

"Captain Darroch, there you are," said General Temple. "I've been looking for you ever since they rang *Comet's* Captain aboard. How have you been?"

"Good, sir. And the General, I trust all is progressing as planned."

"Yes, indeed. You gave us a solid start in that regard. I would say our time at the Red Fox Inn, was time well spent. How is that redhead of yours doing?"

"Annette?"

"Yes, one in the same."

"I fear duty has kept me from her side. Perhaps, this operation will help change that."

"Indeed, success on the Don's home turf could be an important step in bringing this damn war to an end," said Temple. He motioned for an officer behind him to join the two of them.

"Captain Darroch, let me introduce Brigadier General Philip Honeywood. He will be leading our first wave ashore at Vigo."

"Sir," said Darroch extending his hand.

"The ever-pugnacious Captain Darroch of the Royal Marines," said Honeywood. His hand shake was firm and formal. "I've really enjoyed getting to know you through your operational plan. Good work, I must say. My staff made only one change in your approach."

"And what would that be, Brigadier?"

"We are not going to assault Castro in the opening round. Better to break off San Sebastian, and then go for the bigger fort."

"I see. Will you require the services of our Royal Marines during the landings?"

"No, can't say as I have any need for Marines. Damn, that didn't sound right. It is my intent to land with an advance force of regimental size and take the perimeter, before moving against the main defense with increased firepower. We may in fact need Marines for the final assault."

"Well, in order to prepare for the follow-on attack, let me take a small reconnaissance party forward and confirm the planning assumptions in and around Fort Castro," said Darroch. His eyes moved between the two generals.

"How many?" said Honeywood.

"Three."

"Done. That small a force will not tip our hand or compete with boat space for the landing."

"Gentlemen, you know I don't much care for last minute changes to a plan. Get this sorted out and report to me when all the preparations are complete," said Temple. The General walked away leaving the two officers that would be the first on Spanish soil to sort out the details.

*****

Eight days later the fleet made a bold approach on the tidewaters of the Vigo Bay. They sailed straight ahead until they reached an offload point three miles from the city. This distance ensured the fleet would be outside the range of the fortification's guns. The long boats began the circular dance of ferrying troops between the transports and the beach. Unnoticed within the eight hundred soldiers that splashed onto the tan sands, were three men that didn't seem to fit with the rigid organizational structure of those around them.

"Let's get off this beach," barked the Regimental Sergeant-Major. "Come on, lads, keep moving."

The short march to the walls outside San Sebastian took less than an hour. The landing party dug shallow musket firing pits at the base of the fortress. Using the natural folds in the earth, they pushed up barricades of fallen trees, carts, and local vegetation to obstruct the Spanish line of sight into their positions. The bright orange sky behind them, illuminated the bay in like colors. The sight of the setting sun was striking. It would have been the perfect place to enjoy a glass of wine on holiday. If one were on holiday, that is.

"The army attacks this evening," said Darroch.

"At night, sir," said Rutwell.

"How will they see anything?" asked Smyth.

"Balls," added Rutwell.

"You have to feel your way forward for a night attack. Good thing is, the enemy on the ramparts won't be able to see a damn thing either. Most likely a close fight in the making," said Darroch.

"We're not going over the walls, are we, sir?" said Smyth. His tone was nervous.

"Hell, no. When they move out, the noise and confusion that follow, will allow us to get around this fort and approach Castro from the back. That's where you'll earn you pay," said the Marine.

"A lock, sir?"

"Yes, indeed. That will get us through the walls and into the center court. From there, we'll have to feel our way forward to the dungeon."

"A dungeon, sir. We're going inside the fort?"

Smyth slowly turned away from the Marine. He looked down the trail that returned to *Comet*. He slowly slid his foot in that direction. Rutwell grabbed his collar. His grip was firm. He exerted enough pressure to reverse Smyth's movement away from the action. The bright teeth of the Marine were visible in the fading light when he smiled.

"Don't worry, Mister Smyth," said Darroch. "I'll be sure to return you to Portsmouth in one piece. For now, we need to start a slow approach around the fortress walls. Mister Rutwell, you'll follow in trace to ensure we don't get lost along the way."

"Aye, aye, sir," said Rutwell, smiling at Mister Smyth.

Darroch held a single finger across his lips. "Shhh . . ." The sound faded, as he worked to make a stealthy approach to the rear of Castro.

Down the hill, the sound of musket fire and yelling lifted up from Fort San Sebastian. Darroch could hear the sound of footsteps above, all shuffling toward the direction where the noise was coming from. They continued to work along the base of the fort, unseen in the growing darkness.

William ran his hand along the wall. The course rocks scratched the flesh of his palm as he felt his way forward. He counted his steps. On reaching three hundred and sixty, he thought, *that's six hundred yards. The gap with the door should be here. I couldn't have missed it. We moved along the wall well short of where it should be. Now, at this distance it should be right—"*

William stumbled into the door archway. He ground his teeth together when his hand was pierced by a wooden sliver on the door.

"Smyth, over here," whispered Darroch.

Smyth ran his hand along the lock.

"It's of French design. Give me a minute," said Smyth.

The sound of his small pick clicking against the inside of the lock filled the narrows of the doorway. His breathing was intermittent when he listened for the sound of the mechanism aligning. The audible pop that followed, signaled the door was open.

The Captain pulled the door back only enough to allow them inside. Torches burned along the interior of the court, providing a dull light that reflected off the walls. The cold stones of the fortress pulled the heat from their bodies as they continued to feel their way along. Rutwell's body shivered uncontrolled. The ramparts were empty and silent. The three of them worked along the shadows of the castle walls. Darroch looked down the descending stairway. The steps curved away in a tight circle leading into the darkness of the dungeon below.

"Follow me," Darroch said. His voice was whisper soft, but the tone was commanding as always.

He steadied himself with the handrail and started down. Rutwell nudged Smyth ahead of him. The darkness gave way to the light of a single lantern down the hallway. A guard sat reclining at his desk. He leaned his chair back against the wall, with his feet on the desk. The cold stone walls served as his pillow. His beret was pulled down to shade his eyes even in this limited light.

Darroch looked back at Rutwell. He pointed to his eyes with two fingers spread like a vee. Then he pointed with a single finger at the guard. He motioned for both men to remain quiet. The Marine reached into his legging and pulled his dirk from its resting place. He gripped the handle of the blade with the edge extended forward for thrusting. He tip-toed toward the resting Spaniard. His blade aligned at the base of the guard's neck.

Startled, the guard fell forward with all four legs of the chair hitting the deck. He inhaled as if to speak, but Darroch placed a hand across his mouth.

"If you yell, I'll cut your throat. Do you understand?" said Darroch, his words were whisper soft. He repeated the words in broken Spanish.

The guard nodded. His eyes had doubled in size as the realization of the cold steel scraping against his neck was out of his control.

"Where is Annette Armtrove?"

The guard shrugged his shoulders.

"The redhead, where is the redhead?"

"Sir, you mean Copperhead. She's a snake that one. This way, I'll show you," said the guard.

The guard leaned forward to stand but froze until he felt the pressure of the blade ease from his throat. Rutwell took the torch, and the four of them walked by the cells of the dungeon. The sound of dripping water echoed in the background. The breathing of bodies compressed behind the iron doors competed with their footsteps to break the quiet.

"Here we are, Copperhead lives here," said the guard.

"Open it," commanded Darroch.

"Sir, only the Sergeant of the Guard is entrusted with the keys. I can't open this door."

"Smyth."

"Aye, sir. Give me another minute or two."

William took his dirk and drew it across the throat of the guard. The Spaniard's eyes grew wide as the pain registered. His mouth fell open. Darroch covered his mouth and lowered him to the ground. The gurgling sound that bubbled up from his throat now dominated the hallway. The Marine held his hand there until he could no longer feel the breath flow over his flesh.

"Annette?" whispered William.

"What?" she whispered back.

Only Annette would respond like that, thought William.

"It's William. I've come to get you the hell out of here."

"William," said Annette. Her voice was weak but louder than a whisper.

"Shh—"said William. "Please be quiet."

Smyth continued to push and pry with his picks. In the torch light, William could see his lips tighten as he turned and prodded the lock to open. At length, a smile crossed his narrow cheeks.

"That's got it, sir," said Smyth.

William pulled the door back. Annette eased into the torch light. William's mouth fell open. Rutwell gasped. Her auburn hair was matted with mud and dirt in long strands. The once proud dress that had announced her presence at court, was torn and filth ridden. Annette's frame was thin, with her bones more pronounced than her formerly rounded flesh. But her eyes were clear and crisp, green as they had always been. Amid that broken shell of a woman, the same Annette burned beneath.

"Annette, let's get you the hell out of here," said William.

Too weak to respond, she nodded. Annette took a step toward William but her muscles, atrophied from limited use failed to steady her upright, and she collapsed toward him. He caught her and lifted her into his arms. Her head rested against his shoulders and she started to sob.

"It's fine, my love. I've got you now," said William.

"Never wanted you to be seeing me . . . like this."

"Mistress Armtrove, to quote our ship's Captain, 'you are as lovely as a sunset and as refreshing as the trade winds.' Can we go now?"

She once again nodded and let her head rest against his shoulders. Her sobbing stopped.

"Rutwell, take the lead. You know the way," said Darroch.

"Aye, sir. I do indeed."

The four of them retraced their steps up the stairs to the courtyard. Rutwell froze at the top of the stairs. Darroch pushed up alongside him. His lips tightened when he looked into the dim light of the round courtyard. A lone swordsman stood in their way. Rutwell instinctively drew his saber. The sound of the metal being extracted from his sheath rang out into the night.

"Stand aside," said Rutwell. His command voice mimicked that of Darroch.

"I think not young man," said Ernesta. She walked out from the shadows. Her black dress flowed as if she were attending court. Her only accessory was a folded fan held tightly in her right hand. She used the fan to point at Captain Darroch. "William, you should unhand that trash. Your place is here, at my side."

"Well, it's good to see you too Ernesta. However, I don't believe I've ever given you cause to think we had feelings for one another."

"Cause? Damn it William, you gave me a child," said Ernesta. Her voice increased in pitch as she spoke.

"Oh, great," said Rutwell. He let out a long breath.

"I will not allow our child to be banished as a bastard. You will stay here and attend to your responsibilities. You had your night of fun, now it's time to attend to your family and not that pathetic bag of bones across your shoulders."

"I think you know, even if that is all true, I can't stay," said William. He took a step closer to the door. Smyth keyed on this move and pulled along behind him.

"Ildefonso here is a master swordsman. If you do not stay with me, I fear he will have to kill your young friend. Time to think what is best for your family William. Please stay," said Ernesta. Her voice was level and insistent. She lowered her fan in front of her and held it with both hands level to the ground. Her eyes focused on William. Annette's sobbing returned.

"Sir make a run for it. I'll hold this Spanish swordsman—" Rutwell didn't finish his thought.

Ildefonso lunged forward. Rutwell instinctively beat parry the thrusting attack to the side. The Midshipman's eyes widened, attempting to pull in as much of the dim light as possible. He moved forward with a compound attack, feinting to the opposite line and then returning his thrust to the other side. Ildefonso counterattacked avoiding the thrust with a side step and steadying his feet with a straight extension toward Rutwell.

Amid the rattle of steel-on-steel, William lowered Annette to the ground. Smyth stepped forward to steady her upright.

"Hold her," said William in a whisper.

"Yes, sir," said Smyth. His eyes flashed from the duel in the courtyard to William.

The Marine reached into his sash. He fumbled for a pistol.

Ildefonso glided down Rutwell's blade holding constant contact with its edge. As their bodies collided, he drove his pummel into the Midshipman's jaw. Rutwell spun around and retreated a few steps. He felt a small hard object on his tongue. He spit it out but didn't have time to notice part of a tooth hit the deck.

Ildefonso yelled, "Raddoppio." He coupled a lunge with an advance directly at the Midshipman.

Rutwell yelled back, "Passata-sotto." He dropped one hand to the deck. His upper body fell below the oncoming blade. As Ildefonso went by, he raised his sword hand and cut across the side of his attacker. It was not a deep wound, but it was first blood none the less.

Both men stood and stared at each other. Ildefonso lowered his free hand to his side and applied pressure. His smile twisted in the flickering torchlight. Rutwell's breathing was deep and measured.

"You are no amateur, my friend," said Ildefonso.

"You may let us pass, my friend," said Rutwell in reply.

"I fear the time for that has past. The time for dying is upon us, sir"

"As you wish, sir." Rutwell shook his shoulders. *What had he always told Annette, relax?*

A calm washed over Rutwell. He loosened and then tightened his grip on the sword. His breathing was now level. His eyes moved up and studied the wrist position of his opponent. The backward break of Ildefonso's wrist made him think, *slashing attack.*

Rutwell stepped into the attack and met the downward slice with such force he threw his opponent back two feet. Steel flashed in the glow of the torchlight, captivating the full attention of the limited audience in the courtyard. Now the counter, high to low, and then circling around his blade slashed across Ildefonso's left torso. Too light for a killing blow, but the slice returned the oozing of crimson along a horizontal line. The Midshipman rocked on his feet. *Forward and back, breathe.*

Ildefonso recovered. His on-guard stance returned. He motioned with his hand for Rutwell to advance. The Midshipman returned the sign. The Spaniard lunged and engaged Rutwell's blade. He circled the saber in a round sweeping motion, jerking the weapon from his hand. The metallic sound bounced across the stones of the courtyard and came to rest at Annette's feet.

Annette let loose of Smyth and staggered forward to pick up the sword. She was too late. Ildefonso lowered his blade to extend a final lunge at Rutwell. The sound of a pistol shot filled the courtyard. Ildefonso staggered back and dropped to his knees. His hand covered his chest. The blood flowed through his fingers and dampened his shirt. His mouth was round as he looked up at the Midshipman. Smoke drifted in the dim light around Darroch's head. He lowered the pistol to his side and looked over at Ernesta. Her champion fell to the deck. His sword rattled from his grasp bouncing along the stones of the courtyard.

"The time for dying, sir," said Rutwell.

Annette continued to stagger toward Ernesta. She was barely able to keep the blade from touching the deck. Her frame was bent, but her spirit was unbroken. Those eyes, those bright green eyes, were filled with a vengeance that was visible even in the dim of the courtyard.

"Annette, it's time to go now," said Darroch.

Annette continued toward Ernesta. She didn't respond to William. She paused when reaching Ildefonso's saber. She lowered the tip of her sword under the hilt and flicked the blade toward Ernesta. She took another step toward the one that had kept her in these cold stone walls.

"Pick it up," said Annette. Her voice was soft.

Ernesta folded her arms over his chest.

"Pick it up, damn you."

"Bitch, you've been down in that hole in the ground way too long if you think I'm going to touch that thing," said Ernesta. She smiled.

William shook his head, he thought, *shouldn't have called her bitch.*

Annette's eyes widened. From deep inside she was able to muster the strength for one forceful lunge directly at Ernesta. Her skeleton arms extended the arch of the saber over Ernesta's crossed arms. The blade bounced off her rib cage and sliced through the soft flesh beneath, bursting her heart. Ernesta fell to the floor. Her moaning wouldn't last long.

"Nice form, can we leave now?" said Rutwell.

Annette smiled. Nodding she said, "Now we can leave."

"How did you find the strength to finish this?" said Smyth.

"Sometimes, hate can drive us to points beyond our physical limits," said Darroch.

"Not hate," said Annette. Her voice stronger, "Justice. Balance demands justice."

William took the sword from Annette's hand and handed it back to Rutwell. He lifted her once again in his arms and carried her out of the bastion. Smyth pulled shut the door behind them and locked the solid oak portal. The sound of footsteps above them on the ramparts, served to hurry them along their planned retrograde.

The fighting at San Sebastian had subsided. The smell of gunpowder from the spiked cannons on the ramparts drifted down on them as they moved past. Piles of burning debris sent yellow light against the stone walls of the fort. Soldiers of the attacking force moved in what appeared to the Midshipman as random patterns. To William, it was apparent they were clearing the ramparts and moving the last of the Spanish defenders up into the keep. This small band continued by the besieging army toward the boats three miles to the southwest. Rutwell started to run, in order to catchup with Captain Darroch and Annette at the head of the column. His breathing was still heavy when he reached the Marine.

"Sir," said Rutwell. His chest still rose and fell in time with his stride as he addressed Captain Darroch.

"Yes, Midshipman Rutwell."

"Why did you shoot that Spaniard back in the courtyard? I had him, sir."

"Was that before, or after, he sent your saber bouncing across the stones of the courtyard?"

"Sir, I would have dodged his next thrust. Rolled across to my saber and resumed the attack. He didn't have a chance, sir."

"I see," said Darroch. A smirk rose on his lips. "Well, you got the sword of Ernesta's court champion. That should be good for a round of ale or two at the Red Fox Inn when we make landfall at Portsmouth."

"Aye, sir. A round or two, for sure," said Rutwell. He walked just a little more upright.

The moon was sinking in the west by the time they reached the long boat. The soft white light of this orbiting circle sent a long column of light across the still surface of the bay. Its shape on the water rippled with the uneven surface. A dance to welcome home Captain Darroch and crew. The masts of ships rose like sticks from the backlit silhouettes of the Royal Navy, hovering at anchor under a mile in the distance. Only a short boat ride separated Annette from the safety of the fleet.

William handed Annette to Rutwell. The transition woke her, and she looked about. Annette had been in the darkness of the dungeon so long, the limited light on the beach appeared to fully illuminate the scene for her. She looked out across the waters. Her eyes strained to see the outline of each ship in the bay.

"*Comet*, thank God, *Comet* has come," said Annette. Her voice was whisper soft.

Rutwell nodded, confirming her observation was correct. He moved knee high into the waters of the bay and handed Annette over to Captain Darroch. She settled in on his lap at the back of the boat. The two locked eyes. Even in the limited pale glow of the moonlight, William could see the smile form on Annette's lips. They felt the boat rock as the crew pushed it free from Spanish soil.

The light rocking action of the long boat confirmed to Annette she was underway. The oars feathered across the water, before dropping into the bay for a powerful pull. Water would drip from each oar as it was lifted from the bay. Diving back into the dark waters the process was repeated, as the backs of sailors provided the locomotion to glide silently across the sea.

William looked down at Annette. Her cheeks were hollow. Lips that were once lush and moist to kiss, now stood before him as thin chapped vestiges of their former selves. But those eyes, even in the dim of night, they held their stare on him. Unblinking, unwavering, a welcome constant in a confusing world of shifting tides.

"Annette, if I had known they were going to raid the Scottish coast, I'd never have sent you away from *Comet*. I thought you would have been safer up north, away from the channel. Can you ever—"

William's words were cut short. Annette lifted two narrow fingers to his lips to silence him. Her touch on his skin was as soft as it always had been. She held her stare on him.

"I love you, William. I always knew my love would pull you to my side. Please take me away from this God-awful place," said Annette. Her tone was soft and her voice broke as she finished her words.

The long boat bumped against the side of *Comet*. The coxswain gained eye contact with the Officer of the Deck. Cupping his hand around his mouth, he said, "Sir, we have a weak passenger embarked. I'll be needing the boatswain chair to get them on deck."

Block and tackle were run out on a spar and lines tied taut in rapid fashion. Chief White directed the efforts of those around him to pull the passenger aloft. They swung the feminine form onto the main deck. The Chief didn't recognize the body, but he knew well the face before him.

"Welcome aboard, Mistress Armtrove. It has been awhile," said Chief White.

Annette didn't respond. She had to focus the full extent of her physical and mental efforts to steady herself on the moving deck.

Captain Darroch lifted himself from the ladder to the main deck. He moved over to the small group of crewmen that circled around this new passenger. He couldn't help but notice how Annette commanded the attention of those that had gathered around her. These were not lustful glances of sailors too long from home, but the stares of pity for the broken body before them. He pushed through the well-intentioned gawking mass, lifted Annette once again in his arms, and moved next to Chief White.

"Chief, I'm taking Mistress Armtrove to my stateroom. Could you please send a runner to find Doc La Roch? Have him join me there." Darroch said. The normal volume and tone of his command voice had returned.

He headed for the ladder. All eyes followed them as they departed. Annette's head returned to William's shoulder. Her face was buried into this neck. In this initial moment of freedom, all she wanted was to be in his grasp. To feel the warmth of his body against hers. To turn away the rest of the world, that at times, had seemed so intent on keeping them apart. The creaking of the standing rigging echoed in her ears. The sound of William's wooden soles resonated off the deck with a familiar, clip-clop, long absent from the cold stone floor of the dungeon. An unseen smile crossed her face for the first time in years.

The captain's cook had returned to HMS *Comet*. Annette, who was too long absent from William was back in his arms.

Chapter 17 Cadiz Capitulation

Queen Elisabeth Farnese stood by King Philip V. Her dress was artificially extended well beyond her hips by supporting underwire that made her profile appear much wider than those attending her at court in Madrid. She fanned herself as required by formal etiquette, as much as an effort to keep cool amid the fall temperatures. She listened intently to the ministers advising her husband. Elisabeth was more adept in the realm of foreign affairs than many of those that now prostrated themselves before the king, and she knew it would be her role to push Spain in the right direction when the time for decision was reached. She pretended to be uninterested in the dialogue that swirled around these pompous members of the ruling elite. They in turn had always extended a smile and curtesy in her direction, but most viewed her role as limited to producing an heir for the throne. That outcome required little more than for her to remain silent on her back, with legs parted, for the short duration of the king's advances. Or, so they thought.

A figure dressed in red approached her from across the great hall. His steps were measured as he crossed the black and white tile floor. He had difficulty maintaining eye contact as he neared the queen. She dipped at the knees toward her King and took a step away from the tight circle that encased his majesty. The ministers took no special notice of her departure.

The figure in the red robes of a Catholic Cardinal bowed before the Queen. He surrendered eye contact and studied the heavy makeup that concealed the expression of the young queen. She extended him a shallow smile, so as to not crack the thick layers of white make-up that covered her flesh.

"Your Highness, this just arrived from the west coast. I fear events there have not unfolded as we would have thought," said Cardinal Alberoni. "It seems—"

Elisabeth raised a hand to silence her advisor. He lowered his gaze to the tile floor as she scanned down the letter. It was on his counsel that Spain had moved forward to regain territory lost in the last war, and now it appeared that once again news the front was not what he had envisioned. She snapped her finger against the paper. The light popping sound momentarily silenced the curious council attending her husband.

"Are these loss numbers correct?" Elisabeth said. Her eyes now focused on the Cardinal.

"Yes, my Lady. The British have expanded their raid from Vigo to Pontevedra. The garrison there spiked eighty-six cannons and the arsenal was put to the torch," said Alberoni. His voice cracked as he spoke of the cannons.

"Anything else?" Elisabeth said. She was intent on letting the Cardinal twist on the spikes of his own policy.

"Yes, my Lady. The town of Santiago de Compostela paid their commander a sun of forty thousand English pounds to not advance in their direction. I fear the local government does not believe the Spanish army will provide for their security."

"And what would you have me advise the King in this matter?"

Elisabeth had purposely spoken loud enough that such counsel would be unnecessary. The King and his ministers had fallen silent. All eyes now turned toward the Cardinal. A few of the inner circle shuffled a step toward the man in red.

"Gentlemen, it seems we are fighting in three directions," said Alberoni. His eyes moved between the King and his ministers. "None of these battles are unfolding in an acceptable manner. Our troops on Sicily are cutoff by English ships in the Mediterranean. They are being pushed around the Island at the whim of the British army there. Our frontier with France is crossed at will by their armies. We have been able to turn them back each time but now a new threat is positioning to dilute our northern defenses. The English are able to conduct amphibious raids along our western coast opposed by only the local garrisons. Both Vigo and Pontevedra have fallen to troops landing from the sea. They have taken, or destroyed, many of our armaments in the region. Local governments are paying them off to avoid attack. In short, they are growing stronger and we are getting weaker." His voice was downward cast as he finished.

"Perhaps, we could shift their attention back to Sicily and away from our coastline. Can we reinforce the army there?" said one of the Ministers. All members in the inner circle looked to each other to gain some measure of support that the war could, or should, continue.

"Such a course of action would demand enough ships to transport the army. Additionally, the navy would have to be able to secure local control of the seas around the Island to facilitate such a landing unencumbered by English naval action," said Alberoni.

"Gentlemen, I have neither the ships or troops to go on such an expedition. This talk of expanding the campaign is pure folly. Spain retains enough strength in the field to extract a fearful price for military victory. I do not know how much longer this will be so if the direction of the war continues along this line. However, I do know we lack enough troops to take the initiative from our opponents. By God, we have four nations aligned against us. It is time we seek peace. If for no other reason, to gain time for rebuilding our strength," said Philip. He looked over at his bride.

Elisabeth had reached the same conclusion when she read the letter delivered by Cardinal Alberoni. She was glad the boys had caught up to her line of reasoning. The heavy makeup helped her maintain an expressionless gaze, as she gave a shallow nod of concurrence to the King. Other than the Cardinal, those in attendance did not realize the decision to stop the conflict had just been made. Yes, she knew her perceived role was to remain within the confines of the bed chamber, but it was from the four posts of her bed that she would rule an empire.

Maximo Rainerio had not left his hacienda since the fall of Vigo. His eyes were still moist from the pain of having lost his only daughter. His mind wandered to visions of her as a little girl playing in the courtyard. He thought, *I had her betrothed to the next King of Spain. She should have been Queen. I would have dined at the court. Now, she is gone.*

"Sir, you have to decide about the child, William Tonia," said his servant. His voice brought Maximo back into the real world from the soft landscape of memories.

Maximo straightened up in his chair. He looked over at the toddler struggling to take a few steps in his direction.

"What options do I have?"

"Sir, Mistress Rainerio had always planned on raising the child herself—"

"Well, that's not going to happen now, is it!" Maximo said. His curt response reflected the anger still heavy on the loss of Ernesta.

"No, sir. Perhaps you would like to engage him as your ward?"

Maximo looked across at the child. William smiled. It would have been a full tooth grin, if he had a full set of teeth. The light giggle that broke forth from William echoed in the courtyard.

"What about Tonia's relatives. Can't they raise the little bastard?"

The servant's lips tightened. He took a step away from his boss.

"Sir, I'll take care of making the arrangements," said the servant.

He walked over and picked William up. Holding the lad over his shoulder he exited from the courtyard. It was fortunate that William was too young to remember the scene of Maximo staring at him or the red tile roof of the main house. He would never return to live within the walls of the hacienda. Like the Spanish nation, his path to greatness was about to change direction downward.

*****

The English soldier stood above the Spanish girl, looking down at her, he held a slanted grin. It was difficult to know her age, but she was likely not out of school. Her dress remained pushed well above her waist. Her black hair was tangled above her head. Her legs were bent upward and open as she lay on her back sobbing. The bruise on her cheek, coupled with the lone drop of blood that hung in the corner of her mouth, indicated that what had passed between these two had not been consensual. The soldier buttoned the front of his coat but left the top two buttons unfastened. He picked up a bottle of port wine by its neck and took a long swig. He drew his coat sleeve across his lips to clear the moisture.

"I would have rather thought you would be enjoying that," said the soldier in the red coat.

She pulled her dress down across her legs. Still sobbing she sat up and brushed her hair out of her face. She stared at the soldier. Not a normal gaze, but rather one with the intensity of unbounded hate. The kind of stare where the eyelids collapsed half closed, focusing the building venom toward her attacker. She said something in Spanish the soldier couldn't understand.

"No hablar Espanol," said the soldier laughing.

"Private, what unit are you with?" asked a voice behind the two of them.

The private turned and raised the wine bottle to his forehead as if saluting. The motion of turning about unsteadied him. He waivered struggling to stand. He tried to figure out who had disrupted his fun.

"Who wants to be knowing?"

"Sergeant Worth, Royal Marines, from HMS *Comet*. You're in our shore patrol area and accountable to me," said Worth. His normal command tone was just a little more intense.

"Marine, bloody hell. I'm in the army. You don't command me."

"Well, by order of General Chobham, all soldiers are to return to their boats. All wine is now confiscated as a prize of war. Come lad, you've had your three days of fun."

The soldier dropped the bottle and it shattered on the cobblestones of the street. Two Marines came forward on each side of the soldier and pushed him along toward the long boats that hovered near the waterfront. Sailors had to be dragged to boats and returned to their ships. Midshipmen Rutwell and Dugins watched wide-eyed from the main deck of *Comet* as these events unfolded.

"Do you think these men will be held to account?" Dugins asked his counterpart.

"Not likely. England demands their service aboard ships more than the time in detention," said Rutwell.

"What about the crimes against the Spanish?"

"It pays to be a winner. One should always remember that."

"Who told you that?" Dugins asked. His tone was skeptical.

"Captain Darroch, Royal Marines."

"Of course, who else?" said Dugins shaking his head.

William Darroch paced back and forth outside his stateroom hatch. The dim in the passageway appeared just a little darker on this occasion. His mind raced, *I hope she is fine. Damn, they treated her badly in that dungeon. I wonder—"*

"William, would you join us," said Doc La Roch peering out from his stateroom.

The two men disappeared behind the wooden bulkhead. William found Annette flat on her back in his bed. A single blanket had been thrown across her to shield against the damp and cold.

"William, did you put her in here?" Doc La Roch asked.

"Yes. Is she going to recover?"

"I'll get to that in a minute. I wish you had brought her to sick bay first. Annette is covered in lice and some bugs I don't even know what the hell they are. You have to wash all this linen, scrub down the entire stateroom from top to bottom, and one more thing."

"What's that?"

"After you bathe her, you have to shave off her hair."

"No. Her hair?"

"All of it, I'm afraid. It's the only way to kill all those damn lice. They carry all manner of disease and if you don't get a handle on this now, the health of both of you is in jeopardy."

"What if—"

"All of it! I will not let you put the health of the ship at risk because you have some unnatural attraction to redheads. When it comes to the security of the ship, you're the expert. I respect that. When it comes to the health of the ship, I'm the expert. I demand the same consideration."

"Of course, Doc. So, what else ills her."

"Well she is fatigued and malnourished. She'll be fine, if we kill those damn bugs, get her some rest, and force some food down her. Funny thing is, she will not want to eat at first. I'm assigning her to your care for the next seventy-two hours. Are you clear as to what I want, or do I need to repeat it?"

"Clean stateroom and linen, wash Annette, shave her head, and ensure she gets food and rest."

"Great. Now put those Marines to work helping you. They don't have much to do now that we are withdrawing."

William thought, *bathe Annette, I've been given worse assignments.*

The knock on the door was followed by the Bosun's voice, "Sir, I've got that half barrel you requested."

Opening the hatch William pulled the barrel in his stateroom and set it next to his bed. The rich bouquet of a red wine oozed from the oak.

"Boats, where did you find this?" William said.

"Well, one of the lads said he found a barrel in the forward platform. Only problem was, it was filled with wine. But the sailors knew it was for Annette, so they decided to empty the barrel and cut it in half, sir."

"You didn't waste a barrel of wine, did you?"

"Oh, no sir. Like I said the lads knew it was for Annette, so they drank the contents in her honor. They all respect her you know."

"So, I see," said William. A smile returned to his face for the first time since taking on this new task.

The Marines brought up buckets of hot water to fill the tub. William lifted Annette into the vessel and began the process of removing months of filth from her body. His hands bumped across the protrusions of her spine and ribs. The thinness of her arms and legs shocked William as he gently held them up and ran a sponge over their gritty surface. Using a knife, he cut many of the strands of tangled hair from her skull. The remaining locks were washed and separated. He rubbed her scalp, working the soap suds over the skin. He could feel the tiny creatures scurry ahead of the water. He took a deep breath and got his razor. He had shaved the head of new Marines in the past, but this was overpowering in emotion for him. The blade scraped across her head and the last of her once glorious main fell away.

With Annette sitting motionless in the warm water, William went to work scrubbing the bed and the rest of the stateroom. The Purser knocked.

"William, I've got a new mattress for you. I'll leave it outside here," said the Lieutenant. "The linen is washed and waiting as well."

"Thank you, I'm almost done in here," said William.

The Marine stood and surveyed his efforts. This was the cleanest his stateroom had been since he walked aboard. He made the bed, all that had to be done now was get Annette in her dressing gown and let her sleep.

"You had to shave my head?" Annette said.

"Doctor's orders, I'm afraid," said William.

"What does it look like?"

"Oh, not bad. Really, not bad at all. Still same Annette."

"Let me see your mirror," said Annette. Her tone was skeptical.

"No need right now. You need to get some sleep."

"Let me see your mirror."

William lifted the mirror next to his door and held it for Annette to take a look. She bent forward in the makeshift tub and tried to focus on the image. Her mouth fell open. Then it fell wider. The gasp she made was audible in the passageway.

"I look like a blooming egg with lips."

"Miss Armtrove, you're—"

"Don't give me that sunset and trade wind crap. I look like a damn egg with lips."

"I'll get you some food."

"Take me back."

"Where?"

"Vigo, the Castro dungeon. I don't want anyone to see me like this. Ever!"

"You can stay in my stateroom as long as needed. I'll bring you your meals."

"William."

"What?"

"Get out!"

"Annette, it will—"

"Out, damn it. I will not have you be seeing me like this. Out!"

"I think it's a little late for that Annette."

Annette began to cry. She splashed water up on her face to mask the tears that fell freely.

"Look, I'll give you a minute. Promise me you'll dry off, put on your dressing gown, and get in bed," said William.

Annette nodded. William departed and headed up to the command deck. He approached Captain Calder on the back rail and saluted.

"Is everything alright with my cook?" Calder asked.

"Yes, sir. She was more than a little upset at the loss of her hair. Annette just wanted some time alone," said William.

"I sort of gathered that by the volume of her 'out' command. You could hear her all the way up here on the command deck. Perhaps, we should be training her as an Officer of the Deck. She has the command voice for it. I would say her commands would carry forward better than some of my midshipman."

The Marine's lips tightened as he looked at the Captain. He was unsure how to take his meaning. He blinked.

"At ease, man," said Calder smiling. "The Admiralty will never allow women to command ships. What are you thinking?"

Darroch let out a long sigh. He smiled, and thought, *however, they could do a lot worse than Annette on the command deck. At least she knows how to pursue what she wants with passion. Not sure I would ever want to meet her on a hostile quarter deck when she has a saber in hand.*

"Captain Darroch, we have a new mission," said Calder.

"Sir?"

"*Comet* is sailing to Cadiz. We are to accept the surrender of the Spanish forces, both afloat and ashore, in that area. The war is over man." Calder couldn't resist the urge to hit the side of Darroch's arm.

"How do you know, sir?"

"Got the letter this morning, when you were playing house with Miss Armtrove."

He handed the letter to William. He read the letter slowly. His lips moved as his eyes hurried across the text.

". . . receive the complete surrender of all Spanish forces in and around Cadiz," said William as he read the lines. He handed the paper back to his boss.

"Sir, do you know if we have any currier sloops heading back to Portsmouth?"

"Yes, we'll have one alongside in two bells. Do you need to send a letter?"

"No, sir," said William. "However, I do need to get Mister Smyth back to England soonest. He was manifested on the last ship. I need to make this right for him."

"I see," said Calder. "Bosun McKay, would you be so good as to ensure Mister Smyth is on the next boat alongside."

"Aye, sir. But he'd better be a hurrying. That's in like ten minutes."

The frantic activity that followed defied the normal slowness of Imperial administration. Discharge papers were written out on the spot. Calder signed them and added a special note of thanks. Flag signals were sent to the sloop. His baggage was moved topside and lowered away. Smyth smiled from ear-to-ear when he walked up on the quarter deck.

"Thank you, Mister Smyth," said Darroch. He shook his hand. "We could have never accomplished the mission without your skills."

"Aye, and now I know what is more precious than a chest of gold. I wish you both all the love that this world known to man will allow," said Smyth. "Perhaps, the two of you, will buy me a pint of ale in Portsmouth?"

"On that you can be assured, Mister Smyth. I'll see you at your shop in a few months' time."

*****

HMS *Comet* road on a light northwest wind that held directly astern toward the Spanish port city of Cadiz. The brown hills that surrounded the harbor were eager to absorb the passing rain shower that quenched the dry landscape. The high heat of summer had left its mark, but the change in weather refreshed both those ashore and afloat with the possibilities of new beginnings.

Captain Calder tilted his head slightly to the left in a vain attempt to get the water to flow to his back instead of running down his collar. While his oil-skin was keeping his body dry enough, water beaded up on his face and neck. When the liquid found its way beneath his collar, as it often did, a chill would resonate down his spine. The resulting involuntary shiver that rippled through his body reinforced the fact that even a ship's captain could not control all the elements that surrounded him.

"Steer southeast Lieutenant Laurant," said Calder. His hand pointing toward the approach to Cadiz. "I would like *Comet* to hold the center of the channel, if you please."

"Aye, aye, sir," said the Lieutenant.

As Officer of the Deck, he passed these instructions to the Conning Officer, who in turn relayed them to the Helmsman. This seeming clumsy passing of orders reinforced the rigid hierarchy that held sway within the wooden walls of *Comet*. In routine matters, the ship's captain remained aloof and separate from both the crew and the wardroom. Only when the ship was in danger or combat did he feel compelled to directly intervene in her direction. However, his force and awareness were a constant presence of which the crew was fully cognizant.

"It's hard to believe that after these years at war with Spain, we can sail *Comet* directly into the most powerful port on Spain's Atlantic coast," said Calder.

"Aye, sir. With a fort on either side of the channel, this port would have been very difficult to force. What is that gap? Maybe three to four miles?" Laurant said.

"I would say closer to four, Lieutenant Laurant."

A ray of sunlight broke the clouds signaling their pending departure on the wind. Calder held out his hand as if to measure the potential dryness.

"It seems we'll be able to anchor without having to fight the rain, Lieutenant."

"Aye, sir. If the winds hold, *Comet* will ease back into the trades and settle up just fine."

Calder cast his gaze to the star shaped fort on the starboard side. The walls provided just enough elevation that would have given their cannon a distinct advantage in a firefight. He pulled his spyglass from his belt and extended it to full length. He ran his vision along the ramparts counting the number of gun ports. He stopped when he reached twenty. A smile crossed his face when he saw the Spanish fort commander, the one with a white plumed feather in his hat, studying the lines of his ship with his spyglass as he sailed by. *The Dons, always looking for an advantage. That is good.* Thought Calder. *At least it is honest.*

A red uniform pulled up the ladder to the command deck. Darroch walked over to Calder and saluted. The snapped salute between these two marked a level of marshal excellence not always found aboard his majesty's ships.

"Good day, sir," said Darroch. He placed his hands behind his back and interlocked them.

"I see you had the good sense to wait until the rain subsided before venturing topside Marine. Well done. Report, then," said Calder.

"Sir, the honor guard is ready for the ceremony tomorrow. All Marines will be turned out and formed as requested. Does the Captain have any idea what sort of honors will be required?"

"Honors, sir. Well, many I would think. We have all the top brass coming on deck tomorrow. It's not every day you can conclude a war and secure the surrender."

"No, sir. One last point, and I hesitate to bring this up. Weapons loaded or unloaded, sir?"

Calder looked away for a moment. His stare returned to the tall stone walls of the bastion behind them. He held his spyglass with both hands behind his back. He cleared his throat and re-engaged the Marine.

"Loaded, if you please, Captain Darroch," said Calder. The twisted lines on his face indicated the extent to which this decision had caused him pain.

"Aye, sir. Your Marines will be ready for anything the Dons can throw our way."

"I guess we all know," said Calder. His tone was low and reflective. "Force of arms can not only win a war, they are essential to winning the peace. The presence of HMS *Comet*, coupled with the other ships in the squadron, will give them pause before they start anything again. I will see you in the morning, sir."

The sun rose and reinforced the crisp fall air across the bay. The lack of wind flattened the waters into a mirror like surface. The hills along the shoreline reflected a brilliance often lost when the waters rippled in a stiff chop. The crew was formed into a horse shoe shape around the main mast. Each Division occupied a side of the box. A space was reserved for the ceremonial honor guard. Chief White moved among the sailors of the Deck Division inspecting their uniforms. A tuck here, and pull there, ensured the best alignment of their uniforms. It was not all for show. Marshal excellence was a theme to be communicated to those about to sign the surrender documents.

"Forward, march!" said Sergeant Worth. His voice rang from below deck to those waiting topside.

The thump, thump, thump tone of a lone drum resonated deep. The assembled sailors looked in the direction of that hatchway from where the noise broke the quiet of the morning. The red coats of the Marines appeared up the ladder with each step in time with the thumping of the drum. The sound of the drum masked the strike of their feet on the deck as the two sounds were locked in unison. Captain Darroch led the way. Each line of

Marines formed into their tight square, so often seen on the command deck during morning quarters.

"Detail, halt. Order, arms. Right face." commanded Darroch. He turned about and saluted with his saber. "Sir, the Honor Guard is formed."

Calder returned the salute. A few muffled comments drifted up from the sailors. A quick glance from the ship's Bosun returned silence to the deck. The sound of a boat coming alongside, indicated that the Spanish official party was near. Six bells resonated from the quarter deck.

"General Fadrique Gonzalez de Soto, regent's representative, arriving," said the Officer of the Deck.

"Hand salute," said the Petty Officer of the Watch.

Eight side boys lifted their knuckles to their forehead. The official party walked between the saluting sailors. Instinctively, the General returned the salute. The Spanish stopped on one side of a green felt covered table that had been brought on deck. Calder and the Empire's representative stood on the other side. Calder moved forward.

"Gentlemen, on behalf of the King and ruling council these proceedings are called to order," said Calder. He projected his voice so all on deck could hear his words. He forced himself to slow his speech and enunciate each word. A Spanish translator stood next to the General, but he waved him away.

Calder walked to the table and sat on the lone chair. The ship's purser handed him the first document. He lifted the document, paused, and set the document on the table. Silence filled the void, as he pulled his spectacles from his pocket and slid them into position low on his nose.

"On behalf of both parties now engaged in hostilities along the western coastal region of Spain, it is agreed, that all hostile action will cease effective immediately on the signing of this document. It is further agreed, that both parties will abide by such provisions mutually reached in subsequent negotiations at a time and place to be determined," said Calder. He was keen to keep his tone free from emotion.

He looked up over the top of his spectacles at the Spanish General. The General leaned toward his interpreter and the two exchanged whispers. He returned his gaze to Calder and nodded.

"On behalf of the Army, I would invite Major General John Wade to come forward and sign the document."

The General approached and leaned over the table. Calder handed him a quill and pointed to the line requiring his signature. The soldier bent lower and carefully scrawled his name into position. He finished by tapping the quill to the document, standing, and returning to his place in line.

"On behalf of the Royal Navy, I would invite Vice Admiral James Mighels to come forward and sign the document."

The Admiral moved to the table. His sword clanked against his side as he approached. He removed his hat and set it on the green felt surface. Calder handed him the quill. He set his name upon the document with bold script that fully occupied the line provided. He returned the quill to Calder.

"Good job, Delmar. Your performance during this campaign has not escaped those of the Ruling Committee. Keep at it," said the Admiral. His words were whisper soft and heard only by Delmar.

"Thank you, sir," Calder whispered back. He cleared his throat and straightened up in his chair.

Calder looked over his shoulder and waited until the Admiral had returned to the location of the other senior representatives from the Empire.

"On behalf of his majesty the King, I would invite General Richard Temple, First Viscount of Chobham, to come forward and sign the document."

The General approached the table with head held high. He bowed briefly toward Calder. *Comet's* Captain handed him the quill. The General paused over the document, then signed in a rapid manner. His pace back to his starting point was brisk.

"On behalf of the King of Spain, I would invite General Fadrique Gonzalez de Soto to come forward and sign the document."

The General approached with his aide holding one pace behind him. Calder spun the document around, so it would be upright to the General on the other side of the table. He reached forward to offer the General his quill. The General waved him away. His aide opened a small velvet case. It contained a single writing quill. The General dipped the quill in the ink well and signed the document. His signature was bold and filled half the page. His lips that had held a straight line on his approach, now edged downward. He stood erect. His eyes grew glassy, reflecting the light of the middle of the morning. He nodded in Calder's direction, and then his stare tightened.

"Captain, we have come to fear the approach of *Comet*, both along our coast or at any point on the globe. Your ship is mentioned in dispatches from the new world, the Mediterranean, and the icy waters off Scotland. I hope you will accept this as the highest of compliments, when I tell you I hope to never again hear the name *Comet* mentioned in Spanish waters," said de Soto. His English was broken, but his intent was clear.

"Sir, your words are well taken. Well taken indeed, sir," said Calder. He forced his lips together to prevent from smiling as the General departed.

"These proceedings are closed," said Calder.

The crew was dismissed from formation and scattered about the ship. Some went below to sleep, some prepared to assume the watch, and others went back to work under the watchful eye of Chief White. Major General Wade's aide collected the documents and placed them in a leather satchel for transportation back to England. The sound of bells ringing the official party off the ship would last for the next half hour.

Vice Admiral Mighels walked over to Calder. The Captain thought the Admiral looked a little tense on his approach. He thought, *oh, this can't be good.*

"Delmar, nice job today. Your ship was turned out nicely. I must say the Marine detachment looked most sharp," said the Admiral.

"Thank you, sir. The entire ship's company earned the right to hold these proceedings. I want to extend my personal thanks for allowing *Comet* and crew the privilege to do so," said Calder.

"Well . . . that's true. I have one more mission for *Comet* before she is released to Portsmouth."

Calder's mind raced, *what the hell. We have been at this for almost two years now. Another mission, really? I need to get this damn boat some repair time in the yards. Hell, I need to get this crew some time on dry land.* Calder straightened up. "Yes, sir. As my Marine Detachment Commander would say, what's the mission?"

The Admiral reached into his inside coat pocket and pulled a long-folded letter. He handed it to Calder. "You can read it at your leisure Delmar, but the essence of the instruction is assigning you patrol duty."

"Where?" Calder said. His tone was just a little fatigued.

"HMS *Comet* is to patrol the Bay of Biscay for five weeks. We are still suppressing pirate activity if it should bubble this far north. The Admiralty is concerned with the end of hostilities, some of those operating under 'Letters of Marquee' will use the confusion during the transition to peace to attack our shipping. Five weeks, Delmar. I'll get you home after that."

"Aye, sir," said Calder as he took the instructions. He let out a long breath. "*Comet* will stand ready. We always, do."

Below decks Mary approached Captain Darroch's stateroom door. Two crisp knocks announced her request to enter.

"Who is it," said Annette. Her feminine voice made it clear Darroch was elsewhere.

"Mary White, dear. I need to see you."

"Go away. I'm not able to see anyone right now."

"Annette, I really need to talk with you. Please, spare me a few minutes."

Silence . . .

"Annette," said Mary yet again.

She's not going away, thought Annette. *Guess I can't hide away forever.*

"Yes, enter," said Annette.

Mary pushed back the door and stood at the entrance for a moment. The creaking of the wooden beams filled the silence between these two women of *Comet.* Mary pulled the door closed behind her. She reached into her bag and handed Annette a silk scarf. It was red, with flowers printed on one side.

"I wanted you to have this scarf. It's called spring sunset," said Mary. She sat on William's desk chair. She studied Annette's expression.

Annette took the scarf and held it up to the limited light within the cabin. She ran her hand down its length. Each flower unfolded across her hand as it traveled beneath the silk.

Mary stood to exit. "I thought it might help shield the sun from your scalp."

"Thank you, Mary. It's beautiful," said Annette. Her voice reflected some energy for the first time since her return to *Comet.*

"And so are you, my dear. Don't ever forget that. Your hair will grow back, but your beauty will shine all the seasons of the year. And trust me, I'm not the only one that thinks that," said Mary. Her tone was direct.

"But I—"

"You will join me on deck tomorrow when the ship gets underway for a constitutional. After you start to out walk me, which won't take too long I figure, you will return to sword drill with the Marines. But let's just start with the walking tomorrow.

315

For that I think you'll find the scarf useful," said Mary. Her mothering tone implied the topic wasn't up for discussion.

"My saber, where's my saber?" Annette said, as she sat up in bed.

"In the captain's galley," said Mary smiling. "Right where you left it."

"Really, how can that be?" Annette said.

"Captain Calder refused to let anyone touch it. He said to keep it there until Annette's return. And so, here you are my dear. Home once again."

"A ship home? No, that's not home," said Annette.

"Not the ship dear, the people. It's people that define family, and you're among those that love you."

Annette whispered, "Home." A light moisture filled her eyes.

Chapter 18 Homeward Bound

"Helmsman, mark your head," said Captain Calder.

"Sir, steering south southeast."

"Officer of the deck," said Calder. His tone was elevated above the sound of an active swell that collided against *Comet's* sides.

"Yes, sir," replied Lieutenant Martino.

"I believe we have over stayed our welcome here along the southwest coast of France."

"Sir?"

"I have both news and new orders from the sloop that was alongside. Midshipman Dugins, join us if you please."

The Midshipman walked over to join these two. His gait was somewhat widened and awkward, more akin to a bull-legged cavalry trooper. Calder unfolded a letter. He gripped it tight with two hands to guard against it taking flight in the ever-present sea breeze.

"Gentlemen, first congratulations are in order for Midshipman Dugins here. I am pleased to announce that he has been selected for promotion to Lieutenant, effective on our return to Portsmouth. On arrival sir, you will stand detached from HMS *Comet*, and report for duty to the captain of HMS *Britannia*," said Calder. He paused and looked up from the letter.

Midshipman Dugins' mouth was agape. He blinked twice. He looked over at Lieutenant Martino and then back to Calder.

"*Britannia*, sir? Do we even have a ship of that name?"

"Yes, Mister Dugins. A brand-new first-rate ship-of-the-line. I believe she'll carry one hundred guns, if I'm not mistaken. Should be a perfect fit for a new lieutenant, eager to chart his own course."

Martino walked behind Dugins and placed his hand on his shoulder. He rubbed the lad with a light slow rhythm. Leaning forward he whispered in his ear, "Well done, Dugins. You've earned it. Oh, and you're welcome." In one swift move, Martino dropped his hand from his shoulder and slapped him with the flat of his palm on his bottom. Dugins jumped up a few inches.

"Lieutenant Martino, enough folly. Back to your station, while I address our future Lieutenant."

"Aye, sir," said Martino. He walked over to the binnacle and checked the compass.

"Will you miss the southern coast of France, Mister Dugins?" Said Calder pointing landward.

Dugins moved to the port side railing and looked out to the coast. He shook his head from side-to-side. "No, sir. I will not miss this station. We have spent the better part of five weeks sailing back and forth across the Gironde Estuary and the entrance to the Bordeaux region. Not once were we able to sample the local wine or women," said Dugins. His last line drew the attention of Lieutenant Martino.

"Well said, Midshipman. Well said," replied Calder laughing. "Mister Dugins, please join me here at the rail."

Dugins walked with Calder to the command deck railing that over looked the main deck below. They watched the Marines below engaged in their daily sword drill. The clash of steel competed with the slapping of the swell and the creaking of the rigging in a seaward symphony of background noise. One figure below stood apart from those in red and had been long absent from this morning routine on *Comet*.

Five weeks of rest, exercise, and proper meals had fueled Annette's recovery. In the first week, she had begun to outpace Mary on their morning walks around the deck. Now after four weeks of fencing, she was able to regain most of her prowess with the blade. Much of the tone in her limbs had returned. Her strength was on par, but Annette would tire quickly in the heat and sun. She knew her endurance was lacking. The loose fit of her riding pants provided compelling evidence that her weight was still less than when she started her tenure in the Castro dungeon.

Captain Darroch drew his saber and walked to where Corporal Mac Dunn and Annette were sparring. The overhead protection of the sails provided some relief from the strength of the rising sun on this clear Atlantic morning. The rolling of the ship would slide this protection from port to starboard casting this pair in alternating hues of shadow and light. The Marine rolled his shoulders a few times and sliced his blade through the air to loosen his muscles. He took a few deep breaths and then fully exhaled the air from his lungs.

"Corporal Mac Dunn, do you mind if I borrow your fencing partner for a round or two?" said Darroch.

"No, sir. But be warned sir, her speed is fully back now."

"Thank you for the insight, Corporal. Carry on, if you would."

"Aye, sir," said Mac Dunn. The Corporal moved down the line looking for a new opponent to drill against.

Annette leaned her saber against her leg. She tightened the tie of her scarf atop her head. Its red color was a poor substitute for the auburn mane that once commanded the interest of many a traveler to the Red Fox Inn. A few strands of its once former glory peaked out from under the front of the scarf. Its short-cropped length reflected the five weeks of growth from when Annette had embarked *Comet*. She picked up her sword and faced the Marine captain to her front.

"So, you be looking for a rematch my young Captain of Marines?" said Annette. The confidence had returned to her voice.

"Yes, Mistress Armtrove. I think a rematch would do us both well."

"Don't be calling me Mistress."

Annette rolled her blade around toward William's left side. His beat parry was instinctive. They faced each other both holding the on-guard position. Their bodies swayed in time with the roll of *Comet*. This pugilistic pairing immediately drew the attention of Captain Calder on the command deck.

"Not bad, young Captain. Let's see what you got," said Annette.

"Don't call me young Captain, my Lady."

Annette smiled when addressed as "my lady." Her smile quickly flattened out and lips went taught when the Marine lunged at her. She side stepped the thrust. As William extended by her, she slapped his arm with the back of her sword.

"Just a love pat this time. I would imagine your opponent would not be so considerate," said Annette.

William thought, *yes, both her speed and wit have been renewed.*

"So, I see," said William. He recovered to the on-guard position and took a few deep breaths.

Annette lifted her blade overhead and struck directly at William from high to low. He dropped one hand to the deck, rolled under the attack, and drew the back of his saber across Annette's leg.

"Damn it," escaped Annette's lips before she realized it.

"Just returning the love, my Lady."

"On-guard," said Annette. The force resident in her voice exploded with her increased volume.

They stood in opposition rocking forward and back. William extended his blade and Annette parried the movement. They continued to stare at each other looking for an opening. None was forthcoming. Annette lunged forward at the same time William attacked. Their blades collided and rode up over their heads as their bodies crashed together. For an instant, they were face-to-face and kissing close.

"I missed your close embrace, my Lady," said William. He pushed her away and resumed the on-guard stance.

"So, I see, Captain. Close, but not engaged in the fight."

"Not engaged at the moment, my Lady. But this contest is not concluded, On-guard!"

Muscle memory commanded Annette's form as her sword instinctively rose to a perfect forty-five degree angle above the deck. Her grip loosened and tightened. Those green eyes flashed from William's feet to his grip. She remained upright but extended her blade horizontal to the deck chest high toward the Marine. William's saber found direct opposition to this extension and he rolled his hand in a rapid tight circle. Annette's saber rose and was pulled from her grasp. It flew up and William grabbed the hilt on its descent. His stare tightened on her as he held both weapons.

"It would seem I've unarmed you, my Lady," said William. His tone was playful.

"Yes. I concede this round. I'm sure we'll have plenty of time to renew this contest."

William nodded.

"So am I, my Lady," said William. His tone was deeper, more serious now.

He dropped both swords to the deck. The metallic rattling sound drew the attention of the nearby Marines and Captain Calder on the command deck. William unbuttoned the lower two buttons on this red coat. He lowered himself to one knee before Annette. All sword play on the main deck ceased. The Marines began to shuffle in a circle around this couple at the aft end of *Comet*.

"Willian . . ." said Annette. The pause in her voice reflected a forced silence of uncertainty common when facing the unexpected.

"What are you doing?" Annette added.

The Marines continued to tighten around them. William reached into his pocket and pulled out a blue silk cloth. He pealed open the cloth to reveal a gold ring.

"Annette, I had this ring fashioned from a gold coin I got on the Yucatan. It has sailed with us all the way across the Atlantic and I've carried it with me throughout this awful war. I knew this day would arrive. In some ways, I'm just glad it arrived while we were aboard *Comet*," said William.

He paused and looked out at the many faces that now surrounded them. Some of their eyes widened and others nodded. All pressed for William to continue. The only sound on deck was the soft creaking of the standing rigging. All officers on the command deck now hovered on the railing above them taking in the scene below.

William now looked up at Annette. Her green eyes glistened with a light moisture that reflected the mid-morning sun. Her scarf rippled with the wind, dancing in random waves about her face.

"Annette, will you do me the honor of becoming my lady, my love, and my wife. Will you marry me?" William said. The lines were clear and well-rehearsed.

"Yes, William. Yes. It is I that is honored," said Annette.

The Marines gathered around the couple and let loose with a loud and thunderous, "Urauh!" Applause fill the morning air, as William slid the ring on Annette's long finger. Her body shook for reasons she couldn't explain. The mist that had been hovering in her eyes formed tears that now flowed freely.

William stood and embraced her. The kiss that followed would not have sat well with those of prim and proper standing of the ruling elite, but for this couple distant on the waves it didn't matter. Their display of affection resulted in another round of clapping by the crew.

"Three cheers for the Captain and Miss Armtrove, Hip, hip—" said Sergeant Worth.

"Hooray!" thundered the crew.

Hip, hip—"

"Hooray!"

"Hip, hip—"

"Hooray!"

The crew came forward to congratulate the couple one-by-one. The mass of humanity that once encircled them thinned, dispersed, and returned to their stations. With their sword drill complete, Sergeant Worth mustered the Marines below deck.

Captain Calder looked over at Midshipman Dugins. He scratched the side of his face.

"Well Mister Dugins it appears I might once again be losing my cook if our Marine Captain is intent on marrying her and sweeping her away," said Calder.

"Good for them, sir. Given the way the Spanish treated Miss Armtrove during her captivity, one can only wish the best for the both of them going forward," said Dugins.

"Indeed. As for you, have you thought about the potential of a new posting on HMS *Britannia*?"

"Yes, sir. A shock at first, but on review I can't wait to explore my capabilities beyond *Comet's* constraints."

"What do you mean by that Mister Dugins?"

"Well sir, it seems some of the wardroom can be a little exclusive in their dealings with the younger midshipmen. I look forward to observing other officers and how they handle their sailors while underway."

"In that regard Mister Dugins, you shall not be disappointed, sir. I feel that small bit of wisdom may well reflect the level of potential you are capable of reaching given proper motivation and industry."

"Thank you, sir. I will represent both the Captain and *Comet* well," said Dugins smiling.

"Mister Dugins, please inform the Officer of the Deck to wear through the wind and steady up on a northerly course. I would like to go congratulate the new couple on their engagement."

"Aye, aye, sir."

Calder eased about and headed for the main deck. Dugins took a deep breath. He turned and faced Martino to find him closely watching his discussion with the Captain. He walked over to the Officer of the Deck.

"Sir, Captain Calder requests you wear through the wind and settle *Comet* up on a northerly course," said Dugins. His voice was broken as he addressed the Lieutenant.

Charles held a stare on the lad. His eyes squinted down narrow and the muscles around his mouth tightened.

"Aye, a north by northwest course should begin to align us back toward England. You know, Mister Dugins," said Martino. His expression shifted to a calm smile. "We won't have much more time together aboard *Comet*. I was true to my word. I delivered your promotion to Lieutenant—"

"I don't suppose my performance on the board had anything to do with it then?"

"No," said Martino in his curt tone that he found so natural in talking with midshipmen.

"Really, sir. You expect me to believe that you alone determined the results of the promotion board. Not the three Captains that sat across the damn table and grilled me for the better part of an hour."

"Mister Dugins, you would have never gotten to the board had I not told the Flag Lieutenant, you remember Lieutenant Pennycock, do you not?"

"Yes, I recall the Lieutenant. I think the Captain kicked him off the ship last time he was aboard," said Dugins. His breathing was accelerating and shallow.

"Well, I had him fix the board results, so you would finish on the promoted side. He moved your record from the look again stack, to the promoted pile. I want you to think about that when you come around to my cabin after watch."

"Sir?" Dugins said. His rate of breathing continued to rise.

"I expect you to come around after watch. I think we need to work on your breathing, one last time," said Martino. His smile now shifted to a slanted curve across his face.

"Oh, hell no, sir. I've played that role. I shan't be doing so again. More importantly, I would never impose myself in such a manner on others."

"Oh, I see. You may well feel differently when you have been at sea for six months on some godforsaken distant station. Talk to me then. However, let's bring the ship around, shall we."

"Aye, aye, sir," said Dugins. His pulse returned to normal.

Captain Calder approached Annette and William. The smile on his face communicated his feelings about the new engagement before he said a word.

"William, congratulations. It took you long enough to come to this realization. I thought for sure after our carriage ride on the way back to the ship at New Orleans you would have realized Annette was the one. I still remember the look on your face when I put my arm around her shoulders," said Calder.

Annette giggled while recalling the scene. William cleared his throat and pressed his lips together.

"Yes, sir. That was an awkward moment for me. I wasn't sure how I was going to stay out of irons after striking my commanding officer," said William. They both looked over at Annette.

"And as for you, Miss Armtrove. It seems we will all have to address you as Lady Armtrove once these nuptials are complete. I know that is a title you fancy."

"Fancy, sir you don't know the half of it. I have always known my destiny called me to points beyond the waterfront of Portsmouth. Things my mother told me, and more importantly, things she left unsaid all indicated we were from a standing much elevated from that of inn keeper. I would have been your cook much sooner if I knew it would secure me the family I had never known," said Annette. She stood a little taller.

The direction of the apparent wind shifted on deck as *Comet* came through the wind. The shadows of the sails on the main deck moved across this small group as the crew tightened and loosened sheets to spin the spars above them to sequentially align with the wind during the turn. Commands from mast captains echoed from the tops but were only background noise to these three. Captain Darroch handed Annette her sword.

"The sea is settling out as we steady up on this new course," said Calder.

"New course, sir. What's our mission?" Annette said. Her eyes grew wide in Calder's direction.

Darroch chuckled, thinking, *damn she sounds like a Marine. Mission, first. Not sure if that's a good thing or a bad thing.*

"What you be laughing at?" Annette said to Captain Darroch. Her tone was direct.

"Nothing, my dear. I mean, my Lady."

"I really do like the sound of that. Vanity, perhaps, but I really do like the sound of that," said Annette smiling. Looking back at Calder, she added, "Sir, are we leaving France?"

"Yes, Lady Armtrove—"

"I was so looking forward to sampling the red wines of the Bordeaux region," said Annette cutting off the Captain. The sigh in her voice was evident. "I had heard about them back at the Red Fox Inn. Anytime we got merchant sailors from France, that was all they would lament about was how they be missing the reds of Bordeaux. So close, and yet, never to be I suppose."

"*Comet* has just been placed on a course that will take us on a northerly track. I would say we are only a few days out of Portsmouth Annette. I shall have you home within a week my Lady," said Calder.

Annette slid next to William. She took hold of his arm with her free hand, while bringing her saber up over her shoulder. Her green eyes lifted up to engage William. She waited until his deep blue eyes returned her gaze. A smile crossed her face.

Annette said, "But Captain, I'm already home."

53526780R00184

Made in the
USA
Lexington, KY